The Sprog

Denis Leeman

Published in 2011 by FeedARead.com Publishing –
Arts Council funded
Copyright © Denis Leeman

A CIP catalogue record for this title is available from
the British Library.

Introduction

The National Service Act was approved in 1948 and came into force on the first day of January of the following year. It lasted until around 1962, with all fit young men being recruited on reaching the age of eighteen years. The time served was originally eighteen months but this was raised to two years in 1950, supposedly owing to the Korean conflict.

Over its operational years thousands of young men passed through the three services, some being posted to active war zones. However, many considered it – in retrospect – an enjoyable, enlightening experience and its abolishment a great loss for British youth.

The title of this book 'The Sprog' is a slang name given to a raw recruit by those of longer service, a label that remains with him until after the completion of basic training and the grand finale – the passing out parade.

Although this book is a fictional work it is based on research and true factual experiences, and its main intention is to enlighten the reader by describing as closely as possible the life of a home-based recruit – in this instance in the RAF – in the late nineteen fifties. Regarding his working life, after the basic eight weeks military training, this was usually very similar to civilian employment, with regular set hours or shifts.

Trade courses to choose from within the service were numerous, including different types of mechanical and electrical courses, wireless operators, cooks, clerks and accountants, plus many more. In fact, a trainee could even gain diplomas and qualifications beneficial to him in civilian life.

However not all the men were able, or wanted to partake in the learning of a specific trade; these were the general duty workers, officially listed as Admin Orderlies. A man appointed as such could be sent anywhere on the camp to do any job, whether it be digging holes, moving sewage or cleaning windows.

Our hero, Tony Ryan, is one of these men. Tony is a confident, working-class young man who, although granted a deferment from call-up until the completion of his apprenticeship, decides to break it and join the RAF. This story follows his two years as a serviceman, and is portrayed as authentically as possible within a society of similar young men. It includes violence, dirty language and dirty tricks, together with sexual exploits, a love triangle and a belly full of laughs.

In fact the whole book, although it is fiction, is written to show service life in the raw, living in that situation at that time, over fifty years ago.

1

'Come on, Tony, get yerself moving, you haven't struck a bat since snap time, if foreman sees you sat doing nowt, lad, you'll get sack.'

The young man being addressed didn't even raise his eyes from his perusing of the *Daily Mirror*, let alone move as requested.

The older man on the scaffold, Bob Car, a big fleshy chap in his late thirties, a fully qualified bricklayer, was trying to teach the young man his trade. However, he'd finally come to the conclusion that Tony Ryan had no interest whatsoever in laying bricks, or in fact anything concerning the building trade.

They were working on the gable end of a block of semi-detached houses, on a big building site on the outskirts of Leeds; the whole site was buzzing with activity, in the hot late summer sunshine. Bob glanced towards the opposite end of the block with a sigh; working in harmony were his mate, Fred Jackson and young Mick his apprentice, both toiling away in earnest. He felt envious of such a dedicated apprentice as Mick as he gave Tony a quick sideways glance; the lad was still staring at the newspaper.

'Keen as mustard that lad, Mick,' Bob muttered. 'He'll make a fine tradesman, no doubt about that.'

Glancing at Tony, still sitting there on a stack of bricks with his head buried in the paper, he yelled, 'For God's sake, Tony, get your bloody arse off there and let's have you moving. There's Tom Crabtree the foreman down there talking to them navvies trenching, can't you see, lad?' he yelled. Giving another glance down below the scaffold, he went on, 'He'll be coming up here next, I'll bet.'

Tony didn't make a move; in fact he didn't seem to be listening to what was being said to him.

'I've told you, Tony,' Bob hissed menacingly, 'if he sees you sat there reading, you'll get sack, lad – and what's more, he won't think much of me either for letting you lounge about like that doing nowt.

Tony sighed and slowly got to his feet. He folded the paper casually and put it into his tool bag, then turned to Bob and said with a chuckle, 'Okay, mate, I don't want to get you into his bad books.' He bent down and picked up his trowel. 'But as far as my job's concerned, he can do as he likes – in fact, he can stick it up his fucking fat arse if he wants. I'm going for my medical tomorrow. I'm joining up for my National Service. I'm going into the RAF, Bob, what about that then?' He grinned, and started laying bricks at last.

2

'How did you go on then, Tony, my old mate?' yelled the young chap sitting at the bar in the Dog and Gun as Tony walked in; he was a smartly dressed lad about five feet nine or ten, same as Tony, but skinnier.

'Fine,' replied Tony, going over to his mate, grinning. 'Pint of best please, Bernard,' he called out to the short, thickset landlord as he neared the bar.

'Well, come on, did you pass the Service medical okay then?' his mate Dave enquired anxiously.

'Of course I did, you silly bugger, what did you expect? They know a good thing when they see one, believe me.' He laughed.

'Been for your medical today, have you, Tony lad?' Bernard asked, passing him over a big frothy pint. 'What grade were you then?'

Taking the pint glass from him and handing over a two shilling piece, Tony first took a long swig at the ale then, putting it down on the bar top, gave him a prolonged stare. 'A1 of course, Bernard,' he said in an exasperated tone. Pulling a bar stool forward next to his mate, he glanced back at the smiling landlord, shaking his head in disbelief. 'Christ, man, what did you expect?'

Dave sat there on his stool with his elbows on the bar and gave the man a look of mock amazement. 'Bernard, you should have taken it for granted that Tony would be super-fit,' he said. 'With all that pumping iron he does, he's like Superman.'

Taking another swig of ale, Tony said, 'All right, stop taking the piss, Mansfield, you could do with some of it yourself, you skinny bugger.'

Laughing loudly, Dave reached over to him with a mock punch to the shoulder. 'Shut up, you miserable sod,' he said. As the barman moved away to serve another customer, Dave leaned towards his friend confidentially and whispered, 'Hey, Tony, listen, I've got some good news, bird-wise.'

This being Tony's favourite subject, Dave got his immediate attention. Grinning, he asked, 'Good news you say? Come on then, mate, spill the beans, what you been up to now?'

Very seriously Dave said, 'Well, I told you about my older sister Peggy – you know, the one that's just divorced her husband in Canada; well, she arrived home a few days back.'

'Yes, I know about her,' Tony chipped in. 'You said she was coming home, but what's she have to do with us landing some young birds?' he asked . 'Surely all her mates are old buggers in their thirties like her, aren't they?'

'Hey!' Dave said sharply. 'She might be in her thirties, mate, but she's still my sister, and what's more, she's not all that bad looking for her age.'

Reaching over to him Tony stroked his cheek. 'Oh dear, dear, looking after our little sister, are we?' he said mockingly. 'Come on now, joke over, what's this about getting us fixed up with some nice crumpet for the weekend?'

In an exasperated tone, Dave said, 'I'll tell you if you'll let me; now bloody well listen. Our Peg has bought a third share in that new dancing school in that mill complex off main street; she's in partnership with her old friend, Sue and her husband, Tom.'

'Yes, yes,' said Tony butting in impatiently, 'but what's it to do with –'

'Will you shut up and let me get on with it, for Christ's sake,' Dave snapped at him. Taking a sip from his glass of ale, he continued, 'Well, she went down there last night to have a look at her investment and she said it looks great, but Sue told her there are lots of young girls at the dances but there's always a shortage of blokes.' With a smug smile, he went on, 'So I told her we'd help her out there. We can do that, can't we, mate, eh?'

Looking back at him cautiously Tony replied, 'Well, we can have a look at the goods, Dave, obviously. I'm always ready for a bit of the old slap and tickle, as you know, but if they're all a bunch of frumps we'll be out quick, back to the Dog and Gun, okay?'

'Oh sure, of course, mate, I'm with you there without a doubt, but our Peg assured me they get a good mix of nice young girls at them dances down there.'

'Well, they might do, but we can't depend on a woman's judgment when it comes to attractive young birds, can we?' Tony told him with a nod. Then laughing he added, 'I mean your sister won't have been assessing 'em for nice arses and the like, will she?'

Joining in the laughter Dave replied, 'I shouldn't think so, mate. Anyway, the next dance is on Friday, are you game?'

'Sure am,' Tony said, grabbing the empty glasses and pushing them across the bar top towards the barman. 'Same again, Bernard,' he said, slapping two half-crowns down, smiling.

As Bernard was heaving on the big wooded pump handles Tony muttered, 'But don't forget, Dave, if the bloody place is full of thirty-year-old women or frumpy young birds, we're off right sharp, okay, mate?'

'Sure, sure,' grumbled Dave. 'What do you think I am, a bloody masochist or summat?' Taking a long drink from his new pint, Dave sat back on his stool with a contented look on his face. 'Are you certain they're going to put you in the RAF then, Tony? I've heard that it's the luck of the draw where you're put.' He grinned. 'Look well if they've put you down for the Royal Artillery, eh?'

'Don't be bloody stupid, Dave. I passed grade one and sailed through the written test with flying colours; it was obvious I was for the RAF. They put all the best in there, you know,' he told him, smirking. 'Anyway,' he went on, 'my medical report sheet was stamped RAF in the Service column and I was told that I would most likely be posted to RAF Padgate for my basic training.'

'Oh well, that looks final enough then, Tony,' Dave replied, nodding. 'But what made me sceptical was the way they treated that little guy, Nigel Lacy, him that worked at the sewage works, you know. He was in the ATC for about five years from when he was thirteen, got to be a Warrant Officer an' all; then they shoved him into the bloody Royal Artillery.'

'Oh aye, I know all about that silly little fart, Dave. He should have kicked up a stink as soon as he was told, but he did fuck all until they sent him to an army training camp. Mind you, the officer in command of the ATC unit is fighting the case for him; I think there's a good chance he'll get a transfer into the RAF before long.'

'He should do if there's any justice,' Dave said, taking another long swig at his pint. 'Poor little bugger, treating him like that after him training for the bloody air force in the ATC for five years; and what's more getting to the rank he did.' 'Mind you, he told me he only passed grade two at his medical,' Tony chipped in.

'Did he, what's wrong with him then?'

'Bad eyes,' Tony said. 'He wears glasses as you know, but he didn't say there was anything else wrong with him. Mind you,' he chuckled, 'there can't be or else they wouldn't even have had him in the bloody army.'

'Suppose not,' Dave said, turning on his stool to look behind at the doorway where a noisy crowd were filing in.

Following his gaze Tony muttered, 'Huh, it's that bloody apprentice plumber, Chris Simpson and his gang from the bottom end of Canal Road. This could be hassle, Dave. Tony sighed. 'Turn round, mate, we don't want them to see us or they'll be over here, and that'll be trouble for sure.'

They sat quietly with their backs to the flashily attired lads, who were all dressed in full Teddy boy regalia, until Tony shook his head and said, 'Would you believe it? Them bloody suits they're all wearing cost the thick end of a fifteen quid each.' Frowning, Bernard surveyed them with a cautious eye, clearly disapproving of their maroon-coloured, three-quarter-length coats with velvet collars, string ties, and black trousers so tight that they looked as though they were going to bust. Thick-soled suede shoes in various colours completed their uniforms.

'What are we bothering about them silly buggers for?' asked Dave, giving a quick back glance at the noisy gang, who were now standing at the far end of the room yelling for their booze.

'Because,' said Tony firmly, 'if that big-mouthed Simpson comes over here throwing his weight about, as he usually does when he gets stuck into his ale, I'll have to drop him like I did last Christmas at the firm's dance.'

'Well, what's wrong with that, mate?' Dave laughed. 'He asked for it then and if he's daft enough to repeat himself when he knows he can't handle the situation, he's a bloody fool and deserves all he gets, I say.'

'Yes, you're right of course, and I don't mind doing him the service normally, but not tonight, right?'

'Why, what's special about tonight?' A little exasperated, Tony spelled it out for him firmly. 'Because to drop the silly bastard we'll have to have a bit of a scrap, won't we?'

'Yes,' Dave agreed, nodding.

'Then if there's scrapping in a pub, what will the landlord do?'

'Well, he usually gets the cops, don't he?' Dave replied aloofly.

'Full marks.' Tony smiled. 'And that's why we don't want any bother here tonight, because if I get arrested for scrapping now it could go against me getting into the RAF. You see, Dave, they're dead keen on a clean character in the junior Service, any ruffians are usually drafted into the army and nearly always they put them into the Pioneer Corps.'

'Pioneer Corps, what the fuck's that?' Dave asked, shaking his head incredulously.

Tony said, 'It's the Army's bloody navvy brigade, you nit. They do all the digging and shit shovelling, like the heavy gang on the building site, the lowest of the low.' He shrugged.

'Oh,' said Dave.

They were so engrossed in conversation that they failed to notice the tall, slim figure coming purposefully across the room towards them.

3

'Well, well,' a rough voice called out with a cackling laugh, 'if it ain't 'Tarzan and the ape.'

For a moment, the two mates froze; neither turned to see who was interrupting, having recognised the voice of Chris Simpson, slurred by booze.

A silent pause lasting several seconds followed, then Tony, slowly getting off his bar stool, turned to face the intruder. Dave cringed. But what happened next he would never have believed in a million years, if he hadn't seen it with own eyes.

Simpson watched closely as Tony turned to face him, and then stepped back slightly with a nervous smirk on his face. After throwing a quick reassuring glance down the room at his mates, he stood there laughing, bracing himself for the response, which, when it came, surprised everyone.

Smiling broadly, Tony said warmly, 'Hello there, Chris me old mate, haven't seen you out boozing up this way for a bit. Can I get you a pint or summat?'

Simpson stared back suspiciously, giving Dave a quick puzzled look.

'By the way, Chris,' Tony went on in the same friendly way, 'I'd like to congratulate you on your winning the big draw at work; forty quid, weren't it?'

Realising that there wasn't going to be a violent confrontation, Chris spluttered, 'Uh, no, it were fifty quid, Tony.'

'Phew, you lucky sod, Chris. Fifty quid?' Tony gasped in mock envy. 'It's a wonder you're still talking to us hard-up serfs, now you've got that sort of money at your disposal.'

A conceited smile crossed Chris's face as Tony said this. Yes, he really was quite well off, he thought, his weekly wage as a senior apprentice was only around five quid, with overtime an' all. His mate Tom, a fully qualified plumber, was lucky to take home seven; so yes, Tony was right for once, he was a cut above the rest now, Chris concluded.

Smiling and shaking his head, he replied in a condescending tone, 'Don't be daft, Tony my old mate, I'm no snob, you know that, just because I've gone up in the world a bit. No, I'm still the same bloke as I've always been. I'm still one of the lads, Tony, don't you worry,' he added, patting Tony on the shoulder. 'Anyway, what about some ale on me, you guys. If I can't buy you lads a pint, a man in my position,' he said with a loud laugh, 'it's a bugger.'

'Oh, that's very thoughtful of you Chris,' Tony replied. 'We're on best bitter if that's okay, mate.'

'No problem, Tony, old pal,' Chris said magnanimously, pulling a brown leather wallet from the inside pocket of his long maroon velvet-trimmed Teddy boy coat. Then strutting defiantly up to the bar, he called out to the landlord standing at the bottom end talking to a customer, 'Come on now, Bernard; let's have some service up here.'

'Yes, sir, what will it be?' Bernard called back with a smile, realising peace was to prevail.

In a tone of authority Chris said, 'Two pints of your best bitter for my mates here,' nodding at the two of them. A crisp ten shilling note materialised from the wallet, and making sure everybody could see it, he slowly put it down on the bar in front of the landlord. 'And one for your good self, Bernard,' he slurred. With a greasy smirk, he added, 'Keep the change.'

Without any more ado, Chris turned to rejoin his friends down the room, calling out to the two lads, 'See you later, boys.'

Tony and Dave could hardly contain their laughter, watching him walking off with his arse in the air, and his long thin legs encased in the skintight pants.

Bernard stood behind the bar with a mystified expression on his face and the ten bob note in his hand; he leaned forward towards them, and said in a low voice, 'Christ, has he come into money or summat? I never thought I'd see that one tipping and buying you two buggers ale, he must be rolling in the stuff.'

Then as he was pulling their pints, he said, 'The last time he came in here I had to chuck him and his mates out for scrapping. I banned 'em for a month as well.'

'Aye,' said Tony with a grin. 'If I hadn't wanted to keep out of bother for the sake of going into the RAF, he'd have been in one just then, Bernard.'

'What do you mean Tony, why?' he asked.

'Well, didn't you hear him when he first came over to us? He called me Tarzan and Dave here, a bloody ape.'

Laughing as he passed their pints over the bar, Bernard said, 'Good job you are going into the RAF then, Tony lad, or I might have had to chuck you out and ban *you* for scrapping.'

4

'Come on then, mate, knock it back and let's be off down to the fish and chip shop, I'm starving,' Dave said a few pints later.

'Nay, what's the bloody rush, Dave; it's only quarter to ten, we've time for another before we go,' Tony moaned.

Just then the door opened and two young couples came in, one of them a young RAF corporal in his mid to late twenties, the other man of similar age smartly dressed in civvies. The two attractive young women with them were dressed smartly but formally; it was obvious that these people were not rough types like Chris Simpson and his cronies.

As they walked up to the bar the Canal Street gang spotted them; by now having downed several more pints apiece, they were all boisterous and feeling confident.

'Bloody hell,' shouted a little fat member of the gang in a slurry voice. 'Look what the wind's blown in.' Coarse laughter from his companions followed.

They were completely ignored by the little party, the corporal going smiling up to the bar. 'Two pints of best bitter and two port wines please, landlord,' he said politely, as the laughing and taunts continued from the bottom end of the room.

Tony, seeing the man was RAF, felt an alliance with him; he also knew that the gang of idiots making all the noise were well and truly popped up by now and could easily turn violent.

'Hang on, Dave,' he whispered, 'go get us a half each, and let's bide our time for a bit here. I'd like to keep an eye on that lot; they're out to start picking on them folk that's just come in.'

'Well, what if they are, its nowt to do with us,' Dave replied firmly. 'How long have you been so protective over bloody total strangers? It's none of our business, Tony.'

Looking back at him with an expression of amazement, Tony said, 'Are you fucking blind or summat, can't you see one lad's RAF? They all might be for what we know, that's why it's my business. I'm as good as in the service myself, aren't I?' he stated proudly.

'I still can't see why you should bother,' Dave said sulkily, getting up and making for the bar.

'It's what you call comradeship, Dave,' Tony stressed, giving the Canal Street gang a black look as their noise continued to increase in volume.

Still laughing and making insulting remarks about the strangers, the gang were being egged on by the little fat guy with the big mouth who first started the offensive.

'That's Harry Proudfoot who's making all the bloody noise,' said Tony on Dave's return with the beer. 'He wouldn't dare make a muff if he didn't have the gang behind him.' Watching things intently, he slowly slid off the bar stool saying softly, 'Come on, Dave, it's about time we nipped this in the bud.'

He'd noticed the gang suddenly start to wander up towards the two couples, who were now seated around one of the little tables in the centre of the room.

Bernard had also noticed aggro brewing and was standing behind the bar looking very anxious, more so when he saw the two lads making a move. 'Looks like that lot's after bother,' he said, leaning towards them over the bar top. 'Don't you two get involved, lads; if they start their trouble I'll have the bobbies here in five minutes flat.'

'Don't worry, Bernard,' Tony assured him as he made to go over to the noisy, smirking group, 'I think I may be able to stop any trouble before it starts.'

Doubtfully, Bernard stood watching Tony, followed by his mate, walk confidently towards the rowdy lot.

Seeing them approaching, the gang went silent, just standing there, smirking.

'Mind your own business, you two,' yelled out little fat Proudfoot as they got near. 'This 'as nowt to do with you lot; it's only a bit of fun anyway.'

Ignoring him, Tony went up to Chris Simpson, who was not in the jeering group, but standing at the bar watching with amusement, smiling and shaking his head.

Standing very close, Tony said quietly into his ear, 'Chris, do us a favour, mate, cool these lads of yours down. I know we're all a bit lively when we've had a few pints, myself included.' He grinned. 'But look at Proudfoot, it's him that's causing it, I know it's not you.' Nodding in the direction of the two couples sitting talking, he went on, 'They're strangers and they've done nowt wrong, Chris.'

A little surprised at Tony's concern for total strangers, Chris replied with a little smirk, 'I've never been under the impression that you cared for any bugger but yourself, Tony. You'll be telling me next that you've taken holy orders.'

'Well no, not quite that far, mate, but can you see, there's one in that group who's a member of the RAF; they all might be for what we know.'

Glancing over, Chris replied, 'Yes, course I can – so what?'

'Well, I'm going in myself in the next couple of weeks, and if I'm mixed up in any bar room bother and get involved with the cops it could bugger up my chances in the service before I bloody well get in. Especially if it involves RAF personnel being assaulted – see what I mean, Chris?'

Thinking for a second, Chris gave a little laugh. 'I knew you were thinking about yourself, Tony Ryan, you bugger.' Then glaring at Proudfoot in the middle of the room still making noises, he yelled out, 'Hey, you! You fat little twit, shut it before I shut it for you!' Pointing towards the door, he hollered to the gang, 'Out! We're off down Canal Street – we'll just make it to the Golden Lyon before last orders.'
Without another word, they all turned and followed him out of the door like lamb.

5

The door closed behind them and Bernard, behind the bar, gave a little clap. 'Well done, Tony lad,' he said laughing, 'I never took you for a diplomat, come on, you're both worth one on the house for that.'

Back at the bar, the lads were surprised when the RAF corporal got up from his table and came over to them, smiling warmly. 'Yes, and I'd like to say I agree with you, landlord, these young men handled that situation with them drunks admirably. I noticed them as soon as we came in; it was obvious they were in a troublesome mood. Normally that wouldn't bother me, I'm used to handling troublesome characters like them, but this is my first wedding anniversary. We're having a little celebration with my mate and his wife tonight, so I didn't want it spoiled, arguing with rabble like them.' Shaking hands with both lads, he continued to thank them for their efforts.

'Oh, it was no trouble to me really,' Tony said with a confident smile on his face. 'I'm used to that lot.' Nodding at Bernard, he laughed, 'Ask him. Anyway,' he continued proudly, 'got to look after your own, I'll be in that uniform within the next couple of weeks all being well.'

'Oh,' said the corporal with added interest, 'Do you know where your posting is yet, then?'

'Not officially, I only had my medical today. A1 though,' Tony added hastily, 'however on my medical sheet it did say something about RAF Padgate. By the way,' he continued, 'my name's Tony Ryan, my mate here is Dave Mansfield.' He thought it better to be on first name terms seeing they were to be in the same service; who knows, they might be in action together sometime.

'Sounds as though that's your posting then,' the corporal replied, smiling. 'Mind you, it's not forced to be, but it appears most likely. Anyway, pal, I wish you the best,' he said earnestly, 'our paths might cross again sometime.'

Feeling proud, Tony continued seriously, 'Where are you stationed then, Corporal, if you don't mind me asking?'

'Padgate as a matter of fact, I'm a DI there,' he replied casually. After a moment's pause he added, 'My name's Corporal Steve Grimes, I work on B wing.'

'Oh, a DI, Steve. What does that job entail, then?' Tony asked.

A little laughter erupted from behind him; Bernard was nodding, 'You'll soon find out lad, when you get there.'

Laughing, Steve said, 'Sounds as though you're ex-service, landlord.'

'Sure am.' Bernard told him, with pride. 'Twenty years in your mob, I was; ended up a SWO man. Still on reserve, an'all.' he added.

Steve feigned fear. 'Whoa, better watch my step with you then, sir.' Getting up to go back to his table he said, 'Well, best of luck, wherever you're posted, Tony.' He laughed. 'Who knows, you might end up in my flight.'

Pleased with the conversation, Tony took a long swig at his ale, put his glass back down on the bar top, and spoke in a low voice, 'Nice guy that Steve, isn't he, Bernard, but he never said what his job entailed.'

'He did,' chipped in Dave. 'He said he was a DI, or summat.

'Yes, I know he did,' Tony snapped, 'but what the bloody hell's that, that's what I asked him, but he never said.'

'Drill instructor,' Bernard replied bluntly, as he turned to serve another chap, who had just walked up to the bar.

Looking back at his mate, Tony repeated slowly, 'Drill instructor; huh, sounds like some sort of an engineering job, Dave, eh?'

'Oh, I don't know, mate,' he replied, 'and I don't bloody well care. Ask Bernard, when he's served that old bloke; he'll know, being ex-service himself.'

When he did ask him if it had anything to do with engineering, Bernard laughed his head off. 'Drill instructor, nay lad, it's nowt to do with engineering and them sort of drills, a drill instructor in the service is the man who teaches foot drill, you know marching and square bashing in general.' With Tony looking back at him blankly, he started to chuckle. 'He teaches recruits their basic foot drill, you'll find out when you get there, don't worry, Tony.'

'Oh, I'm not worried, Bernard,' he replied cockily, glancing across at the corporal, who sat with his back to them. 'So really he's a teacher then, Bernard, eh?' He finished his pint and put the glass down. 'I thought he looked that type, you know, studious, sensitive.'

Smiling knowingly, Bernard replied, 'Like I said, Tony, you'll find out soon enough when you get to your camp. By the way, Dave, I see that sister of yours is back home, I saw her pass here this afternoon weighed down with shopping bags; big beautiful lass she is and no mistake.'

'Yes, Peg's coming back for good this time, Bernard, she's going into business with her mate, Sue and her husband Tom; she's bought a share in that dancing club of theirs.'

'Oh, has she?' Bernard nodded approvingly. 'Good investment that, I should think.'

'Aye, and she's bought that luxury flat at the back an'all.' Dave added, with a note of pride in his voice.

'She must have plenty of brass,' chipped in Tony.

'She's just got her divorce through in America, they're selling their property over there, that's where she's getting the cash from,' Dave told him. 'She might have to go back for a few weeks to settle the finances between them, though,' he added, 'but she's definitely had enough of that swine she was married to.'

He thumped his fist down on the bar top and muttered, 'I'd kill the bastard if I got my hands on him.'

'Treated her badly, did he lad?' Bernard was sympathetic.

'No, not physically, Bernard,' he replied with a laugh. 'Our Peg could easily have sorted him out that way, no, the local vicar found him in bed with his own wife. The vicar sued him, and divorced his wife.'

'The man must be a bloody fool to want a bit on the side, when he'd got a lovely young woman like Peggy at home waiting for him,' sneered Bernard.

Laughing, Dave said, 'Well, she's my big sis, Bernard, and I love her, but she's not so young any more, she's well into her thirties you know, a bit past her best, eh?'

'What!' Bernard yelled. 'You silly young bugger, old in her thirties, she's only a girl; what about me then at fifty-two, I suppose you think I'm ready for the bloody cemetery. Believe me,' he went on with a nod, 'a woman her age is in the prime of life; especially a big fine-looking lass like her.'

Putting their empty glasses down on the bar, Dave said, laughing, 'Okay, Bernard, every man to his own taste, but my mate and me like 'em young and sweet, don't we, Tony?'

'You're right there, Dave,' he replied, giving Bernard a cheeky wink. 'What's more we've got some lined up for the weekend, Bernard, that would make you change your mind about them old birds in their thirties.' He turned to Dave and winked. 'That's right, mate, ain't it?'

'Sure is.' Dave replied cheerfully, as they made to go.'

'What's more we might even end up with two apiece Bernard,' Tony added over his shoulder. 'How's that, then?'

6

'Smells nice and scented in here, Dave,' Tony remarked, going through the door into the main reception area leading to the dance floor.

'Sure does,' he replied, making for the pay desk. The young woman sitting there painting her nails, smiled seductively as he passed her the two complementary tickets his sister had given him. 'Come on, mate,' he said to Tony, grinning and nodding in the direction of a door behind the pay desk, from where the sound of loud music could be heard. 'Let's get at 'em.'

It was a large dance hall, much bigger than expected for a dancing club. They'd had visions of it being a poky little dump but they were wrong, it was equally as spacious as the local town hall dance floor, and professionally decorated too. 'Oh, very nice, I must say,' Tony remarked, somewhat taken aback, 'but there'd better be some worthwhile crumpet in here, mate, or we're back off down to the Dog, right quick.'

'There will be, don't worry mate; our lass said the men were greatly outnumbered, so we should score in here tonight, without fail. She even said there were some lovely young girls our age, having to dance with each other, men were so scarce.'

'That might be so, but it's quality we're after, Dave mate, not quantity,' Tony said out of the side of his mouth, as he scanned the dance floor for talent.

A radiogram was loudly playing a quickstep, and judging by the smiling faces of the dancers, everybody was really enjoying themselves. He particularly noticed a generously built woman in a loose-fitting floral dress, whirling a tall skinny youth around the floor like a dish rag, giving him firm instructions as she did so.

'Bloody hell!' Tony muttered. 'I wouldn't like to cross that old battleaxe.'

Dave, standing alongside him, suddenly tapped him on the shoulder and nodding behind whispered in his ear, 'What about them little darlings over there sat at that table under the window – you must agree that's the goods, mate, eh?'

Turning to look, a wide smile filled Tony's face. 'Oh, yes, oh yes, I must agree with you there, Dave, a sight for sore eyes, them two little beauties.' Slapping him on the back, he went on, 'I suggest we go over there, my old mate, and make our acquaintance, don't you?'

Dave, grinning as he stared at them, was obviously in full agreement. The beautiful young ladies looked to be about eighteen; both were dressed similarly, in tight-fitting dresses with splits in the sides, showing a fair amount of thigh. This, of course, pleased the lads and contemplating the thighs, Dave remarked that the dresses were a very handy design. Tony agreed and within ten minutes the lads had made the acquaintance of the girls, and the four of them were getting on like a house on fire. There was no doubt that the girls were impressed with the boys, an'all.

After another ten minutes, Tony suggested they all go outside for a walk around to get a breath of fresh air.

'Oh, you're a fast worker, Tony,' cooed Kathy, the one he'd been playing for. 'We'll have to think about that, won't we, Jane?' she giggled, looking over at her mate.

'Now then, girls,' said Dave, in a coaxing tone, himself feeling like a breather outside. 'What's up, don't you trust us to look after you? You'll be safe with us you know, nobody will hurt you, while you're with me and my mate; you can be assured of that, my darlings. That's right, Tony, eh?' he asked, glancing in his direction.

Tony didn't answer; he was standing transfixed, staring across the floor with his back to them. Suddenly without saying a word, he started walking slowly towards the edge of the dance floor.

Dave stood watching him closely for a few seconds, puzzled and concerned. He went over to join him and asked, 'What's up mate? You look as though you've seen a ghost.' Getting no reply, Dave was beginning to worry; he couldn't understand why Tony stayed silent, staring across the floor. Tapping him on the shoulder, he asked Tony again if he felt all right, still with no response.

However, after another few seconds, Tony slowly turned towards Dave, and gestured towards the direction he'd been staring at. 'Just look at that goddess over there, Dave,' he said quietly. 'Now that's what I call a woman.'

Straining his neck to look in the direction indicated, Dave scanned the area briefly, then replied, 'I can't see 'owt to get all that worked up about, mate.'

Surprised, Tony hissed, 'What's up, Dave, are you fucking blind or what? You can't miss her.' Pointing over at a group of women standing talking at the far end of room, he said, 'Over there, look, in that gang of women, gassing. God,' he mumbled, shaking his head, 'she's the most gorgeous woman I've ever seen, you can't miss her among that lot, Dave, surely?'

Looking again intently, Dave replied frowning, 'Which one do you mean, Tony? Honest, mate, I can't see anything in that lot to get excited about. Come on, let's get back to business – we've just about got them two sweeties ready for a bit of fun outside.'

Tony wasn't listening, he just muttered, 'You can't miss her, Dave; Good God, man, if you don't appreciate a beautiful female like that, there's summat wrong with you, mate.'

Beginning to think Tony had lost his marbles, Dave was getting bored. 'For Christ's sake, Tony, which of the buggers is it that's got your bloody fancy; I thought I knew your taste in birds, but I can't see 'owt over there to impress you like this.'

Still staring across the floor, Tony replied, 'That tall athletic specimen in the tight-fitting light blue jeans, white top, and long fair hair tied back.'

Dave gave another quick glance at the chatting group of women, then, suddenly looked back at Tony, with open-mouthed astonishment. 'You must be fucking kidding, Tony,' he gasped.

'I'm bloody well not,' he snapped. 'Don't tell me you don't fancy her, mate, or I'll think you're not the man I thought you were.'

Still in shock, Dave mumbled, 'Of course I don't fancy her, you daft pillock - that's our Peg.'

Spinning around to face Dave in shocked disbelief, Tony yelled, 'What! It can't be; you're bloody kidding, Dave, aren't you?'

'I'm not bloody kidding,' said Dave firmly. 'That's our Peggy over there I tell you, so let's get back to them two young birds now, and forget about her.'

Looking back across at the group of women, he muttered, 'I thought you said your Peggy was an old frump in her thirties.' Noticing the heavily built woman gliding past with the skinny youth in tow, he nodded in her direction, 'I thought that was your Peggy.'

Dave glanced briefly. 'No, that's Sue her business partner, they've been mates for years; anyway, are you coming?' he asked impatiently. 'We'll lose them two birds if we don't get back; there's two slimy-looking hairy arses on that next table, trying to chat 'em up.'

Tony wasn't listening. He was again staring across the dance floor. 'Right Dave, my old mate, you've convinced me; I believe that goddess over there is your Peggy.' He braced himself and grabbing Dave's arm, said firmly, 'So, come on then. Let's get over there, without wasting any more time, and you can introduce me to her.'

Pulling back, Dave argued, 'No, hang on Tony, there's plenty of time for that; I can introduce you to her tomorrow. Come on; let's get back to them lovely young birds, before they fly away with them two toe-rags.'

Tony was adamant. 'Oh, bugger them two, let the bloody toe-rags have 'em, I want introducing to Peggy, tonight, now! Never mind about tomorrow.'
Reluctantly, Dave followed him, as he made his way across the dance floor, weaving in and out of the dancers.

7

Peggy, amongst the talking, laughing group of women, was taller than most, and could easily see the approaching lads. Frowning, she tactfully pushed through her friends to meet them.

Going straight up to Dave she leaned forward towards him, her face close, sniffing. 'You've been boozing,' she chastised, menacingly. 'What did I tell you, you're not drunk I hope?' She nodded sharply. 'Bloody well showing me up.'

Tony felt like bursting out laughing. His mate, who'd stood shoulder to shoulder with him in a scrap with half a dozen of the Canal street gang, was quivering now, like a scared rabbit.

'Course I'm not drunk, sis,' he said meekly. 'We've only had one pint each in the Dog on the way here, haven't we, Tony?' he said, turning to him for reassurance.

'Well, I can't tell a lie, Dave,' Tony said piously, 'I think it was one and a half, mate.'

Dave, knowing full well it was three, said, 'Oh yes, you're right, Tony. I forgot that half the landlord bought us.'

Peggy, not to be fooled, said, 'I don't care how many you had as long as you're not drunk.' Stepping back, she continued sweetly, 'Anyway you both look okay, so you'll be ready for some dancing, eh?' She laughed.

Seeing as he'd passed the beer test, Dave, who had now regained his usual confidence, said, 'By the way Peg, I'd like to introduce you to my best mate here,

Tony,' and winking at his mate, he continued, 'and this is Peggy, my big sister.'

Tony stood smiling and staring intently at her, as she turned to him. Looking straight into his blue, laughing eyes, she returned his smile. 'I don't suppose you could be Tony Ryan, by any chance, could you, young man?'

For a few seconds Tony was speechless, staring at her with adoration and thinking how beautiful she was. At last, he mumbled nervously, 'Why yes, that's right, Peggy, but how did you know?' He forced a little laugh. 'You must be a mind reader.' She was still smiling and staring into his eyes and he was beginning to feel giddy.

'No, Tony, I'm not a mind reader, we've met before you and me – in fact, on many occasions.' He couldn't believe what he was hearing and glanced at Dave, baffled.

'Stop trying to take the piss out of us, our Peg,' Dave said. 'You've never met Tony before tonight and you know it.'

Scowling, she said sharply, 'You keep your language clean in here, you're not on a building site now you know – my friends are not used to that sort of talk. Anyway, I'm not taking the p – what you said,' she continued firmly. 'We have met before, and on more than one occasion.' 'Mind you, it was a long time ago,' she added, looking back at the puzzled Tony, with a gloating smile.

'Look, Peg, I know you've been back home on holiday several times over the years, while you lived in America, but I can't ever remember you meeting Tony, even then,' Dave said, now beginning to wonder himself.

'No, I've never met you, Peggy, and that's for sure, honest,' Tony insisted firmly.

Now beginning to enjoy their bafflement, she laughed. 'You have Tony, but as I said it was a long time ago, love; in fact, it was that long ago, I used to push you and our Dave around the Park Lake in a double pushchair.' Then, with mock sincerity, she continued, 'and what's more, on many occasions I even had to take you both round the back of the duck shed and get your little willies out for a pee.'

Suddenly coughing with embarrassment, Tony spluttered, 'Well, we're wasting time talking about the distant past. What about these dancing lessons? After all, that's what we're here for, ain't it?'

Realising she'd embarrassed the lads, Peggy said seriously, 'Yes, of course it is.' She looked around the room and spotted her big-built mate, Sue, who was standing with the crowd of women, waiting for the next dance tune to start playing. Catching her eye, Peggy waved her over, just as the music struck up a tango.

Sue came up to them smiling cheerfully, 'I suppose you want a hand with these two good-looking young boys then, Peggy love, right?'

'That's right, Sue, this one,' she told her pointing at Dave. 'This is my brother, as you know. Tony here is his best pal; they can both dance reasonably they say, but want to improve.' She smiled at Tony. 'Right, Sue will put you through your paces, Tony, and I'll see to this awkward brother of mine.'

Tony's mind raced like lightning. 'Oh, I'm a bit shy Peggy, I don't know your friend Sue here; I don't think I dare go out on the floor with someone I don't know.' Fidgeting nervously, he ploughed on, 'I thought you might show me this lesson, seeing as it's the first time I've ever had one.'

Dave's ears suddenly pricked up. 'Oh yes, he always has been a bit shy has Tony; I'll dance with Sue.' He went smilingly up to her.

'Okay, then, it makes no difference,' Peggy said, with a laugh. 'I'll take you round then, Tony; Sue can take our Dave.'

Glancing back as he walked on to the dance floor hand in hand with Peggy, Tony felt very pleased. What's more, he nearly burst out laughing when he saw his mate being swung into action behind him, in the powerful arms of Peggy's friend. The tango was not one of Tony's favourite dances, but that didn't bother him – he'd got what he wanted – with Peggy in his arms, he felt he could dance the tango all night. Being of a similar height, their faces were close together and Tony could smell her perfume. The occasional brush of her cheek, as they tangoed back and forth, thrilled him more than any woman's touch had ever done.

After going around the floor a couple of times without saying anything, Peggy remarked softly, 'You're quiet, Tony, don't say you feel shy dancing with me, as well.'

Smiling he replied, 'No, I was just thinking, Peggy, that's all.' Looking deep into her lovely blue eyes, he had a gut feeling that she'd realised how he felt about her already.

Walking off the floor, hand in hand as the music ended, Tony asked quietly, 'Can we dance together again later, Peggy? I enjoyed that.'

Looking into his serious, enquiring face she replied softly, 'Yes, of course we can.' Without another word, she left him standing there on his own, and returned to the little group of women, still talking. Amongst them, Sue, was looking flushed after her bout of throwing Dave around the dance floor for the past ten minutes.

'How did you get on then, mate?' Tony asked with a grin, going up to Dave, who sat at the side of the tea bar, looking hot and bothered.

'You're a lucky bugger, you are, being shy,' he said angrily. 'That big fat cow nearly killed me doing the bloody tango.'

'Oh dear, it weren't all that bad surely, Dave,' he said with mock sympathy. 'She had you going around the floor like a true professional; I noticed you a couple of times when you both went flying past us.'

'It's okay you taking the piss, Tony, but she had me bending backwards and forwards so fast doing that fucking tango – she kneed me int' knackers, I can hardly stand up now – it's bloody agony, I'll tell you,' he moaned.

After he'd subdued his raucous laughing fit, Tony managed to control himself. 'Oh, so I don't suppose you'll be wanting to go outside with them two young ladies now, then, Dave, seeing as you've damaged your tackle, eh?'

'No, I bloody won't and I bet you're not bothered either, now you've taken a liking to our Peggy.'

Cringing and holding his legs close together, he looked up at the still smirking Tony, and sneered, 'Don't think you'll get 'owt from her, mate, you won't blarney her like we do these young birds, you know,' he said defiantly. 'She's a woman of the world I'll tell you, Tony,' he went on, 'She'll make mincemeat out of you, believe me, mate.'

Smiling cockily, he replied, 'Oh dear, poor old Dave's getting protective again, eh?'

'Huh, no need for me to bother about that, mate,' he grunted. 'She can hold her own in a scrap. She's been studying martial arts for three years at a club in America; she's a bloody black belt or summat, in karate and another one of them things,' he told him. This was followed by a groan as he clenched his legs together tighter. On hearing this, Tony's quick mind suddenly jumped into top gear. Martial arts, eh, now there's a thing. We've got something in common then, Peggy, my darling.

After standing at the little tea bar, drinking endless cups of the brew, Tony was beginning to feel absolutely pissed off. Peggy was continually dancing around the floor with different blokes giving tuition, while he stood there drinking tea with Dave, who was constantly grumbling about his sore balls. Then, luck suddenly started to go his way. After a brief pause, the music suddenly struck up with a lively tune and the voice of Tom, Sue's husband, announced on the microphone, 'Ladies and gentlemen! This is an excuse-me quickstep.'

Tony stood scanning the floor for a few moments. Suddenly, he spotted Peggy dancing with a tall bespectacled chap, with whom she was obviously having difficulties. He saw his chance – the bloke was holding her so close and tight, they could hardly dance at all, especially to a lively jig like the quickstep. In fact, Tony thought Peggy looked a bit embarrassed trying politely to loosen his grip from around her waist, while at the same time instruct him in his heavy-footed dancing.

'I think it's about time I continued my lessons, Dave,' Tony muttered over his shoulder, making for the dance floor. Waiting at the side, until Peggy and her pupil had circled the floor and were again approaching, Tony then made his move. Stepping out on to the floor he tapped the man lightly on the shoulder, 'Excuse me, please,' he said politely.

Turning, the man scowled at him, still keeping his tight hold on poor Peggy. 'What did you say young man?' he asked, sounding annoyed in his posh accent.

Tony smiled politely, pointed out that it was an 'Excuse-me' dance, and repeated, 'Excuse me please.'

Looking down into Peggy's face, then back at Tony, the man reluctantly released his vice-like hold, saying, 'Oh – is it?' As he turned to leave the floor, he cast Tony a black look and said to Peggy, 'I'm sorry about this my dear, but we can continue later, no doubt?'

As the man departed, Tony stepped forward and put his arm around Peggy. She gasped, 'Phew, I'm not so bloody sure about that, mate.'

Dancing away, Tony pulled her as close as he dare, saying, 'Hope you didn't mind me butting in, Peggy, but I thought he was giving you a hard time; he wasn't drunk, was he?'

'No love,' she said, looking into his serious face. 'He's my bank manager.' Then with a sigh she smiled, 'He's the guy that gave me a bridging loan, until I get my money sorted out in The States.'

Holding her a little closer, he said, 'Well, that doesn't give the old bugger a licence to take liberties with you, Peggy; I don't know how you could manage to dance at all, with him pulling you so close.'

'With great difficulty,' she said with a laugh.

'Anyway, as far as your loan's concerned,' Tony huffed, 'he'll be getting a bloody good interest on a very secure loan no doubt, or you wouldn't have got it, that's for sure.'

Looking into his angry face as he said this, she couldn't help but feel he was genuinely concerned; she also saw that this was not a young lad she was with. Tony Ryan was a man, a strong, mature-minded man; and suddenly she realised that he felt for her as one. She was complimented, but scared.

Laughing, she said, 'Oh, Tony you're gripping me nearly as tight as he was.'

His face relaxing, he smiled shyly. 'Sorry, Peg, I was just thinking about that fellow assuming that you owed him a favour, for his bloody bank loan.' Tony grinned. 'He didn't like me, though – did you see the black look he gave me, when I tapped him on his shoulder?'

They both laughed and as they continued dancing, she said, 'By the way you and our Dave haven't been getting much practice tonight, have you? Every time I looked over at the tea bar, you were both stood there drinking tea.'

'Well, yes, love, true,' he replied, with a chuckle. 'As a matter of fact, I was keeping Dave company. You see, he's had a little accident, has my mate.'

Looking slightly worried, she asked, 'What do you mean – accident, Tony?'

'Oh, nothing to bother about really, Peggy,' he assured her. 'In fact, I think he'll be okay by now.'

'Well, what's up with him, then?' she asked again, still concerned.

'Well, it happened when he was dancing with the big lass, Sue. She caught him between his legs with her knee as she manoeuvred him backwards and forwards during the tango.' Rather embarrassed, he said, 'Well, to be precise, she accidentally kneed him in the testicles; she doesn't know, though,' he added hastily. 'He didn't say anything to her.'

Noticing that she was smiling slightly, he went on seriously, 'It's very painful I might add; I've experienced it myself not long back, caused by a cricket ball.' At this her face cracked and she burst out laughing, and he joined in. As they whirled around the dance floor, Tony felt good – oh, so good.

Suddenly remembering, he said cheerfully, 'Oh, I nearly forgot, Peggy, Dave told me you're an enthusiast of the martial arts, in fact he told me you'd reached black belt standard in kung fu,' he added, with a note of admiration.

'Well, he told you wrong, then,' she said. 'I haven't got it yet.' Smiling, she continued, 'I was going to take the test, but I went in for a divorce instead; mind you, I intend to take it when I've got my life sorted out again. That's if there's any suitable clubs around here, I can practise at,' she said. Tony couldn't believe his luck when he heard this, but before he could continue on the subject the music stopped, ending the dance. 'Do you know young fellow you're not a bad dancer when you try,' she told him with a smile.'

'Oh, thanks,' he replied, 'I think I'll avoid the tango from now on, though.'

'Yes, talking about tangos, we'd better go and see if our Dave's got over his last try at it,' she laughed as they walked off the floor. Dave, still sitting at the tea bar looking miserable, glanced up forlornly as they arrived. Peggy immediately asked him if he'd got over his little mishap, with her friend Sue.

'Its nowt,' he told her. 'He shouldn't have told you, anyway.' he said, giving Tony a glare.

'Never mind, if you're okay, mate, that's the main thing,' Tony said cheerfully.

He turned to Peggy and went on, 'I was just thinking, Peg, with regard to your martial arts practising, why not come down to our gym? We have a course going down there you could join. As a matter of fact, I've been doing a bit myself lately,' he told her, smiling. 'Mind you, my main sport is pumping iron,' he added, with a note of pride.

Pausing for a moment, she replied, 'I don't think I'll have the time just yet, Tony, but thanks, I'll think about it for later, though,'

Not to be beaten, he continued, 'Well, why don't you let me take you down to have a look around, then you'll know what the joint is like. I'm sure you'll approve,' he nodded. 'They're all nice people, aren't they, Dave?' he said to his mate, hoping for backup.

'Ay, they're okay,' he muttered grumpily.'

'There are quite a lot of women in that class an'all,' Tony said.

'Well, I might go down when I've more time,' she replied, smiling weakly.

Tony noticed Dave giving him a thoughtful look, as he went on, 'Look, Peggy, I'm going down on Sunday morning for a bit of leg work, you know, a few squats and a few sets with the iron boots. Why not come with me? You could have a good look around while I'm training, I'll only be at it for about twenty minutes, then we can pop into the Dog and Gun for a shandy,' he suggested eagerly.

'Well, I don't know really,' she replied, glancing at Dave, with a slight look of guilt on her face. 'It might be better to wait until I know what I'm going to do first, Tony.'

'Oh, come on Peg, you're not doing anything on Sunday morning, surely,' he pleaded.

Looking down at the floor for a moment, she replied quietly, 'No, I don't suppose so.' She shot Dave another cautious glance and asked, 'Are you going, Dave?'

'Phew, not me,' he replied haughtily. 'You won't get me slugging my guts out with them bloody great weights on Sunday morning. I don't get out of my bed until it's time for the lunch-time session at the Dog, you should know that, our Peg.'

'It's no use asking that lazy bugger, Peggy,' Tony said, laughing. 'I'm fed up trying to get him to start working out at the gym and stop that bloody smoking, but he won't have it, love.'

Peggy felt she'd like to go and have a look around the club with Tony, but thought it might not look right, because she was so much older; if Dave had been going it wouldn't have looked so bad. 'I don't know, Tony,' she said hesitantly. 'It might be better to hang on for a bit.'

Not to be put off now he'd got her this far, he said, 'Oh, come on, lass, it isn't such a big deal as that, it's only a gymnasium I'm wanting to take you to, not a bloody shady night club, or summat.'

Dave seeing the situation and thinking it only right to help his mate, butted in, 'Go, on you miserable bugger, get yourself off with him. They're a great lot down there, in fact the secretary of the club, Fred Jackson, was in your class at school; he's married now – eight kids an'all,' he nodded, with a laugh.

'Oh, all right then,' she capitulated. 'Looks as though I've no choice, with you both shoving me. What time on Sunday do we go then, Tony?' she asked him, with an exasperated sigh.

'Are you still living at your mother's, or have you moved into the new flat, yet?' Tony enquired.

'I haven't moved into the flat yet, but I sleep there; I'm moving in on Tuesday, if I can get it ready for then,' she said, with a note of doubt.

'Right, I'll call round there for you about ten fifteen, if that's okay, Peg,' he replied cheerfully.

'Yes, okay, but I'd better get back over there now,' she said, noticing Sue flying around the floor with a short fat young chap, in a full drape suit.

'Don't forget you promised me the last waltz, Peggy,' Tony called after her, as she returned to her duty.

8

'What do you think to our gym then, Peggy love?'
Tony enquired. They were sitting in the quiet little
snug in the 'Dog and Gun at Sunday lunchtime.

'Very pleasantly surprised, Tony,' she replied,
giving him a sweet smile, showing her white even teeth
and making his heart flutter.

'There you are, then.' He smiled back at her.
'What did I tell you, they're a great lot of folk down
there, aren't they?'

'Oh, yes, very nice people,' she agreed, 'but I'll tell
you what, I got a shock when I saw Fred Jackson, my
old school chum. Phew - isn't he a big bugger, he was
always such a skinny little rat at school an'all,' she said,
laughing.

'Oh, aye, he's a big lad is Fred, that's what the
weights can do for you, Peggy,' he said boastfully.
'Does a bit of wrestling as well, old Fred,' he added.

'What do you mean 'old' Fred,' she said with mock
indignation, 'he was in my class at school – don't you
forget that, my lad.'

'Just a figure of speech, Peggy dear,' he said with a
laugh. 'Anyway, let's face facts, he looks twenty years
older than you, and on top of that he's not as good-
looking,' he said with a cheeky wink.

Sitting back in the chair with a slight smile on her
face, studying him across the little table, she said
quietly, shaking her head, 'You know, Tony Ryan,
you're a right bloody charmer you are, and no mistake.'

Smiling a little, he looked her in the eye and said
hesitantly, 'Peggy, I've been thinking, I wondered if
you'd let me take you out for a meal, on Monday or
Tuesday evening? You know somewhere nice and

classy,' he pointed out quickly, 'I don't mean a pub meal you understand,' he added shyly.

'You see,' he continued before she could answer, 'I got my call up papers for Military Service, and I've got to report to RAF Padgate on Thursday, to start my basic training. I won't be home again for about a couple of months,' he finished, smiling weakly.

She sat looking back at him, with a serious expression on her face for what seemed like an age, then said softly, 'I feel very complimented - you asking me, Tony, and I think you're a lovely person.' She struggled on with difficulty, 'but I think you're too young to start getting close to a woman my age.' Pausing again for a moment, she looked down at the table top without raising her eyes and continued almost in a whisper, 'It wouldn't be fair on you, Tony.' He stared back at her in silence, a blank look on his face, as she went on, 'Tony, I'll be thirty-five next birthday, darling, and you'll only be twenty, don't you understand, love?' she pleaded, looking directly into his pained face.

Suddenly he reached over the table and grasped her hands, gently pulling her towards him until their faces were nearly touching. 'Look Peg, I don't care if you're bloody ninety-five next birthday,' he whispered forcefully, 'and what's more, I don't care what anybody else thinks either about age difference; age to me doesn't exist anyway. As I see it we never age ourselves, it's the bodies we exist in that depreciate, some quicker than others,' he told her adamantly. Smiling, he giving her hand a little squeeze and continued, 'Yours must have done well; it only looks about twenty-two to me.'

Peg stared back at him momentarily, then as her face broke into a smile, she said, 'Okay, you bugger, either night will do me; you're right, sod the onlookers. Oh, and by the way, I can't wait to see you in uniform. Mind you,' she continued, as though just remembering, 'really I need every minute I've got to work on my flat, if I want to get it ready for moving in to, on Tuesday.'

'Oh, you worry too much, you women,' Tony said, with a grin. 'What's got to be done anyway, can't be much – you said it's luxury fitted out already, didn't you, Peggy?'

'Yes, Mr Hanson, the last owner was a very well-off chap, he left no stone unturned,' she replied, 'but I've still got quite a few personal things of my own to add,' she said. 'However, if I get down there this afternoon working on it and all day tomorrow, I should manage to get it ready. That's providing I can get that fellow to come and fix them pelmets and bits and pieces,' she sighed.

'What fellow's that?' Tony asked.

'A guy from the paper, my mum arranged with him to do the job last week, so it would be ready for me when I got home, but he let her down twice. I rang him this morning but I got no reply, the swine,' she grumbled.

'Forget him, love,' Tony said sternly. 'I'll be down there with my tools at two fifteen; I'll sort everything out for you, Peg, and if we don't get everything done today, I'm free Monday as well, I've finished on the building site now.'

'Are you sure, Tony?' She smiled at him. 'I asked our Dave if he'd give me a hand but he wouldn't have it, I even offered to give him a couple of quid if he'd help me, but it was no use.'

'Well, he wouldn't, that lazy bugger,' Tony said, grinning. 'He'll be back in bed after he's had his lunchtime drink and his big Sunday dinner.'

Then, glancing up at the wall clock he went on 'Oh, it's nearly one o'clock, if we want to get started down at your flat by two fifteen we'd better be making tracks for dinner, darling.'

'Yes, you're right,' she replied, getting up and grabbing her jacket off the back of the chair.

Tony, seeing her struggling to get into the thick garment, tried helping by lifting her long hair free, from where it was trapped under her collar. 'Oh, you've got beautiful silky hair, Peggy,' he whispered, as he leaned towards her. 'It smells lovely.'

She stared at him in mock shock, and then playfully shoving him back, she laughed. 'Steady, tiger, steady.'

As they walked out of the little room chattering merrily, the only other occupants, an elderly couple sitting at the far end, turned to watch. The old man chuckled to his wife, 'Ee, Freda, these young folk. We were like that at one time, does tha' remember, lass?'

Her reply was firm and to the point, 'Shut up, you silly old bugger, I'm ready for my dinner.'

Overhearing, Peggy giggled. 'Did you hear that Tony?' she whispered to him, 'Young folk!'

'Well, what's wrong with that, so we are,' he replied, playfully putting his arm around her shoulder and giving her a little squeeze.

Dave, sitting on his own at the far end of the bar in the big lounge, caught sight of them going out of the main door acting like two silly kids, 'Well, well,' he mumbled to himself, smiling.

9

Tony alighted from the packed train at Padgate station in a mood of elation, his ambition of joining the RAF had fructified; he'd also got the girl of his dreams – Peggy. Smartly dressed in his well-cut dove-grey suit, white shirt and red tie, and sporting a thick head of dark hair, expertly cut in the latest DA style, he was confident about his appearance. Walking briskly along the railway platform carrying his little weekend case, he joined the bustling crowd of young men, all of a similar age to himself, and like him, all carrying little cases, or packs of some sort, containing their bits and pieces.

Passing through the ticket terminal, a short stocky lad with ginger hair, styled in the same manner as Tony's, enquired in a thick Scottish accent, 'Are you for the RAF camp then, mate?'

Glancing down at him laughing, then looking around at all the thirty or forty other lads, Tony replied, in mock dismay, 'I think every bugger here is, pal by the look of 'em, don't you?'

Looking around, the Scot laughed 'Aye, I suppose your right there, Jimmy; where are you from then? I'm from Glasgow myself.'

'Leeds,' said Tony. 'Well, just outside,' he added. 'By the way, pal, my name's not Jimmy, I'm Tony Ryan.' He grinned, holding out his hand.

The Scots lad replied with a laugh, 'Oh, we call everybody Jimmy in Glasgow. Anyway, very pleased to make your acquaintance, Tony,' he said, taking his hand. 'I'm Gordon Tordoff, but everybody calls me Jock.' As they shook hands warmly both lads felt they had met a friend, which turned out to be the case over the next eight weeks of their military training.

It was a very rowdy, disorganized crowd of young men that wondered through the wide main gates of RAF Padgate later that morning. The single storey building, set back just inside the gates, looked the cleanest place Tony had ever seen. The paintwork was brilliant white, and the windows shone with dazzling brilliance in the bright sunlight. Standing directly in front of it was a notice board that yelled out in big black letters, 'GUARDROOM'.

As the disorderly group of young men ambled noisily through the gates, two tall, very smart corporals with white bands around their peeked headgear, white belts, and armbands saying SP, came out of the building to meet them.

'How's things, my old mates?' shouted a big fat lad, one of the more forward members of the crowd. This was followed by raucous laughter, which several of the others joined in.

The two corporals approached slowly in stern silence, waving them to a halt.

'We've come to join your lot, mate,' shouted the bold chap, grinning, 'Can you direct us to reception, by any chance?'

The two young non-commissioned officers glanced at each other expressionlessly.

'That large hut on the left is reception,' one of them said politely, pointing up the road.

'Thanks, mate,' several of the lads yelled out, as the group made off in the direction indicated.

'By the way gentlemen,' called out the other NCO in a tone of mock reverence, 'I would be very grateful if you could keep your voices down; our Sergeant back there,' he jerked his head in the direction of the guard room and nodded, 'has got a splitting headache, and he's in a very nasty mood.'

'Sure will, pal,' shouted the bold one. 'Give the poor old bugger our sympathy.' Then laughing as they walked away, he called out, 'Quiet lads! Did you hear that? The Sergeant's got a bad head, poor old bugger!' Loud, general laughter followed. As the din died down, he called over his shoulder cheerfully, 'See you later, lads.'

Staring after them one of the young police officers stood slowly shaking his head from side to side in disbelief, 'You bloody well will, mister, no doubt about that,' he said, turning to his colleague and smiling menacingly.

10

Two hours later, Tony sat on his bed in one of the allotted billets, which were large, old and dilapidated, wooden huts. Each hut housed about twenty-five men, and the place was cold, bloody cold, with draughts from every angle. The men's beds were lined up along each side of the hut; the bed head was against the outside wall, the foot to the middle. There was a walking space between the bottoms of the beds going up the full length of the hut, with an iron coke-burning stove situated in the middle. A pipe coming out of the back dispersed its smoke through a hole in the roof; this was the only means of heating in their luxury abode. The time of year being late, they soon found that when the stove burnt out in the middle of the night it got so cold that the fire buckets full of water in there, would freeze solid. Most of the lads began to sleep fully dressed to maintain adequate body heat. This was to be their home for the next eight weeks.

'What a bloody dump,' grumbled Tony, turning to his new mate, Jock, who was sitting on the next bed. 'This place is about as comfortable as the tea hut on the building site I've just managed escaped from.'

Jock laughed. 'What did you expect laddie, the bloody 'Savoy Hotel?'

Sullenly looking around the hut, seeing all the lads sitting on their beds grumbling to each other, Tony muttered, 'No, not quite that, Jock, but I bet it's more comfortable than this in Armley fucking jail.'

Several of the lads suddenly decided to go out and have a look around their new environment. 'Shall we go out for a scout around the camp, Tony?' Jock suggested cheerfully.

'Too cold to go walking around this bleak place tonight, Jock,' he replied, 'but I'll tell you what, we could go down to that NAAFI place at the bottom of the road, it's some sort of café, ain't it?'

'Aye, that's a good idea,' he agreed. 'We can get something to eat in there, and I've heard you can get a pint of Ale as well.'

'Right, what are we waiting for,' Tony said, cheering up. Grabbing his bits and pieces off the bed, he roughly shoved them into his big metal locker; each man had an identical one at the side of his bed.

'Make sure you lock it up,' Jock whispered, glancing around at the other occupants suspiciously. 'We don't know these buggers in here yet, mate.'

Saturday afternoon found Tony, and all the other young airmen living in Number Two hut, sitting on their beds, polishing brasses – the buttons on their new uniforms, and the brass on their caps, badges, belts, and buckles. Elbow grease was also being used in abundance to make their marching boots look like black glass.

The lads all looked quite different now; yes, vastly different to when they first arrived at the camp, a few days previously. First, they were all dressed the same in their Air Force blue battledress uniform, which was called 'working blue'. A dress uniform was also allotted, used mainly on parades and social occasions and referred to as 'best blue'. Oh yes, and all the fancy modern style DA haircuts had gone on the floor in the camp barber's shop; a free service, but unwanted by all.

However to add to their sorrows, they'd been informed by Corporal McGee, the N.C.O in charge of their hut, that foot drill would start on the following Monday morning at nine a.m. on the camp square. He also informed them that they would undergo a full inspection beforehand, and warned them that 'any man failing perfection would be very, very sorry indeed.'

'Have you written home yet Tony?' Jock asked casually, as the two sat polishing.

'Yes, I sent a little note off to my mum yesterday to let her know I was still surviving.' After a pause, a distant smile crossed his face and he added, 'and of course I sent another letter to my girlfriend, Peggy, I don't want her worrying about me, do I now.'

They both worked away in silence for a few minutes, then Jock, without looking up from his task said, 'Serious is it then, Tony, you and this Peggy girl?'

'Oh yes, mate, we think the world of each other,' he replied in a quiet, thoughtful tone.

'You're a lucky lad then, mate,' he replied dolefully. 'I've just been dumped.' Then without looking up from his polishing he went on, 'I've been going out with the lass for two years, Tony. Last week she told me to piss off, just like that; I think it's because I've had to join this lot.'

Staring back at him with a look of disbelief, Tony replied, 'You're kidding, mate, why?'

'I don't know, Tony,' he said quietly, 'but she's started going out with a bloke she met at work.' Screwing his face up, he continued scornfully, 'I can't see what she sees in him, though, he looks like a poof to me.'

Laughing, Tony said, 'Well, if he is, Jock old pal, she'll soon be back if she's like most of the randy-arsed women I've known. That's not including my Peggy, of course,' he added hastily.

11

'Come on get in line, you lot, let's have some order!'
Corporal McGee yelled at the ambling group of men
outside hut Number Two. It was Monday morning, the
first day of their two month training period. 'You've all
done a decent job on your appearance,' the little
corporal continued in a strict tone, 'so don't any of you
let me down, when we get on that square, understand?'
He yelled almost in staccato, startling all the young
recruits with a jerk.

'Yes!' some of the lads called back.

Staring at them standing in complete disarray, he
said in a quiet sarcastic tone, 'Yes what?'
They just stared blankly at him, not sure what to reply.
After a few moments silence, he yelled at them, so
suddenly and so loudly that every man Jack of them
was shocked to the core.

'Yes, Corporal!'

'And don't forget it!' he yelled, with his face red
and his eyes bulging.

The reply was instant and in unity, 'No, Corporal!'
they replied, almost as loud.

The members of Flight Four then marched up to the
camp square in total disarray; the men from each of the
huts housing the flight, were escorted by their own
corporal drill instructors, who led at the front of their
own group. Marching on to the square, they were taken
to their allotted positions, while the other three flights
on the wing, 'One, Two, and Three,' were led to their
spaces at the other three corners of the huge tarmac
area.

The camp square was so large an area that even though each flight contained about one hundred men, they were quite isolated from each other. The flights were also the charge of their own corporal drill instructors on or off duty, who usually bunked in the same hut as their subordinates. This was maintained for the full eight weeks training period. Although the Sergeant DI was mainly in full charge, he rarely intervened.

For all foot drill instruction the ranks were formed in order of height, the tallest man stood at the head of the column, he was the marker man; the next tallest lined up at his side putting his right arm on the first man's shoulder, that was the measured space between them; then so on, right down to the shortest at the end of the rank. Tony, being reasonably average at about five ten, was in the middle of the group. Jock of course, being rather short in stature was always much further down the column. When this manoeuvre was completed, the drill instructor yelled out the order, 'Attention, right turn!' The ranks were then in marching order.

After an hour and a half of intensive basic foot-drill – enough for their first lesson – the men were marched off the square and brought to a halt on the road surrounding it – ironically facing the corporals' club. Here they were told to 'stand at ease' and informed that their instructors were going into the club on business that would take about fifteen minutes.

12

'Aye, I'll bet it's bloody tea business,' Tony grumbled to the lad next to him, 'Leaving us out here freezing, in this bloody cold wind.'

'Selfish bastards,' the other lad grunted.
Just then the instructors from the other flights came walking up the road, accompanied by a slim and immaculately turned out sergeant with a small, dark perfectly trimmed Diego moustache. They were also heading in the direction of the club, no doubt on similar business.

As they got nearer, Tony's face lit up, breaking into a broad smile. 'Bloody hell,' he said in surprise to the lad beside him, nodding towards the oncoming group, 'There's a mate of mine among that lot.' Staring more intently he said, 'It is, it's Steve Grimes – he lives near me, you know, goes to the same boozer, the Dog and Gun.' Grinning broadly, he yelled out 'Hi there! Steve, my old mate - am I pleased to see you.'

The little group of NCOs froze in their stride staring ahead, transfixed. There was a pause of total silence for a few seconds; it seemed like an eternity; then, the sergeant, slightly in front of the main party slowly turned his head towards the source of the cheerful greeting, his face blood red. The corporals, who remained absolutely expressionless, followed his movements with their eyes, obviously wondering what was going to happen next.

Glaring at the ranks the sergeant hissed, 'Corporal Grimes, I presume that that inappropriate outburst was intended for you?'

Still expressionless, Corporal Grimes, glancing quickly at Tony standing in the ranks looking puzzled, replied in a strict military tone, 'Yes, Sergeant!'

The sergeant, now returned to his normal complexion, beckoned the other members of the group on into the club house, saying in a firm voice, 'Right, Corporal Grimes, I'm sure you can sort out this commotion; also the horrible little man that caused it.'

The group continued on its way; Corporal Grimes, cane under arm and poker-faced, turned smartly to face the ranks of silent, anticipating airmen. Tony, standing in the centre of the front rank with a worried expression, cringed as the corporal walked over and stood directly in front of him staring, into his face sternly.

Suddenly, with a violent burst of vocal energy, he yelled, 'AIRMAN! ATTENTION!'
Tony was so shocked by the power in the command, that he shot to attention and stood there like a ramrod, staring ahead and feeling like a right prick an'all.

After a terrible bollocking, plus a warning that if it hadn't been the first day on the training course he would have been on a Form 252 – the RAF charge sheet – and into the guardroom before his feet could touch the ground, he was ordered to remain at attention until his own corporal returned.

Turning to go, the corporal heard a snigger behind him. He froze, then slowly turned and saw the young guy next to Tony, grinning at his belittlement. Corporal Grimes, his face like stone, walked slowly back, coming to a halt directly in front of the man with the snigger.

Glaring into his face, he hissed, 'So you find it funny to see a man stood at attention, then, do you, lad?' he growled.

Suddenly very serious, the young chap replied, respectfully, 'No, Corporal.'

'Well, then,' he hissed, 'You'd better keep him company.' On saying this, he yelled, 'Airman, attention! After which, without further comment, he turned and proceeded on his way, leaving the two young men standing side by side, like ramrods.

13

On Friday evening, Tony and his mate, Jock, were lying on their beds discussing their first completed week in the RAF. They were mainly grumbling about the training and the poorly prepared grub. They both agreed that the food was abundant, but as Jock put it, 'it was thrown at 'em.' Tony pointed out the cabbage had grit in it and both of them didn't like boiled mackerel for breakfast, at six thirty in the morning.

Suddenly going off that subject, Jock asked, 'Have you heard from your girlfriend then, Tony?'

With a warm tone in his voice he replied, 'Oh, yes, mate, she's sent me two lovely long letters this week. It's them that's kept me going through all this turmoil; she says she can't wait to see me in my uniform,' he chuckled.

Pausing for a moment, with a distant smile engrossing his face, he went on, 'I'm sure without Peggy to think about, I'd have gone mad with this bloody lot here.'

Nodding approvingly, Jock said, 'And on top of everything else, you had that bloody showing up by that fucking nasty corporal, who you thought was a mate. I'll tell you, Tony,' he went on, with passion in his voice, 'I felt like thumping that bastard when he was stood there in front of you, yelling his bloody head off.'

With a little laugh, Tony replied, 'So did I mate, I must admit I felt a right prat. In fact,' he said with a laugh, 'I might just do that next time I meet the swine back home in the Dog. I'll tell you what though, Jock, I nearly pissed myself when he made old Ginger Turner jump to attention as well.' Then he went on to tell Jock about how he'd saved Corporal Grimes and his party from being involved in a brawl with big Chris Simpson and his Canal street gang.

Hearing this, all Jock could say was, 'Fucking hell, mate, the ungrateful, mangy bastard.'

Half an hour later, bored to the back teeth of hanging about in a hut full of hairy-arsed blokes, (as Tony so politely put it) the two lads decided to go up to the NAAFI for a little refreshment.

As they walked in, Jock suggested, 'Shall we have a pint of ale tonight, Tony, or what?'

'Aye, why not,' he replied. 'I'm feeling so bloody fed up and missing my Peggy, I might be tempted to have two.'

'Huh!' Jock grunted, 'At least she's at home waiting for you, not like my ex, the bitch that dumped me.'

Standing in the crowd at the little bar, Tony was startled to suddenly feel a firm hand slap on his shoulder, then a friendly voice said, 'Hi there, Tony, old chap. Let me get them; what are you and your mate drinking?' Turning together, the lads were shocked to find themselves looking into the smiling face of Corporal Grimes.

After he'd got over the initial shock, and not believing his own ears, Tony said hesitantly, 'I beg your pardon, Corporal Grimes, but did I hear you right, are you offering to buy me and my mate a drink?'

Laughing, he replied, 'Of course, Tony, come on what are you both supping?' A serious look crossed his face, 'and by the way you two can drop the formalities in here, Tony – Steve will do, mate.'

Glancing at each other, the lads both replied hesitantly, 'A pint of beer please, Steve.'

Sitting down at one of the bench tables in the bar area, Steve said, taking a sip at his pint, 'You know Tony, I felt bloody rotten giving you that bollocking the other morning.'

'Aye, so did I,' Tony said. 'I felt a right pillock, an'all.'

'I really did though, Tony,' he continued, 'but I'd no option under the circumstances, you know, in full view of the others, not forgetting the sergeant.'

With a sheepish grin, Tony replied, 'Well, it's water under the bridge now, Steve. Mind you, I was wishing the Earth would open up and swallow me; as I said, I felt right pillock, I'll tell you.'

Glancing at Jock, who was nodding in agreement, Steve continued, 'I'd no choice – it's my job you see, and if I don't do it right – I'd get booted out, like in any other job.'

Pausing for a moment, Tony's face broke into a warm smile, 'To be fair, Steve, I can see the position I put you in now, but it was a right shock then, on my first day.'

Taking another sip of beer, Steve smiled, 'I was sure you'd understand Tony when you'd thought about it. After all,' he laughed, 'I'd want you on my side, if I ever met that big bugger, Simpson and his Canal street gang, in the Dog and Gun again. However,' he went on in a subdued tone, 'I must point out, lads, apart from in here you'll have to stick to formalities, especially in front of other airmen, we have to maintain respect you see, it's part of the training schedule.'

'Sure, as I said, Steve, I fully understand the position now,' Tony assured him, then laughing, he said, 'but don't start pulling rank in the Dog and showing me up in front of Bernard, or I'll get him to overrule you; don't forget he's a 'SWO man.' (Station Warrant Officer.)

'A what man?' Jock asked, looking puzzled.'

The other two just grinned at him. 'You'll soon find out when you meet one, mate,' said Tony, pushing his empty glass across the table towards him, 'Come on, go and get 'em in, it's your turn.'

As Jock made off to the bar with the three glasses, a young airman came over to Steve and said, with a smile, 'I've been looking for you, Steve; will you take a book of raffle tickets to flog in the Corporals' Club?'

Shaking his head, he smiled. 'You're never satisfied are you, Smithy, what the bloody hell are they in aid of this time then?'

'Local animal rescue, mate,' he said, piously.

'Ok, give us a couple then,' he chuckled. 'They'll be getting bloody fed up of me in there, selling your raffle tickets.'

Hastily passing him two books, he grinned. 'They're always for a good cause, you know that.'

'Go on, Smithy,' he laughed, putting them into his pocket. 'Bugger off, you'll break my heart one of these days, you and your animal rescue charities.'

'I thought you said the airmen had to maintain respect, Steve, he didn't show you much.' Tony frowned, as the man retreated.

'Oh, Smithy,' he said, laughing. 'He's permanent staff, he works in the Airmen's Mess, him.' Noticing Tony's baffled look, he said, 'It's only you trainees that have to be under such strict rule, Tony; after your basic eight weeks training and pass out, it's not much different in the service than in a civvy street job. Observing rank is more lax altogether, as long as you do your job right,' he stressed.

'Huh, it's a nice thought, Steve, but the way that little sadistic Corporal McGee treats us, it takes some believing he could ever behave any different,' Tony grumbled.

'Oh dear, poor old Reg.' Steve laughed. 'He's not such a bad lad really, he's only doing his job; my lads will think the same about me, I'm sure.' Giving Tony a sly grin, he added, 'Well you thought so yourself, when we had that little confrontation the other day, didn't you, Tony?'

'Aye, I suppose you're right,' he chuckled, 'I did, mate.'

'I'll guarantee that after your pass-out parade, Tony, you'll see the RAF in a different light; even your Corporal McGee will treat you like a mate. Don't forget, when his men pass out, it means he's done his job right, don't it?'

'I must admit he's a good instructor, even though he treats us lads like dirt,' Tony said seriously. 'You can see the difference in the lads on the square, after only a week.'

'Well, just think what you'll be like at the end of eight weeks, then.' Steve nodded.

'By the way Steve, talking about our eight weeks training period, will we get any leave before it's completed?' Tony asked, 'One of the lads said we won't be allowed out of camp, until pass-out.'

'Yes, he's right there, but then you'll get fourteen days leave before your permanent posting.' He went on cheerfully, 'I've got a forty-eight hour pass next weekend, though, so next Saturday night I'll be in the Dog and Gun knocking 'em back, mate.' Then laughing, he added, 'I'll be thinking of you back here of course, Tony, sat polishing your brasses.'

Just then Jock came struggling back with a little tray, bearing three pints of beer. 'About time,' grunted Tony, in mock anger. 'Where the bloody hell have you been, we're gagging here, aren't we, Steve?'

14

'Is that you, our David?' Ivy Mansfield called out from upstairs, hearing someone come in the front door with a clatter.

'Yes, Mum,' he shouted back. 'What's for tea, I'm starving?'

After a long pause, she came slowly down the stairs, carrying a basket full of dirty washing. 'Liver and onions,' she replied, frowning, 'but first, I want a talk with you about our Peggy and that mate of yours. I've been talking to his mother this afternoon,' she said, staring at him tight-lipped. 'She confirmed what I suspected and she's bloody livid.'

Looking blankly at her, Dave asked, 'What for, Mum?'

'What for?' she yelled. 'You bloody well know what for, don't come the innocent with me, our David. You know as well as I do that something's going on between your mate and our Peggy; her old enough to be his mother an 'all.'

Sitting down and picking up the newspaper, he said, 'I don't know 'owt; I know Tony likes her, but that's all.' As an afterthought, he went on, 'anyway, even if our Peg is a bit older than him, what's wrong with that?'

'Wrong!' she yelled, 'Fifteen years is not a bit older, you silly bugger, it's a bloody lot older. She'll be the talk of the street, she will, for bloody cradle snatching.'

'Oh, bugger the bloody neighbours, Mum,' Dave grunted, staring at the sports page. 'Anyway, talking about age difference, my dad was twenty years older than you and nobody accused him of bloody cradle snatching, did they?'

'That was different,' she snapped. 'He was a man and don't you be so cheeky,' she said angrily, 'or you'll get your bloody ear clouted.' Then going stamping into the kitchen with a stern look on her face, she called back, 'Did you go up to her flat on your way home, then, as I told you this morning and tell her I wanted to see her?'

'Oh aye, of course I did, Mum,' he whined, still staring at the newspaper. 'She said she'll be down after tea.'

'Huh, I suppose she'll be driving here in that new car she's just bought, she's got more bloody brass than brains that one, I'll tell you,' Ivy grumbled, as she stamped about setting the table.

An hour or so later, having finished his liver and onions and a good helping of rice pudding, Dave was lying on the settee finishing reading the newspaper, when he heard the sound of a car pull up outside.

'She's here I think, Mum,' he called out to Ivy in the kitchen, washing up. Before she could answer, the front door burst open, and Peggy dressed in a pale green tracksuit came bounding in, smiling and looking radiant.

'Hi, Peg,' called out Dave, getting up from the settee and looking her up and down. 'Looks as though you've decided to take Tony's advice then, going to join the sports club, eh?'

'Sure am, little brother,' she said with a smile. 'I'm enrolling in the martial arts group; I want that elusive black belt that I nearly got, over in the States.

The cheery conversation stopped abruptly at the sight of Ivy coming out of the kitchen, face like thunder. 'Oh, so you've arrived at last, have you, madam,' she remarked in an acid tone, looking Peggy up and down. 'All I can say to you is that you ought to be bloody well ashamed of yourself.'

Genuinely taken aback, Peggy just stared at her mother in disbelief. 'Why, what's up, Mum?' she asked, innocently.

Ivy stared back in silence for a moment, then said scornfully, 'You know what's up, you bloody, cradle-snatching Jezebel.'

Seeing the colour drain from his sister's face Dave interrupted in a firm tone, 'Now then, Mum, there's no need to go on like that, I've told you it's none of your business.'

'Anything that brings shame on this family is my business, and you keep out of it,' she snapped at him angrily.

Peggy now composing herself after the first onslaught said quietly, 'I suggest we all cool down and you can tell me what the bloody hell I've done wrong, mother?'

Biting her bottom lip until it went white Ivy hissed, 'Taking young boys to your bed, you bloody shameless vixen, that's what's up.' 'I've what?' gasped Peggy. 'What the hell are you on about, Mum? Have you gone mad or something? I think you'd better explain yourself,' she told her, shaking with anger.

More placid now seeing her daughter fuming with emotion, Ivy replied, 'I was talking to Doreen Ryan today and she was in a right state about it, I'll tell you. She told me that Tony, that young boy of hers, was seen sneaking out of your flat last Monday morning; and he hadn't been home all night either.' Then with an arrogant jerk of her head she went on, 'It doesn't take much to know where he'd spent the night, does it?' Peggy obviously hurt, stood staring back at her mother in silence, then, without further comment turned and walked out of the door, not bothering to close it behind her.

As her footsteps went down the garden path, Dave jumped up out of the armchair glaring at his mother. 'You've done it now, Mum, haven't you,' he said angrily. 'You and that bloody dirty-minded old gas bag Doreen Ryan, you're both a couple of bloody scandal mongers.' At that, he charged out of the house into the darkness, after Peggy.

Reaching the stationary car, he found her sitting behind the steering wheel, sobbing uncontrollably. Charging round to the other side and wrenching open the door, he jumped in beside her. Seeing Peggy so upset shocked him to the core, he'd never ever seen his strong confident sister in this state.

Flinging his arm around her heaving shoulders, as she leaned sobbing on the steering wheel, he gently lifted back her long hair from her tearful face. 'Now then, sis, come on love, don't let them bloody old gossipers get under your skin, they're not worth bothering about,' he told her with disgust.

Fumbling under the dashboard she pulled out a paper tissue, then wiping the tears from her face she said, 'Sorry, Dave love, it's not like me to break down like this, but it was so hurtful what she accused me of, it sounded so lustful.'

'Never you mind, our Peg, I don't think nasty things like that about you,' he told her affectionately. Forcing a little laugh he went on, 'And less of the tears an 'all, I'm not used to seeing you like that, it's usually you wiping my tears away, not the other way about.'

She didn't speak for a moment as she continued to wipe her eyes, then she turned and looking him in the face, she said quietly, 'She was right though, Dave, Tony and I did spend the night together.'

Then, continuing to look deep into his face searching for reaction she continued almost in a whisper, 'But it wasn't planned and it wasn't lustful Dave – it was beautiful, he's grown into a lovely person, Dave.' Telling him this a few fresh tears brimmed in her eyes.

To her surprise, he just smiled, and replied casually, 'Well, what's wrong there Peg, you're both single, adult, male and female; I can't see you've done anything wrong, either morally or against the law; so where's your problem love?'

They sat looking at each other for a moment in silence, and then, for the first time, a smile crossed her face. 'You're a lovely lad, our Dave, I'm lucky to have a brother like you, but all these narrow-minded old devils that live around here, don't see it like that.'

'I've told you Peggy, bugger 'em; it's nowt to do with that lot including my mum and bloody Mrs Ryan. What's more, you being thirty-four and Tony nineteen, you can forget that an'all.'

Before she could reply, he continued, 'because, if it makes you feel better, Peg, I'm the same age as Tony; in fact, I'm six months younger as you know, and I've slept with Mrs Moony on several occasions since her and her husband, Fred, got divorced last year. She's forty-two, an'all,' he added with a cocky grin.

'Oh, you young bugger,' she said laughing. 'You mean the barber's wife on Canal road, the big blonde woman?'

'The very one, and as I said, she's nearly ten years older than you.' Then he grinned. 'Oh dear, I wonder what our dear mother would think if I told her that.'

'Seriously though, Dave,' she said, 'we didn't plan to spend the night together, Tony and me, it just happened after we'd been working on the flat all day. We were sat having a glass of wine and –' she paused slightly, staring ahead before continuing, 'well, we just looked at each other and something was there.' She turned to face him, 'Do you know what I mean, Dave?'

Smiling warmly, he replied, 'I know exactly what you mean, Peggy, because I know my mate through and through. I don't know the depth of feeling you have for him, but I do know he's fallen in love with you, girl. What's more, it was at first sight across the dance floor, before he even knew who you were.'

'Has he told you that, Dave?' she asked.

'Not in so many words, but we know each too well to miss things like that, and I'll tell you this,' he said with a firm nod, 'he's never looked at, or commented on another woman, since he first set eyes on you, Peg, and that's very unusual,' he said, with a laugh.

'Anyway, I thought you women had that bloody 'intuition' thing, couldn't you tell how he felt about you, then?'

'Oh, I knew he liked me, but love's a different thing, isn't it?' she said.

'Well, sis, take it from me,' he assured her, 'he worships the ground you walk on.' As an afterthought he enquired, 'Talking about loving folk, how do you feel about Tony, then?'

Smiling, she replied softly, 'I feel the same Dave, that's why I think I might have to go back to The States and let him get on with his life.'

'What!' Dave spluttered, 'Oh, don't do that, Peggy, don't dump him; it'll break his heart, Peg.'

Looking back into Dave's shocked face for a moment, she said, 'I don't want to spoil it for him love, he's only just starting in life; it wouldn't be fair on a young man his age, Dave, Mum might be right there,' she sighed.

Just then the house door opened and the figure of Ivy came running down the path. 'Oh hell, what's up now,' groaned Dave.

Peggy tensed. 'Oh my God, Dave, I can't stand another session, what can I do?'

However, before anything could be done Ivy had reached the little car and stood motionless looking down at her daughter, sitting behind the wheel. Then, pulling open the door she grabbed her in her arms and sobbed, 'Oh, Peggy darling, I'm so sorry love, I should never have said such terrible things to you, please forgive your stupid old mum, darling.'

'Oh, forget it, Mum, I didn't take it serious anyway,' Peggy lied, in affectionate tone.

As the two hugged each other, Dave, feeling very pleased with the outcome, said to himself as he got out of the car, 'Thank God everyone's come to their senses at last.'

'Good night Peggy,' he called back as he walked up the garden path, 'see you later love.'

15

It was Friday morning at the end of their second week training; the lads had just returned from breakfast and were getting ready for morning parade.

'You're very quiet, Tony, old son,' said Jock, giving a final rub at the brasses on his webbing, 'What's your problem, mate?'

Tony didn't seem to hear him at first, but then muttered sullenly without looking up from his own polishing, 'Oh, nothing really, Jock, well nothing I can do much about anyway.'

'Come on; spill the bloody beans, Tony. What's on your mind, mate?' he insisted.

Nodding at the large photo of Peggy dressed in tennis gear, stuck to the inside of his open locker door, he said, 'It's her, Jock – Peggy.'

'What about her?' he asked. 'She looks fine to me, she's beautiful; you're a lucky bugger, I'll tell you.'

Turning to him with a very worried look on his face he said quietly, 'Oh, I know that, Jock, it's just that I haven't heard from her all this week. I've sent her three letters with no reply, I just can't understand it, Jock,' he said frowning. 'She sent me three letters last week,' he went on, looking down at the floor, 'all normal chatter, you know, just as you'd expect between a bloke and his girl.' He bit his bottom lip, 'I don't like it Jock, something's happened; I can feel it in my bones.'

'Well, I must admit it does seem a bit strange, mate, not answering three letters in one week, but she might have been busy or something,' Jock said, cheerfully.

'No, there's something wrong somewhere,' he replied, shaking his head. 'I can't do much about it chained down in this bloody dump, either.' He thumped his fist into the palm of his hand and said passionately, 'The way I feel, mate, I could just do a runner and jump on that bloody train back to Leeds, to see for myself what's amiss.'

'Now, now, Tony, let's not start thinking down that path, it's not that serious; that sort of thing will get you in jail, mate.'

Nodding and staring at the photo on the back of his locker door, Tony said, quietly, 'Yes, okay, Jock, you're right, but I've got to find out what's up, somehow.'

Halfway through the morning, the men on parade were standing at ease in the usual spot, the roadside near the Corporals' Club; Tony, as usual, was in the middle of the front row. The DI in charge of their lot, Corporal McGee, had just disappeared inside when Tony saw two more instructors walking smartly up the road towards the Club; one of the instructors was Corporal Grimes.

As they drew nearer, the ginger lad at the side of Tony nudged him, sniggering, 'Christ, look who's coming – it's him that gave you the bollocking the other day.'

Suddenly, like lightning, Tony had an idea; he didn't know whether he should risk it, but he decided that desperate situations sometimes require desperate measures.

The two corporals, walking on the other side of the road, had just about drawn level with him, when Tony drew a deep breath and coming smartly to attention, called out, 'Corporal Grimes!'

The two instructors turned their heads, glaring angrily in his direction; he remained stiffly to attention.

Corporal Grimes, seeing who the caller was, yelled back frowning fiercely, 'Are you addressing me, airman?'

Tony called out in true military fashion, 'Yes, Corporal! Request permission to speak to you, Corporal.'

The two instructors stood looking him over for a moment muttering to each other; then the other man turned and went into the club building, leaving Corporal Grimes standing alone, cane under arm, glaring across at Tony. After a slight pause, he hissed, 'Come here, you.'

As Tony broke rank and began walking smartly across the road towards him he yelled, 'At the double! Tony broke into a run, and as he reached him, came sharply to a halt, standing smartly to attention and remaining silent.

'Name and number!' the corporal yelled, staring into his expressionless face.

Staring ahead, remaining rigid, Tony called out, '6726864 AC2 Ryan A, Corporal!'

'Oh dear,' the corporal said, loud enough to be heard by the ranks, 'you're the horrible little man I had to reprimand the other day, aren't you?'

'Yes, Corporal,' Tony replied formally.

'Well, you'd better have good reason this time for your interruption, my lad,' he said loudly and menacingly. Then, in almost a whisper, he muttered out of the side of his mouth, 'What's wrong, Tony?'

In the same fashion, Tony replied, 'Is there any chance I can have a word in private before you go off on your forty-eight, Steve?'

'One thirty in the NAAFI, prompt,' he muttered in reply. Then, drawing himself up to his full height, holding his cane firmly under his arm, he yelled, 'Apology accepted, now get back to the ranks and don't let anything like that occur again, airman, or you'll find yourself in the guardroom.'

Marching back to his place in the ranks Tony noticed the ginger guy who had been leering at him, being disciplined again. This was also noticed by the corporal; going slowly over he came to a halt directly in front of Ginger, and glared into his now, very serious face.

'You seem to be amused airman,' he said softly. With an exaggerated stare, he continued, 'Well, I never, it's you; the funny one I had dealings with before, isn't it?'

'Yes, Corporal,' Ginger replied sheepishly, avoiding eye contact.

Immediately the corporal yelled, 'Stand to attention when you speak to me, you horrible little man!' This he did, like lightning, looking extremely stressed.

'I don't know, some people never learn,' the corporal said shaking his head in mock disbelief. Then glaring angrily at him, he ordered, 'and stay in that position until the return of your corporal.' Saying no more, he proceeded smartly on his way to the club.

16

'Huh, this ain't bad,' Tony remarked, cutting into a thick slice of boiled ham.

'Aye, and they've washed bloody lettuce as well,' Jock replied. He grinned over to the next table where Ginger Turner was sitting eating with his mates. 'I nearly pissed myself this morning when Grimes stood big gob over there to attention again,' he said, laughing with his mouth so full that he nearly choked.

'So did I,' Tony chuckled, 'I don't know how he held it until McGee came back, it must have been fifteen minutes at the least. I thought he was going to pass out; he went right pale, I told him to stand at ease, but he daren't.'

'Aye, and then he got another bollocking from McGee when he did come back, poor sod,' Jock laughed. 'I'll tell you what though, Tony,' he went on, 'you gave me a shock when you yelled out from the ranks like you did; I thought you were in for another dressing-down yourself.'

'It was a spot decision, Jock,' he replied, chewing away. 'It was our friend, Ginger, that brought it to my mind.'

Looking a little baffled, he asked, 'How do you mean, mate?'

'Well, when he saw the two corporals walking towards us he said, look it's him that gave you the bollocking or words to that effect. Anyway, I was just going to tell him to button his lip – or else, when I suddenly remembered that Steve said the other night in the NAAFI, that he was going home on a forty-eight hour pass this weekend.'

'So what?' asked Jock.

'Well, I thought he could look out for my mate, Dave, when he gets home and find out why Peggy hasn't written to me.

'You know, Jock,' he said, pausing in his eating, 'not hearing from Peggy all week, I've been bloody worried to death.'
Jock just sat there, nodding as he went on.

'But then I remembered that Steve would be off home today straight after dinner; I knew I had to catch him there and then, so I took the risk, and it worked,' he smiled.

'Is he going to help you, then?' he asked.

'Yes, I met him in the NAAFI after dinner. He's going to catch Dave in the local and see if there's anything wrong. He'll be back on Sunday after tea, so he said, and we're meeting in the NAAFI at eight. You can come with me and meet Steve again socially, if you want, Jock,' he said with a grin, pushing his empty plate away and taking a swig from his big pint pot of tea.

'Oh, that's nice of you,' he replied sarcastically. 'You are kind.'

Tony's smiling face suddenly froze, as he caught sight of a familiar face across the dining hall. He couldn't believe his eyes as he stared at an airman queuing in front of the long stainless steel serving counter. 'Good God, Almighty,' he gasped. 'It's Nigel Lacy.'

Staring at him in bewilderment, Jock asked innocently, 'Who the fuck's he, then?'

'Oh, he's a lad I know at home; it's a long story – I'll tell you later.' He got to his feet. 'I'm just going over to say hello, Jock, won't be a minute.'

Jock, bored stiff, was getting fed up of waiting, when Tony came back laughing and chatting with a little plump guy wearing thick glasses, carrying his meal and a pint pot of tea on a tray.

Sitting down, Tony introduced them to each other, asking, 'So how did you manage your transfer from the Royal Artillery then, Nigel?'

'It was bloody difficult Tony,' he told him, starting on his meat pie and chips, 'but with me having the rank of warrant officer in the ATC, they didn't have a leg to stand on, when my CO intervened.'

'And you say you've been here nearly a week, Tony said. 'How the hell is it we haven't met before this, you did say you're on our wing, didn't you?'

'Yes I'm in Flight Two,' he told him, munching away. 'We train at the left side of the square, that's why we've never caught sight of each other, I suppose. But, as I said,' he continued, 'I've only been here a few days; I haven't even had time to get to the NAAFI in the evening, yet.

'How's that, then?' Tony asked. 'Everybody else does, there's nowt else to do around here.'

'I know that, mate, 'he replied, 'but I've had that much to do working on my kit; I'm a bit behind the rest of you lot, don't forget.' Still tucking into his bulky meal, he grunted, 'and that fucking sadistic corporal in command of our hut, the bastard, he's got it in for me, I'm sure he has, the swine.'

'Why?' Jock asked, rather amused. 'What makes you think that?'

'Because he knows my background, that's why,' Nigel replied, nodding as he chewed.

'What you mean to say he's been informed of your rank in the ATC, Nigel?' Tony asked him, 'that's none of his business surely, is it?'

'No, it isn't, Tony,' he replied with a grunt, 'but he's a very nasty piece of work is that one; what's more he gives me hell on the parade ground, because he can't fault my foot drill.'

'Well, he won't, will he, Nigel, with all the experience you've had,' Tony said, with a laugh. 'I mean, I've seen you myself drilling your lads down at the drill hall back home, you're probably better than him – making him jealous.'

'That's just what I thought, Tony,' he said, banging the knife and fork down on his empty plate and shoving it back on the table. 'Oh yes, mate,' he went on, 'he's a right nasty bastard is our bloody Corporal Grimes, I'll tell you that, Tony.' Tony and Jock exchanged glances as he continued. 'You'll give that one a wide berth if you take my advice lads, he seems to hate every bugger except himself; he's a right cunt he is, I'll tell you.'

Walking back to their hut, Tony told Jock the history of Nigel, and the way he'd been drafted into the Royal Artillery, after serving years in the ATC and attaining the rank of warrant officer. They both agreed that, joking apart, it was out of order.

17

Walking into the billet laughing about the unfortunate Nigel, their mirth stopped abruptly at the sight before them. 'Christ Almighty,' gasped Tony, staring in disbelief.

Sitting white-faced, on one of the beds halfway up the hut, was Corporal McGee. He was minus his jacket and one of his arms was bleeding profusely. Tight-lipped, he was staring wildly up into the face of an airman, who was menacingly brandishing a long-bladed knife. Four of their fellow residents were standing with their backs to the wall, watching, but clearly too terrified to intervene. It was plain to see, that the airman had lost control of himself completely, by the way he was cursing, swearing, and threatening the injured corporal, with the long, razor-sharp butcher's knife. As the newcomers entered, he swung around with the large knife held aloft, his eyes blazing. The two didn't recognize him, but realised by his glaring expression, that he was out of his senses.

'Get back to the wall; keep out of my way you two twats,' he ordered. Spitting at them, he leered, 'or do you want your bloody throats cut, like I'm going to do to this cocky little bastard of a corporal here?'

Without hesitation, Jock ran straight at him as he stood there with the big knife held aloft. The man was momentarily shocked at this unexpected move, as everyone else was. Without hesitation Jock went in, delivering into him a powerful determined kick in the balls. With a scream the knifeman doubled up, dropped the knife and leaning forward grasped the painful section of his anatomy. Jock however continued the attack with his fists next, raining a flurry of heavy blows to the man's unprotected face, which knocked him to the floor. He remained there, flat out. His Scots blood now up he charged at him again, intending to put the boot in, even though it was obvious that the man was no longer a threat. Tony, himself shocked at the speed and ferocity of the onslaught, now realised Jock had no intention of stopping, the man could be killed.

Charging in, he grabbed his mate around the shoulders to restrain him. 'Come on now, Jock, that's enough,' he said. 'We don't want you getting into trouble for a scab like him.

Fortunately, after a few seconds of pulling and tugging and shouts of 'Let me at the murderous bastard,' Jock cooled off.

Sitting on the bed, Corporal McGee got slowly to his feet holding his bleeding arm out before him. 'Good man, Tordoff, that was brilliant,' he told him. 'I'll make sure your quick thinking and prompt action is reported to the Wing Commander.'

The madman, coming round from his beating, was holding on to his groin and moaning. No doubt, this was giving him more pain than his blood covered face and broken teeth. McGee, by now appearing back to his usual cocky self, picked up the big knife, and ordered the four chaps who'd been watching, to make sure that the madman remained where he was, and caused no more trouble until the Service police arrived.

'He'd better behave himself or he'll get some more,' called out Jock, now sitting on his bed talking to Tony. The corporal went back to his bunk, wiping the blood off his forearm with a piece of his torn shirt sleeve, and then contacted the guard room by phone. Within ten minutes two stern-faced police officers arrived and arrested the man. They offered the injured corporal transport to sick quarters for treatment, which he gladly accepted.

'He'll get time in Colchester for that,' called out one of the lads, as the door closed behind the party of police, prisoner and injured.

'He'd have needed a bloody wooden box – if my mate here hadn't held me back,' called out Jock, laughing.

'You took a big risk though, you know, Jock charging in like that,' Tony said, with a shake of his head.

'I don't know how you had the courage to do it,' said another of the lads. 'What, a madman wielding a knife with a bloody twelve inch blade; you deserve the VC Jock.'

Laughing, he replied, 'Oh, you sound like a load of old women, that was nothing; in the part of Glasgow where I come from, that sort of thing happens all the time, but mainly they use cut-throat razors and chainsaws,' he said, casually.

18

'Thank God you're here,' Tony called out to Steve Grimes, walking up to their table in the NAAFI on the Sunday evening. 'I thought you might have decided not to come back until morning.'

He was dressed casually in civilian clothes carrying his weekend case, looking as though he'd just got off the train; which he had. 'Sorry I'm so late, Tony,' he apologized, 'but that blasted train was held up, we've been stood out in the middle of nowhere for over twenty minutes; some sort of trouble with the signals, the guard said. Then I'd to call in the bloody club,' he went on. 'I'd some raffle ticket money for Smithy to pick up, he'll be in here later for that no doubt,' he sighed. Glancing down at Jock sitting quietly with his elbows on the table listening, he said, 'I've just been told by Corporal McGee about that incident on Friday, Jock, seems as though the bloke went mad; McGee needed ten stitches on his forearm, he told me. He can't get over the way you disposed of the chap,' he chuckled. 'He said you went straight through him, knife and all.'

'Oh, it's commonplace at home that sort of thing,' Jock said, with a conceited smile. 'A way of life, like.'

'Did you manage to see my mate, Dave then, Steve?' Tony interrupted, unable to contain his suspense any longer.

Sitting down Steve replied, 'Yes, we had a few pints together on Saturday night, Tony. I was on my own, and my wife had gone down to her mother's for the evening, so I was glad of his company.'

'Well, what did he say about Peggy?' Tony asked impatiently. 'Did you tell him that she hasn't written to me for over a week now?'

'Yes, I asked him all you said, Tony.' He reached into his inside jacket pocket, pulled out a scrap of paper and passed over to him. 'That's the new phone number of the public phone in the 'Dog and Gun; Dave said to tell you he'll be in there tonight from eight 'till closing time. He said to give him a ring and he'll put you right in the picture.' Then he added thoughtfully, 'I thought he seemed a bit upset about something though, Tony, but he didn't tell me anything.'

Jumping to his feet Tony made for the phone booth in the corner of the room. 'I'd better ring him, then,' he called back, he's sure to be there now, it's a quarter to nine.'

Fifteen minutes later a very worried looking Tony came walking back. The other two, drinking tea, looked up at him expectantly as he pulled out a chair and sat down in frowning silence.

Sympathetically Jock said, 'Oh dear, you don't look very pleased with yourself mate, what's up?'

Leaning forward, elbows on the table, chin in hands Tony said quietly, 'Everything's up, she's bloody well gone back to America, and to make things worse it seems like my own bloody mother was the cause of it.'

'How do you mean, Tony?' Steve asked in amazement, looking very concerned.
Tony explained all he'd been told by Dave adding, 'Wait until I get my pass-out leave, I'll sort the bloody lot of 'em out, I'll tell you.'

19

 One of the nastiest, most feared corporal drill instructors on the camp was a man called Corporal Snowdon. He was a man of about twenty-eight of average height, as thin as a lathe with a complexion that was as white as a ghost. Tony Ryan first met him while bollock naked in the bath house. Although a large training camp like Padgate obviously had a gymnasium, it was not very easy for the trainees to get access to it in the evening; at least that's what Tony found. So, being a lad not to let things stand in his way, he compromised by using one of the bathrooms in the airmen's bathhouse to get some sort of a workout, so as to keep in shape. He went down there three times in the week and performed sets of push-ups using the bath as a push-up bench. It was after one such workout session that he bumped into Corporal Snowdon – literally! He'd just finished his workout and was swilling himself down in the bath, when he thought he heard a noise outside the door.

Glancing up at the fanlight over the door he saw something flash then disappear. 'That looked like a mirror,' he mumbled to himself, 'a bloody peeping Tom.' Then quickly drying himself, he charged out of the bathroom, not bothering to dress in his eagerness to catch the offender. Glancing up and down the empty passage, he thought he heard a slight movement; suddenly he noticed a lone, skinny figure dressed only in a pair of baggy underpants, standing silently up at the far end.

'Oi, you there, can I have a word?' he yelled angrily, charging over towards him.

'What's your problem?' the man said nervously, as Tony reached him.

'Have you seen anybody else in here, just now?' Tony asked.

'No, the place is empty as far as I can see,' the man answered, looking the naked, muscular figure of Tony up and down.

Glaring at him, Tony said angrily, prodding him in the shoulder with his forefinger, 'Right mate, so it must have been you peeping into my bathroom just now with a mirror, eh?'

Smiling and openly eyeing him up and down, the man replied, 'I wasn't, anyway no need to go to that trouble is there, when of your own free will you're running around the bathhouse, showing your naked body off.'

When Tony's fist hit him he fell back to the wall with a grunt. 'Don't give me that sort of lip, Mister or I'll give you a real clout next time. You look like a bloody puff to me, mate but you've picked the wrong bloke here,' he told him, angrily.

The man, now terrified, was standing with his back to the wall; a little trickle of blood was coming out of his nose. He groaned as he wiped it away with the back of his hand. 'I hope you realize, airman, you've just struck a superior officer.'

'Oh, and how do I know that mate?' Tony asked with a laugh, nodding down at the man's baggy underpants. 'I can't see any stripes on the legs of them. Anyway, how do you know I'm only an ordinary airman?'

'Easy,' the man answered, 'because I've seen you before in the NAAFI with your mate,'

'Oh, have you,' replied Tony. 'You're one of them big-eyed buggers that miss nowt, eh?'
Staring into the chap's eyes he said, threateningly, 'Well, I don't like nosey bastards; I'd give you a bloody good hiding for your cheek, but it might kill you if I did, you being no more than a fucking bag of bones.'

Feeling a bit more confident now, the man relaxed and replying cockily, 'I'll have you know I'm a corporal and I could have you arrested for this assault. He straightened up to his full height, 'You could get Court Marshalled for assaulting a superior officer.'

'Aye and a superior officer could get Court Marshalled for peeping into bathrooms at naked men,' said Tony, with a laugh. Turning to go and get dressed, he said, 'Go on, piss off, whoever you are and don't cross me again, or delicate as you are, I'll thump you good and proper next time, mate.'

A little later, as he walked back into the smoke-filled hut that was his home, he yelled, 'Christ Almighty, open some windows, it stinks like an opium den in here.'

'Shut up!' came back a chorus from the lads with mock aggression. 'It's about time you started smoking yourself,' called out one of them, laughing. 'You don't know what you're missing, mate.' Ignoring them, he went over to his bed space in the corner, and threw the window behind wide open.

'I've put mine out, Tony don't worry,' said Jock, who was sitting on his own bed reading. 'Have you had a good workout, then, mate?'

Sitting down on his bed, Tony replied solemnly, 'I've just thumped a bloke in the bathhouse Jock; he said he was a corporal, I don't know if he was, though.' He laughed. 'He only had a pair of long, baggy underpants on and I couldn't see any stripes on the legs of them. He then went on to tell him the full story.

'Oh, I shouldn't worry, Tony. He's not forced to be a corporal, he was most likely saying that so you wouldn't go to town on him and give him a real good thumping,' said Jock, laughing. 'Anyway whoever he is, he won't know who you are in a bloody big place like this, we all look alike in uniform,' he said reassuringly.

After a thoughtful pause, Tony said quietly, 'He knows me all right, Jock, he'd seen you and me in the NAAFI he reckons.' Looking melancholy, he added, 'and I made his nose bleed, Jock.'

'Oh, fuck him, Tony,' he replied sharply. 'Anyway, mate, he won't dare say anything about it if he's been peeping at you starkers in the bath; will he? He must be some sort of a bloody pervert anyway,' he added, grimacing. He jumped to his feet. 'Come on; let's nip over to the NAAFI for a cuppa tea before bed time.

20

It was the morning of the pass-out parade, the final challenge.

'Christ Jock, the most important day since we've been here and I feel bloody half asleep,' Tony groaned. He, Jock and most of the other lads in the billet, were sitting on their beds putting the final touches to their kit, before the great climax of their eight weeks' training. Yes, they were the end of their eight weeks of Purgatory, just before the big final parade; after that it would be home and fourteen days leave.

'Never mind about that, you'll soon waken up when you get out on that square, Tony,' said Jock. 'We'd better hurry up anyway. Old McGee will be in here any minute, yelling his bloody head off.' Glancing up at the big round clock on the wall, he gasped, 'Bloody Hell, look – it's nearly half eight.'

'Stop worrying,' Tony replied calmly. 'The parade doesn't start until nine fifteen; we've bags of time yet.'

'I know that,' he said, struggling to get into his best blue jacket without creasing it, 'but we've got to be inspected by McGee before we go on the square don't forget. Then we've to march up there and get in regimental position before the Officer in Command comes on with the band.'

Just then the door of Corporal McGee's bunk opened and the corporal came striding out; his attire was perfection.

'God,' whispered Tony 'look at him, Jock, he's like a bloody tailor's dummy.'

By eleven thirty, it was all over, with everybody in a state of elation. All the airmen had been dismissed and were standing in their own chosen groups talking and complimenting each other on their magnificent display. 'I suggest we make our way over to the Mess so as be first in the queue for lunch,' Jock whispered in Tony's ear, as they stood talking in the middle of the elated crowd.

'Good thinking, mate,' he replied, 'I want to be off by one fifteen, the Leeds train leaves here at two; come on, let's go before the rest of this lot get the same idea.'

'Hello, look who's coming up the road Tony,' Jock said with a grin as they were on their way. 'It's your friend Corporal Grimes with some of his mates.'

'Aye, so it is,' Tony replied. 'They look like three SS men with their little canes under their arms,' he said, laughing.

As the three corporals, walking abreast, got nearer, Tony said, quietly, 'Hey, Good God, that one at the far side, Jock, that's the cunt I thumped in the bath house the other night. Oh, bloody hell,' he muttered, 'he is a corporal, then,'

'Aye and he looks a nasty bugger, an'all,' said Jock, staring at the trio advancing on them.

'Just keep looking ahead Jock, they'll probably ignore us,' Tony said hopefully.

However, this wishful thinking was not to be; as the three conversing corporals were about to pass by, Steve Grimes spotted them, a wide smile crossing his face, 'Hi there, Tony,' he called out, 'Can I have a word?' Mumbling something to his companions, he came walking briskly over to the two lads. They came to a halt, rather shocked at the informal greeting. As the other two corporals continued on their way, one of them gave Tony a steely glare.

'Pass-out went like a dream, Tony, eh?' said the immaculately turned out Corporal Grimes, as he approached them grinning.

'What's up? You don't seem very pleased to see me,' he added.

'Oh, I am Steve,' he replied, 'but I'm just a bit shocked at your familiar greeting, in front of the other two corporals, while on duty.'

'Aye, that's just what you told us not to do, that night in the NAAFI,' said Jock.

Laughing, he replied, 'Oh, you can forget most of that bullshit, now you're out of your training lads.' He slapped them both on the shoulder and said, 'You're not Sprogs now you know, you've passed out with the full approval of the RAF.'

'That's a relief to know, Steve,' Tony said sarcastically. 'So we can talk to you in the open now, without fear of a bollocking, eh?'

'That's about it Tony, yes,' said Steve. 'Except on formal occasions of course, but that also applies to the airmen who are permanent staff on the camp. Anyway, Tony,' he went on, 'I wanted a word with you about getting home; my mate Bob Peters has offered me a lift home in his car, he lives in Yeadon. He says that you can have a lift if you want; it'll be quicker and easier than the train, and door to door.' He smiled. 'We're off straight after lunch if you're interested.'

'Count me in, Steve,' Tony replied, grinning enthusiastically. 'I'm very grateful, so long as your mate doesn't mind a minion like me in his car.'

'Oh no, he's a grand chap is Bob, that was him, the sergeant who was with us the day I had to give you a bollocking,' he said, laughing.

'Him, the sergeant?' gulped Tony. 'Sure it'll be okay, Steve?'

'Of course it will,' said Steve. 'No airs and graces, Bob, he's a first class NCO but off duty he's a right card, I'll tell you.' Turning to follow his two colleagues he added, 'I'll be off then, Tony, see you outside the Sergeants' Mess at two fifteen, okay?'

'Just hang on a moment, Steve,' he called out. 'Before you go, who was that corporal you were with just now, the pale-faced, skinny built one?'

Pulling a face he replied, 'Don't tell me he's had you up for dirty shoes or haircut or something. He's a bugger is that one, mate. That's Corporal Jeffery Snowden, he works to the book on or off duty.' Giving Tony a long, thoughtful look, he asked, 'He hasn't pulled you over for something has he, Tony?' I noticed he gave you a funny look as he walked away just now.'

'Not really,' Tony chuckled. 'You get yourself off, Steve. I'll tell you all about it on the way home.'

21

'Hi there, Tony, old son, I thought you'd decided not to bother coming,' Dave called out from his barstool, as Tony walked into the lounge of the Dog and Gun that evening.

'Sorry I'm a bit late, Dave, but I've just been having a row with my mum. I'll tell you about it in a minute,' he said. He was dressed in his best light grey, handmade suit, with a sparkling white shirt and bright kipper tie, plus a pair of thick-soled blue suede shoes.

'Wow, you look smart and with it, Tony,' remarked Dave, as he came up to him at the bar. 'What are you having, the usual, eh?'

They walked away from the bar with their pints, making for a little table in the corner. Tony said quietly, 'How do things stand now then, Dave, has she come back then?'

As they sat down, Dave glanced quickly at Tony. 'No, Tony, I'm sorry, she hasn't written either, well, that's what my mum told me anyway,' he said, frowning doubtfully. 'I can't understand it, Dave.' He stared down at the table top. 'I just can't believe she'd dump me like this, we got on so well together. Her last words to me were that she couldn't wait to see me in my uniform.' He stared across at Dave for a moment, before saying quietly, 'You know I love Peggy, don't you, Dave.'

Looking back at his brother in all but blood, Dave silently nodded. 'Yes, I realise that, Tony, and if it means anything, it's hurting me like hell to see you so upset. I tried my bloody best to persuade her to take no notice of the old women, mate,' he replied solemnly, shaking his head, 'but as I told you on the phone, they really upset her. I've never seen our Peg crying like she did in that car, I had to cuddle her for ten minutes before she stopped. But one thing, I know for sure, she loves you, Tony,' he assured him firmly.

'But if she does, why has she buggered off like this, Dave, it's a bloody conundrum,' he sighed. 'Do you think she's written to your mum, Dave and she hasn't told you?' he asked optimistically. 'You know, thinking you might want her address to give to me?'

'There's no might about it, mate, I bloody well would want it to give to you,' Dave said angrily. 'But I'll tell you what, you've got me thinking now; I'm going to have a real good look around that house in the morning when my mum goes out: I might find summat, you never know.' He smiled arrogantly.

'Christ, Dave, look who's just walked in,' interrupted Tony suddenly, nodding towards the entrance door.

Turning in his chair, Dave said smiling, 'Oh, it's Steve and he's on his own again.' He stood up and waved him over.

'By Gum, Steve you're looking smart tonight, I like that blazer,' remarked Tony, when Dave had gone up to the bar. 'I've got one very similar to it, but where did you get that RAF emblem on the breast pocket from? I've looked all over for one of them.'

'Oh that,' Steve said, glancing down at it proudly. 'It's a nice one isn't it, I got it in the store at the Corporals Club, Tony, four and six it cost. I'll get you one when I get back if you like,' he offered.

'Oh, thanks a lot,' he said gratefully. 'That's very nice of you, it's a beauty. Do you want the brass now then?' he enquired, reaching for his wallet.

'No, you can give me that when I bring it, Tony.' He looked at Tony's flashy tie, and grinned. 'That tie won't match your blazer, you know. How about me bringing you an RAF tie like this one I'm wearing? They sell them an'all, in the club, half a crown each.'

'Good thinking, mate, I might as well show my respect for the service now I'm a fully fledged airman, even though I'm still only an AC plonk.' He laughed loudly and Dave, coming back carrying a tray with three foaming pints on it, called out, 'What's so funny then?'

They'd been talking for no more than five minutes, when Tony, suddenly sat bolt upright and stared past the others towards the door. 'Christ!' he muttered. 'I've never seen him in here before; he always uses the Golden Lyon.' He stood up quickly and laughed. 'Don't look round Steve, little Nigel Lacy has just walked in, let's have a lark with him; he's a great admirer of yours, you know.' He walked around the table, and placed himself where he could block Nigel's view of Steve. 'Hi, Nigel,' he called out smiling and waving his arms, 'Come on over and join us.'

Smiling broadly, Nigel called back, 'Oh, it's you, Tony,' and walked over to him, still maintaining the smile of a Cheshire cat.

Looking him up and down as he got nearer, Tony said, 'I see you've decided to show your uniform off tonight then, Nigel, I'd have thought you'd have wanted to get it off and relax a bit now you're home.'

'Oh, I can relax just the same in uniform here, Tony,' he said cheerfully. 'There's no bugger here to eye me up and down.'

'What do you mean mate, eye you up and down?' Tony asked innocently, maintaining his position and still shielding Steve from view. 'Like telling you your buttons need a rubdown, eh?' he said. 'Which they certainly do, Nigel,' he added with a laugh.

Laughing with him, then looking down at the brass buttons on his jacket, he said, 'You're right there, Tony. I wonder what that nasty bugger in charge of our hut would say if he saw them now.'

'What's his name again, Nigel? You did say the other day but I've forgotten,' enquired Tony, pretending to look baffled.

'Grimes, Corporal bloody Grimes!' Nigel muttered menacingly. 'Huh, him and his bloody bullshit,' he sneered. 'He nearly drove us fucking mad in our hut for the full eight weeks' training; aye he's a right nasty cunt that one, Tony, I'll tell you.'

Hearing a chair move behind him, Tony moved to one side and watched Nigel's face going white as he stared ahead, mouth agape. Then turning away, hardly able to hold himself from exploding into laughter, he saw Steve standing there with a venomous look on his face, glaring down at poor little Nigel.

'What's all this about then, Lacy?' he said in his strict DI tone of voice, as he glanced down sneeringly at Nigel's tunic buttons. 'Them buttons look as though you've been polishing them with cow muck, they're a disgrace, man!'

Standing stiffly to attention, Nigel replied in a squeaky voice, 'Yes, Corporal, sorry Corporal, I'll return to my home at once and polish them, if that's all right with you, Corporal?'

Steve stood glaring at him for a few seconds in silence without further comment, while Nigel stood to attention, staring back at him like a fart. Observing the performance, Tony had nearly bitten through his bottom lip to prevent himself laughing and the customers sitting nearby were fidgeting, and beginning to wonder what was going on.

Steve suddenly made a move and walked slowly up to the poor lad, with a smile breaking out on his face. He put his hand on Nigel's stiff shoulder and said in a friendly voice, 'Come on, you daft young bugger, we're only winding you up. Come on let's go over to that bar and get you a pint. You can polish your bloody buttons tomorrow, if you're that keen.'

Nigel was almost dumbstruck and could only mutter, 'Yes, Corporal, if that's all right with you, Corporal.'

'By the way, Nigel lad,' he replied, with a laugh, 'You'd better call me Steve from now on, when off duty, or you might after all find yourself on a form 252.'

Half an hour, later all were friends and having a good time, even Nigel, who, by now was on his third pint and finding it easy to be on first name terms with his hated ex-drill instructor.

Suddenly a loud voice called out across the now crowded room, 'Hi there, Tony Ryan. You back home, then? Have they made a man out of you yet, in the RAF?' This was followed by a coarse laugh and the owner came walking over to the group of friends. 'Oh and look here, our little Mr Lacy, what a smart little chap he is in his uniform,' he said scornfully.

'Stop piss taking, Chris Simpson,' Tony called out. 'It doesn't make you look big with us.'

Chris was just going to continue his verbal attack on Nigel, when he caught sight of Steve sitting there quietly, sipping his pint and listening to the banter. 'Oh, who have we got here, then?' he said laughing, a gloating look crossing his face, 'It's the cocky little RAF corporal who you talked us out of thumping that night, isn't it, Tony?'

Tony just replied, without turning to look at him, 'Shut it, Chris, or piss off.'

Steve, looking up at him from his chair smiled, saying politely 'Good evening, yes, you're right, I'm the very same chap.'

'Look here, Chris, I hope you haven't come over for any aggro, mate,' interrupted Tony sternly, 'because if you have I don't advise it tonight, I'm not in the mood for playing games.'

'Me neither,' called Dave over his shoulder, emptying his glass and putting it down on the table with a bang.

'No, no, you've got me wrong, lads,' Chris said hastily. 'I've just come over to let you boys know the good news.'

'Good news,' Tony said suspiciously. 'What's that, then? Don't say you're moving house down to 'Lands End' or somewhere like that, eh?' He laughed.

Chris pulled himself upright and said sneeringly, 'You're not as far out as you'd think, Mr. Know-all, Tony Ryan.' He smirked proudly. 'Yes, I'm moving all right in a couple of weeks, I've completed my apprenticeship and I'm joining your lot. I had my medical two weeks back and I've got to report to my training camp a week next Thursday.' He sniggered. 'So what do you buggers think to that, then?'

Steve replied casually, 'Good for you, Chris. Which camp are you posted to?'

'Padgate,' he replied proudly, 'and I'll straighten the buggers out when I get there an'all,' he said, with a loud raucous laugh. Nigel, who was just taking a swig from his pint, nearly choked on it when he heard him say this; Steve and Tony just exchanged glances smiling knowingly.

22

Back at Padgate after a very enjoyable two weeks leave, the lads were eager to hear about their postings. This was to be their final week together at Padgate. They would soon have to say sad farewells to their mates of the last eight weeks as they were about to be posted to a variety of destinations. Some would be sent on the specialist trade courses they had chosen; others, without a trade choice, would be sent to different camps around the country. There they could be put on general duties as required and these men were officially called Admin Orderlies. Tony had decided to put this down as his choice of occupation, because he'd had enough of bloody trades, working on the building site. However, being a well built athletic man, he'd been posted to join some sort of special athletic display team that the service was preparing for. He hadn't been told anything else about the venture, but he liked the sound of it. Better that than bloody bricklaying, he thought – at least he'd most likely be spending lots of time in the gym – in fact he couldn't believe his good luck.

23

It was a bright sunny afternoon as Tony walked up to the reception window of the guardroom on his appointed camp. It was situated in a beautiful country location in the South Midlands and Tony liked the look of it. No rushing and pushing crowd here; he was the only person in sight, apart from a few people some distance further inside the camp, going about their business. He stood there smartly dressed in his best blue uniform, kit bag resting on the ground beside him and pressed the shiny brass button on the window sill, as the notice beside it instructed.

After a good two minutes, a corporal SP came casually up to the window, munching at a pork pie; sliding it open a few inches he said in a friendly voice, 'Yes, can I help you, airman?'

A little surprised at such a casual, hospitable reception, Tony stood up straight and smiled. 'I've come to report to the display training unit, I'm 8726864, Ryan, posted from Padgate.'

The police corporal, still munching his pie, raised his arm and pointed up the road further into the camp. 'That red brick building on the right, that's where you want, mate, that's special courses Reception. You're one of the physical training guys, then,' he said. 'They'll run you to bloody death on that course, mate,' he said, grinning. As he slid the window shut he called out, 'Best of luck, anyway.'

The Reception people were friendly, and helpful. Tony was appointed to a billet of great luxury, compared to his last one. Furthermore, on going to the Airmen's Mess for his tea-time meal, he had another pleasant surprise. The Mess hall was the usual size as one would expect, but the décor was better; it looked more like a good class restaurant them an Airman's Mess. The seating was set out around small, four-seater dining tables, with wooden, yet comfortable chairs, unlike Padgate, with its big oblong four aside tables and bench seating. The stainless steel serving counter was not the scene of rowdy bustle that he'd been used to either; although serving a long column of men, the servers behind the counter maintained good service and politeness.

After Padgate, Tony could hardly believe it all. The selection on menu was very good, the aroma of it tantalized the hungry lads on the course as they walked in, but the biggest surprise of all was the serving concession. Automatically they headed straight to the end of the long, orderly queue.

'No need for that you lads,' the corporal PTI accompanying them called out cheerfully. 'You chaps on the display flight are exempt from that, you've got corporal's privileges.' Noticing the men hesitating, he said, 'Go on then, lads. Get yourselves to the serving counter, nobody expects you to wait, you're in a privileged flight, no queuing for you lot.'

Other privileges included immunity from most normal camp disciplining; this had to be done by their own officers. They were also exempt from queuing in the NAAFI, together with several other minor concessions. However, on the down side, all men on the course were subject to severe, regular medical checks. Yes, they were in a privileged flight as they were about to find out, but by God, they were to earn it over the next fourteen weeks of the course.

The living quarters were roomy and comfortable, and furthermore, each contained only fifteen men. All the men on the course were of similar average height, approximately between five foot eight and five foot eleven; as this was the requirement for team work and general display. Tony was one of four trainees to be selected out of the flight to be appointed acting corporal for the duration of the course; there was one for each billet. He was picked out for this privilege because of his physical training experience; the other three men were semi-professional Rugby players in civilian life. The idea of their temporary unsubstantiated promotion was to aid the training staff, and to help with billet control. Tony thought that other lads in his billet were a decent bunch; however, all had only one interest, and their conversation was continually about it – football. The one exception was John Foster, a slim studious fellow. Tony hated football; so, consequently the two made friends, and to the delight of both they discovered they shared many common interests. These included astronomy and several related subjects such as space travel, etc.

'Come on, you lot, get your kit on and be smart about it,' Tony called out to his mates in the billet, glancing down at the two stripes on the armband on his right arm. 'The PTI will be here any minute, so come on, move it, lads,' he yelled with authority.

Two hours later, Tony was running in the front row of a group of men with his new friend, John, running alongside; both beginning to get bored and fed up with it. The men were all dressed in shorts, vests, thick socks, and heavy marching boots; they were also browned off, and sweating buckets.

'This is getting a bit much for my liking' muttered Tony out of the side of his mouth as they jogged along. 'We must have run about ten bloody miles up to now.

I've got a hell of a blister on my right heel, an'all,' he grunted. 'It don't half fucking hurt John, its red hot,' he moaned.

'I think I've got one on both mine,' he replied, puffing and blowing as he struggled along, obviously under great strain.

By the time they'd got back to camp the lads had completed a fourteen mile run. This didn't fatigue Tony much as he was used to regular heavy workouts in the gym, and the rugby lads didn't show much distress either. However, the majority of the men, not being used to such violent exertion, were – as Tony put it – well and truly buggered. That evening, while his mate Jon and most of the other lads in the billet were flopped out on their beds still recovering from the day's toil, Tony decided go down to the camp gym for a workout.

24

He found it easily, as the camp was only a fraction of the size of his former one. On entering, he was also delighted with what he saw. It was the most luxurious gymnasium he had ever been in; there appeared to be equipment in there for nearly every type of sport. But for such a luxury as this, with all its terrific equipment, he was very surprised to see that it was almost devoid of personnel. Noticing a chap in ballet tights practising his art, Tony, was at first rather surprised, he'd never expected to see ballet dancers in the RAF. However, as he was the nearest person out of only three others in the place, he went over to seek information about the establishment.

'Excuse me, mate,' he called out to the dancer, who at first was so intent on his practice that he didn't hear him. 'Excuse me, mate,' he repeated, a little louder this time.

The man stopped in his movements, glancing at Tony with indifference. 'Yeah, what you want, pal?' Tony was rather taken aback by this response; he'd expected a very refined, effeminate reply from a male dancer in tights. However, he was to find out over the next few weeks while training alongside Jeff, as his name later turned out to be, that his training for ballet dancing could be equally as strenuous as his own weight training. The dancer also proved to be very friendly and helpful, directing Tony to the men's changing room and showers, etc. These also shocked Tony with their luxury quality.

Walking out of the changing room fifteen minutes later dressed in track suit and trainers, Tony made his way over to the weight training area at the top corner of the large gym. Here he saw, that although the whole floor area of the hall was covered with polished wood parquet flooring, the weight training area was fitted out with thick impact matting. It really was a dream, thought Tony, marvelling at the sight of the shining barbells, dumbbells, and the other modern equipment. Then with a start, he caught sight of another dream, and this one really did grab his full attention.

Walking on to the mats in the weight training area was the most beautiful girl – well nearly – that he'd ever seen. She was of average height, and although she was wearing a stylish pale grey track suit, he could see that the figure it concealed was something special, and what's more, her tied back, fair auburn hair, encased the face of an angel.

Walking over to her as she was preparing a pair of dumbbells ready for use, he said cheerfully, giving her his best come-on smile, 'Hello there; so I've got a training partner, have I? My name's Tony.' It was then he found out that she was definitely no angel.

Slowly pushing the dumbbell she'd been loading to one side, she stood up and looked him full in the face, her deep blue eyes boring into him. 'No, you haven't,' she said quietly, 'and I don't care what your name is. Furthermore, I hope you're not going to interrupt my concentration, while I'm working out Mister!'

Taken aback slightly, but still smiling, he replied courteously in his best English,' 'Oh, I'm sorry, dear, but I was only trying to be friendly. I don't like anyone interrupting my concentration when I'm working out either.' Having said this he turned away and started loading one of the five-foot barbells. The two then worked out in silence for the next hour, without even exchanging so much as a glance. When Tony decided that he'd just about done enough, he thought he'd finish up with a few sets of bicep curls and then go for a shower.

He'd just loaded a pair of dumbbells and started his first set, when the young lady, having finished her own workout, came over and stood right in front of him, smiling sweetly. 'I'm sorry for snapping at you like that earlier, I hope you understand?'

Glaring at her as he strained in the exercise, he yelled through clenched teeth, 'Bugger off, can't you see I'm busy?'

25

Later, back in the billet, Tony told his mate, Jon, all about the quality of the camp gym, and about the beautiful but bloody cocky, young bird who'd been training alongside him.

'Aye, after she'd nearly bitten my head off telling me she didn't want interrupting when she was training, she'd the bloody cheek to come over to me when she'd finished herself, and interrupt mine,' he said, with a laugh.

Laughing with him, John said, 'Well, I bet you didn't say much to her Tony did you, her being such a sexy piece, eh?'

'Huh, you bet I did, mate, I told her to bugger off, nobody interrupts my training; if it had been the Group Captain himself, I'd have told him the same,' he stated adamantly. 'Anyway, you'll see the gym yourself on Wednesday, John, we've got the full afternoon doing some sort of gymnastic training for the course, haven't we?'

'I don't know what we'll be doing, Tony, but whatever it is I'm sure I won't be much good at it, that's for certain,' he said, grinning.

'I don't mind what the Hell it is we've to do,' Tony said, 'as long as it doesn't entail doing them bloody back flips and somersaults – I can't stand that sort of thing, too dangerous,' he said shaking his head. A bloke I know back home broke his neck buggering about like that, poor sod's in a wheelchair now for life,' he said sadly.

To Tony's delight his fears were not realised. The Wednesday afternoon session in the gym turned out to be just a session of stretching exercises and formation movements, which all the lads appeared to be really enjoying; Tony, of course, found this sort of stuff very elementary and boring. The group was supervised by the two corporal PT instructors, who, being very friendly, allowed the lads quite a lot of freedom. This allowed them to have a good look around the place and to try out any equipment they fancied. Most of the boisterous lads were attracted to playing about on the two big trampolines.

Everybody was enjoying themselves and making a hell of a din, when suddenly, a loud feminine voice called out from the open door of a little office at the far end of the hall, 'Corporal Hudson! Corporal Black! What the hell's going on here?'

The two corporals were sitting on a bench at the side, talking and having a crafty cig; on hearing this they both jumped their feet, at the same time dropping their half smoked weeds on to the polished wooden floor and quickly standing on them. 'We're just giving the men a short break, Sergeant,' one of them called out to the now advancing figure of a young woman. 'They've just had a strenuous hour's training,' he told her.

On reaching the crowd of men she walked straight up to the corporals, who were both now looking a little on edge. 'Oh, have they now,' she yelled. 'Well get going and give them another, they won't learn much running around the hall like madmen, will they?' Then quietly she said, 'By the way, don't let me catch you two smoking in here again, you both know full well it's not permitted.

'Come on, you lot,' she called out, turning to the men, some of whom were still running around in disorder. 'Let's have you back in formation, and be quick about it!' he yelled.

'What's up with you Tony?' John asked Tony, noticing that he'd gone very quiet and was trying to keep well behind him, as the sergeant walked towards them, on her way back to her office.

'Don't move, mate,' he muttered. 'Keep well in front of me, for Christ's sake – don't let her see me; she's the bird I told to bugger off the other night down here.' However, with his heavily muscled physique, Tony stood out like a sore thumb. As she passed their eyes met, and he was sure he saw just the slightest hint of a smile on her lovely face.

26

Friday evening was Tony's next workout session with the weights; on his way down to the gym he couldn't help wondering if he might have another encounter with the lovely sergeant. However, he had a very good workout and really enjoyed it but, there was no sign of her, nor was there on his next training night, which was the Monday of the following week.

'Was she there tonight, then, Tony?' John enquired, grinning, as Tony returned to the billet on the Monday night.

'No,' he replied aloofly, throwing his training gear down on the bed. 'She most likely does her workouts in the day, the other night must have been a one-off,' he said.

'It would be nice to see how you got on with her though, Tony, you know, meeting her without her stripes again. What would you do, pretend you didn't know who she was?'

'Don't be bloody daft, lad,' he said. 'I told you, she recognised me the other day when she came in bollocking the two corporals.' He reached into his locker, and taking out a packet of biscuits, he pulled one out and offered one to his friend. 'Anyway, there's no chance of landing that one now, mate,' he sighed, 'her being a bloody sergeant.'

'But you said you liked her, didn't you?' John replied innocently.

'Aye of course I did, you daft bugger,' Tony grunted, 'but I didn't know, then, she was the sergeant in charge of all our lot. She wouldn't look at a bloody Sprog like me anyway, they keep to their own kind our superiors, mate, believe me,' he said with a knowing laugh. Then putting the packet of biscuits back in his locker and locking it up, he said with a sneer, 'Anyway, John I've gone off her since I found out who she was; I wouldn't bother with her now, if she threw herself at me with her panties in her hand. Come on let's go down to the NAAFI for a snack. I've just burnt off about three thousand calories pumping iron down there.

Just then there was a movement at the bottom end of the long hut. 'Right you lot, cut the noise and stop buggering about and stand by your beds,' Corporal Black yelled, coming out of his private bunk room at the bottom of the billet. Walking into the centre of the room in his usual strutting way, he stood there near the old iron stove for a few seconds in silence, before beginning to speak in a very serious tone.

'Gentlemen, I have just been reading our schedule for next week, and, I'm pleased to inform you that Monday a.m. will be fully taken up with your first full medical examinations.'

After a long pause he continued in the same serious manner. 'When I say, 'full medical', gentlemen, I mean 'full medical'. Do you understand?'

Without a word, the men stared back at him expressionlessly. 'You don't, eh?' he hissed with raised eyebrows. 'Well, I'll tell you; the medical you had when you first came into the Service was to make sure you were fit to be an airman, right?'

'Yes, Corporal,' a few of them replied, in unison.

'Okay then,' he said, looking at them with a gloating smile. 'Well, the medical you're going to get on Monday is to make sure you're fit to be bloody supermen!' he yelled.

All the lads visibly jumped at the sudden yell he'd emitted. 'That's why I'm here now, to forewarn the lot of you that I want every man in my command to be so clean, that I could eat him – right! I want everyone soaked, scrubbed and polished up to a high standard. Should any of the doctors down at the medical centre have any cause to complain to me regarding the lack of hygiene of any one of you lot, that man will wish he was dead.' As he turned to go back to his own room, he continued in a quieter tone, 'I'm telling you all this to save you embarrassment, believe me boys.' He smiled. 'They'll be poking you all, in the most intimate places including having a right good look up your arses.' Grinning over his shoulder as he disappeared into his room, he called back, 'so make sure that's spotlessly clean an'all won't you, lads.'

On Monday morning the men lined up inside the big sterile-looking waiting room on the ground floor of the Medical Centre – the first batch waiting quietly to be called into the examination room. They were to go before a team of four doctors, who were about to give each one of them that terrifying individual medical examination, as promised by Corporal Black. Tony and his mate, John, had managed to get into the first batch of twelve men to be called into the examination room.

As they walked in, they were overwhelmed by the strong smell of disinfectant; the general hygiene in the long, sparkling room was impressive. It had six separate cubicles within it, each containing an examination table surrounded by a red curtain. On entering the men were instructed by one of the doctors to strip naked, then wait to be called into one of these cubicles. This didn't bother Tony, he'd always been used to walking around starkers at the gym back home, but Jon was a little more modest, and said so.

Tony laughed. 'Don't be daft, lad. No bugger's going to be looking at us with lust in here.' He then pretended to survey all the other chaps in the room, with mock concern. 'Well, I hope not mate, or there'll be sparks flying.'

Leaving the examination room half an hour later, their respect for Corporal Black's altruism had grown somewhat. Each man had been given the most thorough examination imaginable, and all said how glad they were it was over. Filing out into the main waiting room, the lads couldn't help but laugh as they passed the next group cheerfully going in; they thought it more merciful though, not to enlighten them about their good times ahead. However, what they themselves didn't know at that time was, this specialised medical examination was standard on the course, and was performed weekly throughout its duration.

27

The rest of the week was normal procedure, running fourteen miles in the morning, general training and course instruction in the afternoon. The lads were beginning to find this repetitive and boring, particularly Tony, who was concerned about all the miles of roadwork, and the harm it was doing to his weight training schedule. When he checked his weight, he found he'd lost nearly half a stone since starting the course.

'I wonder if there's any way to dodge some of these fucking fourteen mile runs, John,' Tony moaned on the Friday night, as they were sitting talking in the billet.

'The only way I can think of is to go sick or something,' he replied, 'but then, if you did you wouldn't be able to go doing your weight training down at the gym.' He laughed. 'They'd soon see you weren't sick when they saw you humping them bloody great weights about.'

'Oh, I don't know,' Tony said, with a thoughtful look on his face. 'That might not be a bad idea, John my lad.' He smiled slyly. 'Anyway,' he went on, 'who the hell would know, there's only that dancer, Jeff, goes down there in the evenings these days and he's got nowt to do with our lot, he's permanent staff.'

Pausing for a moment, John said, 'What about Sergeant Stanhope?

'Never seen her since that first night, John,' Tony replied casually. 'As I said before, she most likely does her exercises in the daytime, the night I met her must have been a one-off.' He thought for a moment.

'Anyway, I could always go sick with a strained muscle in my leg; that might get me off the bloody running.'

As he said this, he got up off the bed and went over to his locker and pulled out his training kit. 'Right, mate, I'm off down there now for a workout. See you about nine; then we can go over to the NAAFI for an hour, if you like.'

28

Walking cheerfully into the brightly lit gym hall the first person Tony saw was his friend, Jeff, the ballet dancer. He was working away like hell, stretching and jumping about the place like a fairy.

'Evening, Jeff.' Tony called out, making for the changing room at the top end of the hall.

Half-way there he saw her. 'Oh Christ,' he muttered as he went in, 'so the beautiful sergeant has returned, eh.'

She was in the weight training area working away like a beaver, with two lightweight dumbbells. She was still hard at it when he came out. Changed and ready to start himself he didn't speak; because of course, he daren't interrupt, she'd obviously tell him to bugger off – of that he was certain. Over an hour passed while both Tony and the sergeant worked in silence, apart from the clanging of the equipment. Suddenly she stopped and giving Tony a quick glance, as he strained on the incline bench with two fifty pound dumbbells, turned away from him without a word and walked towards the ladies shower room. Obviously she didn't want to be told to bugger off, either.

Fifteen minutes later, Tony decided he'd finished; banging down the barbell he'd been using he stood there in his tracksuit bottoms, wiping the perspiration from his face and chest with a towel.

Suddenly, a voice behind him said sweetly, 'Hello, Tony, I hope I'm not breaking your concentration.'

Spinning around with the towel in his hand and smiling broadly, he replied, 'Oh no, no, Sergeant. I've finished now.' She stood there smiling, dressed in a pair of denim shorts and a white sweater, looking all fresh and glowing, straight from the shower. As he looked

her up and down, his pulse instinctively quickened.
God, she even smells good, he thought.

'You can drop the Sergeant stuff, Tony seeing as
we're both weight trainers,' she said smiling. 'While
I'm off duty, anyway,' she added, 'and my name's
Becky.' Hearing her say this, Tony felt elated; he was
beginning to think that he might have a chance after all
with this very sexy young lady, even though she was so
much his superior in rank.

Giving her an exaggerated mock bow, he said
smiling, 'Very pleased to meet you, my dear Becky.
Shall we dance?'

Laughing and pretending to hit him she said, 'Oh,
we've got a comic have we?' She pretended to sniff and
said, 'Go and get your shower and sweeten your self up,
you stink of sweat.' She looked him up and down. 'I
must say though, your muscle definition is looking
good,' she added.

'Yes I know, it is it's all this road work,' he sighed.
'I've lost half a stone. Too much running doesn't go
down well with bodybuilding, Becky, as you'll no
doubt know.'

'That's true I suppose,' she agreed, with a smile. 'If
you'd like a cool drink when you've showered you can
come down to my office and join me, I'm gagging for
one myself.'

Unable to believe the invitation, he replied, 'I'll be
five minutes, my dear.' As he hastily made for the
shower room, he called back with a grin, 'I can't refuse
an invitation like that.'

Shaking her head smiling, as she watched him go,
she called after him, 'Don't rush it lad, have a good
scrub and don't forget to wash behind your ears.'

'Cheeky little bugger,' he muttered on his way to the shower room, unable to believe his good luck.

'Come in,' was the response to his tapping on the door marked, 'Sergeant Stanhope'. Tony went gingerly in, wondering what to expect.

'Come through, Tony,' she called out from inside an adjoining room at the back of the little office area.

Going in he was very surprised to see that this was a fully fitted out living area and bed space, containing a comfortable single bed and a wardrobe. Becky was reclining on a small sofa in front of a radiogram playing an Elvis record and there were two bottles of beer and two glasses on a little table beside her. She was smiling as she surveyed him, and he thought she looked edible.

'Come in, sit down have a beer and listen to this new record I bought the other day; it's great,' she said, giggling like a school girl.

Bloody hell, he thought as he went over to join her, those two corporals wouldn't believe their eyes if they could see their boss like this.

Getting up from the sofa she proceeded to open the bottles enquiring over her shoulder, 'I suppose you do like beer, Tony, don't you?'

With a laugh, he walked over to the table to help her, 'That's a bloody silly question to ask a Yorkshire man, Becky, darling.'

Sitting on the comfortable sofa, listening to Elvis belting away, Tony slyly began to slide his arm around her shoulder. She ignored the move for a moment. Suddenly, as the record changed to Blue Suede Shoes, she jumped to her feet and pulled at his arm. 'Come on let's rock,' she said, with a giggle.

'I don't know how to do it, love,' he replied, trying to stay on the sofa as she pulled at him.

Insistently she continued, finally getting him to his feet, 'Come on, I'll teach you how to do it,' she said, grabbing his hand. He suddenly froze as she said this, standing motionless, with a blank stare on his face.

Still holding his hand, Becky looked up at him puzzled, 'What's up Tony, are you all right?'

After a slight pause, his face relaxed. 'Yes, Becky, yes, I'm fine,' he replied. 'It was just something that crossed my mind.' He grabbed her in his arms with a smile. 'Come on then, we're wasting this record, I was only kidding, I can rock.'

As they were sitting, drinking their beer after the Elvis record, Tony tentatively said, 'I suppose a good-looking girl like you has a bloke hanging around somewhere, Becky, eh?'

She reached for her glass and replied hesitantly, 'Yes, I've been going steady with a boy for over a year now.' Then she added, 'Well, he's a man really, he's quite a bit older than me.'

'Oh, is he?' Tony was thoughtful. 'How much older, if you don't mind me asking?'

'Well, I'm just twenty-one and he's thirty-six; he's a divorcee,' she said, giving him a cautious glance.

Looking warmly into her face, he said almost in a whisper, 'He's a lucky guy, Becky, he really is.'

For a few seconds she made no reply; then she asked softly, 'I suppose you've got a steady girlfriend, Tony, haven't you? A good-looking guy like you must have,' she said, with a coy smile.

'Huh, I thought I had,' he grunted, staring down at the floor, 'but she dumped me, she's buggered off back to America, where she's been living for several years, not so much as a goodbye,' he said sadly.

'Good Lord, she must have gone out of her mind dumping a bloke like you, Tony, and I mean that,' she said adamantly.

'Don't worry, Becky darling I'll get over it. Tony Ryan has never been known to be beaten by anything, let alone a woman,' he said, with a grin.

He got up from the sofa and finishing his beer he said, 'Much as I hate to, I'd better get back to my billet, it's nearly ten thirty; that corporal of ours will be yelling at me, if I'm not in for lights out.'

Smiling, she replied, 'Yes and I'll be yelling at him an'all if he starts smoking in my gym again.'

'Aye, I saw you tell the pair of 'em off the other day,' he said, with a laugh. 'I agree you were right though; bloody smoking, especially in a gym, it's not on in my book. If they'd dared to smoke in our gym at home the lads would have thrown the pair of them out – physically an'all,' he said firmly. 'Anyway I'd better get off, love, I've really enjoyed our time together here tonight.' He smiled, and asked hesitantly, 'Dare I hope to see you again socially, Becky?'

Looking up into his face with a glowing smile, she just nodded slowly.

As she escorted him out he felt elated; pausing as he opened the outside door which led into the main gym he turned and looked down into her face, 'You know, Becky, he really is a lucky bugger that bloke of yours,' he said softly. Without replying she went up to him, cupped his face in her hands, pulled him to her and kissed him firmly on the mouth; he eagerly responded.

As they hung on to each other she whispered, 'You're a lovely guy, Tony Ryan; when are you coming down again?'

Holding her firmly to him and kissing her upturned face, he muttered, 'As soon as possible, darling; tomorrow night, if you'll be here.'

'I'll be here,' she said; pulling herself together, she gently pushed him away. 'Go on now, you sexy beast,' she said, giggling, 'before I weaken and drag you back in and lock the door.'

Laughingly, Tony replied, 'You wouldn't have to do any dragging, darling, believe me.'

29

The following morning being Saturday was a half-day; the men were engaged in general light exercise movements in the field adjoining the gymnasium, attended by the two corporals. It was a beautiful sunny morning and everybody was enjoying the activity – even the two instructors were laughing as they worked away with the lads, putting them through their routine.

Suddenly, a voice called out from the back door of the gymnasium building, 'Corporal Black! Corporal Hudson!'

'Oh God,' Tony heard Hudson groan. 'It's bloody Sergeant Stanhope, what the hell can she want now?'

'Come on,' replied Corporal Black. Let's go and see before she starts yelling again; she can be a funny bugger if she's rubbed up the wrong way.'

'You've no need to tell me that,' Hudson muttered as they both made off hastily to answer her call.

'Morning, gentlemen,' the Sergeant greeted them as she drew near. 'How are your men faring – any obvious failures showing up yet?'

'No, not really, Sergeant,' Corporal Black replied formally.

'What do you mean 'not really', Corporal,'' she said sternly. 'Have you noticed any weakness in any of them or not? We have a surplus of eight men on the course, you know, so we do expect some failures,' she said, staring at the two blank-faced men. 'Okay, keep a close watch on them next week,' she went on after getting no reply. 'Any that show chinks in their armour, let me know before the weekend. The sooner we get the failures posted off the course the better, we don't want any wasted time,' she said positively.

Both corporals agreed, and said so.

'Right, I've been planning a few changers in routine as from Monday,' she continued, passing them several large sheets of typed paper. 'These are my new instructions – study them over the weekend,' she ordered. 'I also want you to pick out of the ranks, six of the strongest men to train as bearers to back the gymnastic team. However, make sure they are also of reasonable intelligence, a bearer has a lot of responsibility with regard to the safety of the team – as you'll understand, of course,' she added, nodding firmly.

'Oh, definitely, Sergeant,' agreed Corporal Hudson confidently. He glanced at his mate. 'I'm sure we can pick six strong intelligent lads out of that lot, can't we Corporal Black?' he said, looking back over his shoulder at the men frolicking about in the field like school boys.

'Who's that weight trainer that uses the gym in the evenings, the one you made a head man, has he any common sense, or is he like most of these muscle men – thick?' she asked, smiling.

'No, he's definitely not thick that one, Sergeant, his name is Ryan; he's told me that he's got a certificate to be a Weight Training Instructor.'

'Has he?' she replied. 'Include him in then, Corporal. I think we could make good use of him.' When the two corporals continued to remain there motionless, she snapped, 'Well, go on then, get over there and see to your men. By the way,' she called out, as they turned to go, 'Bring that man, Ryan, over here when you break up this morning. I'd like to asses his mental capabilities for myself, before we give him any extra responsibilities.'

'We'll have him over within half an hour, Sergeant,' called out Corporal Black, as they strode back to join the noisy crowd.

30

'I see the good-looking Sergeant's back with us then, Tony,' John said, grinning as they stood watching the two corporals in discussion with her.

'Aye, I wonder if she's giving 'em another bollocking, like she gave 'em the other day in the gym for smoking,' he replied, laughing.

'We haven't seen her since then, have we?' John pointed out. 'Did you see her in the gym last night Tony?' he asked.

'Aye, I did catch sight of her messing about with them light weight dumbbells,' he replied casually.

'She didn't get flirty with you then Tony, eh?' he teased.

'Nobody interrupts my concentration, while I'm training John my lad,' he replied. 'I've told you that before, haven't I?' He laughed, hoping that would be the end the subject.

'No, but I thought by the way you were talking the last time you saw her – '

'Look, look the corporals are coming back,' Tony interrupted to stop the probing. 'By the look on their faces, there's something going off, mate.'

Later as the men were being dismissed, Corporal Black called out in a loud voice, 'Head man, Ryan; come here, please.'

Rather surprised, Tony said, 'Now what's up, John?' and then proceeded briskly over to the corporal, who by now had been joined by his colleague Corporal Hudson; both were stern-faced. On reaching the two, Tony was told briefly about the assignment he was to be a part of, as from Monday, and also about his present interview with the Sergeant. The three then walked to the gym in silence. Corporal Black who was leading, knocked tentatively on the door of the Sergeant's office.

'Come in!' She called out. She was sitting at her desk on the phone; miming to them that she wouldn't be long, she continued her conversation. Actually it took about fifteen minutes, during which time the three men began to feel rather fed up standing there in silence, as she chatted on and on, occasionally laughing, in between a great deal of feminine small talk.

At last she put the phone down and looked over at them blank-faced. 'So this is the man you recommend to head the bearer team is it, Corporal Black?' she said casually, as if it were of little concern.

'Yes, Sergeant, this is AC Ryan. He tells me that he is a lifelong member of the Health and Strength Organisation, also of the National Federation of Body Builders; he claims to hold an Instructors Certificate issued by the latter.'

Getting up from her chair, the sergeant stood looking Tony up and down for a moment, remaining expressionless. He, staring at the wall behind her, could hardly believe that only a few hours ago, he'd been holding her in his arms, kissing her passionately. 'Very, very impressive credentials, Ryan, I must say,' she eventually said, nodding slowly, 'I don't suppose you could let me see them, could you?' she asked. Tony, glancing at the two corporals next to him, noticed a slight smirk had crossed their faces.

'No problem there, sergeant,' he said in a firm voice. 'I'll ring my friend at home this evening; with luck, you'll have everything you want on your desk by Monday morning.'

'Thank you, Ryan, I'd appreciate that,' she replied. Tony glanced again at the corporals, and noticing they were no longer smirking, gave them a faint smile.

'Well, Ryan,' she went on, 'I think Corporal Black will have put you in the picture as to what will be required of you as from Monday.'

'Yes, Sergeant, you want me to put the other bearers through a bit of strength training in preparation for the job, I'm sure I can handle that, provided the right sort of men are selected. It's not all men who are psychologically suitable for strength training, as you'll no doubt appreciate,' he emphasized.

'Yes, you're right, Ryan,' she agreed. 'Anyway, you'll need to get yourself prepared for Monday. Could you manage to do a little preparation this afternoon, so you'll have everything firmly in your mind? I'm sure Corporal Black will be more than pleased to give you a couple of hours down here after lunch.' Raising her eyebrows, she looked questioningly over at the corporal; pursing his lips and scowling slightly, he replied abruptly that he'd be delighted.

'That's very dedicated of you, Corporal Black,' she said. 'I know you usually play snooker in the Corporals' Club on Saturday afternoons,' she continued with a sigh, 'but, as we all know, duty comes first. I'd give Ryan here the instructions myself,' she told him, 'but I've got to go into town this afternoon to pick up a new dress I ordered earlier in the week. It's for a Ball I've been invited to next weekend.' She picked up a sheet of glossy paper from her desk top showing a model in a light blue dress, and held it up in front of them, smiling.

'This is it, isn't it sweet?' she said, looking at it with pride. The corporals both agreed in a formal tone, that it was. Tony couldn't help smiling at the situation.

Tony was back down in the gymnasium at two fifteen, the time agreed with Corporal Black. The corporal was obviously not in the best of moods, having to miss his snooker session, and made some very derogatory comments about his superior.

'Fancy her putting a fucking frock before my match Final,' he complained loudly. Further derogatory comments followed. Tony didn't like the nasty names he was calling her, but he could appreciate the corporal's point of view and just laughed.

After about half an hour, he'd been given all the instruction required with regard to the job of bearer, and as far as the strength training program was concerned, Corporal Black knew very little compared to Tony, and was fully aware of it.

'I think I've got all the information I'll need to know now thank you, Corporal,' Tony said. 'I'm sure I'll be able to manage the job without any difficulty,' he assured him, smiling.

The corporal looked up at the wall clock. 'We can't pack up just yet, she'd never believe we'd finished in half an hour; if she came back and found us gone, she'd play up like hell.'

Tony, seeing a softer side of Corporal Black, felt a little sorry for him. 'Why don't you get off to your snooker game, Corporal,' he said. 'I'll stay here and do a few abdominal sit-ups, and if she comes back before four o'clock, I'll say you've just gone.'

After a moment's thought, the Corporal began to smile. He patted Tony on the shoulder and said in friendly tone, 'That's very nice of you, Ryan. I won't forget this, you're a good bloke.'

'Anyway, I don't think she'll be back for ages, if she's anything like my sister when she goes shopping for clothes,' Tony told him, grinning.

Corporal Black had only been gone about ten minutes, when Tony heard the sound of a car pulling up outside the main door. 'Bloody hell,' he said out loud. 'She hasn't been long with her shopping.' Jumping up off the mat where he'd been doing his sit-ups, he charged to the window; peering through, he saw the Sergeant leaning into the back of her little car, struggling to unload some large parcels off the back seat. Charging back to the mat, he picked up the instruction sheet the corporal had left for him to study and he sat down, pretending to be reading it with great interest.

When he heard the main door opening, followed by the sound of someone struggling in, he called out, without looking up from his instruction sheet, 'Hello, is that you Sergeant?' There was no reply, just the noise of parcels being dropped down on the floor, and then the sound of footsteps walking slowly towards him. Not quite knowing what to do next, he remained sitting, pretending to be engrossed in his studying.

The footsteps stopped right behind him and she said quietly 'No, it isn't the Sergeant, Tony; it's Becky.'

Throwing the paper down, he jumped up facing her and smiled. 'Glad to see you, love,' he said, with a mock sigh. 'That bloody Sergeant frightens me to death.' Looking at her, as she stood there dressed in a tight leather skirt and a low-cut blouse, he thought again, it was hard to believe she was the same person

that stormed about the gym bollocking the corporals –
or anyone else in sight for that matter.

'I'm not that bad, am I?' She laughed as Tony,
grinning, made for the shopping she'd dropped in the
doorway.

'I'd better help you with this lot, Becky, eh? Looks
as if you've been buying the whole of the shop up, as
well as that fancy dress you told Corporal Black and
Hudson about,' he said, laughing.

'Oh thanks. By the way, talking about Corporal
Black, he didn't spend much time with you, did he?
I've just seen him going into the Corporals' Club, as I
came back on camp,' she told him, with a frown.

'Oh, we soon got everything sorted out okay dear;
we could concentrate on the job better with the gym
being empty,' he told her. 'We came back a bit earlier
than two fifteen as we'd arranged, anyway,' he added
casually.

As he was picking up her parcels in the doorway
she said with a little sarcastic laugh, 'You can't have
got here much before – I didn't leave for town until five
past two, myself.'

'Didn't you love?' he replied, going into her office,
loaded up with the big parcels. 'We must have just
missed each other.'

Following him in and pushing the door shut behind
her, she spoke in a mock strict tone. 'Stop making
excuses, for that crafty scoundrel, Corporal Black – and
come here, Tony Ryan.'

Tony put the parcels on the desk and turned
towards her with a sheepish grin and open arms. Pulling
her to him, he said softly, 'Do you realize, Sergeant
Stanhope, I'm beginning to fall for you – in a big way.'
Their lips met.

Later, when they were sitting in her living quarters behind the office sipping cups of tea, she said, 'Did you really mean what you said earlier, Tony?'

'What – about falling for you? Yes,' he said seriously, 'I did, what's more, I've got to admit I can't help feeling bloody jealous of that other bloke of yours, Becky,' he said, gazing down at the floor like a sulky child.

Smiling slightly, Becky leaned forward in her chair and looked into his face. 'There's no need to upset yourself over Conrad, Tony; I'm not married to him you know.'

Still with a sulky look on his face, he replied, 'I know that, but I can't help feeling that he's there between us all the time, Becky.'

Rising from her chair, she went up to him pulled him to her bosom and stroked his hair. 'Look, Tony, there's nobody between you and me,' she said. 'I've known Conrad for just over a year as I told you before; he's a lovely guy, we've had some good times together, but there's never been anything deep or a commitment between us.'

She looked down into his face as he sat there frowning, and gave him a little kiss on the forehead. 'We've never slept together or anything like that you know, darling,' she said softly.

'How did you meet him then, Becky?' He had now clearly cheered up somewhat.

'We met at my last camp, the one I was posted from, to come here,' she replied.

'Oh, so he's in the service then, is he?' Tony said. 'Is he a Sergeant PT Instructor, like you?'

'No, not him,' she laughed. 'He's far from the physical type – him, no, he's in Intelligence, is Conrad;

he got posted to Cyprus three weeks before my posting on to this course.'

'Oh, so he's in Cyprus then,' Tony replied more cheerfully, feeling the competition diminishing. 'What's his rank, Becky,' he asked again. 'Is he the same as you, then?' He laughed. 'Whatever he is he'll easily be superior to me, a bloody AC plonk, won't he.'

'No, he's not a sergeant,' she went on hesitantly, 'as a matter of fact, he's a wing commander.'

Staring at her for a moment open-mouthed, Tony said quietly, 'Christ! A bloody wing commander – that puts me in my place then – an AC in competition with him.'

Laughing, she said, 'Don't be daft, Tony. You're not in competition with anyone; anyway he's only a man like you.' She put her arms around his neck and smiling into his face, whispered, 'Anyway love, I'm here with you now, aren't I? And that's where I prefer to be.' Releasing him, she changed the subject. 'By the way, Tony, this Ball I'm going to next weekend; I had two tickets given, would you like to accompany me?'

Hearing this, his face lit up, 'Sure would, darling; where is it held, anyway?'

'It's the Annual Hospital Ball held in the recreation hall at the General Infirmary in town. The physiotherapist down at our sick quarters got them for me last week,' she told him. 'Have you got any civilian clothes here though, Tony,' she asked?

'Of course I have, don't worry, my darling, I won't show you up, having to go escorted by a poor simple AC plonk.' Tony laughed.

31

'You're in, then, John, my old mate.' Tony grinned, as he walked up to his mate, who was lying on his bed in the billet, reading. 'I got Black to put you in the bearer team as I promised I would, but we'll have to improve your form a bit; there's some heavy lifting involved, you know.'

'Now you're getting me worried,' he said, with a chuckle. 'What does the job entail, anyway?'

'It's nothing to bother about,' Tony told him. 'We just help the lads as they go over the vaulting horse, prevent accidents, you know that sort of thing. Oh and we move the bits of equipment about as the display proceeds,' he added. 'We'll get all the training we need, John, don't worry.' He shook his head. 'I can't see the need for the bloody job myself though, but it gets me out of that fucking running – that's all I'm bothered about.'

'It was funny how this job came up out of the blue, just when you wanted to get out of all that lot, Tony, wasn't it?' John said, thoughtfully.

Tony grinned. 'Aye, they say the devil looks after his own, John, lad. He probably told the good sergeant that I was running all my muscle bulk off.'

'By the way, who are the other four guys picked for this bearer job, Tony?' he enquired.

Tony who was busy delving about in his overfull locker, threw his shorts and sweat shirt on to the bed, and replied without turning, 'Oh, there's just us two from this billet, Shaw and Bailey from next door and Fleming and that thick set mouthy bugger Brown from across the passage; they're all a bit thick, but they're strong lads,' he added dolefully. Then he glanced back at his mate and laughed, 'but I'm sure us two can make up in brain power for them silly buggers.' Meanwhile, having sorted out his gear and stuffed it in his training bag, he said with a smile, 'Well, I'm off then, mate, see you later.'

John, with a look of surprise called out, 'I've never known you go to the gym on Saturday night before, Tony, we usually go over to NAAFI for a pint, don't we?'

'Well, yes, I know, John, but I want to get a bit of extra arm work in, I've been neglecting it a bit lately.' Then storming off out of the door swinging his gym bag, he called back over his shoulder, 'See you later, mate.'

32

'Stop acting the bloody goat Bailey, there's nobody laughing,' yelled Tony at the young airman who was showing off. The little group of six men were standing waiting to start the afternoon training session in the gym. The morning had gone well, under the supervision of Sergeant Stanhope, she'd given them the full outline of their task as bearers; she had also suggested several safety measures to be employed when using the vaulting horse and other equipment.

'Is the Sergeant taking us again then, Tony?' John asked him, looking down the empty gym hall towards her office.

'I don't know,' he replied, looking in the same direction. 'She seems in no bloody hurry to start does she, we've been here waiting ten minutes,' he complained.

'Shush – she's coming,' whispered one of the lads, seeing her office door opening.

Walking briskly up the hall towards them she called out, 'Right you lot, I hope you've digested all I told you this morning.'

'Yes, Sergeant,' some of them replied.

'Right, well this afternoon I'm leaving you in the hands of Ryan here,' she said, nodding in Tony's direction. 'He's going to put you through a bit of weight training to get you in condition for the job.' She looked at Tony. 'By the way, Ryan, thank you for the qualification certificates you left on my desk, very impressive, Ryan, I must say.'

Straight-faced Tony replied, 'Thank you, Sergeant.'

'I'm going to a meeting now,' she told the group, 'so I don't want any skiving while I'm away, and Ryan – ' she continued firmly, her eyebrows raised, 'I'm leaving you in charge, as head man – anyone not cooperating and I want his name on your report sheet, is that clear?'

'Yes, Sergeant,' he replied, with a sharp nod.

As she turned to go, she added cheerfully, 'By the way Ryan, don't let any of the men overdo it at first, will you, we don't want anyone reporting sick in the morning with muscles full of lactic acid, do we now?'

'Don't worry, Sergeant, I'll handle them with kid gloves,' he called after her in true military tone, as she strode off briskly down the gym hall.

Without wasting any time, Tony got the other five lads to stand in line on the matted area used for weight training, and began instructing them in stretching and bending exercises to warm up, prior to using the weights. Meanwhile he himself set about loading the barbells, ready for the serious strength training routine. Suddenly there was a loud wolf whistle from one of the trainees; looking up Tony saw them all staring across at the side door leading to the shower rooms. Coming out was Jeff, the ballet dancer dressed as usual in his silk tights.

The wolf whistle was followed by raucous laughter and the voice of Brown, one of the rugby players yelling, 'I like your undies, darling.'

'That's enough of that, you lot,' shouted Tony, 'and you keep your comments to yourself, Brown,' he said firmly.

'Sorry about that, Jeff,' Tony called over to him, surprised to see him training at that time of the day.

'Huh, no apology necessary, Tony, I just ignore fools,' he called back indignantly, preparing to start his dancing routine.

'Okay now, get on with your warm-up, while I get the bars ready,' Tony shouted out, as he continued loading the weights.

'Tell you what, Bailey,' he heard Brown say as they were working away exercising, 'I'd rather see our sergeant in her fancy undies, than that creep of a dancer in his, wouldn't you?' This was followed by muffled laughter. Tony, although angry, pretended not to hear, and continued with his task.

All was quiet for a couple of minutes apart from the sound of puffing and blowing by the men, then with a dirty little laugh, Brown muttered again to his mate, ' Oh yes, I'd love to see the Sergeant's lovely bottom in frilly panties – without a doubt, Bailey.' Bailey had no time to reply

Tony, fuming, jumped up from what he was doing and stormed briskly up to the loud-mouthed Brown. All training stopped abruptly. 'How many times have I to tell you to keep that big gob of yours shut, Brown; nobody wants to know the contents of your dirty little mind. What's more,' he went on angrily, 'I hope you realise that the person you were ridiculing is one of our superior officers and if I put this lot down on my report sheet, you're in shit street, mate – understand?' he yelled.

Brown just stood there looking back at him with a sneer on his face. Then, grinning back at the other four lads, he turned back to Tony and pointed at his corporal's armband. 'Oh, the makeshift corporal speaks, lads,' he said sarcastically. 'He's protecting our sergeant's lovely bum.' He laughed. 'She would want someone to protect her if I got my hands in them fancy panties of hers, I'll tell you.' Tony would normally have taken firm action by now, however, under the present circumstances he just managed to control his natural instincts; after all, this was an RAF gymnasium, not the Dog and Gun pub.

Staring straight into Browns eyes, he said quietly, 'Okay, Brown, you've asked for it, I'm going to put you down on the report sheet.'

A big grin spread across Brown's broad features, and taking a sharp step towards Tony, he hissed, 'You, my friend, aren't man enough to put me down on anything, even with all your big muscles,'

The effect was like lightning. Tony shot his left arm up in front of the Brown's face and as the man turned his head sideways in a reflex action, he brought the cupped palm of his right hand around with a violent crack on Brown's now exposed left ear hole. The force was such that the big fleshy man went down with a thud on the thick matting, yelling in agony and holding on to his obviously ringing ear.

'You fucking bastard, you bastard Ryan,' he yelled, rolling on the mat still holding on to the painful ear, 'You've bloody well buggered up my ear, you fucking bastard, it's stone deaf now.'

'Shut up you pillock and get to your feet,' Tony said as though nothing had happened, 'before I deafen the other bugger for you. That might teach you to have some respect for women an'all,' he added, with a satisfied smile on his face.

Getting slowly to his feet, Brown, the bear with the sore lug, replied menacingly, 'I'm the one that's going to do the reporting now, Mr Bloody Clever Ryan, for common assault, that's what!'

Tony stood surveying the pathetic sight before him, the figure of Brown struggling to his feet, holding his sore ear and making threats. 'You must be a mind reader, Brown,' he said, shaking his head and grinning. 'That's the type of thing I intend to put on the report sheet.' He nodded. 'You were the one that made the move first, intending to assault me; that's why you got your lug cracked, it was self-defence,'

'Oh, balls!' said Brown, rubbing his ear.

'Apart from that,' continued Tony, ignoring the comment, 'there's the improper remarks you made regarding a superior officer, Sergeant Stanhope – it should make an interesting report when it's finished,' he concluded, with a chuckle.

'Huh, bollocks,' Brown grunted scornfully. 'All that's just your word, you assaulted me with no provocation; as far as the other thing's concerned – you've made that up, I never said anything about Sergeant Stanhope and you know it. Anyway,' he called out to the other men standing silently by, 'these lads can witness to that, can't you lads?'

There was silence from them for a few seconds and then Bailey, his pal and another man muttered, 'That's right, Brown,' while the rest remained silent.

Brown stood smirking at Tony for a moment, until another voice called out calmly, 'I did though, Brown, I saw you make a move to strike Ryan, prior to him having to take evasive action.'

Turning towards the voice he glared into the face of John Parks. 'You bloody grass,' he yelled. 'You'll side against your mates, will you? Well, I won't forget this, you skinny little rat, believe me – I'll have you for this,' he said threateningly.

'Oh,' Tony interrupted in mock surprise. 'That's another one to put on the report sheet then, threatening a witness, eh?' Brown stared back at him speechlessly, not quite knowing what to do next, and looking a little forlorn.

Tony, seeing the steam was out of the lad, started laughing. 'Look, Brown, I'm willing to forget all this if you behave yourself from now on. Just keep your thoughts to yourself okay, after all we've got a job to do and we're all in it together – ok?

With a look of relief on his face, and still holding his ear, Brown nodded and growled, 'Fair enough, I see your point.'

Hearing a clapping of hands from across the gym, they all turned in that direction to see Jeff the dancer coming towards them with a wide smile. 'Now that's what I call common sense and diplomacy,' he said.

'Well there's nothing to gain with unnecessary aggro, Jeff,' replied Tony cheerfully.

'No you're right, Tony, if you'd put that report in Brown would have, without a doubt, been in the guardhouse; that could then have interrupted the course.'

Brown, who was looking a bit disturbed at the interference said curtly, 'Look we've sorted it all out now, we can do without your advice mate, so just get your silk knickers back over there and get on with your fairy dancing, will you?'

'For Christ's sake, Brown shut it and stop being so insulting,' yelled Tony. 'Jeff here is a training mate of mine and he's only being friendly. I'd like to see you do an hour or so ballet training with him, I'll tell you, it'd bloody kill you.'

'What! You wouldn't get me dancing around with a ponce in silk knickers, Tony, I'd rather be in the bloody guardhouse, mate.' Brown laughed, pointing at Jeff's ballet togs.

Walking slowly up to him, Jeff said quietly, 'Look lad, for your information I'm a member of the RAF ballet team, what's more I'm a married man with two daughters.' As he said this, he reached into the top pocket of his training shirt and pulled out his 1250 (RAF identity card) with his photo on it. He held it up in front of Brown's sneering face and hissed, 'and this is who I am – airman!'

As he looked at the card, Brown's expression immediately changed, and he went red. 'Oh, oh – I didn't realise, Sergeant,' he spluttered. 'I was only joking of course, please accept my apologies, I thought you were just one of the lads, Sergeant.' The man had been severely shocked without a doubt; all the other lads had too, including Tony.

Turning to return to his part of the gym, Jeff said, 'Well, just watch who you pick on to insult in future, Brown, that big mouth of yours will get you into real trouble one of these days.'

The experience made Brown a different man, and what's more, the other lads began showing an extra keenness in the training, and this of course made Tony's task much pleasanter. The rest of the afternoon went smoothly, as did all the other training periods from then on. By the end of the first week they were all genuinely enjoying the sessions and making very good progress and Brown's ear had also stopped ringing.

33

On Friday evening as Tony came out of the dressing room ready for a training session, he was surprised to see Jeff smiling and waving him over. 'Hello there, Jeff,' he greeted him, 'I haven't seen you down here for a few days; I hope you haven't been ill or something?'

'No, I've been away for a few days, Tony, for an interview. By the way, have you had any more bother from that cocky, young bugger, Brown?'

Laughing, Tony said, 'No, I think you broke his rebellious spirit when you showed him your 1250 the other day; he's been a most polite fellow since then. Though I suppose I should be calling you Sergeant now, too. I didn't know your rank either, until then.' He grinned.

'Don't be bloody daft, Tony, we're training mates.' He laughed. 'I don't look much like a sergeant in these silk ballet tights, anyway, do I?'

Laughing with him, Tony replied, 'Well you put the wind up Brown the other day, wearing 'em, Jeff.'

'Anyway,' Jeff went on, 'if the interview I've just had has been successful, I won't be a sergeant any more Tony,' he smiled. 'I'll be getting a crown on top.' 'Flight Sergeant Davis, eh,' he said with mock self-importance. 'Also I'll be a bit better off money-wise, which will be very welcome, seeing the wife's expecting again.'

'Congratulations, Jeff on both counts,' Tony said. 'I'm sure you'll have been successful with your promotion as well as the other.' Then glancing around the otherwise empty gym he said casually, 'No sign of Sergeant Stanhope, Jeff –she's usually working out around this time of an evening, isn't she?'

'She'll be up at the 'Sergeants' Mess,' he replied. 'There's another bloody meeting going on up there tonight, I got out of going being on call at the Airmen's Mess,' he told him.

'So she'll be up there all evening, I suppose then?' Tony enquired.

'Yes, those bloody things usually take hours, they bore me to death,' he replied, pulling a face.

The conversation paused for a few minutes as Tony began loading one of the barbells, but he was obviously deep in thought. 'I don't suppose there are many women sergeants at this meeting, Jeff,' Tony called out over his shoulder. He forced a little laugh and said, 'She'll be out of her depth with all them blokes, eh?'

Jeff didn't reply for a moment, then looking across at Tony, he stopped dancing and went over to him where he was squatting on the mat, adjusting the barbell. 'Tony' he said quietly, squatting alongside him, 'I'd like a confidential word – if you don't mind, mate.'

Turning to face him – looking puzzled, Tony replied, 'Sure, Jeff, what's on your mind?'

Fidgeting slightly, Jeff continued, 'Well, Tony you can forget rank and tell me to mind my own bloody business if you like, but I mean well, it's about Becky Stanhope, actually, Tony.'

Tony's mind began to race, and with a slight note of panic in his voice he asked, 'What do you mean Jeff – she hasn't been hurt or anything, has she?'

'No, no, nothing like that, Tony.' Jeff patted him on the shoulder. 'I told you she's up at the Sergeant's Mess for the meeting.' Recognising the look of concern and relief on Tony's face, he went on with a smile, 'However, as I said at the start, it's none of my business really, but I couldn't help noticing that you and Becky seem to be very good friends.' He hesitated as though expecting a reaction before continuing, 'There's nothing wrong in that, you're both nice young people, but I just thought you'd like to know that Becky's got a very persistent admirer up at the Mess, whom she's having difficulty shaking off.' He paused and looked into Tony's frowning face. 'What's more, I think the bugger could get dangerous, with her continually rebuking him an'all, especially if he's been on the booze.' Tony face was by now taut with anger, as Jeff went on, 'What's more the bloke came down here one night and I had to tell him he was out order and show him the door,' he said. 'I'm telling you this, Tony,' he said seriously, 'just to put you in the picture in case he ever comes again when I'm not about.'

Tony jumped to his feet, his eyes flashing, and said menacingly, 'Who is the bastard, Jeff? I'll soon put a stop to his little games, mate, believe me!'

Shaking his head, Jeff replied, 'No, that's not the way to handle this one, Tony. He's a sergeant technician, he lives in the Mess and most of the time when he's off duty he's in the bar, on the booze; that's his problem,' he told him, frowning.

'Well, how would I recognise him, Jeff, if he shows his face and you're not here?' he asked.

'He's a big ginger-haired bloke with a moustache,' Jeff replied. 'About a couple of years older than me, about thirty-five; his name is Sergeant Jim Webster.' He became serious. 'If you do have to intervene, you must control your emotions, be very polite, and just firmly show him the door. But for God's sake,' he emphasized, 'don't get heavy with him or he'll have you in the guardhouse, Tony,'

'Okay, Jeff, I'll remember what you say,' he replied. 'I fully understand what you mean, but if the swine hurts her, I'll say bugger the bloody guardhouse, Jeff, I'll put the bastard in sick-bay – or worse,' he promised, nodding vehemently.

Two hours later, Tony had finished his workout, and had finished his shower. Jeff had already gone; the gym was silent and empty, but he couldn't leave himself until he was sure that Becky was safely back. Sitting down on one of the benches he started reading an old copy of a 'Health and Strength' magazine he'd found lying about, but he couldn't stop turning over in his mind what Jeff had just been telling him. It must have been half an hour later that he heard the sound of a car outside. 'Oh, thank God, this must be her,' he muttered to himself. Almost immediately she came walking briskly through the main door. She was dressed very smartly in her best blue uniform, carrying a brown briefcase, but she looked angry and fed up.

On her way to her office she caught sight of Tony sitting on the bench, and she called out, 'You still here, are you, Ryan?' He heard the sound of the briefcase being thrown down on the table and she called again, in a very formal tone, 'Ryan, in here please, at the double, man!'

Tony was genuinely startled, he couldn't believe his ears. What's the problem now, he thought. He jumped off the bench, and hurried to her summons. Solemn-faced, he charged into the office to see her standing there facing him, looking stern, cap in hand.

Before he could say anything she threw her cap down on the desk angrily. 'I'm bloody fed up; that lot up there are enough to drive anyone mad.' Frowning she ordered, 'Shut that door behind you, an'all.' Tony did as he was told and as the Yale lock clicked into place, he was just about to ask what he'd done to upset her, when a smile broke out on her tired, but still lovely face.

'Now come here, Tony Ryan,' she cooed seductively, stepping towards him, with her arms wide. 'Cheer me up – and that's an order.' Tony obeyed that order, promptly and without complaint.

34

'Christ, Tony! You're looking smart.' John was watching him preen himself in front of the mirror on his locker door.

Tony was unashamedly admiring himself as he dusted down his light grey, cavalry twill suit with a clothes brush. He wore with it a white shirt, formal mustard coloured tie and highly polished brown shoes – he looked like a young country gentleman. 'Thanks, mate,' he replied with a wink. He grabbed his black gabardine raincoat from the back of the locker and put it on. 'Got to keep the ladies happy you know, old son.'

'You must think a lot about that bird you picked up, Ryan to dress up like that for her,' called out one of the lads from across the room. Where did you say she works, Tony?' he asked.

Before he could reply, John chipped in with a knowing air. 'She works in Marks and Spencer in town; we met her and her mate in the café there, didn't we, Tony?'

Tony was making for the door. 'That's right. See you, lads,' he called back as he left, slamming the door behind him.

Walking down the main road leading to the camp gates, he spotted Becky's little car parked just outside; it had the parking lights on, and as he drew near he could hear the engine running.

'Jump in, Tony,' she called out, as he leant forward to open the door. 'Oh, darling, you smell good,' she said, as he dropped down into the seat beside her.

'Yes,' he replied smugly, 'It's that new aftershave I bought it in Marks and Spencer the other day; 'Old Spice' it's called, pet; glad you like it.'

Patting his thigh as they drove along, she giggled. 'I wouldn't mind if you'd used turpentine darling – on you I'd even like that.'

As Tony came out of the men's cloak room into the large dance hall, the sight of his Becky, standing waiting for him in her new dress, took his breath away; he'd never seen her look so beautiful. Her reaction to him seemed to be the same; she came up to him smiling, telling him he looked every inch a Country Squire, and as they walked further into the crowded hall, many eyes turned in their direction.

'What a beautiful young couple,' whispered a middle-aged lady to her male partner, as they walked passed hand in hand. Becky had several friends at the occasion, mainly from the Physiotherapy Department at the hospital, one being Tom, the young guy that had got her the tickets. Tom was standing at the bar when they walked in and waved them over, with a smile. Becky mentioned who he was and Tony liked the look of him from the start.

'Looks a nice lad,' he said, as they were walking over to join him. As soon as they were introduced, it was obvious that the two young men where going to get on well with each other.

'Can I get you and Tony a drink, Becky?' Tom asked.

'Well, yes, thanks, Tom,' she replied, glancing around, 'but where's your girl friend?'

'Oh, she'll be back soon, she just popped down to the Department for something,' he told her, smiling.

'Why don't you and me have a dance, Becky, until she gets back,' suggested Tony, putting his arm around her shoulder affectionately.

Dancing around the big hall, Tony felt happier and more contented than he'd felt for a long time; what's more it never entered his head to do his usual thing of scanning the floor for talent. No, all his attention tonight was in one direction, and looking down into his lady's deep blue eyes, he was sure that she felt the same.

Pulling her closer, and feeling her firm athletic body against his, he whispered in her ear, 'Sergeant Stanhope, I think I've fallen in love with you.' A faint smile crossed her face as they danced along and she gently slipped her arms around his neck and kissed him lightly on the mouth, to assure him it was mutual.

Making their way back to the bar area where they'd left their friend, Tony said cheerfully, nodding ahead, 'Oh look, Becky, that must be Tom's girl.' Tom was chatting to a big, good-looking ginger-haired girl, about the same age as themselves.

'Nice looking lass,' Tony remarked casually.

'You control your roving eye, mister,' Becky replied, feigning anger.

'Not in your class of course, pet.' He grinned as they drew near to the other couple.

'Oh, you're back then you two, did you enjoy your dance?' asked Tom cheerfully. Without waiting for an answer he smiled and nodded in the direction of his girlfriend. 'Tony, Becky, this is my girlfriend, Peggy.'

Tony's smiling face momentarily went blank; then, after a pause, he regained his smile and took her hand. 'Very pleased to meet you, Peggy dear,' he said politely. Becky and Tom exchanged a quick glance, before Becky took Peggy's hand, with a warm smile.

Later in the evening, the four were sitting around one of the small tables. Tom suddenly grinned. 'You and I haven't had a jig yet, Becky, I'm sure Tony won't mind me having just one dance with you, will you Tony?'

Tony laughed. 'No, it's okay with me, mate, but I'll be keeping my eye on you.'

'Tell you what, Tony,' Tom went on, 'Why don't you take Peggy on the floor, ballroom dancing is her hobby. I'll bet she'll be able to teach you a few fancy steps, old chap.'

Smiling hesitantly, Tony looked over at the young lady with a sheepish grin. 'That okay with you Peg?'

35

'Sure it's okay, me coming in at this late hour, Becky?' Tony asked, as they went into her living quarters on their return to camp.

'Of course it is, she replied. 'This is where I live and I can invite anyone I want in here; it's not as if I live in the women's block, is it?'

'No, I see what you mean, love,' he replied. 'I just didn't want you to get any hassle, though, it being half past one in the morning, you know.'

Walking up to him with a coy smile, she tapped him playfully on the end of his nose with her finger. 'Shut up worrying and let's make some tea,' she said. 'Anyway, there's something I want to talk to you about, Mr Ryan,' she added, giving him a long, thoughtful look.

'Tell you what, Becky, I could murder a nice, big sandwich,' he said, lying back in the little armchair, as she passed him his tea in a yellow beaker.

'Huh, I'd have thought you'd have eaten enough tonight with that big buffet at the dance,' she said, getting up from her chair and going over to the little kitchen area in the corner. 'What would you like – will cheese do, love?' she asked, without turning.

'Beautiful darling,' he replied, smiling. 'With tomato, if you have any, please,' he added.

Passing him a plate with two slices of bread, full of Cheddar cheese and a thick cut slice of tomato between, she said, with exaggerated mock courtesy, 'There you are, my love, be careful it's heavy.' Then, settling back in her chair, nursing her tea in a red beaker, she sat silently watching him attack the big sandwich. Finally finishing it off, he was sitting back with a contented sigh, sipping his tea, when, out of the blue, Becky broke the silence. 'So her name's 'Peggy', is it, darling?'

Still lying back with a relaxed look on his face, Tony replied, yawning, 'Of course it is, love, that's what Tom said, and she's been answering to it all night, an'all.'

'I don't mean that Peggy and you know it, Tony Ryan,' she said, looking him in the eye,' I'm referring to the girl you told me dumped you and went to America, her name's Peggy too, isn't it now, eh?' she smiled, seeing his face tense slightly.

Looking away with the expression of a naughty child, he said quietly, 'Well – yes, as a matter of fact, love it is, but however did you guess, Becky?' She thought he looked so boyish sitting there looking slightly embarrassed – she could barely stop herself from bursting out laughing.

However, controlling herself, she staring smilingly into his face. 'I didn't guess, Tony baby, you as good as told me when Tom introduced us to his Peggy.' She jumped out of her chair and went to sit on his knee. 'Your face dropped a mile when Tom said her name, even he noticed it.' She laughed and put her arms around his neck.

Pulling her to him with one arm and pushing back her long hair with the other, he kissed her lips. 'Okay, we don't want any secrets between us, do we, Rebecca Stanhope. Still holding her close he continued, 'Right, I'll fill in all the bits you don't know about my past now, how's that?'

'Carry on, then,' she said expectantly, snuggled up within his arms. 'Then I'll tell you mine,' she added. Ten minutes later sat in the same position Becky said softly. 'I didn't realise you felt so much for her Tony; it must have been hell for you caged up at Padgate training camp with that on your mind, darling. But I don't know how she had the strength to leave you like that if she said she loved you.' She looked away from him and said softly, 'Or why.'

'I still have a photo of her in my locker, Becky, if you'd like to see it,' Tony said eagerly, trying to be helpful, 'I don't have it pinned up, though,' he added hastily, 'that's all in the past now, pet.'

Becky was silent for a moment, then without looking at him, she replied, 'No thanks, Tony, I don't think I want to see it yet, but it's kind of you to offer.'

Noticing a tear running down her cheek, he pulled her closer and kissed her forehead. 'Now then, baby, don't get upset, there's no need for that – I told you that's all in the past now.' Turning her face towards his, he saw that her beautiful blue eyes were brimming with tears. 'Oh, my baby, my baby,' he murmured, holding her to him, cupping her face in his hands and kissing her warmly.

Slipping off his knee and taking a small handkerchief from her pocket, she wiped her eyes with a sniffle. 'Now, Tony, I've something I'd like to tell you,' she said determinedly, it's about Conrad and I.'

Tony's heart missed a beat as he heard her say the name. 'You mean that boyfriend of yours, Becky, the wing commander?' As he spoke his voice wavered nervously, he couldn't bear to think of any other man having any part of her emotions; Christ, what sort of a shock was he in for now? Looking back at him expressionlessly, she replied, 'Yes, Tony, I rang him up long distance last night, while I was up at the Sergeants' Mess and we had a long talk.'

Tony chipped in, 'God, Becky, don't say you're going to dump me now for him, why have you waited until now to tell me you'd been talking to him, anyway?'

'I wanted us to have a good time at the dance, with nothing on our minds. Anyway, the conversation we had concerned only him and me, your name didn't come into it Tony,' she assured him smilingly.

'Oh, I see,' he mumbled sulkily, ' After all, I'm only a bloody ACI, aren't I, not a posh wingco, I don't suppose he'd think a bloody minion like me worth a thought, anyway.'

Becky looked back at him for a second; then she chuckled. 'You're a big sulky thing, Tony Ryan, you'll be crying next.' Getting off her chair, she went over to him and took hold of his hand. 'I couldn't dump you for anybody, you silly boy, I love you too much.'

Tony looked up at her smiling face, threw his arms around her and pulled her close, burying his face in her bosom. 'Oh, Becky, you gave me a bloody shock, though, I don't think I could have stood it again,' he whispered.

'And as far as I'm concerned, darling, you won't have to,' she assured him, with a kiss on his brow. 'No, the reason I rang Conrad last night, was to tell him that I'd met someone else who I'd fallen in love with, and to end the situation between him and me, absolutely.

36

 Loud cheers broke out from John and the other lads, as Tony walked into the billet on the Sunday morning about ten thirty, still dressed in his best suit and looking a little bleary-eyed.

'Oh, the prodigal lover boy returns, then,' said John, laughing.

'I got held up,' said Tony grumpily, opening his locker.

'Aye, and you'll be held up a bit more, Ryan,' warned one of the other lads, 'when Corporal Black's finished with you; he said you've got to report to him in his bunk as soon as you come in. He said you should have asked permission from your senior officer to stay out all night.'

'Oh, bugger him,' Tony said, hanging his coat in the locker. He sat down on his bed and proceeded to take his pants off and change into uniform. 'Christ, it's Sunday,' he said angrily. 'What's up with the guy anyway?' he grunted. 'We've nothing to do today; so fuck him,' he said.

'Bugger who, Ryan?' called out a loud voice from the bottom of the room.
Turning to look, Tony was shocked to see Corporal Black in his shirt sleeves, standing up very straight in the doorway of his bunk, with a stern expression on his face.

'Oh hello, Corporal Black; my mate here, just told me that you wanted to see me as soon as I got back.' Tony forced a confident smile.

'I do,' the corporal replied, menacingly. 'Just get yourself dressed and report to me in my bunk in ten minutes, Ryan, you're in trouble, man,' he told him, turning to go back inside.

As the door closed behind him, John said quietly, 'Sounds as though you're in for it, Tony. I hope that bird you took out last night was worth it, mate.'

Tony chuckled. 'She certainly was, John, I can assure you of that, pal.'

'Come in!' shouted Corporal Black in response to the tap on his bunk door. As Tony entered the pristine little room, the corporal threw down the 'News of the World' he was engrossed in and turned to face Tony with narrowed eyes. 'Shut the door behind you, Ryan, there'll be flapping ears out there,' he said in a rather friendly tone. As the door clasped shut he went on, 'Right lad, I think you're in the shit this time; unfortunately there's not much I can do to help you, even though I owe you one for the snooker cover up; all the lads in the billet know you were absent last night without permission.'

'Well, I would have let you know Corporal, but I didn't intend to stay out all night,' Tony said, submissively. 'It was just an accumulation of unforeseen circumstances that cropped up, Corporal, I assure you.'

The corporal stood there for a moment in silence, thinking that Tony had missed his way in life. 'You're very convincing, Ryan,' and he grinned. 'You should have been on the bloody stage, but it's not going to do you much good this time. I'm afraid you're still going down on my report sheet for being absent overnight without permission; I've no choice,' he said, shaking his head. 'You know what that means, Ryan, don't you man, you're up in front of the sergeant first thing in the morning and believe me – she won't like a breach of discipline like this.' He gave a greasy grin. 'I'll bet she'll throw the bloody book at you to make an example to the others, especially with you being a head man with a two stripe armband,'

Tony stood there subserviently, looking very sorry for himself as he listened to all this, and then he lamented, 'Oh hell, must you report it, Corporal? I'm back now and it is Sunday; I mean, I haven't missed any of my training.'

Looking back at him with the hint of a smile on his face, the Corporal shook his head slowly. 'Sorry, Ryan, I would if I could; seeing as you helped me the other week when I wanted to play snooker, but I can't. You see my hands are tied – all the lads know you've broken standing orders; sorry, Ryan, I just daren't, she'd have me over a barrel, if she found out I'd condoned such a thing.'

Looking back at him with sad eyes, Tony said quietly, 'Yes, yes, I understand, Corporal. I suppose I'll just have to take what's coming; what'll happen now then, will I be on a 252 do you think?'

Sitting down, Corporal Black said in a more friendly tone,' I don't really know, Ryan. I'll put your case down in the best light I can, I assure you, but I've got to do my duty; whatever action is taken is the decision of the senior NCO.'

He paused and gazed at Tony standing there in front of him, looking so forlorn. 'Come on, Ryan, it's not that bad,' he said cheerfully, 'she won't have you shot at dawn or anything like that.'

Forcing a laugh, Tony replied, 'Huh, knowing my bloody luck, Corporal, even that could happen.'

'Go on, Ryan, get back to your mates,' he said, with a laugh. 'Just forget it until tomorrow morning, it's no use worrying. She might even let you off if she's in a good mood.'

'Aye, and she might not,' Tony grunted, as he made for the door – but his worries were not for himself. Going back into the billet Tony was genuinely worried; he was wondering how Becky could get around this, was there any possibility it could hurt her in some way?

'Here comes the criminal,' shouted one of the lads, as Tony went back in with an arrogant smirk on his face.

'Shut it, you lot,' he grunted, going over to his bed. He sat down and stared at the floor, scowling.

John sitting on his own adjacent bed, reading a newspaper, said quietly, 'How did it go, mate?'

'Oh, he's booking me, I'm in front of the sergeant in the morning,' Tony moaned.

'The rotten bastard,' said John. 'He could have overlooked it, seeing as it's the weekend.'

'Well, I can see his point John,' he replied. 'He's not all that bad really; he'd be risking his own job if he was found out covering up for one of us, wouldn't he?'

Thinking for a second, John sighed, 'I suppose you're right, but it seems so unfair, you've done nothing wrong as far as I can see. If he hadn't popped in here first thing this morning, he wouldn't have known you'd stayed out all night.'

'But he did, John, my old pal, didn't he?' said Tony, sullenly.

37

'Right, AC Ryan, the sergeant is ready for you now,' called out Corporal Black, standing in the open doorway of Sergeant Stanhope's office.

Tony, who was instructing the other five lads with some light bar-bell work, immediately walked towards him briskly, and followed him back into her office, wondering what to expect from this very unusual confrontation. Corporal Black was dressed in track suit bottom and the usual RAF PTI's white training jersey, Tony was in shorts and vest. However, in contrast, Sergeant Stanhope, at her desk reading the report sheet, was immaculately attired in full best blue uniform.'

'Attention!' the Corporal yelled at Tony, as they reached the centre of the room in front of her desk. Corporal Black then informed him that although this was an informal interview, the consequences would be the same. The sergeant never flinched, even though Corporal Black had yelled out with such volume that it had nearly deafened Tony; she continued reading for at least two minutes, while both men stood before her, staring ahead in silence.

Eventually, she slowly raised her eyes, staring coldly in Tony's direction. 'AC Ryan, I hope you realise that you have committed a very serious breach of discipline,' she said quietly. 'You were absent from your billet overnight without permission. Didn't it cross your mind, man – that you should have informed your NCO, Corporal Black – of your intention to stay out all night?'

The Corporal, still facing straight ahead, glanced at Tony out of the corner of his eye.

'Well, as I told Corporal Black, Sergeant, I didn't intend to be absent from my billet all night, it was just a matter of unforeseen circumstances.'

Still staring at him, she said in a rather raised voice, 'Whatever the circumstances are, Ryan, you've still committed a serious breach of discipline, I hope you understand that.'

Looking back at her expressionless face, Tony replied, 'Yes, I realise the situation, Sergeant, but all I can say is, that I'd been out with my girlfriend to an Annual Ball, and when I took her home we got talking.' He looked away for a moment. 'Well, when a man loves a woman as I love her, time just flashes by; suddenly it was daylight,' he said.

Hearing him out the sergeant said with a sigh, 'I don't know, Ryan, you can certainly state your case, and although I do believe what you say, you've still breached discipline; you've got to be made an example of. We can't have all the other men breaking the rules and thinking that they can get away with it,' she said with a sharp nod. As she said this, Corporal Black cleared his throat, nodding in agreement. 'You do realise, Ryan,' she snapped, 'you could be put on a 252 for this, don't you, man.'

Tony replied quietly, 'Yes, Sergeant.'

'However,' she continued, as we are a separate unit on this camp, I prefer to isolate ourselves from the main camp procedure as much as possible. But that doesn't mean you're not to be punished, Ryan,' she said sternly, staring up at him over the desktop. Looking at the report sheet again for a moment, then glancing back at him, she said, 'Actually, your corporal has been very lenient with you on his report sheet, considering the seriousness of the charge. I'm still going to make an example of you all the same, Ryan.' she slapped her palms down onto the desk top and stared up into his face, frowning. She looked at him blankly for a moment, before continuing in a very firm voice, 'You're deprived of liberty between seven and ten pm all this week, five nights –Monday to Friday. You'll spend the three hours between seven and ten p.m. each evening down here in the gym, practising your training – do you understand, man?' she said in raised voice.

'Yes, Sergeant,' Tony replied solemnly. He felt like laughing.

She looked over at Corporal Black. 'By the way, Corporal, from now on all requests by any of the men for concessions like this, are to be made directly to me; I'm not having any more of this carry on,' she said, shaking her head.'

'I still say you ought to be on the stage, Ryan,' said Corporal Black, laughing as they walked back into the gym.

'Why what do you mean, Corporal?' Tony asked innocently.

'You know what I mean,' he said, still chuckling. 'That blarney you spun her, about being in love and all that shit; do you think she's daft, man, she won't have believed a word you said.'

'Well, I hope she did because it's true,' said Tony seriously, as he walked back over to his five companions training on the big mat.

'You still got five nights' loss of privileges, though, Ryan, whether she believed you or not,' called out Corporal Black, laughing.

The other lads also had a good laugh at his expense, when Tony told them the outcome of the situation. 'You're to spend three hours every night this week on duty training down here,' said one of them, laughingly. 'Bloody hell, you'd have only got a couple of nights in the guardroom, if you'd been put on a 252, Ryan.'

'Anyway it's all over now,' sighed Tony. 'I'll take my punishment like a man,' he added, shaking his head sadly. Getting the lads working again, he stood back watching their movements closely. John, who was standing nearby, leaned over to him and whispered in his ear, 'I don't know about taking your punishment, you bugger; you spend all your time down here in the evenings, anyway.'

'Shut up, you, Parks, or I'll put you on my report sheet for taking the piss,' Tony whispered back, pretending to threaten his mate.

38

'Well, have you enjoyed your punishment this week then Tony?' asked Jeff the dancer, walking over to him, as he was taking a breather between training sets.

'I've managed Jeff, thanks, mate; only another day to do now though; she's a strict one is our boss, you know,' he said, with a laugh. 'But you've finished off early tonight, Jeff,' he continued in some surprise. 'I'll be all on my own in an empty gym when you've gone; it's only just gone nine thirty and I can't go myself, until ten p.m. even if I wanted to.'

'Where is Becky then?' Jeff asked. 'I thought she'd have been in here working out tonight, Tony.'

'Paperwork, mate, she's in her office scanning through a pile of it for the second half of our course; I wouldn't like her job, Jeff, I'll tell you, I hate paperwork,' he said frowning.

'So do I,' he replied. Then he smiled. 'But I've got some to do when I get back tonight that I'll love doing, Tony.'

'Oh, what's that then, Jeff, if you don't mind me being nosey?'

'My reply to the CO concerning my promotion,' he said, grinning broadly. 'Yes, Tony, I've got my crown today, you're now talking to Flight Sergeant Jeff Davis,' he told him proudly. He turned and headed for the shower room, as Tony called his congratulations after him.

Ten minutes or so later, Tony was lying on the press bench, performing the final set of his night's training, when he suddenly heard the main door open and close, and the sound of heavy footsteps walking briskly across the floor. Straining with the heavy barbell, he gave a quick glance down the gym and saw a tall, burly, uniformed figure walking towards the Sergeant's office. Although it was rather late, he thought that it wasn't unusual, as she was still working; it was most likely something to do with her task, he deduced. After finishing his workout, he was wiping the sweat off his face with a hand towel and he glanced at the wall clock, noticing the time was nearing ten. So, as Becky seemed very busy he thought he'd go have a nice long shower, then get back to the billet for an early night; she'd be exhausted too, no doubt, he thought.

Suddenly, he heard Becky shout, 'Sergeant Webster! Will you please leave my office or I'll call the guardroom.'

Immediately, there was a loud raucous laugh and a man's voice called out, 'Don't be so silly, Becky you know you want me, come here, you little devil, give us a kiss.'

Throwing the towel down on the bench, Tony sprinted down to the office and gave the door a hard knock. He yelled out, 'Everything all right, Sergeant Stanhope?'

'Bugger off!' came a loud, angry reply from the man.

But almost at the same time, Becky shouted, 'No! Come in, AC Ryan.'
Tony grabbed the door handle and pushed but it was locked; the man must have dropped the catch as he went in. Without hesitation, Tony raised his leg and hit the door just under the lock with the flat of his foot, delivering such force that it flew open violently, banging back and rebounding off the wall inside.

Bursting in, he was confronted by a big ginger-haired man who turned to face him, hatred burning in his eyes. 'Get your bloody self out of here at once, airman,' he yelled, 'or I'll have you in the guardhouse before your feet can touch the ground.'

'No, you get out, Webster, you're drunk,' said Becky, obviously upset. Tony, seeing the stress in her face was on the verge of charging at the man and getting stuck into him, whatever his rank.

However, recognising him from Jeff's description, he just said as calmly as possible, 'Come on, Sergeant, you heard what Sergeant Stanhope said, please leave.'

'Bollocks! You're the one that's going to leave or you're for it,' the man yelled back, his speech slightly slurred. 'You'll be behind bars tonight without fail, if you cross me, boy, I'll tell you,' he threatened menacingly.

Tony took another glance at Becky and noticed the top part of her shirt appeared to have been torn open. Eyes blazing he stepped forward, grabbed the man by his arm and wrenched him towards the door with such violence that he nearly went down. He was a big man, two or three inches taller than Tony, and although slightly overweight and out of condition, he could still prove to be a very dangerous opponent, especially after alcohol. Regaining his balance, the man swore and drunkenly aimed a huge fist at Tony's head, which Tony was easily able to dodge. He shoved him out of the door into the gym hall, and called out to Becky, 'He's not going to go peacefully, Sergeant, I'm going to have to drop him before he does some real damage, I've no choice.'

Before she could answer, a voice called from the direction of the changing room, 'Hold it, airman, I'll take over now.' Jeff, now back in uniform, came hurrying down the hall towards the men who were still struggling violently. Jeff spoke authoritatively, 'Right, Sergeant Webster, I see you're making a nuisance of yourself again, and after what I told you the last time you came down here disturbing Sergeant Stanhope.'

'Bollocks! he yelled, as he continued his struggle to free himself from Tony's grip.

'Oh, I see, it's like that is it?' Jeff replied. 'Well this time you're in serious trouble, Webster.'

'And who the fucking hell do you think you are, you can't give me orders, Mister,' he yelled back aggressively. 'You're not talking to a bloody AC plonk now, you know, you're talking to your equal, don't forget that Davis.'

Staring into his drunken face, Jeff slowly raised his arm in front of him, and tapped his new shining crown above the three sergeant's stripes. 'This says I can give you any orders I think appropriate, Webster, right?' he yelled at him.

The man stared at it and attempted to calm down. 'Oh, I didn't know you'd got your crown, Jeff, congratulations,' he said.

Angrily, Jeff replied, 'I can do without your congratulations, Webster, just pull yourself together. You're in trouble, man, and don't you forget it.'

He looked over at Becky, noticed her slightly torn shirt front and frowned. 'Has this man assaulted you in any way, Sergeant Stanhope?' he asked, staring at the now subdued drunk.

She hesitated for a moment. 'Well, he made a determined grab at me and I shoved him away, which wasn't too difficult, considering his condition.' she replied scornfully. 'He tore the buttons off my shirt, though, in his attempt.' Tony's eyes flashed as she said this and he glared at the drunken sergeant, hardly able to contain himself from doing more than just holding his arm in a vice-like grip.

Going into the office, Jeff picked up the phone and was about to dial, when the culprit, in a very subdued voice asked, 'What are you going to do Jeff? Come on, mate, it was only a bit of a joke.'

'Not in my book, Webster, it looked more like attempted sexual assault on a female officer,' he replied, 'and I'm about to have you arrested.'

'Come on, Jeff, please!' he pleaded. This'll be the end of my career; I've a wife and two little girls to think of, you know, come on now please,' he said, almost with a sob.

'You should have thought of that man before you started all this; don't forget it's the second time you've done it,' Jeff told him, starting to dial.

'Hold it a second, Jeff,' said Becky, thoughtfully. 'We don't want to make all this fool's family suffer for his drunken behaviour; God knows – they've most likely suffered enough with him already.'

'What, you mean you don't want to press charges, Becky?' said Jeff surprised. 'You're too soft-hearted, you are,' he told her.

'Not for him, I'm not,' she said, 'but I wouldn't like the thought of those little kids and his poor wife suffering for his stupidity.'

Putting the phone slowly back down on its cradle, Jeff glanced doubtfully at the now quiet, shocked looking Sergeant Webster, still being held firmly by Tony. 'You've got Sergeant Stanhope to thank for your future in the service, Webster,' he said sternly. 'If it was up to me, pal, you'd be on your way down to the guardroom now under arrest and a court martial at the end of it; believe me. Release him, AC Ryan,' he said to Tony quietly. 'Let him be on his way.'

'Thanks, Jeff,' he said, almost in a whisper as Tony released his grip.

'Don't thank me, man,' Jeff replied with disgust. 'I've told you where you'd be if it had been my choice; just get out quick, and don't ever let me see you in here making a nuisance of yourself again or it will be the end of your RAF career, I promise you that, lad.' He pointed to the main door and glared at him. 'Now on your way, before I change my mind,' he hissed.

The door closed behind him and the three looked at each other. Jeff gave a sigh and shook his head; while Tony went over to Becky and put his hands on her shoulders. Looking into her face, he said affectionately, 'The drunken sod didn't touch you, did he love? I think Jeff was right, he should have been reported,' he said.

Shaking her head, she replied, 'No, he didn't, Tony.' Smiling, she leaned over the desk top and gently stroked his face. 'He didn't have much chance, did he, with you nearly kicking the door off its hinges to get at him.' She suddenly realised that Jeff was still in the doorway and she straightened up saying formally, 'By the way, AC Ryan, I've no lock on my door now.'

Jeff, turning to go, said, with a knowing smile, 'Oh, I'm sure Tony can do an emergency job on that for you, Becky, he told me he worked in the building trade for a couple of years before he joined our lot.'

When he'd gone she said, 'Do you think Jeff suspects we're personal friends, Tony?'

Going round the desk and taking her in his arms he replied, 'I'm bloody sure he does, and by the way,' he added, pulling her closer, 'I hope we're a bit more than just friends, you little temptress.'

Snuggling up to him she whispered in his ear, 'I think we've already proved that, Tony Ryan, you sexy hunk.'

'Good morning, Ryan,' called out a sarcastic voice behind him, as he walked into his darkened billet later.

Turning, he saw Corporal Black standing in the open doorway of his bunk room, smoking a cigarette.

'You're a glutton for punishment, Ryan, aren't you, lad,' he sneered. 'You know lights out is eleven o'clock on weekdays, don't you; it's now twelve thirty, ain't it?' He gave a little laugh. 'So you're in the mire again, lad, right?'

Tony walked over to him, reached into his breast pocket and handing him a slip of paper, smiled broadly. 'No, Corporal, wrong this time, I've been doing an emergency repair job on Sergeant Stanhope's office door; some fool banged it so hard that the lock broke.'

Reading it, the Corporal said, 'Oh, I see, carry on then, get to bed Ryan; at least you've been doing something useful for once.'

39

'Right men, can I have your full attention, please,' called out Corporal Black. The men standing at ease before him on the road in front of the billet block went silent, awaiting his response. 'As you will all be aware, this is the last instruction week of your course,' he said in firm military tone. 'And I am to inform you that we, your instructors, including Sergeant Stanhope, are very pleased with the standard of training you have achieved.' He pulled himself up to his full height and said proudly. 'Furthermore, I personally feel sure, that when we get down to the display hall in London we're going to do our Service, the RAF, proud, by bringing back the Diploma.'

There was a little cheer as he said this and a similar one could be heard from up the road, proving that Corporal Hudson was telling his lads the same story. Corporal Black stood still in front of the ranks for a moment silently, enjoying the reception, before continuing. 'Now more good news; hard work this week as usual, then you are all on seven days home leave until the following weekend.' There was a muttering of excitement among the lads on hearing this, and the corporal went on, 'Then, we have a few days following your return from leave to perfect the display routines. Sergeant Stanhope will obviously be in attendance most of the time, so I've no need to tell you that she'll expect no less than perfection.' He scowled aggressively. 'So you'd all better be on your toes and be warned, don't let any man disappoint her or he'll be for it. We go down to London to win the Diploma the following Saturday morning by coach.' He smiled and called out, 'Any questions?' There weren't any, so he dismissed the ranks and told them to make their own way down to the Airmen's Mess for the midday meal and to report back for duty at one thirty prompt.

There was a buzz of excitement within the large group, making their way to the airmen's mess; the conversation was mainly about the seven days leave, as it was the first break they'd had since the start of the course.

'You don't look so pleased with the good news, Tony,' said John cheerfully. 'You have got a home to go to, I hope,' he teased.

'Of course I'm pleased, you daft bugger,' he replied grumpily. 'Why shouldn't I be?'

'I don't know, I just thought you looked a bit fed up,' John replied, with a laugh.

By early Friday evening, John still didn't know what was up with Tony. In the billet there was an atmosphere of great excitement; their efforts were now to be rewarded. All the lads were buzzing around preparing themselves for the seven days leave starting the following day – that is, all but Tony Ryan, who was assembling his training kit ready to go down to the gym for a workout.

'Aren't you going to get yourself sorted out for tomorrow, Tony,' John asked him. 'It'll be a mad rush in the morning, you know.

'Don't worry I'll manage,' he answered, cheerfully picking up his training bag and heading for the door. See you later, mate, he called back as he left, leaving John staring after him, baffled.

'Hi, Jeff,' Tony called out, walking into the gym. As usual, Jeff was on his own in the hall, working away at his dancing schedule.

'Hi there, Tony,' he replied, smiling. 'I didn't expect to be seeing you down here tonight. I thought you'd have been getting ready for tomorrow.'

'Well, I decided I'd just come down and do a bit of stretching exercise,' he replied, glancing around the empty gym as he spoke.

Noticing this, Jeff said casually, 'She's doing some typing in her office, Tony, if you're looking for Becky.'

Smiling sheepishly, he replied, 'Well, I did think she might be out here tonight, Jeff, she hasn't been doing much training all week.'

'It'll be all the paper work she's got concerning the display, Tony. She told me she's snowed under with it,' he said, with a friendly smile. 'Why don't you go down and have a chat with her, go on cheer her up mate; I should think she'd like that – she must be fed up, being cooped up in there on her own, most of the day.'

As he gently tapped on the office door, Tony could hear the frantic banging of a typewriter, which stopped abruptly when he knocked.

'Come in,' called out Becky.

She was sitting at the desk behind a big black Olivetti typewriter, still in uniform and looking tired and bedraggled. 'Good God, Becky love, you look all in.' He sounded concerned. 'Do you realise it's nearly eight o'clock, how long have you been behind that thing?' he asked, indicating the big machine.

Pushing her chair back, she stood up and rubbed her eyes. 'Since just after lunch; then, giving him a weary but plainly welcoming smile, she said lethargically, 'Oh, I've bloody well had enough, Tony; come here, give me a hug.' He didn't need asking twice and as he cuddled her to him, she said, 'I saw you instructing your little team this afternoon. You've done a good job with them, you know, why don't you try to get on to my job? You'd be a natural at it, Tony.'

Kissing her forehead he replied, 'If I could be working with you, darling, I'd be at it like a shot.' Then he went on, 'but seriously, Becky, I've thought about it, but I don't think I'd have much chance as a National Serviceman. They'd want me to sign on for five years to go on that course, I'm sure,' he said despondently.

Reaching up putting her arms around his neck and pulling his face close to hers, she smiled, 'So, what's wrong with that? I did.'

Without replying, he pulled her closer, then after a long lingering kiss, he said with a smile, 'I promise I'll give it a lot of thought, pet, as soon as we get this project over.'

Pausing for a moment, but still holding her in his arms he was suddenly melancholy. 'I was just thinking, Becky, we're going to be broken up anyway, aren't we, after the display?'

Breaking away from him, and going into her living quarters, she called over her shoulder, 'Not necessarily, darling. Come on, let's have a cuppa, you're not working out tonight, are you?

'No, I've only come down see you,' he said, following her.

'Do you want anything to eat, love?' she enquired, handing him a beaker of tea.

'No thanks, pet, this'll do fine,' he replied, sitting down on the little sofa. He took a sip, and glanced up at her with a worried look. 'It's right what I just said though, Becky; we've only got another couple of weeks together here, then we could be posted anywhere, hundreds of miles apart even,' he added, frowning.

'Oh, yes, there's that possibility,' she agreed. She went on in a more optimistic tone, 'but that's what I was going to say, Tony, by the end of our final week, I should have the list through for the men's postings after the display. So,' she went on with a sly smile, 'as soon as I find out yours, I'll request a posting for myself to the same camp, or one as near as possible. It shouldn't be too difficult – I think I'd have a good chance,' she said reassuringly.

'Woo! Tony yelled, 'That would be great! So you think you'd have a good chance, pet?' he said excitedly.

'I'm definitely going to try my best, darling, believe me,' she said. Then, changing the subject, she went on, 'Anyway, forget all that now, we'll sort it out when you get back from your leave; you don't want to be worried about that sort of thing, when you should be enjoying yourself at home, do you?' She gave him a cheerful smile.

'No, I suppose not. As a matter of fact, Becky,' he said seriously, 'There's something official I'd like to ask you about, I've been wondering about it all week as a matter of fact.'

'Oh, and what's that, love?' she enquired, a puzzled look crossing her face.

Looking down at the floor, then glancing up at her, waiting for his reply, he said, 'Well, I wondered if I was forced to go on leave? I'm not particularly bothered about going, Becky. I'd rather stay here with you.' He grinned. 'We could have a good free week, you know, get around the district a bit; it would be like a little holiday together.'

Smiling warmly, she sat down beside him stroking his face affectionately. 'No, you're not forced to go, you big soft thing, and I definitely don't want to be separated from you either, but it's only for a week and it'll do you good to see your family and your mates at home, won't it? Anyway darling,' she pointed out, 'I'll be so busy with Corporal Black and Hudson getting all the preparations ready for the display; I won't have much free time.'

'I suppose you're right,' he agreed half-heartedly. 'Okay, I'll go, but I might not stay the whole week,' he stated adamantly.

It was Sunday lunch time, and Tony and his mate, Dave, had just walked in to the Dog and Gun. 'Christ Almighty, I'd never have believed it in a month of Sundays,' called out Bernard from behind the bar. As they went to the bar to order their ale they glanced at each other, wondering what he meant.

'What the hell are you on about, Bernard? Come on, we're thirsty, two pints please, before we take our custom elsewhere.'

Tittering as he pulled the beer, Bernard said, 'I just couldn't believe it, though, Tony, when Dave there told me, it seemed impossible – a randy young bugger like you.'

'What's he on about, Dave?' Tony asked, turning to his mate, baffled.

By now, Dave had realised what Bernard was on about, and a guilty smile crossed his face. 'I don't know Tony, you'd better ask him,' he replied, smiling sheepishly.

'Come on, Bernard, stop taking the piss,' said Tony, as the two foaming pints were planted down on the bar top. 'Let's be having it, what are you on about? What's this silly bugger here, been telling you about me, that's so funny?'

'Well, as I said, Tony, old love, I just couldn't believe it about a bloke like you,' and he chuckled.'

'What?' Tony yelled, now getting a little fed up with the situation.

'Well, Dave here told me the other day that you'd told him, you'd fallen in love with – ' he stopped and spluttered with laughter – 'you'd fallen in love with your senior NCO, a sergeant physical training instructor.'

Glancing sideways at Dave, who'd maintained his sheepish grin, then looking back at the still laughing landlord, Tony reached into his inside jacket pocket and pulled out his black leather wallet. 'Yes, that's quite right, Bernard,' he said. 'I'm not ashamed of it either; I have fallen in love with my sergeant PTI.'

As Bernard wiped the tears of mirth from his eyes, Tony pulled out a postcard-sized photograph, and passed it over the bar to him smiling proudly. 'This is her, do you blame me, mate?'

Bernard immediately went silent as he studied it. 'Bloody hell, Tony, lad, they didn't have sergeants like that in my squad, I'll tell you, or I'd never had come out,' he said, shaking his head.

'Now then, you lot, what's all the shouting about?' called out a voice across the room.

'Hi, Steve,' replied Tony, turning to see Steve Grimes, the corporal drill instructor at Padgate, walking towards the bar, grinning.

'Long time no see, mate. By the way, did you manage to get me one of them blazer badges, like the one you have on your blazer there,' he said, pointing at it. Nodding at Bernard, he said, 'A pint of best for him, Bernard, he looks thirsty.'

'That's nice of you, Tony, thanks, that'll do me fine,' he said, 'and about the badge, yes, I got you one, it's at home – I didn't know you were on leave or I'd have brought it with me. I'll bring it tonight; I suppose you'll be in here, won't you?'

'Sure will, Steve, you know me,' He took a long swig from his pint.

Laughing, Steve said, turning to Bernard, 'Now then Bernard, what was all that commotion about as I was coming in?'

'You'll never believe it, Steve,' replied Bernard with a pious expression, 'but our friend Tony here, has fallen in love with his sergeant in command.'

Steve stared back at him for a moment with in disbelief, then glancing at Tony, he said, 'What? Come on now, is someone trying to have me on?'

'No, it's true,' said Bernard, his face breaking into a grin as he passed the photo over the bar together with his pint. 'This is his sergeant, Steve,' he said, 'and I don't blame him, what do you say?'

'Come on now, landlord, stop showing my girlfriend's photo to all and sundry,' said Tony, with mock sternness.

Returning the photo to Tony, Steve said seriously, 'Congratulations, mate, she's a lovely young girl.' Just then there was commotion in the doorway, as a group of men came charging boisterously into the bar.

'Oh, bloody hell, here we go,' said Dave. It's that bloody Canal Street lot, and look who's leading 'em,' he said with amazement, 'that big-mouthed little bugger Harry Proudfoot; he must have taken over, now Chris Simpson's not here.'

'I doubt if you'll ever find him in that gang again, now,' Steve chipped in, 'we made a man of out him at

Padgate; he's grown up and learnt some sense.'
Laughing he said, 'Took some doing at first, but we managed in the end.'

'Don't tell me you got that bugger in your flight, Steve,' said Tony.

'Not in my flight, Tony, but he was on our wing and I had a few skirmishes with him over the training period.'

Laughing, he went on, 'Poor bugger, he had the shock of his life when he came out on his first parade and saw me there in front of the ranks, staring back at him like thunder.'

'I'll bet he did, I experienced similar from you, if you remember, but I bet he didn't threaten to thump you, as he did in here, did he, Steve?' said Tony, with a laugh.

'He bloody didn't, Tony, but I'll tell you what, without joking, he turned out to be one of the best recruits in his flight. When he got settled in, he got really keen, and being a tall lad he was always one of the markers, I reckon that made him all the keener.'

'Do you know where he got posted to when he passed out, Steve?' Tony asked.

'Went on a course somewhere, but I don't know what it was, but he did sign on for five years, so his corporal told me at the pass-out parade.'

'Must be keen then, good luck to the lad, anyway,' Tony said with a nod.

'Do you want another before we get back for dinner, Tony?' Dave asked him later, when they were on their own after Steve's departure.

'No better get off,' he replied. 'Mum said not to be late.' After a slight pause he asked casually, 'By the way, Dave, have you heard anything about your Peg, lately?'

Dave, giving him a quick glance picked up his glass, and after taking a long swig replied, 'Not a dickybird, mate, since she went; mind you I've kept looking out for letters but I've never seen any. I've even gone though my mum's drawer to see if she'd had contact and not told me; you know, thinking that I'd tell you about it, which of course I would,' he stressed. He lifted his glass again and drained it, while Tony sat there in silence. Banging the empty glass down on the table, Dave went on, 'Anyway Tony, my old love, I'm glad you've got her out of your system at last, and realised what a mistake it all was.'

Tony froze for a moment, glaring into his mate's face with a look Dave had never seen before; a deep piercing stare that sent a shiver through him. 'I never said anything like that, David,' he said coldly. Then, immediately getting to his feet he said, 'Come on, let's get off, Mum will be playing hell, if I'm late for my dinner.'

40

Early on Thursday evening of that same week, Tony was back in camp, sitting on his bed in the deserted billet, sorting through the personal effects in his locker. Finding what he was looking for, he put it in his wallet, picked up his training bag, closed the locker and made for the door. Walking into the gym hall he found it deserted, not even his friend Jeff the ballet dancer was there. However, looking down in the direction of the sergeant's office, he saw there was a light and heard the sound of voices. Although he'd come to see Becky, he thought that, whoever it was in there with her might be someone official, so he'd better be very tactful in his approach. Tapping on the office door, training bag on his shoulder, he heard Becky say something, and the sound of footsteps inside. The door opened and he was confronted by Corporal Hudson, who looked stern when he saw Tony.

'AC Ryan, what the hell are you doing here man? You're not due off leave till the weekend,' then smirking he went on, 'What's up – have they kicked you out at home?'

'Yes, Corporal,' Tony replied, quite loudly, so that he could be heard inside the office. 'I've had a row with my dad; he caught me taking a young bird up to my bedroom after I'd been out on a pub crawl.'

Immediately the voice of the sergeant called out, 'What's all the chatter about out there, Corporal Hudson, fetch that man in here.' The corporal ushered Tony in, remaining standing behind him as he went up in front of the sergeant, who was sitting at her desk.

Tony was hardly able to refrain from laughing as he looked at her glaring up at him. However, before she could say anything, knowing that Corporal Hudson couldn't see his face, he gave her a little smile and a cheeky wink, to show her he was joking.

'What do you want down here, Ryan?' she asked, looking more relaxed.

'I've just come for a workout, Sergeant and to let you know I'm back on camp; hope it's okay, me returning early,' he said.

'No problem there, Ryan,' she told him formally. 'That's up to you if you've been kicked out at home as you say; anyway, carry on with your training session,' she added, nodding towards the door.

As he went out, she gave a tired sigh. 'You'd better get off too, Corporal Hudson; we've done enough today on this lot, we can finish it off tomorrow,' she said.

The main door banged behind the corporal, the office door opened and Becky stood there smiling. 'Tony Ryan, come here. I want you,' she called out.

Running down the gym he followed her in to her office, grinning. 'Yes, at your service, beautiful lady – anything you want?'

Falling into his open arms she said, as he pulled her close, 'I've just told you what I want, I want you, Tony Ryan.'

After a prolonged affectionate greeting, they were sitting in the living area drinking tea. Becky asked casually, 'Have you had a good time on your home leave, then, Tony?'

'Not bad, I got a bit fed up by Monday, though,' he replied, shaking his head.

'What, you got fed up by Monday,' she echoed, with a chuckle. 'I thought you'd have been glad to get out enjoying yourself with your mate, Dave, after being cooped up here for weeks.'

'You know why I got fed up so soon, you she devil,' he growled in mock anger. 'By the way, Becky,' he continued seriously, 'did the postings come through this week, as you expected?'

'Yes, I got them today, but we haven't had time to go through them yet, love,' she said. 'I intend to sort them out in the morning. I'll let you know where you're going, but keep it quiet, Tony, you're not supposed to know till next week.'

'Becky, I'm not daft. I don't tell the lads anything regarding you and me, love, even my best mate, John Parks, thinks I've got a girlfriend who works in Marks and Spencer.'

'I hope you haven't,' she said menacingly.

'No, no,' he laughed. 'We met two sales girls from Marks and Spencer in the café there one Saturday afternoon, and he thinks it's one of them that I go out with, when I'm with you.'

'You're making me begin to wonder about you, Tony Ryan, I'm beginning to think you're a womaniser,' she said, pretending to doubt him.

'Course I'm not,' he laughed, 'but it's useful when you and I go out anywhere, he just takes it for granted that I'm out with her, saves me having to tell him lies, Becky.'

Walking over to the little sink in the corner, Becky rinsed out her now empty tea cup. After a brief pause she said, 'By the way, did you see anyone else of interest at home, Tony?'

Without saying anything he got up from his chair and going over to her, standing at the sink, put his arms around her waist, and gently kissed the top of her head.

'No, I didn't, darling,' he said softly, 'and don't you think, if I had seen her, it would have been the first thing I'd have told you when I got back?'

Looking back over her shoulder into his face, she said with a little smile, 'Well, I just wondered love; anyway Tony, I think I'd like to see that photo of Peggy sometime, if you can remember to bring it with you.'

'I must be bloody psychic, pet,' he said, chuckling. Releasing her, he went over to his jacket hung on the back of the door, pulled out a postcard sized photo from the inside pocket, and without looking at it, passed it to her. 'There you are, darling, that's Peggy on the tennis court; she told me she'd just lost the match to a Chinese girl,' he said, with a little, forced laugh.

Taking the photo from him slowly, she stared at it in silence for a full minute, then passing it back she said softly, 'I can see why you fell so hard for her, Tony, she's a very attractive athletic woman; I should think most men would do the same.'

'Well, don't look so dismal, pet.' He put his hands on her shoulders and pulled her face close to his. 'You've no need to worry about any woman being attractive and athletic, darling, believe me. How long is it since you took a long look at yourself in the mirror, anyway?' She looked back at him for a moment, then, with glazed eyes she flung her arms around his neck, and pulled him to her, kissing him hard on the mouth.

41

'Well, the training is all over, Tony, old son; all that's left now is the real thing,' said John Parks, with a grin. 'We're off to the big smoke in the morning for the week of real action.'

Tony, sitting on his bed cleaning his brasses, just grunted. 'Don't worry, mate, we'll come out on top, you'll see.'

'Oh, I'm sure you're right, Tony,' he replied confidently. 'We've worked hard enough training for it, anyway.' He started to undress. 'I'm going to have an early night – them bloody coaches are coming to pick us up at seven in the morning, don't forget.'

It was the following Friday evening, the display, so long prepared for, was over. A very close victory on points was gained by the Army, followed by the RAF. The Navy – the 'Senior Service', ran a close third. The narrow margins had been expected, owing to the quality of the first class training methods in each of the three Services. In celebration, the teams were now enjoying a buffet reception in the main entertainment hall at the host camp, on the outskirts of London. Tony and his pal, John Parks, were in their usual position, propping up the bar.

'Good ale this, considering we're in London, what do you say, Tony?' John remarked, after they had taken long swigs from their pint glasses.

'Very nice,' he replied, licking foam from his lips.

'Good show lads, eh?' called out a voice. They turned round to see Corporal Black, accompanied by his colleague, Corporal Hudson, coming to join their group, followed by more of the team, all making for the bar.

'Well it's been a hard four months, lads,' said Corporal Black, addressing the crowd of drinking airmen, 'and this is the end of it. After tonight we are all going our separate ways, and I wish the lot of you the very best of luck for your future in the service.' He ended by raising his glass, with a warm smile.

'Very nicely put, Corporal Black,' rang out another voice behind him. 'You've taken the very words out of my mouth.' The lads all went quiet as they saw Sergeant Stanhope coming towards them, smiling radiantly.

'Good evening, Sergeant, said Corporal Black very formally. 'Very close finish, Sergeant,' he added with a smile.

'Sure was,' she replied, easing her way through the crowd of lads around the bar, 'and I'm sure ready for a drink, now it's all over,' she said. Tony, standing with his mate at the bar, didn't make a move as she came through the crowd of airmen. Then he caught her eye and to his surprise – and that of all the others – she made straight for him, smiling. On reaching him she slipped her arm through his and looking up into his flushed face said affectionately, 'Hello, Tony, darling, aren't you going to get me a drink then?' The lads all began to mutter and the two corporals just stood transfixed. Continuing to hang on to his arm, she gave a little laugh as she surveyed her rather baffled-looking subordinates. 'No, I haven't gone mad, boys. Tony and I are very close friends, and have been ever since we first met at the beginning of the course.' Then looking back at Tony, flush-faced and smiling, she gave him a peck on the cheek. 'We are 'very' close friends, aren't we, darling?' she said, smiling up at him.

Tony slipped his arm around her waist pulling her to him. 'Couldn't be closer, love,' he said, looking into her eyes affectionately.

After the cheers had died down, Corporal Black said, grinning, 'You kept that very quiet, Sergeant, if you don't mind me saying so.'

'Well, the Service always comes first, you should know that, Corporal Black,' she told him seriously. She took a long drink from the pint of ale that Tony had acquired for her. 'We kept it quiet to maintain discipline, Corporal; of course, now we're all breaking up, there's no need for secrecy,' she smiled.

Later, as they sat on their own at a small table in the corner of the bar, Tony said softly, 'Thanks, Becky love, I was very proud of the way you let them all know about us.' Looking into her eyes and shaking his head, he continued, 'but I don't know how I'm going to get on without you, if you're posted miles away.'

'Well, my dear, I don't think you'll have anything to worry about,' she told him, cheerfully, 'because I got a message through from our camp personnel today, regarding my requested posting. It's been granted.' Tony's face lit up. 'However, she went on, 'not the same camp as you, though, but I'll only be about ten miles up the road.'

'Great!' he said, grinning broadly. 'Super, Becky, but you're on leave as soon as we get back, aren't you?'

'Yes, I've got ten days, but I'm not going until you go to your new posting on Monday; if you can come back early, then I can go late.' She laughed and leaning over the table, she tapped him on the nose with her finger. 'Then we can have a nice long weekend together,' she whispered seductively, 'can't we, Mr Ryan, eh?'

Giving her a knowing look and a wink, he replied, 'Good thinking, baby.'

42

'Right, I want all airmen who have applied for general duties, to fall out at the far end of the room,' shouted one of the two sergeants in the large assembly room at Tony's new camp.

The room was full of men of many trades, from mechanic to cooks; all were being allocated their employment positions on the camp. The group ordered to fall out included Tony; their trade being down as 'Admin Orderlies,' virtually the dogsbodies. These men could be sent to anywhere on the camp that required anything from scrubbers in the Airmen's Mess, to gardeners, or assistants to anyone requiring unskilled labour – they were the men with no trade. Tony and another young lad called Jeff Baxter, who came from Cornwall, were ordered to report to a Sergeant Pike for general duties in the Sergeants' Mess.

'Well now, Jeff lad,' Tony said, as they went through the big front door of the Mess building. 'What now, mate?' Little did he realise that their luck was in. Going into the big entrance hall, the first thing they noticed was the shiny polished floor and furniture.

'Christ, there's some elbow grease gone into this lot,' Jeff remarked, glancing around the place.

Just then a voice called out from a doorway half way up an adjoining passage, 'I suppose you're the two men sent from the distribution centre, aren't you?'

Noticing his stripes, both called out, 'Yes, Sergeant.'

The sergeant came walking briskly down the passage towards them, he was a small upright man of about forty, with a bald head and a friendly, yet no-nonsense smile on his face. He was dressed in a well-pressed working blue uniform; his general appearance was very smart.

'Morning chaps,' he said as he reached them, 'They told me on the phone that you were on your way here. Ryan and Baxter, that right?' he asked, scanning their faces.

'That's right, Sergeant, I'm AC Ryan and this is AC Baxter,' Tony told him, nodding towards his companion.

The little sergeant looked the pair up and down for a moment, then without further comment, yelled behind over his shoulder, 'West! West! Wherever you are, come down to the main entrance, immediately.'

There was a scuffle above on the next floor and almost at once a figure came hurrying down a wide stairway at the very far end of the corridor. The young man that came into view was a little taller than Tony, of average build and although pleasant-looking, Tony thought he had a rather cocky expression on his face. He looked Baxter and Tony up and down contemptuously.

'Right, West, this is AC Ryan and AC Baxter,' said the sergeant, pointing to the two. 'They're new staff, I want you to show them around the Mess, explaining the duties entailed, then bring them back to my office in one hour, okay?' he told him sternly. Without further comment he then turned and marched back briskly up the corridor, disappearing into the doorway, from which he had previously emerged.

As the door closed behind him, West smiled slightly and shaking his head, mumbled, 'Bloody windbag.' Without another word he about turned, calling out authoritatively, 'Okay, you two follow me.' Giving each other a quick glance and a smirk they obeyed, marching off up the passage on the highly polished floor, in true military fashion.

'I suppose you two lads have noticed everything in here is clean and polished like glass,' the leader of the marchers called over his shoulder. 'That's how it's always got to be and that will be one of your jobs.' Round the bend at the end of the long passage, West turned into a doorway, 'This is one of the resident's ablutions,' he told them in firm tone, 'there's one on each floor of the Mess.' Waving his arm around and pointing he continued, 'There's ten washbasins and six WC's in each ablution, as you can see and everything must always be hygienic and sparkling, do you understand?' he stressed, giving them a long stare.

By now Tony was beginning to get a bit fed-up of being talked too like a fool by someone he'd already realised was a one. 'Excuse me, West,' he said going towards him smiling, 'What rank did you say you were, are you a sergeant who's forgot to put his stripes on, or what?' he asked, feigning ignorance.

A little taken aback, West replied, 'No, I'm not, but I'm the longest serving man on the Mess cleaning staff, also the head man; all the cleaning staff in here come under me,' he said, arrogantly.

Glancing across at Jeff Baxter, who was beginning to wonder what was going to happen, Tony said, grinning, 'Oh, so everybody takes orders from you do they, sweetheart, well there's one here that don't, mate.'

'Count me in that, an'all,' called out Jeff, laughing.

West, not used to being stood up to like this from the other staff stood silent, his mouth agape, not knowing what to say next. 'Well, come on, man,' yelled Tony. 'I thought the sergeant told you to show us around the Mess and point out our duties; we won't learn much stood here in the shithouse all day, will we.' The following half-hour passed in near silence as far as West was concerned; apart from any details regarding the Mess layout or questions asked by the other two, he hardly uttered a word.

Finally he said meekly, 'Well, chaps, that's it – have you anything more you'd like to ask me, before we go down to Sergeant Pike's office?'

Tony, seeing the man had now been well and truly deflated, gave him a warm friendly smile. 'Yes, what's your name? I'm Tony Ryan.' He smiled and nodded towards his companion, 'This is Jeff Baxter. Now, I suggest we start off on friendly terms, seeing as we're going to be working together. Okay?'

His face relaxed and he held out his hand, with a smile. 'I'm Ted West. Pleased to meet you, Tony and Jeff. Welcome to the Mess, the pair of you.'

43

'Well, chaps, do you think you're going to like your duties here in the Mess?' Sergeant Pike asked, from behind his desk after signing in his two new members of staff.

'Yes, Sergeant,' they both replied, almost in unison. They were hardly able to believe what a nice bloke he was for a sergeant.

'Very good, very good that's what we like, keenness for the job and full cooperation between the staff; that's imperative,' Sergeant Pike impressed upon them with authority.

'Oh, definitely, Sergeant,' agreed Tony, wanting to get in his good books. AC West introduced us to the other cleaning staff and I'm sure, together, we'll be able to keep the Mess up to the high standard that you so rightly demand, Sergeant.'

Smiling, and looking very pleased with himself, the little sergeant replied, ' Well, as long as you all understand what a big responsibility the upkeep of this establishment is, I'm sure we're all going to get on well together.' Noticing West, standing motionless at the back of the room he said sharply, 'What the hell are you standing there like a zombie for, West? Go on, man get back to your duties.' To the two newcomers, he added firmly, 'and you two report back here straight after lunch, one thirty, and don't be late.'

'He doesn't seem a bad little bugger that Sergeant Pike; does he, Tony?' Jeff remarked later.

'He'll do,' muttered Tony, frowning as his eyes scanned around their new billet. It was dinner time on the following day; the two were now sitting on their beds in the billet block they'd moved into the day before, when they first arrived on to the camp.

'Aye, he seems right enough, but that's more than I can say for this billet we're in,' Tony said, screwing his nose up.

'What do you mean?' Jeff asked. 'What's wrong with it?'

'It's scruffy and it stinks of engine oil, that's what's up lad,' he grunted.

'Well, that's to be expected, seeing as all the lads we've met up to now living in here are mechanics, working down in the transport department,' he replied.

'Just what I mean, Jeff; they all stink of engine oil, that's why they're known as grease monkeys.' I know a lad at home in that trade and he stinks the same; even when he's dressed up on a Saturday night at the dance, you can smell the bugger a mile off.' He glanced around the billet again and said firmly, 'that's why we're going to find somewhere else, a bit more up-market, Jeff.'

'What do you mean, Tony? We've only just moved in.'

'What I say, we're going to move out soon as possible; I suggest we go and have a peep in that block near the Sergeants' Mess, Jeff. It looks a nice clean place and it's next door to the Mess, very handy; we won't have far to walk from there. In fact, we can pop in and have a look around before we go into work this afternoon,' he added. 'What do you say, Jeff?'

'Will it be okay for us to go moving around like that, though, Tony, they might not like it?' he said meekly.

'Who are they?' Tony asked, laughing. 'You're not at a bloody square-bashing camp now, you silly bugger,

we're permanent staff on this camp, not bloody
trainees; a corporal's nowt here, not like at Padgate, a
god on a pedestal.'

Later that afternoon, as they were cleaning one of
the sinks in the ablutions, Jeff remarked, 'Nice clean
block that, Tony, it would be great if we could get in
there, wouldn't it?'

Tony, polishing the mirrors, shook his head and
laughed. 'I don't know, Jeff lad, you're a born defeatist
– what do you mean – if we could? Look, Jeff,' he said,
smiling. 'We're moving in tonight, straight after tea and
I'm having that bed in the corner on the right as you
walk in, you can have the next one up, okay, mate?'

Just then, a tall man in his mid to late thirties with
dark wavy hair, dressed only in vest and trousers, came
in with a towel over his arm. 'Which one of you is the
Yorkshire lad?' he asked, grinning.

Stopping his polishing, Tony turned to see who it
was. 'That's me,' he said with a smile, 'and who's
asking?'

The big man now started to lather his face with a
shaving brush. 'Sergeant Jerry Banks,' he replied,
brushing away. 'I heard you talking as I was coming up
the passage. Where are you from, then, Yorky? I'm
from Doncaster myself,' he told him, pulling a face, as
he starting scraping away at his chin.

After Tony had told him he was from the Leeds
area, he mumbled, staring into the mirror, 'Well, we
might get this bloody place running smoother, now
we've got a Yorkshire man on the staff.'

When he'd finished his shaving and gone, Jeff said,
'Bloody hell, fancy a sergeant talking to us like that,
Tony; I thought he was going to give you a bollocking,

when he asked which one of us was from Yorkshire, didn't you?'

'For Christ's sake, Jeff, when are you going to realise, mate, that you're not on the bloody square-bashing camp, any more,' Tony said exasperated. 'A corporal or a sergeant isn't going to attack you on sight here, like they did there, you know, lad.'

Saying this, he started to polish away at the mirrors again. 'Come on, now,' he went on. 'Let's get this place looking good, I want to impress old Pike. I've got some big ideas about this place that I think he might help me fulfil if I can get in his good books,' he added with a sly smile.

44

'Are you moving out already, you two?' called out one of the lads, from where he was sitting on his bed on the other side of the billet room.

'Yes, we've got a place nearer where we work,' replied Tony, transferring his things from locker to kitbag, ready for the off.

'Huh, they think they're too good to live in here with us mechanics, Benny,' called out a gruff voice from behind a newspaper.

Tony knew who it was; a big rough-looking guy with ginger hair, lying on his bed further up the room. He'd noticed him the first time he walked into the billet yesterday, and didn't like the look of him then; a bully if ever there was one, he'd thought.

'Oh, I don't think they do, Sam,' replied Benny with note of subservience in his voice.
Tony, sensing the possibility of trouble, and having seen the size of the man earlier, beckoned silently to Jeff to hurry with his packing.

'I'm right, aren't I, mister smart guy,' said the big lad, now off his bed and walking down the room towards them. He was staring at Tony filling his kit bag and stopped behind them, silently scowling.

However, the two lads ignored him and continued what they were doing, and a silence fell over the whole billet. The other half a dozen lads present sensed bother too, as they'd seen similar before, when big Sam was after a bit of fun at the expense of somebody he thought he could easy manage. Jeff, the nearest to him, suddenly got a kick in the arse as he bent over, emptying the bottom shelf of his locker; falling forward he hit his head with a bang on the metal door, and gave out a loud yell. 'Don't ignore me, punks,' hissed the big guy, menacingly giving him another kick.

Tony turning to face him, yelled, 'Cut that out, mate, we don't want any bother; we're moving out so as be nearer our place of work, that's the only reason.' He got no further, the big lad shot out his fist, aiming it at Tony's face. Tony, saw it coming, and dodged to one side with lightning speed, but still caught a glancing blow to the side of his head, forceful enough to make him see stars. With no choice left, Tony retaliated. Stepping forward, he stamped down on to the instep of the man's right foot with a crack. As the man bent forward with a yell of pain, Tony braced himself rigid and shot out his right arm, hitting him with the heel of his palm, straight between the eyes. To Tony's surprise, he just stood there motionless, with a silly smile on his face. Thinking he was going to have to fight for his life, Tony clenched his fists, and was just about to give the man a pile-driver under the ribs, and then follow with another to the head, in his usual way, when he noticed the man's eyeballs slowly roll to the middle and his long legs start to fold beneath him. Tony held back at the last moment, and saw him flop back on to Jeff's bed and remain still. He lay there without moving, his feet hung over the end, while all in the room stood staring at him amazed – he was clearly out for the count.

The silence was suddenly broken and a muttering went round the billet, 'Christ, mate, you've dropped him,' gasped Benny, walking across the floor and looking down at the bully on the bed, with disbelief. 'I can hardly believe it, Sam's an all-in wrestler you know in Civvy Street,' he said, still staring down at him. 'He's in charge of the camp wrestling team as well,' he added continuing to stare down at the unconscious figure, mouth agape.

'I suppose he uses the camp gym a lot, then, eh?' Tony said.

'Oh, aye,' replied the lad. 'He goes up there most nights; he trains all the new boys – as I said, he's a professional.'

Picking up his kit bag, Tony replied, with a sigh, 'That's all I need, having his company every time I go for a training session. Come on, Jeff,' he said urgently, looking down at the motionless figure, 'let's get off, before he comes round.'

'What if he don't,' Benny asked nervously. 'I don't like the look of him; he should have come round by now.'

All the other lads in the billet came closer to have a better look at him and one of them said, 'He could be dead you know, look how his face is swelling up.'

'He'll be okay,' Tony said cheerfully, although he was beginning to wonder himself. 'If he were dead his face wouldn't be still swelling, would it, everything stops when you're dead,' he told them confidently, but he didn't know whether he was right or wrong.

'Tony's right,' called out Jeff, pointing at the suddenly stirring sleeper, 'Look, he's coming round.'

'Told you he'd be okay,' repeated Tony with a smile of relief. He turned and made for the door, with his mate close behind him.

In their new billet, Jeff fell back on to his bed and said, 'Well, you were right, mate, I think we've done a good thing moving in here.'

'You should know by now, old son, I'm always right,' chuckled Tony, shoving the last few items of kit into his locker, before dropping back on his own bed, with a sigh. The new abode they had moved into was far superior to the last, it was lighter, cleaner and the lads there were, in general, a much more pleasant lot.

'Hi, there you two, welcome. Have you just moved onto the camp, then?' one of them enquired, coming over to them, smiling, 'My name's James Clark. I'm in pay accounts.'

Getting up off his bed, Tony smiled and offered his hand, 'Pleased to meet you, James. I'm Tony Ryan and my friend here is Jeff Baxter, we both work in the Sergeants' Mess.'

After a further half-hour chatting to their new friend, the three lads found they'd got quite a lot in common. Tony went on to tell him about the first block they'd tried and what had happened. James agreed that they had made the right choice. With regard to big Sam, he said that he was well known on the camp as a bully; also that he was once arrested by the Military Police for thumping a guy in the Mess hall. He thought that the reason for his aggression was that nobody had ever dared to stand up to him. Hearing this, the two pals glanced at each other and smiled.

45

'Where are the other two lads you introduced me to yesterday, Ted?' Tony called out, spotting him coming up the passage, toilet brush in hand.

'They're down in the dining hall talking to one of the waitresses,' he replied with a shrug. 'They take some starting them two, Tony, I'll tell you.'

Without reply, Tony marched briskly passed him calling back over his shoulder, 'I'll bloody well start 'em, Ted lad, believe me, mate.' Reaching the big dining hall, he saw the two men in question, flirting and showing off in front of a tallish, good-looking young woman, setting out the tables.

'Now don't try and kid me, Ruby,' called out one of them, while the other stood grinning. 'You know you'd like to get your arms around my manly neck and hug me to death.'

'I don't know about your manly neck, you pillock,' yelled Tony, 'if you don't come and get on with some work like the rest of us, I'll kick your manly arse.'

Spinning round, the man glared at Tony with a look of aggression, then deciding he wouldn't have much chance of fulfilling what he'd like to do to the intruder, he turned to his companion and forced a smile. 'Come on, Frank, let's be off upstairs,' he said with a sneer. 'We'd better get on with the landing floor, I did promise old Pike it would be done by ten thirty.'

As they marched out of the dining hall Tony went up to the nice-looking young woman laying the tables, and smiled. 'Hello, darling, what's your name then?' he asked, turning on the Ryan charm.

'ACW Prichard,' she answered, giving him a coy side glance, as she continuing setting the tables.

'Ruby, ain't it, love?' he said, having heard the other lad call her that. 'Lovely name,' he added with sincerity.

Stopping her work, she turned to him with a knowing smile on her face, 'and you're a bloody fast worker, mate, what's your name, anyway?' she asked, staring into his face.

Shocked at having a response like this from what he'd thought was a timid young girl, he replied, after clearing his throat, 'Tony Ryan, love, I'm one of the two men that's just started.'

Breaking into a laugh she said, 'For a new bloke on the job, Tony Ryan, you're certainly full of yourself – but I'll give you one thing, Tony, you made them two lazy buggers jump; I've never seen them move so fast, not even with Sergeant Pike behind 'em.'

'Aye,' he replied grinning, relieved at her change of attitude. 'I meant what I said, that's why they moved; they'd have got a kick in the arse if they hadn't got going I assure you, love.'

'Oh, one of them dominant male types are you, Tony Ryan?' she replied, giving him another sexy glance, as she walked away with her tray, through the swing door into the kitchen.

'I'll see you later, you sexy little devil,' Tony called after her with a laugh, as he set off after the other two.

By the end of the first week in the Sergeants Mess, Tony was beginning to wonder why he'd had no letter from Becky; anyway, he reasoned, she'd be busy with her family, she'd contact him, he told himself, as soon as she got to her new camp.

One of the jobs Tony had volunteered for was looking after the bedding store; this was a nice big room about the size of a sergeant's bunk room; here all the bedding was kept, for allocation to the residents as required. The store was handled by Tony in working hours, but Sergeant Pike was on call if bedding was required after five pm and he didn't like the inconvenience of it at all. Tony realising this, decided to turn the matter to his own advantage. Knowing that Sergeant Pike did one of his inspections between four and five in the afternoon, Tony made sure that he was in the bedding store tidying up at that time.

Spot on four thirty he heard footsteps coming briskly up the passage; within seconds the sergeant came striding in through the open door.

Seeing Tony hard at work stacking blankets on the shelves at the back of the room, he called out, 'Oh, hello, Ryan, I see you're busy, sorry to disturb you.'

Pretending he'd been surprised, Tony spun around. 'Oh, hi, Sergeant Pike, I was just thinking about you and what you said the other day about being called out in the evenings, and also sometimes late at night; it must be very restrictive for you,' he said sympathetically.

Looking back at him with a sigh and shaking his head he replied, 'That's an understatement Ryan, I've got virtually no freedom sometimes. It's been known for some bugger to come knocking on my bunk door in the middle of the night, if they arrive late. It's very rare that, I admit, but it's still a strain when you've got the responsibility I have to bear, all day,' he moaned. 'Mind you, I shouldn't complain I suppose,' he continued, with a pitiful little smile. 'When duty calls and all that, you know, Ryan. I'll just have to put up with it I suppose,' he said, shaking his bald head.

Walking slowly towards him stood in the doorway, Tony said 'Well, that was what I was just thinking about, Sergeant, there's no need for you to have that weight on your shoulders any longer.'

'What do you mean, Ryan?' he asked, a puzzled look crossing his face.

'Well, I handle the bedding store in the day and I love the job, Sergeant, so why don't I take it over full time?' He smiled. 'I don't go out anywhere in the evenings, only up to the gym for a couple of hours occasionally and I'm always back by ten,' he said.

His face lighting up, the little sergeant replied, 'Would you? Ryan, are you sure?' Then, frowning he said, 'Oh, but what about the buggers that turn up in the middle of the night, though?'

'No problem there, Sergeant,' Tony replied, waving his hand around the room. 'Plenty of space in here, I could put a bed in the far corner over there behind the door.' With a grin, he added, 'Twenty-four hour service then, Sergeant, no problem, as I said.'

Rubbing his chin and thinking for a moment, Sergeant Pike replied quietly, 'Great idea, Ryan, I must admit, but would it be in order for you to sleep in the Sergeant's Mess? That's the problem; others might object.'

'Oh, I can't see that happening,' Tony replied nonchalantly. 'I mean I'd be on duty wouldn't I? What's more I'd only be sleeping in here when late arrivals were expected, everything official then,' he stressed, with a shake of his head.

'Well, yes, I see that point, Ryan, but some of the buggers turn up out of the blue without notice,' he pointed out firmly.

'Just what I mean, Sergeant,' Tony replied cheerfully. 'They can be expected anytime, so there's no problem is there? I'd be on official duty whenever I stayed in here.'

Still looking thoughtful, the Sergeant stroked his chin and stared into space. 'That's true, yes, that's true, Ryan. It isn't often folk come very late, but they sometimes turn up without warning, yes, yes, I see your point,' he said.

'So, whenever I slept in here I'd be on official duty, Sergeant, nobody could complain then, even if they wanted to,' Tony said knowingly.

By now, losing track of Tony's explanation, in fact feeling rather baffled, the little Sergeant said, 'I suppose you're right there, Ryan, not knowing when any anyone might turn up, you'd have to be on bedding call duty twenty four hours a day. So, if anyone was expected you'd have to be here to admit them officially; yes, yes you're right there,' he said, staring down at his boots, frowning.

Then with a little smile, unable to believe his good luck, he said sharply, 'Are you sure you don't mind volunteering for this, though, Ryan?'

Smiling back, Tony replied, 'Well, as you've just been saying, Sergeant – when duty calls and all that.'

Grinning broadly, he replied, 'Great idea, Ryan, we'll give it a go. Get looking around for a bed, there'll be one somewhere in the Mess and get it all sorted out as soon as possible.'

'Oh, I've got a bed lined up already, Sergeant,' Tony told him casually. 'That room on the top floor that's being converted into a drying room, there's a single bed in there; I've told a couple of the lads to bring it down, before they go off for their tea.'

'Good, that's sorted out, then,' replied the Sergeant, giving him a puzzled second glance as he turned to leave.

The following morning, Tony was sitting at a small table, alongside a comfortable -looking single bed in his new abode, the bedding store. He was listening to a small radio beside him and writing a reply to a letter he'd just received from his mate, Dave. The little kettle on the sink side was just coming to the boil, when there was a tap on the door. 'Come in, it's not locked,' he called out authoritatively.

The door opened slowly and Jeff came cautiously in, standing there like a bewitched prick. Looking around the place for a moment, he said with a whistle, 'By hell, Tony, this is home from home, mate; you've made a right comfortable bunk for yourself here.'

Tony just looked back at him smugly grinning, then as the kettle began to whistle he asked, 'Would you care for a pot of tea with me, Jeff?'

They'd only been drinking their tea for about five minutes, when there was another tap on the door. 'Oh, hell, go see who that is, Jeff, 'Tony groaned.

Peeping out into the passage, Jeff smiled sweetly. 'Oh, hello there, Ruby, love – it's Ruby from the kitchen, Tony,' he called over his shoulder.'

'Fetch her in then, are you daft or what?' he yelled back. 'Now then, darling, what can I do for you this bright morning?' he asked in his best flirty manner, as she shyly entered.

'Sergeant McNabb sent me to see if the tablecloths have got back from the laundry yet,' she said, looking slightly embarrassed at being in the room with two men, who were both eyeing her up and down.

'Yes, they have, love,' said Tony, stripping her with his eyes, 'but we haven't had time to get them all unpacked yet, it'll be later this afternoon before I can get them sorted out, I'm afraid.'

The young woman was quiet for a moment, then smiling shyly, she explained, 'She said she wants them now, she said to tell you they were promised for yesterday, we've used up all the reserved ones, you see,' she pointed out, blushing a pleasant pink.

'Who the bloody hell is this Sergeant McNabb, Jeff?' he grunted, turning to his mate.

'She's that big well-made woman in charge of the kitchen staff,' he replied.

'Oh, I've never met her, anyway we can't get them ready until after dinner,' he said firmly.

'You'd better be careful, Tony,' said Jeff. 'She looks like a nasty old bugger; she wants pensioning off, if you ask me, she must be going on for forty.'

'Anyway,' Tony continued adamantly, 'whoever she is, she'll have to wait until we've time to get them unpacked, won't she; we're under orders to see to that van delivery this morning. Sergeant Pike's our boss, not her,' he stressed, looking at Ruby and grinning. 'You tell the old bugger that, darling, but you can come back here anytime you like,' he added, with a cheeky wink.

'She's a nasty old bugger you know, Tony,' Jeff repeated seriously, when the young girl had left.

'Oh, to hell with her, Jeff, sup your tea and relax, man. We've a lot on this morning; don't forget there's a van load of new blankets being delivered.

No sooner had they settled down again, when there was a loud banging on the door. Jeff, who was nearest, jumped up with a start, spilling his tea. 'I'll get it, Tony,' he called out, rushing to answer it. He opened the door and his face dropped.

'Where's this AC Ryan?' a very loud angry female voice enquired; before he could answer she barged in, pushing Jeff effortlessly out of the way.

Jumping out of his chair, Tony found himself looking up into the glaring face of a tall woman, well over six foot – at least four inches taller than he was himself. She was on the well-built side, although she would, in the right attire, look quite sexy, he thought. Now, she was dressed in a long, baggy white smock with three stripes on each arm and wearing a white cook's hat. She stood looking at him for a moment in silence, and then to the surprise of both lads, she said quite softly, 'Are you AC Ryan?'

'Yes, Sergeant, that's right, what can I do for you?' he asked.

A coy little smile crossed her face. 'That's a bold thing to ask a girl when you first meet her, Ryan, isn't it? But I could think of a few things if you ask me nicely.' She giggled.

Beginning to get a little worried, realising the way her mind was working, Tony said, with a forced smile, 'I suppose you've come about your tablecloths haven't you, Sergeant; me and my assistant here, were just about to make a start on unpacking them, seeing as it's so urgent.'

Giving Jeff a black look, she said, 'What are you stood there for, airman? Get off to your duties.' She looked at Tony – now frantically trying to unpack a huge cardboard box at the far end of the room – and continued 'I'll help you to sort my cloths out, Ryan, I'm more nimble than him.'

'No, no don't go, Jeff,' Tony shouted out, panicking slightly. 'You know what Sergeant Pike instructed, about two of us having to witness all deliveries – we must stick to the rules,' he added. Jeff, realising the situation, rushed to help him and five minutes later, Jeff and Tony, their arms loaded with tablecloths, were following closely behind Sergeant McNabb, as she stamped her way to the dining room.

'Put them over there on that bench,' Sergeant McNabb yelled. They did as they were told without comment and beat a hasty retreat back along the passage.

Ruby, who was clearing the dining room tables called over her shoulder, 'Oh, they managed to get them sorted out for you then, Sergeant, however did you manage it?'

'You've a lot to learn, AC Prichard,' she told her smiling. 'I used my female charms, you'll learn when you get a bit older,' she added gruffly, making her way back into the kitchen.

Safely back in the bedding store, Tony flopped down with a sigh on an old armchair he'd found for his abode. 'Christ, Jeff, I've never been scared of a woman before in my life, that big bag put the shits up me, mate, I'll tell you; did you see the lust in her eyes, Jeff?

'I certainly did, she wanted your pants down, old son.' He laughed loudly. 'If I hadn't have been there I'll bet she'd have had 'em down an'all, and given you a real good fucking.'

'Christ,' he sighed, 'she'd have killed me if she'd rolled on me, with them great big legs wrapped around my arse.' Then he said more seriously, 'but joking apart, Jeff, a woman like that could be dangerous you know.'

'How do you mean?' he asked. 'You could easy stop her, Tony, big as she is, I'm sure of that.'

'Of course I could normally,' he said, 'but don't forget, Jeff, we're in the RAF and she's a sergeant – I couldn't just give her a slap and tell her to behave herself, now could I?'

'Why not, if she was trying to take advantage of you, I would,' he replied firmly.

'Aye and you might be the one to end up in the bloody guardhouse, mate.' Tony told him. 'She'd obviously deny it and who do you think they'd believe, a long term serving female sergeant or a bloody AC plonk like us.'

He sat back in the chair with a worried look on his face. 'No, Jeff, I've seen her sort before, mate, big frumpish buggers. Once they take a liking to a bloke, they take some bloody shaking off. No, mate,' he muttered with a nod, 'the only way with that type, is to give 'em a wide berth, old lad, I'll tell you.

Suddenly brightening, he said in his usual chirpy manner, 'but you can send that Ruby up here, if you like Baxter; I assure you I won't struggle if she tries to force herself on me.'

46

By the back end of the following week, Tony hadn't heard a thing from Becky; naturally he was beginning to get very worried indeed. He knew she should back from leave by now and had expected contact from her, to arrange a meeting for the weekend. However, the weekend passed with still no communication, leaving him in near panic. Had she had an accident, or been taken ill, he thought? He just couldn't understand it, they loved each other – he knew that – so why hadn't she contacted him, where the hell was she, he pondered? Then his mind went back to Peggy – Oh God, he suddenly thought, please don't let that happen again, please!

For the next few days he could think of nothing else, but by the Thursday there had been no letter or phone call. He decided there was no chance that he was going to go through the mental anguish he'd gone through at Padgate. He would follow the advice he always gave to others with worrying problems and he would shut his mind off the subject completely; in other words – forget it. After all, he reasoned, Becky knew where he was, and even though she didn't know his mail address was the 'Sergeants' Mess,' she could easily find out from the camp Personnel Department.

By Friday morning Tony was managing to keep cheerful, even though it was a struggle. His little episode with the big cook, Sergeant McNabb, also seemed to have been forgotten, although she did give him a cheeky wink once, when he went down to the kitchen with a delivery of floor cloths.

'Late mail, lads,' called out Ted West, coming along the top landing towards Tony and Jeff, who were changing curtains. Both dropped tools and Tony's heart raced. Could there be a letter from her, he thought?

'Three for you, Jeff and two for Tony,' Ted smiled, handing the letters over. Glancing at the handwriting, Tony's excitement ceased; one was from his mum and the other from Dave. Ripping open the one from Dave and looking at it for a moment, he turned to Jeff in disbelief.

'Bloody hell, Dave, my mate at home has joined the Royal Marines; he signed on for five years – the silly bugger! Shaking his head at the news, he turned to go. 'Come on, Jeff, let's go down to the bedding store and have a cuppa; it's half past four and I'm knackered.'

'What if old Pike comes up here and finds us gone,' replied Jeff. 'He'll play hell.'

'Bugger him,' Tony said, walking away. 'We've put in a bloody good day's work up here on these windows. I'm calling it a day, whatever he says. Anyway, he's gone for a new uniform fitting this afternoon, so he won't be back in the Mess yet,' he told him.

The little kettle was just coming to the boil, when they heard footsteps coming briskly along the passage.

'AC Ryan. AC Ryan!' called out a voice urgently.

'Christ, its Pike,' gasped Jeff, 'He's back.'

'What the hell does he want me for now?' Tony grumbled. 'It's nearly finishing time, anyway.'

'Don't know – but it sounds urgent, Tony, by the tone of his voice,' Jeff replied, jumping to his feet and pretending to be sorting blankets out on one of the storage shelves.

The sergeant came hurrying into the store, 'Oh, you're there, Ryan,' he said breathlessly. 'Get down to the front hall, quick, there's a long distance phone call for you from a camp in Cyprus; the caller has been trying to trace you all week, apparently. I hope you haven't been getting yourself into any trouble, lad,' he added, with one of his squeaky little laughs.

Tony's heart missed a beat when he heard this and he made for the door like a shot, mumbling, 'Oh my God, is this really what I think it is?'

Back in the billet, Tony lay on his bed in silence.

'Will you bloody well tell me what's up, Tony?' Jeff asked, looking down at him.
'You've been lying there since tea time, staring at the bloody ceiling like a zombie. What
the hell happened, what was that blasted phone call about to upset you like this?'

After a long pause, Tony replied as if in a dream, 'It was from my girlfriend, Jeff. I've a feeling I've lost her.'

'What do you mean, lost her?' he asked sympathetically.

Tony told him about the earlier phone call, which had been from Becky. She'd received a telegram while at home on leave; her posting had been changed and she was to report to a local RAF camp, within two hours. She'd been booked on a transport plane going to her revised posting, a camp in Cyprus. Tony went on to tell him about Conrad, the Wing Commander, her ex-boyfriend and his own suspicion that Conrad had engineered the change.

'Well, what does Becky think about it all then, Tony,' he asked, after hearing the details.

'Same as me,' he replied, looking melancholy. 'She also said it won't do him any good; but she told me not to write to her for the time being, as she doesn't want him to find out who I am.'

'Why's that?' Jeff asked, 'How could he ever tell who'd sent her a letter, anyway?

'Jeff, as I told you, he's in Intelligence, and don't forget his high rank; he could easy find out the name of anyone that sent a letter through the camp Post Office, even before it was delivered to her at the gym.'

'You mean he could have a private letter intercepted?' Jeff said, stunned.

'Well, let's say there's a possibility,' he replied, 'but she's going to write to me regular, she said that she'll post it off camp. Anyway,' he went on optimistically, 'she's going to try and get that posting reversed, which I don't think she'll be able to do, myself,'' he moaned frowning.

'Look on the bright side, mate, you never know,' Jeff reassured him.
'Huh, a Wing Commander in Intelligence,' Tony said, scornfully. 'He'll be able to pull fucking strings all over the place, that's how he got her posting changed without a doubt; I might never see her again,' he mumbled gloomily.

Jeff stood silent for a few seconds then laughing, said cheerfully, 'Anyway, you miserable bugger, come on, cheer up. You're not going to make things any better lying there moaning. It's Friday night, let's go over to the NAAFI; you can cry on my shoulder over a few jars.

47

Several months later, with Christmas fast approaching, Sergeant Pike was putting all the lads who worked in the Sergeants' Mess, under extra pressure preparing for the festive occasions on top of the usual everyday cleaning work; everyone was in top gear. Tony Ryan had by now got himself firmly settled in a self-appointed supervisory position and this was accepted by the other cleaning lads. He considered himself to be their boss, under Sergeant Pike of course, and got their full respect.

Since his phone call from Cyprus he'd received several letters from Becky, in which she still assured him she was trying to get a UK posting. However, this, he was beginning to think, would not be forthcoming. Furthermore, as he wasn't able to reply to her letters, he was also pondering the possibility that the whole affair might be starting to wear thin. Even though he still loved her deeply, there were many things he would have liked to discuss with her and this was also playing on his mind.

Christmas time on an RAF camp is celebrated in the same way as in the rest of the country, but although the camp almost comes to a standstill, it never does completely; each department maintains a skeleton staff, the Sergeants' Mess being no exception.

'Right, Jeff, we're volunteering to stay on duty over Christmas; we'll have two holiday breaks instead of one then, okay?' Tony said. They were in the bedding store having their mid-morning break; they'd been busy putting up the Christmas decorations in the main bar since starting work that morning and both felt ready for it.

'Well, if you say so, mate,' Jeff replied reluctantly, 'but how do you mean get two breaks, instead of just the one?'

'Well, look at it this way, Jeff, over Christmas the camp is only operating at emergency level, so, it's virtually shut down as far as we're concerned, right?'

Jeff nodded. 'Well, I suppose so.'

'So, by staying here we still get all the Christmas celebrations, including the big Christmas dinner and all the boozy times, plus the annual dance; on top of that Pike's buggered off,' Tony said. 'Then after all that, when the others come back after their Christmas leave, we go on our leave for the New Year celebrations at home; see what I mean mate?' he winked.

'Aye, you're right, Tony, good thinking boy.' Jeff smiled in agreement. 'I never thought of it like that, good thinking, mate.'

'By the way, Jeff, there might be a few lonely ladies knocking around over the holidays; I wonder if the lovely Ruby will be staying?' Tony said, giving him a sly smile, as he passed him his tea.

'Well she'll be the only Scottish member of staff in the Mess that doesn't,' Jeff replied. 'They all go home for Hogmanay, the Scottish folk, as a rule.'

'Of course, of course they do, so you see we should have plenty of good company here in the Mess as I said. Laughing he went on, 'I'll have to make sure I've got my bedding store all nice and cosy for the occasion then, Jeff, old son, won't I.' Tony became more serious. 'If you're a good lad, I might lend you the key for an hour, if you can manage to pull that little ginger bird from the kitchen, you fancy.'

'What about Pike, is he going off for Christmas, for sure?' Jeff asked, ignoring the offer.

'Of course he is, I've just told you, he's a family man, is Cyril; he's got stockings to fill at home, him,' Tony replied, with mock sincerity.

'How do you know he's going for Christmas, Tony, and how do you know he's got kids? Jeff asked, puzzled.

'Oh, he told me when I went down to his office yesterday, to let him know you and I we're volunteering to stay on duty over the Christmas period,' Tony replied casually. 'He was very grateful actually. He also told me that now I was staying, he could go and enjoy his Christmas with a contented mind,' he added, with a conceited little smirk.

Looking more puzzled, Jeff enquired, 'How did you know I'd volunteer to stay, though, you've only just asked me?'

'Oh, I knew you'd think like me, mate, we've both got logical minds, we're not bone heads like the rest of the buggers in here, Jeff,' he said.

'No, no, I see what you mean, mate,' Jeff agreed, sipping his tea, with a thoughtful frown.

48

Sergeant Riley was a man in his early thirties; he was an aircrew navigator on transport planes; his bunk in the mess was on the top landing and for some unknown reason he seemed to hate Tony Ryan. Every time he met Tony around the building he would give him a long stare, then pick some sort of minor fault to reprimand him about. Tony had mentioned the situation to Sergeant Pike, but he had been reluctant to confront the man, brushing it off with a laugh, and so the victimization continued.

'I'm getting right to the end of my tether with that bastard upstairs,' Tony complained, walking into the empty bar, where Jeff and two of the other boys were busy cleaning.

'You mean Riley,' Jeff asked, with a sigh. 'What's up this time, Tony, dirty sinks again?'

'No bloody dusty window sills this time; I don't think I can stand much more or him, you know, Jeff – he's been picking on me like this for weeks now. I only wish I knew why he hated me so much,' he mumbled, as he joined in their work.

Riley had frequently directed unjustifiable criticism at Tony over the past weeks; if it wasn't dust it was dirty sinks, or furniture not polished enough, or even streaky windows. He'd always find something to fault in the cleaning work, and always blamed Tony. None of the other residents were treated in this way – it must be something personal, Tony was sure of that. Sergeant Priest, a police sergeant temporarily living in the next bunk to Riley on the top landing, never complained like him, he was just the opposite. Tony had always been on very friendly terms with him, as with most of the other residents in the Mess. Sergeant Priest was a Service police sergeant in charge of the main guardroom, and, as was to be expected in his position, always immaculately dressed with his little black moustache groomed to perfection. He was a strict disciplinarian and the terror of the camp; even in the Mess he got respect from all the other residents, regardless of rank. Tony thought if a man like him found no reason to complain, Riley must be making things up. Eventually he came to the conclusion that Riley must be some sort of a nut case, and all he could do was try to keep out of his way; this of course, was difficult in such a confined area.

'Okay, Yorky?' Sergeant Banks called out as Tony passed his open bunk door, almost straight opposite the bedding store.

'Yes fine, Sergeant,' he called back, pausing in his stride. 'Are you going up to Doncaster for Christmas then, Sergeant?'

Coming to the door in his pyjama bottom and vest, still looking half asleep, he replied, 'No, I'm staying on camp over Christmas, kid, I'm on duty; I'm going home for the New Year.'

'Oh, me too,' Tony told him with a smile. 'You'll be at the Mess dance on Christmas Eve then, Sergeant, eh?'

'Sure will, no doubt I'll be pissed by the end of it an'all.' He grinned. 'By the way, Yorky, my name's Jerry to you in the Mess, bugger the titles – we're both Yorkies, aren't we? We've got to stick together, us.'

'We definitely have, Jerry; there's some funny buggers around here and no mistake,' he told him, with a laugh.

Nodding knowingly, he replied, 'Like that silly little fart, Riley, on the top landing, eh? Didn't I hear him playing hell with you the other day, over dusty windowsills or summat?'

'Aye,' Tony said. 'He gets me most days; if it's not one thing it's another, I'm fed up of him. He bloody well hates me and I don't know why; I've always been respectful and tried to be obliging towards him, with his bedding and laundry.'

'Aye, I was in the upstairs ablutions having a bath, when I heard him going on at you; they were all in use down here,' he added, 'but for that, I'd have come out and told him to grow up and belt up – bloody dust,' he mumbled.

49

'Morning, Ryan,' called out Sergeant Pike, coming into Tony's office (the bedding store), one morning later in the week. 'I've just been having a good look around the Mess and I'm very impressed; you lads have done an excellent job,'

'Well, I knew what you wanted, Sergeant,' Tony replied in a business-like tone. 'I made it plain to the others that you'd only tolerate the best.'

Smiling at the implied respect, the sergeant continued, 'Good man, Ryan, I can see you know how to handle these chaps, that's a big help to me, you know, with all the responsibility I have here.'

'I can appreciate that, Sergeant,' Tony replied. 'I sometimes wonder how you manage, what with all the cleaning and organising, not to mention the running of the dining room and the bar. Now, with the festive season to prepare for, you must be worn out,' he said, shaking his head.

Nodding in silence for a couple of seconds, a look of self-pity on his face, he said, 'You're so right, Ryan, I am, but that's partly what I came to see you about. I've decided to go on leave a day earlier, if you can manage without me. You see, I've got a lot of sorting out at home – it being Christmas; kids' stockings and that sort of thing,' he said, with a weak little smile.

'Don't you worry, Sergeant, you'll be missed obviously,' said Tony, 'but I'll make sure your high standards are maintained.'

'Good man,' he replied. 'Oh and don't forget what I told you yesterday, Ryan, there's a chance we might get an odd late resident moving in over the holiday.'

'That's all in hand, Sergeant,' Tony replied, reassuringly. 'I'm staying in the Mess myself the whole period, so there's no problem there.'

'Good thinking Ryan, that solves everything then, I'll be able to get off tomorrow with a contented mind now.' Turning to go, he added, 'Thanks for your consideration, Ryan, I won't forget this.'

The following morning, Ted was at the top of a ladder, adjusting one of the curtain rods on the big centre window.

'Ted! Have you a minute,' yelled out Tony, across the large dining room. 'Coming, Tony, I've finished here now, what's the problem?' he asked, as he walked over.

'Sergeant Pike's going off on leave at dinner time,' Tony told him. 'He's doing his inspection at eleven thirty before he goes, so you'd better take Eddy and Frank up onto the top landing and start polishing – and make them floors shine, okay?' he said, with a questioning look at Ted.

'Don't worry, mate, we'll send him home on leave happy,' Ted replied with a laugh, and scurried off to find the other two.

Late that afternoon, Tony was sitting alone in the bedding store with his feet on the table, reading a newspaper and listening to his radio, when suddenly there was a sharp knock on the door.

'Is that you, Jeff? Come in and stop fooling about,' he yelled.

The door slowly opened and looking up from his paper, Tony was confronted with the smirking face of Sergeant Riley.

He stood there in the doorway for a few seconds looking around the room, before saying sarcastically,

'Very cosy, Ryan, I must say.' He nodded in the direction of the nicely made up bed and the kettle nearly on the boil, and went on with a raised voice, 'So you've taken the liberty to move into the Mess as soon as Sergeant Pike's back is turned, have you, Ryan?'

Getting up out of his chair Tony went up to him and quietly replied, 'I'd like to inform you, Sergeant, that the idea of making part of this store into a living area, was Sergeant Pike's. The reason being, I am on "bedding duty" when called, for twenty four hours a day; consequently, as new residents are expected over the holiday, I'm on duty over the full Christmas period.' Then, giving him a little smile, he said, 'So, I shall be residing in here over that period.'

'I don't believe you, man,' Riley yelled, obviously very annoyed at Tony's calm explanation. 'I'll have a word with Sergeant Pike on his return, and if you're lying I'll personally put you on a 252 charge, for lying and insubordination.' In a calmer voice he continued, 'Anyway, that's not what I came to see you about, come on, follow me,' he hissed, turning, 'there's something on my landing I want to show you.'

'It can't be dust again, Sergeant,' Tony said, following him out onto the passage. 'We've had three men up there this morning for over two hours cleaning, and Sergeant Pike passed their work on his inspection, before he went on leave.'

'Just follow me and shut up, Ryan,' he yelled. 'It's something more serious than dust this time,' he told him menacingly.

'Oh dear, something worse than dust, Yorky, you bad boy,' called out a voice as they approached Sergeant Banks' room on the corridor. He came to the door grinning, in pyjama bottoms, sleeveless singlet and carpet slippers.

'Whatever can it be that you've found up there, Riley, that's worse than dust, it must be summat bloody terrible,' he said, laughing.

Riley walked on briskly, ignoring the interruption, with Tony following closely behind expressionless. Laughing, Jerry, fell in behind Tony; the three then marched in single file along the passage, heading for the top landing.

'This looks interesting,' Jerry said, still laughing. 'You don't mind me tagging along, Sergeant Riley, do you?' he called out, as they marched on their way. 'I can't wait to see what this nasty thing can be that's caused you such distress.'

Reaching the top landing, Sergeant Riley, without a word went marching down the corridor and stopped abruptly in front of one of the large windows, smirking at Tony. 'There you are, Ryan,' he said sarcastically, pointing at one of the middle panes of glass. 'Disgusting, eh?' He grimaced.

Staring at the window, Tony looked puzzled. 'What? What's the problem there, Sergeant?'

'That, man!' he snapped at him, pointing at a big white smudge in the middle of the glass, 'are you blind or something, Ryan?' he yelled.

'Well, that's only a bit of bird shit, Riley,' chipped in Jerry Banks, laughing.

Glaring at him, he replied scornfully, 'I know what it is, Sergeant Banks, and it's a disgusting sight, apart from being unhygienic.'

Shaking his head grinning, Jerry said, 'Bollocks, it's only a bit of bird shit and it's on the outside of the window an'all, it's nowt to do with these lads. They're employed to clean the inside of the building, the outside is the responsibility of the window cleaners; they come under the general camp maintenance department.'

Glaring at Jerry, standing there smirking, the now very angry Sergeant Riley gave the motionless Tony a quick nasty glance and turning on his heel, marched away up the passage to his own room, without another word.

Giving Tony a wink, Jerry said loudly, 'Come on, Yorky; let's get back down to civilisation.'

This was followed by a loud bang, as the very upset Sergeant Riley slammed his door in their faces, as they walked past.

50

Christmas Eve was a very busy day for Jeff and Tony; the other three cleaning staff had gone off on leave and although most of the preparation for the celebrations had been done, finalising things ready for the Christmas Eve dance and buffet still proved a formidable task. Part of the large dining hall had been cleared for a dance floor and several long tables put at each side of the room to accommodate snacks. In fact by the time it was all set out, the lads, although tired, were proud of their work.

'Well, I think that's about as good as we can make it, Jeff, old chap,' Tony said, flopping down on one of the dining chairs. 'It's four thirty now,' he said, looking up at the wall clock. 'I say we go and get an early tea, then have a rest. We've got a very busy night, you know: we've got to be back here at seven, best blue uniform an'all tonight; don't forget we're on security duty.'

'Phew, it'll be bloody hot, walking around in that when the dance warms up, Tony.' Jeff frowned.

'We can always take our jackets off later when things get going,' he told him. 'Everybody else will. When the booze starts flowing, formalities disappear. By the way, Jeff, we've got to keep sober tonight, you know; we can't be getting pissed on duty.'

'Sounds as though every bugger, will be enjoying a good, old knees-up, but us,' moaned Jeff, as they made their way out of the building.

'Well, we might be able to manage a few pints later on when everybody else gets pissed,' said Tony, smiling, 'and don't forget your little ginger bird is waiting on tables tonight, so you might score there if you play your cards right.'

'Aye, and don't you forget the lovely Ruby will also be present, so you might not do so bad either,' he replied, grinning.

That evening, Tony was walking down the passage from the bedding store dressed in his best blue uniform; with his athletic build he looked very smart indeed. Jeff was already there when he reached the dining room, come dance hall, and the instrumentalists in the little quartet were tuning up for the event. The two smartly dressed lads standing in the doorway, surveyed the nearly empty room, and felt proud of their earlier toils.

'Not many in here, Tony,' Jeff remarked.

'It's early yet, 'he replied. 'The bar's throbbing though, I noticed that as I passed coming down the passage, they'll all be getting oiled up before they come in here,' he laughed.

Just then Jeff nudged him, whispering, 'Look over there, mate, we're being watched.'
Glancing across the room Tony saw Sergeant McNabb standing in the kitchen doorway, staring in their direction with a lustful look in her eyes.

'Oh, hell, aye, I see what you mean, mate,' he said out of the side of his mouth. 'She looks a different person dressed up, doesn't she; quite an improvement an'all.'

'Aye, I never thought she'd a figure like that under her baggy smock,' Jeff muttered.

At that moment a very small, skinny warrant officer of about fifty went up to her, and greeted her affectionately. Although hardly up to her shoulder, he grabbed her arm firmly, said something in her ear and then led her onto the dance floor, looking up into her face smiling warmly.

'Who's that little Warrant Officer, that's just got her on the floor?' Tony asked, watching the happy couple go gliding around. He laughed. 'What the hell's he doing dancing with a great big bugger like her for? She could pick him up and put him in her pocket.'

'Oh, you wouldn't know, Tony, that's Warrant Officer Bloomer, he very rarely comes in the Mess, he's got a flat over his office in the working area; she's his long time lady friend, Ted West told me; they've been courting for about two years,' he said.

'Poor little sod,' Tony gasped. 'It's a wonder she hasn't killed him before now, getting them great big legs around him.'

'Yes, I bet they're a right sight when they're on the job, mate,' Jeff said, laughing.

The evening progressed well and uneventfully until about ten o'clock, when the dining room suddenly filled up with the previous bar customers. That's when things started to get lively. The senior NCOs, their wives and girlfriends, now full of Christmas cheer, all made for the dance floor and the room began to throb.

'Right, come on Jeff,' said Tony, making for the door.

Following behind, Jeff asked, 'Why, where are we going, mate?

'Up to the bar old, son, for a pint, it'll be just about empty now – they've all come down here.'

After a couple of very nice pints served by Corporal Jackson, the Steward, Tony said, 'Okay, Jeff, that's enough for now, mate, I think it's about time we went back down to the dining room for a check-up,' adding with a sly smile, 'and I want a word with long-legs Ruby.'

Leaving the bar, they heard a hell of a din coming from the dining room. 'Christ! Jeff, what the fuck's going on in there?' Tony said, breaking into a run.

Barging through the door they were confronted with what looked like a mad house; everybody stood with their backs to the wall looking shocked, and two men in the middle of the floor were knocking hell out of each other.

'Oh Christ, just look at 'em,' muttered Tony, pausing in the doorway and shaking his head in disgust. 'Makes me feel homesick; come on, Jeff.' He charged over towards the two pugilists.

Stepping between them and pushing them firmly but gently apart, he said in a friendly tone, 'Come on, gentlemen, let's cool it shall we?'

'Mind your own business, twat,' one of the obviously drunken sergeants yelled, as he tried to push past Tony, to get at the other chap.

Grabbing his wrists, Tony called to his mate, 'Grab that one, Jeff, but be careful, let's have 'em out, before they do any damage.' Eventually out in the passage, they cooled down somewhat, but being so drunk were still very aggressive.

'You're in trouble you two bastards, big trouble,' slurred one, prodding his finger into Tony's chest. 'I know who you are and I'm putting the pair of you on a charge for assaulting a senior officer.' He then slowly dropped back into one of the armchairs at the wall side and passed out.

The other one, although drunk himself, mumbled, swaying slightly, 'Take no notice of him, lad, he's pissed; you lads haven't done anything wrong. He'll

have forgotten all about it in the morning; silly bugger.'
He stared into nothing; then flopped down into a chair
alongside his opponent, a silly smile on his florid face.
The pair turned out to be the sergeants billeted on the
top landing, also known to be the best of mates.
Leaving the fighters snoozing where they'd fallen, the
two lads went back into the dining room; which was
once more buzzing with peaceful activity.

The first person they bumped into was Ruby,
carrying a tray full of empty glasses. 'Hello, darling,'
Tony whispered in her ear, as she walked past.

She gave him a coy look over her shoulder and
said, with a smile, 'You did a good job there with them
drunks, everybody gave a sigh of relief when you got
them out; they nearly frightened me to death, Tony.'

'Oh yes, darling, I always try my best to please.'
He winked at her. 'You come up to my bedding store
when you've finished at midnight, and I'll show you
how I do it.'

'You're a cheeky devil, Tony Ryan,' she said,
flushing. However, as she walked off she giggled, 'I'll
think about it.'

'Very smoothly done, Mr. Ryan,' said Jeff,
watching her tripping away through the crowd, with her
tray full of empty glasses.

Tony looked at with a conceited smile. 'Just keep
watching, Mr Baxter and you'll soon learn how to
handle women yourself. Come on now,' he said
sharply, 'we'd better have a walk around the Mess to
make sure everything's okay, you never know what
these drunken buggers could have got up to, the state
some of 'em are in.'

Later, as they were going into the bedding store,
Jeff said, 'Do you think we did right to ignore them

sergeants taking women into their bunks, Tony? We
had authority to stop it, you know.'

'Aye, why not, live and let live, Jeff, that's what I
say, mate. You wouldn't like some bugger to pull a
sexy female from under you, would you? Come on in,
and have a cup of char before you go back to your bed,
lad.'

Jeff followed him in. 'Well, I was just thinking
what Sergeant Pike would say if he knew; he told us no
women were allowed in the men's bunks after six
thirty, didn't he?'

'Yes he did, Jeff,' Tony replied in a bored voice, as
he filled the kettle, 'but he's not here is he, mate?
Anyway I'd be a bloody hypocrite if I'd have said
anything to them, when I'm hoping to do a little
entertaining in here myself tonight, wouldn't I, Jeff?'

'Oh, you mean Ruby, eh?' He grinned. 'Do you
think she'll come, then, Tony?'

'Oh yes, I'm sure she will,' he told him
confidently. 'They always come when Tony calls,
you'll see,' he assured him, passing him a cup of tea.
'Anyway, sup that up, mate and then bugger off – she
could be here any minute.'

As soon as Jeff left, Tony had a good wash and
dabbed a little after shave on his face in preparation for
when Ruby arrived – he knew what the women liked,
did Tony. After waiting on edge for about fifteen
minutes, he began to think he'd been let down; after
another ten he decided she wasn't coming and
concluded he'd have go to bed on his own. He'd just
taken off his shirt and was standing in front of the
mirror posing and admiring his muscles, when there
was a tapping on the door. His heart throbbed with
excitement. 'Coming, darling,' he called out. Opening

the door with a broad smile on his face, he said, 'Hi there, I was –' the words froze in his throat as he surveyed his visitor.

'You cheeky boy, you've been getting ready for me, have you? I've seen you eyeing me up all night,' she said, stroking his bare chest as she barged passed him into the room, and pushed the door shut behind her, with a bang.

The Yale lock clicked and Tony moved back, shocked. 'Oh, Sergeant McNabb, I'm surprised to see you at this time of night,' he said shakily. 'What can I do for you, Sergeant?'

Giving him a wink, she giggled. 'You know what you can do for me, you young devil.' Saying this, she stepped forward stroking his manly chest again with one hand, and slipped the other down the front of his pants. 'You get yourself all stripped off like this,' she continued, still stroking him, 'making yourself smell so nice,' she cooed, 'and then you ask a girl what you can do for her. Oh, you are a devil,' she whispered into his face. She flung one long arm around his neck, while still fumbling down the front of his trousers with the other one and started to manoeuvre him towards the bed. She was suddenly interrupted by another tapping on the door.

With a gasp of relief, Tony said, 'Someone at the door, Sergeant.'

Holding on to him as he tried to open it, she hissed, 'Bugger 'em, they'll go away.'
Struggling out of her stranglehold, he managed to lift the catch lock, and opening the door he saw Ruby standing there, looking beautiful. She'd obviously been making an effort to look her best, he could see that.

'What the hell are you doing here, Pritchard?' yelled Sergeant McNabb, coming to the door to see who it was that had disturbed her lusty desires.

Thinking fast, Tony said, 'I told ACW Pritchard to come up and collect the clean tablecloths for tomorrow, Sergeant; I noticed most of the tables were covered in spilt beer tonight and thought you'd be short of them for breakfast in the morning.'

Then going to the back of the store he slipped his shirt on and picking up two big parcels brought them back the door. 'I'd better carry them down for you, Pritchard, they're heavy,' he said, giving Ruby a wink behind her boss's back.

'Hurry back, Tony,' the sergeant said gruffly, 'but I can't see why Pritchard couldn't carry them herself,' she grumbled, glaring at poor Ruby standing there like a scared rabbit.

Seeing that she intended to remain in the store waiting for him to return, Tony said, 'I'm sorry, Sergeant, but my orders are, that only me and Sergeant Pike can stay in here on their own.'

'What the hell do you mean,' she yelled. 'Do you think I'm going to pinch your bloody blankets or something, man?'

'Sorry, Sergeant, but that's my orders,' he replied. 'I'm afraid I'll have to lock up when I leave,' he told her, apologetically.

Coming out into the passage glaring at poor Ruby, waiting in silence, she turned up the corridor heading away briskly for the women's wing. 'Well, if that's the case, then I'd better be off, hadn't I?' she called back, haughtily.

Tony face lit up into a smile, which soon faded.

Suddenly pausing, she turned and yelled out, 'You, Pritchard, had better come as well and get to your billet; he can manage to take them bloody cloths down, himself.'

As the two disappeared through the outside door, Tony marched off in the other direction loaded with tablecloths and mixed feelings of relief and frustration.

51

'What, you mean to say you refused the sexual favours of Sergeant McNabb, Tony?' Jeff said, laughing, the next morning. The two of them were clearing away the little temporary stage used by the musicians the previous night.

'Don't try to be funny, Baxter, it don't suit you,' snapped Tony, grumpily. 'It weren't no lark, I'll tell you; she was half drunk,' he moaned. 'The big cow, she got hold of my old man an'all, you know. I don't know what I'd have done if Ruby hadn't come just when she did,' he frowned and shook his head.

'You lost your chance with Ruby, an'all then, did you, mate?' Jeff said. He had stopped laughing, realising Tony was really perturbed by the experience.

'Of course I did, I've just told you, the drunken old bag made her leave with her, sent her back to her billet; anyway I explained to Ruby this morning what happened.'

'What did she say about it all, then?' he asked,

'Well, just as I expected, Jeff, she appeared to be as disappointed with the situation as I was.' He sighed. 'She said that the big bugger's been giving her hell this morning.' Regaining some of the usual confidence in his voice, he added, 'She's coming up tonight though, I told her I'd make her a nice nightcap.'

'I thought you said you had a steady girlfriend that you were serious about, though, Tony?' Jeff asked.

'I have, well I think I have,' he said. 'This is different though, it's only a bit of fun with Ruby, you know, a bit of slap and tickle,' he said, smiling. 'Anyway, she's engaged to be married next August,' he said, with a shrug.

'What, you mean to say she told you she's engaged to another poor bugger, and she's having bloody leg over with you,' he said, in disgust.

'Who said anything about getting leg over, Mr Baxter?' Tony smiled. 'I said she's coming up for a nightcap, didn't I? '

'Aye, but we all know what your nightcaps end up with, when there's a nice-looking bird involved, don't we?' Jeff said, grumpily.

'Don't be a bloody a prude, Baxter. You're only jealous, anyway how are you getting on with that little ginger bird down there in the kitchen, have you had her pants down yet?' He grinned.

'Don't be fucking crude, Tony, Betty's a decent girl. You wouldn't get your way with her, you know,' he said angrily.

Laughing, Tony replied, 'Do you want me to try, Mr Baxter just to make sure you're right?'

Ignoring him, Jeff said, 'What time shall we go over to our Mess for Christmas dinner then? I can't wait to get my teeth into one of them great big turkey legs.'

They hurried over to the Mess dining room, and were soon finishing off the first course of the big Christmas dinner.

'By, that were grand,' Tony sighed, 'I like a bit of turkey,' he added.

'Aye and served straight away,' replied Jeff.

'That's because there's hardly anyone to serve, it's nearly empty in here to day, or hadn't you noticed?' Tony grinned.

'Anyway, I told you what a good move it was to volunteer for Christmas duties if you remember,' he nodded. 'With only a skeleton staff on camp everything's simple, no hassle.'

'You were right this time, I'll give you credit there,' Jeff replied, pushing his plate back with a look of contentment. 'Are you ready for a nice big portion of Christmas pudding now, then?'

'No,' Tony replied, pulling a face. ' I don't push loads of stodgy rubbish like that in my stomach, mate – they put suet, sugar, and all sorts of shit in them puddings; I'd rather have a couple of apples or something like that,' he told him.

'Oh, faddy are we?' Jeff said, getting up from the table. 'Well, I'll go and get my portion of stodgy Christmas pudding, then.' Grinning as he made for the serving counter, he called back, 'I might as well get yours while I'm there, I'm sure I can manage two lots, seeing as it's Christmas.'

'Greedy bugger,' Tony smiled, shaking his head.

'Is everything to your satisfaction, airman?' he heard a soft nervous voice said behind him. Looking over his shoulder, Tony saw a small thin youth in the uniform of a Pilot Officer – it was the Orderly Officer on a routine mealtime inspection.

'Yes sir, everything was very nice,' he replied.

'Good, good' he said passing on to the next table.

'By, he's only a young lad, ain't he?' Jeff said coming back with two plates full of Christmas pudding on a tray; he only looks about fourteen, don't he?'

'Aye, he does, but he must be eighteen or he'd only be in the ATC,' Tony replied, glancing at the full tray Jeff had put down on the table. 'You greedy bugger,' he chuckled. 'You're not going to eat all that lot, are you? You'll bloody well bust.' Sitting there talking as Jeff got stuck into the first big plateful of Christmas pud, they were suddenly alerted by a loud disturbance coming from the kitchen behind the serving counter.

Almost at once a man came charging out yelling at the top of his voice, 'I'll kill the bastard, I'll kill the bastard.' He jumped over the counter with a meat cleaver in his hand.'

'Oh my God, it's Corporal Freeman, one of the cooks,' said Jeff. 'He's gone bloody mad by the look of him, he's going for the orderly officer with that bloody meat cleaver; he'll kill the poor little bugger, Tony.'

As the corporal came charging past their table, red-eyed and holding the cleaver aloft, in hot pursuit of the young officer, who was running for the door, terrified, Jeff jumped to his feet, picked up the big metal tray still holding one of the Christmas puddings, and smashed it full into the corporal's glaring face. Stopping dead in his tracks, he dropped the meat cleaver and fell back on his arse with a bang, the pudding temporarily blinding him. By now the flight sergeant in charge of the Mess had arrived with one of the other male staff, a big stout corporal. For a moment they stood alongside him, sitting there on the floor with custard running down his face, then one grabbed hold of him and dragged him to his feet, while the other took possession of his lethal weapon. By the main entrance door looking shocked, the young orderly officer saw that the man was being safely restrained by the two big men and walked across the hall towards them.

'Wow, he's for it now,' muttered Jeff. 'He deserves all he bloody well gets, an'all, I'm sure he'd have killed that lad if he'd got near him, Tony,' he said, shaking his head.

'Well, he certainly got your Christmas pudding, mate, didn't he?' chuckled Tony. 'Quick thinking, though, Jeff to use that metal tray like you did, mate, I must congratulate you there. I was baffled myself how to get at him with that bloody thing in his hands. I was going to trip him up as he went passed, then thump him, but you beat me to it, quick thinking, mate,' he repeated.

'Very sorry about this, Sir,' called out the sergeant, as the officer approached them. 'I'll ring the guardroom immediately, sir, and have this man arrested.'

Looking at the now very subdued man, held under restraint with his face covered in plum pudding and custard, the officer's expression took on a look of pity. 'No, don't do that Sergeant,' he said softly. 'This man is obviously not in control of his mental faculties; ring sick bay and tell them I say they've to send transport up for him, he must have a thorough examination.' He shook his head sympathetically, still looking at the pathetic trembling corporal.

'But are you sure, Sir, he could have killed you, Sir,' replied the astounded flight sergeant, staring back at him wide-eyed.

'Definitely,' he replied. 'I'm not pressing any charges, do as I say.' A hint of a smile crossed his face. 'After all, Flight Sergeant, it is Christmas Day, isn't it?'

He nodded in Jeff's direction and smiled. 'Oh, and I think you should ask that quick thinking airman over there, the one who sacrificed the second course of his meal on my behalf, if he would care for another portion of Christmas pudding.'

52

Feeling drowsy after their exiting Christmas dinner, the two had no alternative but to return to the Sergeants' Mess and continue cleaning up after the previous night's drunken festivities. They were still on duty of course – no relaxing for them. The afternoon was spent cleaning in general and collecting beer glasses left around by the over-indulgent residents, which were scattered around on shelves and window sills up and down the corridors. They were found even in the ablutions, mostly empty, but some partly full, left by people with eyes bigger than their bellies, according to Tony.

After a couple of hours tidying around, it was decided that it was time for a cup of tea. Heading for the bedding store, Jeff said, 'I wonder what was wrong with that cook, then, Tony? He looked to have gone bloody mad to me.'

'Aye, mad or not, he's a lucky bugger that young Officer let him off like that,' Tony replied. 'If Sergeant Priest in the guardroom had got his hands on him, he wouldn't have been so bloody lucky, I'll bet.'

'Christ, I'll say! He's a horrible bugger that man; everybody on the camp hates him, don't they?' Jeff said, pulling a face.

'I don't, he's only doing his job,' Tony replied, adamantly. 'I think he's a nice bloke, we often have a natter when we bump into each other around the Mess; he's got a right sense of humour him.'

'He doesn't live in the Mess, does he?' Jeff asked.

'No, he's got a semi on the new married quarters now,' Tony told him. 'I'll tell you what though, his wife's got a lovely arse, mate.' He grinned lustfully.

'Huh, trust you to notice that,' Jeff mumbled. 'You're bloody sex mad, you are, Ryan.'

'No, I'm not, Jeff. I'm just a fit young bloke who has a weakness for the ladies. Anyway, let's go and put that bloody kettle on, I'm gagging,' he said, with a laugh, as he unlocked the door.

'Aye, well, you'd better not let Sergeant Priest hear you talking about his wife's arse like that, or you won't be doing any more joking with him when he calls in the Mess.'

'Oh, shut it, Baxter, you're a bloody prude you are,' he said, with a laugh. 'I'll bet you have all sorts of dirty fantasies that you'd love to fulfill, if only you'd the nerve, eh?'

'That's what I mean, you see,' Jeff replied scornfully. 'You think everybody's the same as you Tony, if they're not they're prudes. Anyway, let's drop the bloody subject now,' he grunted. 'I'm fed up of arguing with you, you awkward sod, you're only taking the piss, I know that,' he said, as he filled the kettle. Will you be seeing your mate, Dave, when you go on leave then, Tony?' he asked, obviously determined to change the subject.

'No, he's taken Christmas leave, he's in the Marines, as I told you, he'll have spent it all in the Dog and Gun getting pissed, I suppose,' he said, with a laugh.

Suddenly, pausing for a second, he said, 'Blue devils! That's it, blue devils – that's what was up with that bugger that tried to cut the orderly officer up at dinner time, Jeff, I've just remembered. A bloke in the Dog went off like that once and Bernard floored him with a bottle of Bass; Bernard said afterwards that the bloke had blue devils.'

'Blue devils?' enquired Jeff, looking baffled. 'What the bloody hell is that, Tony, is it a fever or something?'

'No it's nowt like that you silly bugger,' he replied. 'Bernard, the landlord at the Dog, said he's seen quite a bit of it, especially at holiday times. It's when a bloke is on the piss and gets sodden in whisky and strong stuff like that, Bernard said; their body can't get rid of it as fast as they're shoving it in and their brain goes, they just go bloody mad. I saw the one that Bernard dropped with the bottle of bass and he was really gone, just like that bugger in the dining hall today,' he said, nodding.

'Well, let's hope you're not haunted with any blue devils in the Dog and Gun when you go home for your New Year, mate,' said Jeff. 'By the way,' he continued in a more sombre tone, 'have you heard anything from that Becky of yours, lately?'

'Aye, a Christmas card and a letter the other day,' he moaned. 'She just said the usual, that she loved me and was still trying to get a posting back here, but I don't know what to think,' he said, frowning gloomily.

'Well, if she loves you and she's trying her best to get another home posting – you should be pleased,' Jeff told him cheerfully.

'Aye, well, we'll see,' Tony mumbled. 'I don't know mate, but I've been hurt before as I told you and I don't want any more of it.'

'Oh, I think you're looking on the black side of things again, Tony. Anyway, mate, you've always got Sergeant McNabb to fall back on.' Laughing, he added, 'Literally.'

'I'll bloody do for you, Baxter,' Tony yelled out, pretending to be angry, and made a grab for his collar.

Dodging and still grinning, Jeff said, 'No, but seriously, Tony, I do think you're looking on the black side; you want to cheer yourself up and go and have a good time at home – you'll come back seeing life a lot brighter. Who knows – that other beautiful lady from your past, might be home for the New Year celebrations.'

Without commenting on this, Tony turned to pour himself another cup of tea, and stood in silence staring down at the table top for several seconds.

'What would you do mate, if she was home?' Jeff asked, breaking the silence. 'Do you still love her, Tony?' He sounded genuinely concerned. 'You can tell me to mind my own business if you like,' he added.

Without turning, Tony replied quietly, 'Oh yes, yes, Jeff, I'm afraid I do, I always will.'

'And what about Becky then, Tony, if you still love Peggy so much,' he asked.

'That's the big weight on my mind, Jeff,' he replied, turning to him with a strained look on his face. 'I love them both like hell, I'd die for either of 'em', he whispered, his eyes filling with tears.

53

Feeling knackered as he signed in at the guardroom, on his return to camp from his New Year's leave, Tony felt he'd had enough. He'd travelled by rail down from Leeds, on a slow train that stopped at nearly every station on the way. It was so crowded that he'd stood in the passage for the whole journey, alongside a group of sobering up corporals, who were continually letting off high pitched farts of foul beery aroma.

Adjusting his greatcoat and cap, he walked smartly away from the guardroom, making his way across the public road into the main gates of the domestic section opposite. The footpath alongside the private road within at this part of the camp was raised about three feet, and bordered by a grass verge that sloped down to the road. Suddenly he heard the band strike up, then through the trees ahead he saw it coming marching off the square, followed by the morning parade. This consisted of three flights of airmen, each flight headed by a corporal, with the whole group being led out front by a tall, very smart, olive skinned squadron leader of Middle Eastern origin. As the parade got nearer, with the band playing a lively march, Tony did the correct thing; stopped in his tracks, and coming to attention, smartly brought his right arm up to salute the parade and held it as the column advanced towards him.

However, to his amazement, instead of just marching past ignoring him – as was the rule, the squadron leader at the front did a very smart 'eyes right', and returned the hand salute to Tony as he stood to attention on the raised foot path. Furthermore, the whole parade followed his gesture with a sharp 'eyes right'. This would have been appropriate, of course, when passing a group of high ranking officers, on an inspection or similar, but never a very tired AC1 with his knap sack on his back returning from leave, slightly bedraggled. However, Tony held his salute until all the parade had passed. He felt like a wing commander, or even of higher rank. I bet Becky will never believe I took the morning parade with full ceremony when I tell her, he thought, as he stood there proudly.

Tony, back on duty after lunch, walked into the Sergeants' Mess ready for his afternoon's work. He was immediately cheered by the sight of Ruby, who gave him a beaming smile. She waiting at the tables of the late diners, and when she'd delivered the food, he nodded and smiled back, but before he could speak to her, a voice rang out from behind him.

'Ryan! I want a word with you, come here, man, and hurry up.'

Spinning around, he was confronted by Sergeant Riley, walking slowly towards him and scowling menacingly. 'Don't you ever learn, Ryan,' he said as they met. 'You're in trouble this time, man, I'll tell you,' he growled.

Looking back at him with a look of exasperation, Tony enquired, 'What's the problem, Sergeant? I don't know what you mean.'

'Insubordination!' he yelled, glaring into Tony's face. 'You've completely ignored what I complained about last time I had to reprimand you, regarding hygiene on my wing. Disrespect for a superior officer that's what it sums up to,' he snapped, 'and you're going to pay for it now, man. I intend to put you on a 252 for this insult to my rank, do you understand?' he hissed into Tony's baffled face.

Genuinely wondering what the man was on about Tony replied, 'No, Sergeant, I'm afraid I don't, would you mind enlighten me, please?'

His eyes standing out with anger, he replied, 'There you go again, trying to be smart, you know bloody well what I'm on about, man, it's the same thing I had to complain about the last time, negligence. Those window sills and shelves on my landing haven't been cleaned for the last three days, the bloody dust on them is a foot thick, and I think you've done this just to spite me.'

Just then, seeing Sergeant Pike coming through the door, Tony called out, 'Excuse me, 'Sergeant Pike, have you a minute, please?'

Coming over, smiling, the Sergeant said, 'Oh, hello, Ryan; had a good time, then?'

'Yes, thanks, Sergeant,' Tony replied, then gesturing at the other sergeant, he said courteously, 'I gather from Sergeant Riley here, that there's been some negligence with regard to the cleaning on the top landing, while I've been on leave, Sergeant.'

A look of annoyance crossed his superior's face as he glared at the now puzzled looking Sergeant Riley. 'What the hell are you on about, Sergeant Riley? I've been checking up on the cleaning myself over the New Year, while Ryan has been away; don't you dare say I'm negligent regarding cleanliness in this Mess.'

'Well no, no, Cyril, I'm not insinuating that,' Riley spluttered. 'It was just that I noticed some dust on the window sills up there.'

Fuming now and showing it, Pike yelled angrily, 'Well, it must have accumulated in the past hour then; I did my morning inspection just before I went for my dinner and the whole area up there was pristine, then.'

Turning to go he added, curtly, 'So if it's that important to you, Sergeant Riley, go and dust the bloody window sill yourself.'

54

'Well, you should have seen his face, Jeff, when he realised that I'd just come back off leave, and when old Pike told him he'd just inspected up there himself, I nearly pissed myself, mate.

Laughing, as he rubbed away at the greasy sink he was cleaning, Jeff said, 'I bet that took the wind out of his sails, Tony. What did he say when Pike flew at him like that?'

'Nowt,' said Tony, laughing. 'He was too shocked, I think. I've been up to have a look since, and everything up there's polished like glass. Ted and the lads did a very thorough job on it this morning as far as I can see.'

'One thing's for sure, mate,' Jeff said, 'he definitely don't like you for some reason or other.' Pausing in his polishing for a moment, he said casually, 'unless he's a bloody closet queen, Tony, and he fancies you.'

'You: what?' Tony yelled. 'You mean he might be some sort of a pervert, a bloody poof?'

'Well, it's possible, he might hate you because he fancies you,' Jeff replied with a shake of his head. 'It's been known before, you know, and also for men to be married with a family and be like that.'

'Oh, I don't know much about them,' Tony said pulling a face.

'Oh aye,' went on Jeff knowingly, 'some keep it a secret all their lives; mind you, some of them really like women as well as men, you know.'

'Huh, I didn't know that, Jeff,' he grunted. 'I thought they just went around flogging their arse to any dirty bugger that would have it.' A stern look crossed his face. 'I'll tell you this, mate, if he is like that, and he comes near me, I'll bloody well drop him there and then, stripes or no bloody stripes.'

'Now then, who's the poor bugger you're going to drop, Yorky?' called out Sergeant Banks, coming through the door stripped to the waist, with a towel around his shoulders.'

'Oh, hello there, Sergeant,' Tony replied, turning to face him with a smile. 'How's Doncaster then, have you had a good New Year – plenty of good old Yorkshire ale down your neck, eh?'

'Oh, aye,' he said, laughing. 'Went to a mate's party on New Year's Eve and got pissed. Ten pints of Tetley's best, by God, but I paid for it next morning. Anyway, who's the poor bugger you're contemplating to drop then, Yorky, and why?' he asked cheerfully, as he filled the sink.

Realising the strong geographical bond of friendship he shared with the other Yorkshire man, Tony went over to him as he was scrubbing his hands and told him about the latest dusty encounter he'd had with Riley, and what his mate Jeff thought could be the cause of his uncalled for treatment by the nasty sergeant.

Sergeant Banks didn't say anything for a moment when Tony had finished explaining, and then looking thoughtful, he said in a low voice, 'Well, Yorky, your mate there could be right; there's something funny about the man to find fault with you all the time, when it's obvious there's nowt wrong. I mean take that bird shit on the window for instance, that was on the outside of the glass, it was clearly easy to see that.'

'Yes, and all this invisible dust,' called out Jeff from the other side of the room, as he polished away.

'I'll tell you what Yorky,' Sergeant Banks went on, without acknowledging Jeff's intrusion. 'I'll put some discrete feelers out around the Mess, see if I can find 'owt about him being inclined that way. Mind you,' he said, 'I know he's got a lovely little girl friend, he's been going out with her for over a year.' He grinned at Tony. 'Anyway, Yorky, don't get yourself worried about it, he wouldn't dare do anything to you even if he is one of them: he'd get kicked out of the service if even he tried.'

Scowling, Tony replied, 'Aye, they would if they could find him, believe me there'd be nowt left of him to chuck out of the service, Jerry, if he tried owt like that on me, I'll tell you. By the way talking about women,' Tony went on, with a grin, 'who was the little beauty you were entertaining in your bunk after the dance on Christmas Eve, Sergeant Banks?'

'Oh, you saw her, then,' he replied, surprised. 'That was Molly, she's one of my clerks down in the transport office.'

'Aye, of course I saw her, you weren't on your own entertaining either,' Tony said with a laugh, 'believe me nearly every other bunk in the Mess had a nice bird residing in it that night.'

'And you didn't say owt, Yorky, eh?' Jerry replied, with a smile. 'Pike's very keen about not allowing women in the bunks after six thirty in the evening. I'd have thought that would have been his orders.'

Laughing, as he resumed his polishing, Tony said, 'They were his orders of course, Sergeant Banks, but he wasn't there, was he?' Still laughing, he said, 'Anyway, I'd have thought myself a bit of a hypocrite to uphold it under the circumstances.'

Jerry shot him a quick sideways glance, accompanied by a sly smile. 'Oh, I see what you mean, Yorky – you stayed in the Mess right over the Christmas period, didn't you?'

'Yes, I did, Sergeant,' Tony replied with mock formality, 'but I was on duty don't forget, and I don't believe in mixing business with pleasure.'

'I'll bet you don't, you bugger,' grinned the Yorkshire sergeant, knowingly.

Later, Sergeant Pike passed Tony and Jeff walking along the top landing with mop buckets in hand. 'Oh, Ryan!' he called out. 'Will you call into my office when you've finished what you're doing; I want a word with you about parade duties.'

'Yes, Sergeant, will do,' he called back, without interrupting his stride.

'What do you think he wants you for this time, Tony, sounds like something to do with that big annual job that's coming up next weekend, don't it?' Jeff said.

'Yes, I'm sure that's what it is,' replied Tony in a matter of fact tone. 'It's a very big do, you know, the Air Officers' Parade.' No doubt old Pike will want me to help him pick out a couple of us lads to send, as he did on the Church Parade just before Christmas.'

'Well, don't let the old bugger pick me this time if you can help it, Tony,' Jeff said firmly. 'The Church parade only lasts for about half an hour, but this bloody thing is a full morning job. It'll be fucking murder marching up and down the runway all togged up, for that length of time; apart from that, think about all the bull shit involved for preparation.'

'Don't worry, old son,' laughed Tony. 'I'll tell him we can manage the work here without two of the others this time.'

'Come in,' shouted Pike in his usual authoritarian voice, when he heard the light tap on his office door.

'Well, we've got everything done up there now, Sergeant,' Tony said cheerfully as he walked in. 'We'll make a start on the downstairs after dinner.'

'Good show, Ryan,' he replied, with a smile. 'Now then, about the Air Officers' Parade: it's next Friday morning, as you no doubt know, and as you appreciate, I'm obliged to send two of my men to take part.'

'Oh yes, I'm aware of that sergeant,' Tony replied in a confident voice. 'I suggest West and Jones, Sergeant; they're both very good at foot drill.'

Pausing for a moment, the Sergeant replied, 'No doubt, no doubt Ryan, but this is a very special event, the Air Officer in command is a very important man and this is a very important annual parade.' Pausing momentarily, as though thinking how best to put it, he went on, 'Consequently, we must contribute the *best* personnel we've got, Ryan, you must see that.'

'Of course I do, Sergeant, that's why I suggested West and Jones; two very smart chaps them,' he said, with a nod.

'Yes, they are, I must agree,' he replied, 'but as I said, we must send the *very* best, Ryan on this one.'

Smiling he went on, 'That's why I think on a big important job like this, you should go yourself, Ryan, you can take any one of the others you choose; I'll leave that to you.'

55

'Stop your bloody laughing and piss-taking, Baxter, don't forget what I told you. Pike said I could pick any one of you lot I wanted to join me; if you're not careful I'll bloody well pick you,' he told him grumpily.

They were having dinner in the Airmen's Mess discussing the big forthcoming parade, when Jeff suddenly glanced across the table behind Tony and stopped eating abruptly. 'Look who's just walked in,' he said urgently.

Turning on his seat, Tony muttered, 'Well, well, if it isn't our friend, big Sam, the ginger giant; I haven't ever seen him in here before.' As he spoke the big man caught sight of him; in the brief moment that their eyes met, Tony could see a burning look of hatred oozing from him, however he continued on his way to the serving counter without incident.

'Did you see the look he gave me, Jeff? If looks could kill they'd be carrying me out of here now on a stretcher.' Tony forced a short laugh and continued to eat. However, inside he knew he'd have to keep on his guard, with a man like that bearing him a grudge.

'It's the first time I've seen him since we moved out of that block across the square when you knocked him out, Tony.' Jeff laughed. 'He most likely thinks you're going to do it again,' he said, still laughing.

'Don't underestimate him, Jeff,' Tony said seriously. He glanced across at the man, whose broad back was to them as he was being served his meal. 'That guy could be very dangerous, he's a professional wrestler don't forget. Just look at the size of the bugger, he must be at least six foot four and a lean seventeen stone plus.'

'You've no need to bother about that, mate, you easy sent him to the land of nod before, I'm sure you'd easy do it again,' Jeff said confidently, as he ate.

'As I said, don't underestimate him, Jeff, it was more luck than anything else that time,' Tony told him, glancing at the big figure now walking away from the counter with a tray full of food.

'I just happened to catch him unawares by stamping on his foot, then followed it up quick, before he realised. I'll tell you what, mate,' he added, 'I won't be looking for any bother with him if I can avoid it, I'll tell you that, old son.'

'Well, this is the first time I've seen the guy since the day we moved out of that block he lives in,' repeated Jeff. 'To tell you the truth, I thought he'd been posted or something.'

'Oh, I've seen him regularly up at the gym,' replied Tony, 'but he's never caught sight of me; the workout room where I train is separate from the main hall and he's always out there on the mats, training his wrestling lads. He most likely uses the weights sometimes, but we've never bumped into each other up to now,' he said. 'Anyway, bugger him,' he went on, pushing his empty plate away and getting to his feet. 'We'd better get back to the Mess; old Pike will be on the war path if we're late today, we've got to prepare the bar for that little party tonight, don't forget.'

'How could I forget? The old bugger's been going on about it all week, ain't he?' Jeff sniggered.

56

'Christ I'm knackered, I thought I'd finished with bloody square bashing when I left Padgate,' said Tony, walking into the billet the following Monday dinner time, after three hours on the square, practising for the big parade.

Jeff, was sitting on his bed waiting for him. 'It'll do you good, mate, you were getting soft, but don't forget I did my turn before Christmas on that Church Parade.'

'Huh, that was a picnic compared to this bugger,' scoffed Tony. 'You'd no rehearsals to do for that and the parade itself only lasted about half an hour anyway. We've got another two practise sessions this week before the big do on Friday, an'all,' he added, flopping down on his bed with a sigh.

'Come on, get off that bed and stop pitying yourself, you lazy bugger,' said Jeff, laughing. 'I'm starving; let's get over for some dinner.'

Later that afternoon, he was busy cleaning the glass panels in the bar room door and feeling a bit browned off, when he heard the sound of Ruby's voice.

'I saw you on the square this morning, Tony, as I was coming back from my dental appointment down at sick quarters,' said Ruby, going up to him coyly.

Tony was instantly cheered up. 'Oh, did you, darling,' he replied, pausing in his work. 'And what did you think then, did you like what you saw, love?' He gave her a cocky grin.

'Oh, you looked lovely, Tony,' she told him, smiling shyly. 'You looked so smart and elegant, marching across the square in your best blue uniform.'

'I stood out from the others then, did I, Ruby, darling?' he replied proudly.

The conversation got no further. 'Ryan! I want a word with you, come here, man,' a voice called out from the end of the corridor. It was Sergeant Riley, all dressed up in his best blue uniform, with his usual sour expression on his face; the sight of him was enough to finish Tony's day.

'Oh, my God,' he muttered and Ruby turned and slunk back to the kitchen.

Later on, he met Jeff in the dining room, and told him all about it.

'What, you mean he's had you again, mate, what was his complaint this time, then?'

'Mucky bath in the top ablutions,' Tony replied, 'I said I'd go straight up there and clean it, but he said he'd had to do it himself before he could have a bath.'

'Aye, he told you that because there was no mucky baths up there,' Jeff said angrily. 'Me and Ted did that place out like a new pin this morning, he's just wanting to find something to get at you for, mate, he's a fucking nutcase,' he said shaking his head in disgust.

'Bugger that silly twat,' Tony said, smiling. 'I've just got a letter from Becky; she's made an application for a transfer to this camp; failing that, to any camp in this county. She says she doesn't mind where it is so long as we can get together, even if it's only now and again; she said she's missing me so much.'

'Great, Tony,' he smiled. 'I told you it would work out okay; do you think she'll be successful, then?'

'Well, she says she's trying on compassionate grounds this time, her dad's been in and out of hospital all this year with ulcers or something, and she thinks that might help,' he told him hopefully.

'Well the best of luck to her then, mate,' Jeff said. 'I'm longing to meet her, Tony; she sounds a right nice girl.'

'That's an understatement as far as I'm concerned, Jeff, but wait till you hear this mate,' he said excitedly. 'She sat her promotion exam last week and if that goes okay, she'll get her crown,' he told him proudly.

'Bloody hell, a flight sergeant at her age, that's an achievement I must say, Tony,' Jeff said, shaking his head.

'Well, I suppose it is really, but it's a thing to be expected from a girl like Becky, with the education she's had,' Tony boasted nonchalantly. 'She's never had any other job you know, Jeff; she went straight from college into the Service.'

'Watch out, here comes our lord and master,' whispered Jeff, nodding towards the door.

'Hello, chaps,' called out Pike, as he approached them. 'Everything going all right, then?' he enquired in his usual brisk manner. Without waiting for an answer he said, 'By the way, Ryan, how did the rehearsal on the square go this morning?'

'Oh, fine, Sergeant,' Tony replied cheerfully. 'You should have been with us; it was a nice feeling to be back in military guise again after all this domesticity.'

'Was it?' he said, after a slight pause. 'I would have volunteered obviously, but with all the responsibility in here, I can't indulge in such luxuries.' Saying this, he marched briskly away towards the kitchen, calling out to one of the other cleaners in his path.

'I think you shamed him there, Tony,' said Jeff, watching him speedily walking away.

'He bloody well deserves it, he was happy enough to get me out there, wasn't he?' Tony said. 'By the way Jeff, I forgot to tell you, he told me yesterday that he's got one of them new houses they've built on the extension of the married quarters estate. He said his wife and kids are moving down here this weekend, so we should be shot of him for a few days, while he's busy moving them in there,' he chuckled.

'Huh, that'll be a Godsend, anyway,' Jeff replied. Looking at his watch, he added 'How about going up to your place, Tony for a cup of tea; we've nothing more to do here now.'

Later, they were in the bedding store drinking tea and discussing their favourite subject – women, when there was a tap on the half-closed door and Ted West burst in. He was red-faced and smiling nervously, holding aloft a pair of green silk, lace trimmed, French knickers.   'Just look here,' he called out waving them in front of the two other lads, 'I've never known anything like it.'

The pair sat looking back at him for a moment with baffled expression, then Tony started to laugh and said, 'What's the idea, West, coming in here waving your fancy underwear in front of us like that – showing off as usual, are you?'

'These aren't mine,' West replied scowling. 'I found the buggers in the waste bin outside little Warrant Officer Keyes' bunk on the top floor; they were wrapped in an old newspaper to hide 'em,' he said.

'Well you can keep 'em if you want, Ted, if you like that sort of thing,' Jeff laughed.

'I prefer 'em when there's a nice arse inside 'em,' Tony said, grinning. 'A woman's, of course,' he added hastily.

Going redder still, as the other two sat laughing their heads off at his expense, Ted replied angrily, 'I don't bloody well want 'em, and stop taking the piss you lot, what do you think I am – one of them bloody poof boys?'

'Well, green does suit you, Ted, you must admit that,' Tony told him, accompanied by more loud laughter from the pair.

Throwing the fancy garment down on the table in front of them, Ted turned and stamped out, telling them where they could go.

'Do you want us to send them to the laundry for you with the other things, then, Ted?' Tony called after him. The request got the same instructions as before, which was followed by more raucous laughter.

'Oh dear, poor old Ted,' sighed Jeff, as their laughter died down, 'I think we might have upset him, Tony.'

'He'll get over it,' Tony replied, his laughter petering out. 'I wonder though, Jeff, if that little Warrant Officer Keyes up there does wear fancy knickers like them under his trousers? I saw him on the square this morning; he was in charge of one of the flights.' Laughing again, he said, 'I can just imagine him marching around giving orders on the A.O.C.'s parade at the weekend with a pair of them on, can't you?' The laughter again got so loud that they failed to hear footsteps marching briskly up the corridor.

'Now, what's so funny then?' asked Sergeant Pike, striding briskly through the door. He saw the bright green garment on the table and paused, then picked it up and examined it thoroughly.

'What have we here, then?' he said, holding the frilly knickers aloft and glaring at the two, now solemn-faced, airmen. 'Come on, then,' he went on frowning at the knickers, 'who brought these in, Ryan? I thought all the laundry from the female wing went through the general women's block for laundering; you only handle the men's in here, don't you?'

'That's right, Sergeant,' replied Tony in dutiful tone, 'but that garment doesn't belong to any of the female residents, Sergeant; it was left in here by AC West.'

Looking back at him dumfounded for a second he yelled, 'What! You mean to say these ladies frilly knickers belong to AC West; you don't mean that he wears this sort of thing do you, Ryan?'

'Well, I don't know what he wears under his trousers, Sergeant,' Tony replied, straight-faced, but bursting to laugh – as was Jeff, 'but I assure you he brought them in just before you arrived.'

Still holding them out at arm's length and scrutinising them minutely, the now exasperated little sergeant said authoritatively, 'Anyway, he's not allowed to put his personal laundry through the Mess, so you'd better give them back to him, Ryan, and I'll have a quiet word with him about this matter.' Saying this he threw the knickers down on the table and marched smartly out of the store. As the Sergeant's footsteps died away down the corridor, the two piss-takers exploded in mirth.

'Hope we haven't put poor old West in the shit, Tony,' Jeff said, wiping his eyes. 'Poor bugger, he won't know what to say when old Pike asks him why he wears French knickers.'

'We didn't tell any lies about him, Jeff, 'Tony stated, piously. 'He did bring them in, didn't he? Seriously, Jeff, I wonder if that little dandy, Warrant Officer Keyes, really does wear them things under his uniform, when he's on parade?'

'I don't know, mate, but every time I see him now walking about with his arse stuck out, I'll be wondering if he has a pair on.' With that the laughter recommenced.

57

'Ryan, can I have a word?' called out Pike, as Tony walking into the Mess the following morning. 'Catastrophe, Ryan,' he said, as Tony approached. 'Catastrophe,' he repeated. 'Some silly drunken bugger has pulled down the curtains on the big window on the top landing. They've broken the rail and all the fittings an'all, it's a bloody mess,' he said, shaking his head with a look of desperation on his face.

'Don't worry, Sergeant,' Tony told him reassuringly. 'I'll go and get one of the other chaps, we'll soon have it sorted out; have they damaged the curtains themselves?' he asked.

'No, I don't think so,' Pike replied, 'apart from beer stains. They'll want changing of course,' he added, with renewed authority.

'No problem there, Sergeant. We've got a clean replacement in stock; I'll get the situation sorted out immediately.' He turned and walked briskly away up the corridor. Meeting Jeff standing outside the bedding store, Tony informed him of the crisis, and told him to proceed to the damage zone and start taking the beer-splashed curtains down. He added that he himself would sort out the replacements and follow as soon as possible. After having a leisurely cup of tea and a few biscuits, Tony picked up the replacement curtains and made set off to join his mate. Going up the wide stairway, he saw that the soiled curtains had been taken down, but there was no sign of Jeff. Reaching the top he heard the sound of scuffling and cursing coming from the ablutions further along the passage. Dropping the replacement curtain on the window sill, he charged towards the disturbance; rushing into the ablutions he saw Jeff and Ted West rolling on the floor locked in combat, both cursing and swearing at each other.

'Stop it, you silly buggers,' Tony yelled, grabbing each by their arm and hauling them to their feet – still trying to get at each other. 'Don't you realise you'll end up in the guardhouse, if any of the residents come in here and see you acting like this,' he hissed.

'He started it!' yelled Jeff. 'He flew at me as soon as he saw me, he's fucking mad.'

'It's all right for you two piss-taking buggers,' Ted snarled angrily, shaking himself loose from Tony's grip. 'I've just had a long lecture from Sergeant Pike, offering me help and advice.' he told them with venom in his voice.

'Well, what's that got to do with us, Ted, what's it about anyway?' Tony asked innocently.

'You know what about, Ryan,' he replied, curling his lip. 'You are nothing more than a bunch of rotten swine, the pair of you. Do you realize that Pike thinks I'm some sort of a pervert? You led him to think that I'm one of them blokes that cross-dress; he offered to get me help to overcome the habit, he wouldn't believe me when I denied it.' Turning, he rushed out into the passage, obviously very upset; in fact almost in tears.

Tony and Jeff stood looking at each other in silence as he left. 'We've let this go too far, mate,' Tony said quietly, staring after him.

'I agree,' he replied with genuine sympathy. 'He's in a right state with it, isn't he, but what the hell can we do about it now? After all it was only a joke.'

'Yes, it was, Jeff and come to think about it not a very nice one, so the only thing we can do now is to try and undo the damage we've done.'

'I agree,' he replied, 'but what shall we do, Tony?'

'Come on, I'll show you and no time like the present,' he said making for the door. 'Let's go and get this thing sorted out before it escalates any further.'

Following in his wake, Jeff enquired, 'How do you mean, Tony, where are we going?'

'As I said, we're going to try and undo the damage we've done by being thoughtless,' he repeated, hurrying along the corridor without turning. 'We're going to explain everything to Sergeant Pike, and hope he's in a bloody good mood.'

'Come in,' Pike called out from behind his desk, when Tony tapped lightly on his office door, which was slightly ajar. 'Hello chaps, everything going smoothly up there?' he asked, smiling as they entered.

'Yes, fine, Sergeant, we've got it all in hand now, we'll have it finished within the hour.' Tony returned the smile and paused momentarily as he considered how to continue. Faltering slightly, he went on, 'Sergeant, er – we haven't come to see you about the window, it's about AC West, Sergeant,' he said, looking nervously down at his boots.

'Don't be so worried about him, Ryan,' he replied, looking up from behind the desk, smiling. 'I've had a quiet word with him about his weakness; it's nothing really, you know,' he said, condescendingly. 'I've seen this before on several occasions,' he added, nodding slowly.

'Yes, oh yes, I understand that, Sergeant,' replied Tony, giving Jeff a quick nervous glance. 'The point is Sergeant, West is not like that; it's all been a big mistake, it's all my fault, Sergeant,' he told him, looking him in the eye.

Holding eye contact for a moment with a blank look on his face, Sergeant Pike said, 'Your fault, Ryan? I don't understand, how do you mean, man, your fault?'

'I was just as much to blame, Sergeant,' interrupted Jeff.

'Ignoring the interruption, Tony replied. 'I failed to fully explain to you the situation regarding the French knickers, when you came into the bedding store yesterday. They weren't the personal possession of AC West. He found them in one of the waste bins on the top landing; he'd brought them in to ask me what to do with them.' The sergeant sat staring up at him as Tony continued, 'It's my fault, Sergeant. I let you think the worst about West, it was a sick joke, which I now regret. I've no excuse, but I couldn't let it go any further,' he said, with genuine sincerity. Staring down at the floor for a moment, he continued firmly, 'I personally accept full responsibility, Sergeant Pike.' He stood smartly to attention and awaited the deserved reprimand.

Sergeant Pike sat in silence for several seconds, tapping on the desk top with his pencil and staring at the two before him –Tony, standing to attention with an expectant look on his face and Jeff, slightly behind him, pale and anxious.

'Well, so that's the situation then is it?' Pike eventually said. 'I think you're both equally to blame for this stupid schoolboy prank, causing not only your colleague to be humiliated, but also me to look like a bloody fool trying to help him with advice which was not needed.'

He got to his feet and leant forward, his palms flat on the desk top and stared into their faces. 'However,' he continued, 'You've shown strength of character by coming to explain your stupidity and for that I'm willing to overlook the matter, on this occasion. Of course, you'll appreciate I'll have to have another talk with AC West and explain to him your stupid, childish behaviour.'

'Yes, Sergeant, thank you, Sergeant,' said Tony, still at attention.

'Thank you, Sergeant,' agreed Jeff, humbly.

Shaking his head, sitting down again, Pike said curtly, 'Go on, get on with your work and no more school boy pranks or you'll both be for it, do you understand?'

'Yes, Sergeant,' they both called out, turning to leave.

'By the way, Ryan,' he called after them. 'If you see AC West up there, ask him if he would come down here when he's got a free moment, I'd like a quick word with him. I'd better let the poor chap know it was all the doing of you two fools,' he muttered, continuing with his desk work.

'Phew, that was a close shave,' Jeff whispered, as they walked down the corridor away from the office. 'He could have put us on a fizzer for that, you know.'

'Aye, I know that,' Tony replied. 'We'd have bloody well deserved it an'all, the distress we caused poor old Ted.'

Jeff made no reply as they ascended the stairs back to the task in hand. They'd no sooner started on it, when Eddy Jones came walking along the corridor towards them, with a very serious expression on his face, concealing something inside his jacket.

'Ryan, look what I've found,' he whispered as he reached them. 'They were in the waste bin outside Warrant Officer Keyes' bunk.' As he spoke, he pulled out a bright red, rolled up garment and glanced over his shoulder to make sure nobody was coming. He held it out at arm's length before him. It was another lady's undergarment, more ostentatious than the last that Ted West had found.

'Oh, my God!' moaned Tony, seeing the pair of frilly cami-knickers being waved in front of him. 'Put the bloody things away, Jones, for Christ's sake.'

'Well, what shall I do with 'em then? They were all wrapped up in newspaper,' he said wide-eyed.

'You can do what the fuck you like with 'em,' Tony told him, as Jeff stood laughing. 'Chuck 'em back in the bin you found 'em in, or as far as I'm concerned you can wear the bloody things yourself, Jones,' he yelled, turning away from the lad.

As poor Jones walked meekly off, stuffing the bright garment back under his jacket, Tony mumbled, shaking his head, 'Christ, this place is getting like a bloody ladies' lingerie shop.'

'I reckon we ought to see if we can find anything out about old WO Keyes, Tony,' Jeff said, with a frown. 'It's a bit unusual for the lads to keep finding women's fancy knickers on the male wing, you know; you can't blame 'em for being a bit surprised.'

Thinking for a moment, he replied, 'Well, as I see it, Jeff, it's just a matter of an old bloke that likes to wear that sort of thing for some kinky reason or other, as Sergeant Pike told us, there's a lot of them about.'

'That's fair enough, mate,' Jeff replied, nodding seriously, 'but I should think a bloke like that would normally want to conceal his secret perversion, not flaunt it. I mean, putting the bloody things outside his own bunk and in his own waste bin, it's obvious who they belonged to, ain't it?

'True, true,' agreed Tony, 'but what the hell can we do about it, mate, it's not a crime for a bloke to wear ladies' fancy knickers in private, you know.'

'I know that,' Jeff replied firmly, 'but it's not quite the thing to openly leave them scattered about the place in a male section of a Sergeants' Mess, Tony. I'm half inclined to ask the advice of Sergeant Pike about it,' he stated arrogantly. 'I mean look at the hassle we've just had with the green pair, and then, within minutes of getting out of that trouble, Jones appears with a similar pair of red ones.'

'I agree with you, it's a bit out of order,' said Tony, 'and I know you – a bloody old prude who don't like the sight of sexy knickers lying about.'

'I'm not a prude, Ryan, you know it,' Jeff interrupted angrily. 'I like ladies' knickers but in their right place,' he grunted.

'Oh, don't say you like wearing them an'all, Jeff,' Tony ribbed him. 'Anyway, mate, I don't want Pike being consulted about it,' he said. 'I'll find out about old Keyes through other channels. Hang on Jeff,' he said suddenly. 'I've just had a brilliant idea about how to capitalise on them bins; there's easy money going to waste there, boy.' He winked.

Jeff's ears pricked up when heard this; the thought of making money had always been attractive to him. 'How do you mean, Tony,' he asked eagerly. 'How can we make money by finding a couple of pairs of knickers?'

Tony delayed his reply for a few seconds until he'd finished an intricate part of the curtain hanging, and then looked at him thoughtfully. 'I'm thinking more than knickers, Jeff lad, they just gave me the idea. No,

I'm thinking about a bit of general dealing, mate: 'owt we can find.' He grinned. 'Interested?'

'Of course I am, if there's money in it, Tony.' he replied with enthusiasm. 'What have you in mind?'

'Simple,' he said, with a superior smile on his face. 'You get the lads to look through all the bins in the Mess as they go about their duties; anything that looks worth 'owt, tell 'em to bring it to the bedding store; mind you, tell 'em not to let Pike see anything,' he added hastily.

'But what do you think we'll find of any value, Tony?' he asked.

'Look mate, Tony replied seriously. 'Forget the knickers now, joke's over. I'm talking about serious business now. Haven't you ever noticed that the blokes in here chuck lots of bloody good gear out into them waste bins, not only women's knickers? For one thing, don't forget, they get paid a lot more wages than us, and if they get fed up with a shirt, or jersey or 'owt, they chuck the bloody thing away and buy a new one. Also, they throw parts of their military kit out too, shirts, parts of their uniform, even shoes and boots; look, Jeff, as I said, anything like that – bring it in, we can always throw the bugger out again if it's no use,' he told him with a stern nod.

'What if they're not clean, though, Tony?' Jeff asked him. 'They won't wash and press 'em to throw the buggers away, will they, we can't sell 'em mucky, you know.'

'No problem there,' Tony smirked. 'We send them off with the laundry, don't we? Don't forget, I'm in charge of that in here, so that'll cost us nowt. Furthermore,' he went on, 'as far as the boots and shoes are concerned – the same thing, they can be sent off to the cobblers for repair; there again,' he said, laughing, 'free of charge as far as we're concerned.'

Smiling broadly now, Jeff said, 'Brilliant idea, mate, brilliant. I'll get the lads going around after dinner, I'll also get them red knickers off Eddy Jones for you as well, Tony,' he told him in a business-like tone of voice. Pausing, he gave Tony a doubtful look, asking with a frown, 'By the way, how are we going to market the goods, though, Tony?'

'Simple,' he replied. 'We lay out a stall on our beds every Thursday or Friday evening after tea, when the boys have just been paid; they'll be like bees around a honey pot, when word gets around about all the bargains.'

Jeff thought for a moment and gave Tony another doubtful look. 'You know, Tony, I was just wondering, the lads here collecting all the stuff out of the bins might get a bit jealous, if they see us building up a thriving business and them getting nothing out of it.'

'Who said anything about them getting nowt out of it?' Tony replied with raised eyebrows, sounding very hurt at the thought of such a selfish assumption. 'I intend to run this in a fair, business-like manner, Jeff; I've worked out the financial side too,' he told him piously.

'Oh, have you Tony? I didn't realise that: you only thought of the idea a few minutes ago,' he said, looking a little baffled.

'Definitely,' Tony replied haughtily. 'I get fifty per cent, as organiser, you get twenty, and the other lads get ten each; providing they do the job right and pull their weight,' he added with a firm nod. 'By the way, Jeff,' he continued, 'As you know, I'll be occupied most of this week with that bloody ceremonial parade, so I'm afraid you'll have to take a bit more responsibility, both here in the Mess and also for the collection of goods for the new business.'

'Aye, Tony, I realise that, mate, don't you worry it's all in good hands. He laughed. 'You go off and represent the Mess with pride.'

58

By twelve thirty on Friday, the great A.O.C.'s Parade was over; the men had been marched back from the airfield where the ceremony and inspection had taken place, and were now standing about on the camp square.

Dismissed and exhausted, Tony was walking off alone, thinking about the start of his new business idea, when he was suddenly startled by a voice behind him calling out, 'Hello, there, Ryan. Very good show you put on today, I could see you haven't forgotten your basic foot drill, laddie.' Looking back, he was surprised to see the heavily-built figure of Warrant Officer Cox – the station warrant officer – whom he knew quite well in the Mess, coming up behind him.

Stopping and turning smartly, he replied, 'Thank you, sir, it's very nice to know I've managed to keep it up to scratch, sir.'

Seeing Tony at attention, the officer said smiling, 'Drop the formality, Ryan, it's over now, lad.' They walked alongside each other and he said with a smile, 'Haven't you ever thought about getting something better than that job you do in the mess, Ryan?'

Rather taken aback, Tony replied, 'Well, I did once think I'd like to take a PTI course, sir, but only being a national serviceman, I don't think I'd have much chance.'

'I suppose you're right,' the WO replied, 'but haven't you ever considered making a career in the Service? You're only a young man, if you signed on for five years for a start, you'd have no difficulty getting on a PTI course, I'm sure, an athletic man like you,' he told him.

'Well, as a matter of fact, sir, I have thought about it, as I said,' Tony told him. 'My girlfriend is a PTI and she suggested it to me, too.'

'Oh, I see,' he said with renewed interest. 'Is she on this camp, then, Ryan?'

'No, sir, I only wish she was,' he replied, with a note of sadness. 'She's abroad in Cyprus.'

'She'll obviously outrank you, then, Ryan,' the WO said, with a laugh. She'll have a couple of tapes up, won't she, eh?'

'Oh aye, she definitely outranks me, sir, she's a sergeant at the moment, but she's just taken an advanced exam and should have her crown up within a week or so she says – and she's only a year older than me,' he added, grinning proudly.

'Seriously now,' the WO said, 'there you go, Ryan. It's about time you started to catch up on her, ain't it? You think about what I said and if you do decide to stay on in the Service, now or in the future, contact me; I'll help you in any way I can, lad.'

59

'Excuse me, Yorky,' called out Sergeant Banks, as Tony walked passed his half-open door later that afternoon. 'Have you got a minute?'

'Yes, Jerry, what can I do for you, sir,' said Tony, stopping in the doorway of the room with a smile.

Lying on the bed with a book in his hand, Jerry said, 'I just wondered, Yorky, if you'll be on duty in the Mess over the weekend?'

Still smiling, Tony replied, 'I'm always on duty, Sergeant, when required, you know that.'

Getting off the bed and throwing the book down, he went on seriously, 'I know that, but I mean are you staying the full weekend, you know, overnight, like?'

Wondering what this was leading up to, Tony said, 'Well, as a matter of fact, yes, I am. I've got two people moving in on Saturday or Sunday evening, a male flight sergeant, and a woman sergeant; I'm not sure when either will arrive, so I'll be here all the weekend, but why do you ask, Jerry?'

'Oh, so Pike won't be hovering around this end of the Mess, then,' Jerry said, grinning.'

'No, he never comes up here when he's off duty,' Tony replied. 'Anyway he's got his family on camp now, you know, he's got a house on that new section of married quarters,' he told him. 'What's the problem, Jerry, why do you ask?' he repeated.

'Well, Yorky, I've a little favour to request, it's for Saturday night,' he said, looking very pleased with himself. 'I've got the chance of an overnight guest; I was hoping that you would be on duty and that you would turn a blind eye,' he said, giving a little wink.

Grinning broadly, Tony said, 'It wouldn't be that hippy young bird from your office in transport division, would it, Sergeant Banks?'

Laughing out loud, he replied, 'The very one, AC Ryan, however did you guess?'

'Well, I think we can make sure I don't see anything out of order, Sergeant, seeing as it's you,' chuckled Tony, 'but if you could bring another one like her, and shove her into my bedding store as you pass, that would make doubly sure,' he said, returning the wink. By the way, Jerry,' he continued, suddenly becoming serious, 'Come to think of it, I've had a little problem crop up in the last few days, that you might be able to help me with.' He then told him all about the women's underwear the lads had found, but omitted to say whose bin they had been found in; he thought that it would be unfair to divulge that.

'Oh, bloody hell,' Jerry muttered, when Tony had finished telling him. 'It sounds as though we've definitely got one of them queer guys in the Mess, then, Yorky. Any idea who threw the knickers out then? Whose bin were they found in anyway?' he asked with a frown.

Tony remained silent for a moment then said cautiously, 'Well, I don't know if it would be fair to say who I think it is, Jerry, I might be wrong. It was a couple of the other lads that found 'em, they brought them into the bedding store asking what to do with 'em.'

'Yes, I see your point, Yorky,' Jerry replied, 'and I admire you for it, but I've known most of the chaps in here for a few years now and I can't think of any one of them that's that way inclined. Unless it's one of the new chaps that moved in over the last few weeks,' he added. 'I don't suppose it could be your friend, Sergeant Riley's bin, they found them in, Yorky, eh?'

Grinning, Tony said, 'No, I'm afraid not, I can't pin this one on him.' Then, silent for a moment in thought, he said, 'If it's just between you and me, Jerry, I'll tell you whose bin both pairs were found in, but you do understand my position, don't you?'

'Certainly I do, Yorky. It would be between you and me, but it's the only way I can help really, ain't it?' he said with a shrug.

After another think, Tony said quietly, 'Both pairs of knickers were found in the same bin on two consecutive days.' He hesitated, with a guilty look on his face and said, 'I feel bloody awful giving his name, I might be wrong you know.'

Jerry was now keen to find out who the culprit was. 'Well, come on then, Yorky, whose bloody bin were they, then?'

'That little Warrant Officer Keyes at the far end of the top landing, but don't say 'owt, though, will you?' he stressed. 'I wouldn't like to embarrass him, I mean it's not a crime after all is it,' he said, wide-eyed.

Looking back at him for a moment expressionlessly, Jerry's face suddenly creased, as he broke into uncontrollable laughter. 'Christ Almighty, little Charley Keyes,' he muttered, amidst his mirth.

Tony was staring at him, looking baffled. 'What's so funny about that then, Jerry?' he asked.

'Funny, funny it's a scream, Yorky; don't you know that Warrant Officer Keyes is head of the camp entertainment society, he organisers all the charity shows that are put on, pantomimes for the kids that sort of thing.' With another little laugh, he said, 'You'll most likely find some more unusual things in his bin from time to time; he gets all sorts of gear given for his shows. Anything he doesn't want, I suppose he chucks it out,' he chuckled, 'but I'm sure Charley won't be wearing the fancy knickers.'

'Seeing the funny side himself now, Tony joined in the laughter until he was interrupted by the sound of someone clearing their throat in the doorway behind him.

'Hello, Ryan, what's so funny then?' asked Sergeant Pike, with a sickly smile on his face.

Before Tony could answer, Jerry called out from inside the room, 'Is that you, Cyril? I was just telling AC Ryan here a funny joke, come in, lad, and I'll tell it to you; it'll have you in stitches,' he promised, gleefully.

Scowling and refusing the invitation, Sergeant Pike replied, 'No thanks, Sergeant Banks. I'm too busy for jokes. Come on, Ryan, we've got work to do; we can't lounge about joking all day like some,' he said turning and marching off.

Next morning, as Tony entered her busy kitchen, Sergeant McNabb greeted him warmly. 'Hello, AC Ryan, or should I call you, Tony,' she whispered in his ear as he came up to her.

'Either is fine with me, Sergeant, he replied formally. 'I've come to request the loan of one of your girls to get a room ready on the female wing; I'm expecting a lady sergeant sometime over the weekend.'

'Oh, I suppose so,' she replied in a bored tone. 'Take one of the dining room staff, but I want her back for eleven thirty,' she added firmly.

'Thanks, Sergeant,' he replied, turning and walking out into the big dining room. Ruby was laying the tables and he called to her, smiling, 'Come on, Ruby dear, I've got a nice little job requiring your personal attention.'

Coming over to him smiling shyly, she enquired, 'What sort of a job are you wanting attending to then, Mr Ryan.?'

Giving her a cheeky grin he said, 'Just you come with me, darling, I'm sure you'll enjoy this one.'

'Oh, I will, will I? What is it, Tony?' she asked, as they walked out of the room side by side.

'I'll give you a clue,' he said glancing at her grinning. 'It's to do with a bed and we've got plenty of time to sort it out, you haven't to be back down here until eleven thirty.'

Ruby walked a few steps further, while Tony's words sank in and then her face flushed. Giving him a playful shove that nearly knocked him off his feet, she said bashfully, 'Tony Ryan, you cheeky devil, that's all you think about, you've a one track mind you have.'

Still staggering from the playful shove, he laughed. 'Come on, Ruby don't play the angel with me, you know you'll like the job once you get at it.' She made no reply, apart from giving him another playful shove, accompanied by a giggle.

60

'Come in,' Tony yelled in response to a shuffling sound out in the passage followed by a knock on the door. He was sitting in his old armchair in the bedding store reading a newspaper.

Ted West pushed the door open noisily and staggered in, his arms full of mixed clothing, plus two pairs of boots tied together, with their laces hung around his neck. 'Yesterday's collection, Tony,' he said, struggling with his load.

'Oh, good work, Ted, old son,' Tony replied, giving him a quick glance before resuming his reading. 'Put them on the back bench, I'll have a look through them when I've had my tea break; would you like a cup of tea, Ted, lad?' he asked.

'That's nice of you, Tony,' he replied gratefully, dropping his load on the bench. That done, he said hesitantly, 'Er, Tony I was wondering how the sales of this stuff we keep collecting, is going on? I know we all got fifteen bob each, the week before last, but the business has been going for over four weeks now and –'

Without looking up from his paper, Tony cut him short. 'You aren't I hope, doubting my abilities as a business man, Ted?' he said quietly.

'Oh no, no, nothing like that, Tony,' he replied hastily. 'No, it was just that I was talking about it to Jones, and we were thinking that fifteen bob wasn't much for over a month's work collecting the gear.'

Still lying back reading, Tony spoke in a hurt tone. 'Don't tell me you lot have been ganging up on me, Ted; you know I've been working my fingers to the bone on the venture; you must realise a businesses like this takes time to get off the ground.' Then throwing the paper down and slowly getting to his feet smiling, he said condescendingly, 'Come on, let's get you that cup of tea, tell the lads to stop to worrying and leave the thinking to me.' As he was filling the old kettle he called over his shoulder with a laugh, 'There aren't any fancy knickers among that lot you've just brought in, are there, Ted lad?'

'Well, if there are you can wear the buggers yourself,' he replied, feigning anger.

61

Later that evening, Jeff and several of the other lads were lounging about in the billet, with the radio playing softly in the background. Suddenly the door burst open and Tony came in, his training bag hanging from his shoulder and a large swelling over his left eye, together with a bloody nose.

'Christ Almighty!' Jeff shouted, jumping off his bed and rushing over to him. 'What the fucking hell has happened to you, mate?' he asked, taking Tony's sports bag, as he scanned the swelling.

'Some bastard jumped out from behind a hedge and took a swing at me, as I was walking down the lane from the gym,' Tony said angrily. 'I just saw a shadow flash before me in the dark, then an almighty thump and a thousand stars, followed by the sound of some bugger running away.'

'Didn't you see who it was?' asked one of the other lads, who were now all crowding around him.

'No, I didn't see a thing it was all too quick, and it was black as pitch in that lane.' Then wiping the blood from his nose, he said menacingly, 'but I've a good idea who the bastard was, though.'

Taking his coat off, he threw it down on the bed, grabbed a towel from his locker and made for the door. 'See you in a bit, Jeff, I'll just go and clean up,' he called out.

Jeff followed with a concerned look on his face, 'Are you sure you're okay, Tony? Your face has blown up like a balloon, you know.'

'Yes, I'm fine, stop bloody fussing, Jeff,' he replied, as they made their way in tandem to the ablutions. 'I've had many a thump like this on a

Saturday night down at the Dog and Gun,' he told him, trying to be cheerful. 'Mind you,' he continued, 'I'm lucky, this one caught me mainly on the forehead – if he'd caught me a bit lower down – he'd have smashed my face in; the bastard wasn't going to show his fucking stinking face though, the swine,' he growled.

'Don't you think you ought to go down to sick quarters for a check up, Tony, with it being your head that caught the full force of the blow?' Jeff asked, still very concerned.

'Jeff, the forehead is the hardest part of the head,' Tony told him. 'It'll be fine within a couple of days, mate; stop worrying. I've had worse than this from the Canal street gang back home, believe me,' he said forcing a laugh. Grimacing with pain, he filled one of the wash basins with warm water, and splashed his swollen face gently to sooth the delicate area.

Jeff, in front of the urinal at the far end of the ablution having a piss, called out, 'You're going to report this though, aren't you? After all, it's common assault; whoever did it to you deserves catching – he might be some sort of a nut that goes around doing that sort of thing for kicks.' Tony continued, swilling the soothing water over his now rapidly swelling face, without replying.

Jeff, then shaking his cock, put it away and went over to Tony at the wash basin. 'Well, what do you think, mate, are you going to report it?' he asked.

Tony, patting his face delicately with the towel, replied, 'I can't do that, mate, this is a personal thing; we both know who the culprit is though, don't we Jeff?' he muttered, giving him a sharp look.

'Do you think it was him though, Tony,' Jeff said, frowning. 'You do mean big Sam Barns, the wrestler, don't you?' .

'Who else could it be? He hates my bloody guts because I put one on him that night, even though I'd no option,' Tony replied. 'What's more that punch had some bloody beef behind it, mate; it was a very strong man that delivered that, I'll tell you.'

'Well, if it was me that had caught it, Tony, I'd go down to the guardroom and report him to Sergeant Priest; he's done this sort of thing before, don't forget he thumped that chap in the Airmen's Mess a few months back.'

'That was different,' Tony replied. 'That was just an argument, off the cuff job, this is a grudge, Jeff, and it's got to be sorted out mutually and with decorum, or it'll never end. After all's said and done, I did knock him out,' he said, gently patting his swollen face dry.

Walking back to the billet, Jeff said. 'What do you intend to do about it then, mate, you're not just going to let it slide by, are you?'

'No, I'm not Jeff, I'm going to have a quiet word with the big cunt next time I see him up at the gym, that's what,' he told him adamantly.

62

'Bloody hell, what a shiner,' said Ted West, with a laugh, when he saw Tony coming into the Sergeants' Mess the following morning.

'Stop taking the piss, Ted, or you might get one yourself,' Tony replied, pushing him and walking briskly away. After several more comments about his swollen face and slightly darkened eye, Tony eventually reached the sanctuary of his bedding store. He immediately put the kettle on as was usual and while he was waiting for it to come to the boil, Jeff walked in grimacing.

'Christ, Tony, you've never seen anything like it in the top floor ablutions; some mucky bugger's shit all over the floor, diarrhoea an'all,' he moaned.

Laughing, although it hurt his sore face, Tony said, 'Oh, lad what are you getting so upset about? A bit of shit won't hurt you.'

'Aye, it's okay for you, I'll bet you won't be rushing up there to clean it up, will you, you bugger?' he grumbled. Glancing at the singing kettle, he added cheerfully, 'I see you've got the kettle on anyway.'

'Yes, and would you like to join me in a cup before we start our labours, Mr Baxter,' he replied, grabbing two pint mugs from the sink shelf.

'Definitely, Mr Ryan,' he replied, plonking himself down on an old stool near the table.

'Hold on a minute, mate, before you start making yourself comfortable; there's the matter of that shit to attend to, first,' Tony said, smiling as he mashed the tea.

'What! You want me to go and get stuck into that lot on my own,' Jeff yelled.

'No, of course not, Jeff, don't be daft, lad, I want you to go up there and find West and tell him to get one of his mates to help him to get it scraped up, then they can mop out all the area with carbolic disinfectant before Pike goes on his rounds. I'll have your tea all ready for you when you get back,' he promised.

'I knew you wouldn't want to get your hands dirty with a job like that,' grumbled Jeff, as he went lumbering sulkily out.

Ten minutes later, he came hurrying back through the door, red-faced and scowling. 'They're playing hell up there, Tony,' he said. 'Pooh! Christ the stink,' he added, screwing up his nose. Then he laughed. 'I got Ted West and Eddy on the job, I left them arguing over who was going to do the scraping up and who was going to do the mopping.'

'They sound keen to get at the job then, Jeff,' Tony replied mockingly. 'Anyway, it sounds as though it does smell nice in there, don't it, mate? It'll give 'em an appetite for their dinner, that's for sure,' he said, trying not to laugh, because of his swollen face.

'I don't suppose you've any idea who the mucky bugger was that dropped that lot, have you, Jeff,' he asked, as they sat down with their tea cups.

'No, but I gather there was some sort of a celebration in the bar last night, a birthday or something,' Jeff told him.

'Oh well, we're not going to let a thing like this pass without saying something about it, Jeff, I'll tell you,' Tony said firmly. 'I'm going to complain to Sergeant Pike as soon as we've had our tea. Dirty, drunken bastards,' he continued angrily. 'Leaving a mess like that for us to clean up.'

'Ted and Eddy – you mean, don't you, Tony?' Jeff said, laughing.

Tony ignored his comment and sat back in the old armchair with a thoughtful expression on his face, sipping his tea. 'By the way, Jeff,' he said after a few moments pause, 'As far as what happened to me last night, it was an accident – I walked into a tree on the way back down from the gym, okay?'

'Why – the secrecy, Tony? You've done nothing wrong,' he replied in surprise.

'Because, as I told you before, this is a personal matter, I want no hassle, right?' Tony emphasized.

'Fair enough, if that's what you want, a tree it was, mate,' he said, shrugging his shoulders.

Meeting them later in the dining room, Sergeant McNabb said sympathetically, 'Oh, dear me, AC Ryan, whatever has happened to your face, dear?'

'Just a bit of an accident, Sergeant,' he replied casually, continuing to walk past her.
Barring his way with a concerned look on her face, she said, 'Oh, it looks so sore.' She reached out and gently stroked the swollen area. 'You should go down to sick quarters and get something to reduce the swelling, dear; it must be so painful,' she cooed.

'Oh, it's nothing to bother about,' he told her forcing a smile. 'It'll be okay in a couple of days, Sergeant.'

'I've got some ointment in my room that I know would soothe it,' she said. 'I can bring it down to your bedding store later, if you'd like me to,' she told him, with a warm smile.

Before he could answer, Ruby, who was coming out of the kitchen area with an empty tray, on her way to clear the breakfast tables, caught sight of him. Giving a little gasp at the condition of his face, she came over and asked what had caused it. He repeated the story, whereupon, she also reached out gently and stroked his swollen brow sympathetically.

Seeing this, Sergeant McNabb looked down at her and frowned. 'Right Pritchard, 'she said curtly, 'you've had your say now, go on, get on with your work.' Smiling at Tony, she continued in a much kinder tone. 'Would you like to come into the kitchen, Tony for a tea, or a coffee, perhaps?' Tony made his excuses, blaming Sergeant Pike, and hurried out on his way down the corridor. As he walked past the bar room, he heard several voices within. The bar itself was not open for business until noon, so being inquisitive he opened the door and went in. The scene he was confronted with was quite a shock.

63

In front of the bar stood two smartly dressed Service police corporals, wearing their white tunic belts and white topped peak caps. Behind the bar was a very stern-faced Sergeant Prince conversing with a tall, middle-aged and bespectacled, commissioned officer. The two were looking through the bar record books with great interest, while the Steward, 'little Corporal Barney Jackson', stood alongside them motionless, his face as white as a sheet.

'Who are you, airman?' asked one of the corporals, sternly.

As Tony began to reply that he was staff, Sergeant Prince turned to see who the interrupter was. After giving Tony's bruised face a surprised stare, he said, 'Could you leave the cleaning in here for the next hour, Ryan, I'll let Sergeant Pike know when we've finished.' Tony apologised for the interruption and as turned and walked out, he glanced at the white-faced Steward, wondering what the hell he'd been up to.

That afternoon the whole mess was buzzing. Corporal Jackson, the bar steward, had been arrested; news had leaked out that he'd been fiddling the till for months. The rumour was that the bar accounts were short to the tune of two hundred pounds, at the very least. Sergeant Pike had taken the event very seriously, and was obliged to take over the bar duties for the rest of the day personally, until another corporal barman could be found.

Tony thought he could be of service and offered to help, saying he had once helped out at the Dog and Gun back home, when Bernard the landlord was ill. Reluctantly, Pike told him he appreciated the offer, but informed him that only NCOs could work behind the Mess bar. However, he assured him that the thoughtful offer would not be forgotten. Several days later it was officially reported on the Mess notice board that Corporal Jackson had been sent to the Military Detention Centre at Colchester and that a temporary steward had been appointed, a Corporal James Conway.

'He'll get two years for that,' stated Jeff, as the matter was being discussed in the bedding store, shortly after the notice had been put up. 'I always thought he looked a slimy little bugger,' he added, frowning.

'I don't know what to think about it really,' Tony replied, shaking his head. 'If it had been going on for several months, as I heard, why wasn't it spotted before now? There's been some negligence somewhere. I must admit, though, I felt sorry for the poor little bugger that morning, standing there behind the bar between Sergeant Prince and that investigating officer – he looked shit scared.'

'Well, he'd asked for it, Tony, the man knew what he was doing, 'Jeff said, without sympathy. 'I heard one of the sergeants saying that he'd fiddled just over two hundred quid, that's big money, mate,' he added, shaking his head.

'Over two hundred quid, you say, Jeff?' Tony echoed, with a whistle. 'It sounds as though that rumour was right, then. Christ, that is big money, mate; how was he able to get away with fiddling like that for so long?'

'Makes you wonder, don't it?' Jeff replied. 'I'd have thought the accountants would have spotted it sooner than they did.'

'It certainly appears some negligence was involved,' said Tony. 'I'd have thought Sergeant Pike himself would have checked the bar finances at least once a week; he's responsible for the whole Mess.'

'You don't think Pike could get reprimanded for negligence or something, do you Tony?'

'I wouldn't think so, but when that sort of money's involved, you never know what the bloody hell could happen, Jeff,' he replied, with a worried frown.

'Don't say it would bother you, if old Pike ended up in the shit as well, Tony?' Jeff said, laughing at Tony's thoughtful expression.

'It bloody well would, mate,' he replied adamantly. 'Better a devil you know, Jeff, lad, if he went we might get some sour old fucker that would make our lives hell. Anyway, Pike's not a bad old bugger really, you know,'

'I suppose you're right,' he agreed. 'By the way, did he ever ask you about your swollen face?'

'Yes, and so did Sergeant Prince; I met him coming out of Pike's office the other day –they asked if I'd been scrapping.' He laughed. 'I told them I'd walked into a tree.'

'But do you think they believed you, Tony?

'Pike did, I think, but Sergeant Priest just stared into my face with his little, black, snaky eyes and smirked – he didn't, I'm sure of that.'

Three weeks later it was officially announced in the Mess, that Corporal Jackson had been found guilty of the pilferage of bar takings. He was sentenced to six months detention at Colchester Military Jail; followed by dismissal with dishonour from the Service. The case then closed with no involvement of any other person, thus finalising the matter – or so it was thought.

64

Coming out of the Mess kitchen one Saturday lunch time, arms laden with dirty laundry, Tony was beckoned over to one of the tables at the far end of the room, by a small, scowling warrant officer. Looking across at him, Tony thought he recognised him from somewhere, but couldn't place him at that moment. Putting his load down on an empty table, he went over and politely enquired what he wanted. Without replying, the little man got slowly to his feet, walked over to the window and waved at Tony to follow. When they were out of earshot of the other diners, he spun round to face the puzzled Tony, with a venomous black look on his face.

'Ryan,' he hissed, looking up at him with flashing eyes. 'When are you going to stop leering at my girl friend? I've seen you on several occasions now, looking her up and down –every time you see her you're eating her with your eyes; I've had enough, lad, do you understand?' He stared into Tony's bewildered face.

Looking back at him in stunned silence for a moment, not knowing what he was on about, Tony said, 'Er, sorry, sir, but I don't know what you mean, sir, I don't know the lady you're referring to either sir, honest.'

'Do you think I'm a bloody fool lad?' he snapped, red-faced and shaking with rage. 'I've watched you and I've seen the lust in your eyes when you look at her; I've had enough I tell you. What's more,' he raved on, 'if you don't keep your eyes off her, I'm going to teach you a lesson you won't forget, my lad.' He prodded him hard on the chest with his finger. Again Tony proclaimed his ignorance of the accusation, stressing firmly that he didn't know the lady in question.

'You can't wriggle out of it, Ryan,' the little man replied venomously. 'You certainly know who and what I mean all right,' he muttered, glaring up at him. 'I'm referring to the torment you're putting my little love through with your lust for her, and in her place of work, an'all.' He nodded rapidly, his eyes bulging so much that Tony shuddered, thinking the eyes would fall out, such was the man's anger.

'She can't avoid you, man,' he hissed into Tony's face, emitting a spray of spittle from his ill-fitting dentures, 'much as she may want to – the poor darling girl.'

Tony was mystified, and just stood there in silence as the man raved on. Surely he can't mean Ruby, he thought? Oh no, she wouldn't look at an old fart like him; but who else could it be?

'Mind you,' the little officer said firmly, 'she hasn't complained to me herself – tolerated it in silence – the little darling; but *I've* noticed you at it for weeks now, though.' Cooling down somewhat, a slight smile crossed his face. 'She's too proud a person to admit having noticed you herself,' he said quietly.

'I'm sorry, sir,' Tony said insistently, 'but I don't know the lady you're referring to, sir and that's the truth, sir.'

'You bloody well do,' he said with a slight whistle through his stained dentures. 'I'm referring to Sergeant McNabb, that's who she is, lad, you bloody know it, an'all.' Taking a step nearer to Tony, and staring up into his face menacingly, he went on almost in a whisper, 'It's got to stop. Do you hear me, lad? This infatuation you have for her has got to stop.' He curled his lip and stared venomously at poor Tony. 'If it doesn't, I'm not going to pull rank, I'm going to take you up to that gym and teach you a few boxing lessons that you won't forget for a long time, my lad.' For a few seconds he glared at Tony's shocked face in silence, then with a note of disgust in his voice, he hissed, 'Go on, get on with your work and don't forget my warning, lad, you won't get another – you'll be in that bloody boxing ring –you'll cool off then – when I've finished with you.'

The bedding store rocked with mirth later that afternoon, as the lads, having their tea break, sat listening to Tony telling them of his warning from the little warrant officer.

'Oh, Christ, I can't believe this,' Jeff gasped, amidst laughter, 'I bet you nearly shit yourself, mate, when he threatened to get you in the boxing ring, didn't you?'

'I didn't know what to think at the time,' Tony replied. 'I was too shocked with the accusation; I thought the silly little bugger had gone round the fucking bend or something,' he laughed.

'Didn't you recognise he was Warrant Officer Bloomer from the dance at Christmas, Tony?' Jeff asked. 'He was there with McNabb, surely you remember, we remarked at the time they looked a funny couple, him about five foot two and her about six foot two.'

'No, I couldn't place him, he's very rarely in the Mess, you know. I knew his face, but I just couldn't place him until he mentioned Sergeant McNabb, then I thought bloody hell, he's that little lover boy of hers.'

Anyway, Ryan, it looks as though you're in line for another shiner, if you don't keep your roving eye off his girlfriend.' Ted West laughed, glancing at his two mates for back up.

'Aye, and as I've told you before, West,' Tony emphasized, 'you'd better stop trying to be witty and taking the piss or you might be in line for two shiners, dear boy.'

When the other three had left, Tony said, 'I know it seemed bloody funny, Jeff, and I felt like putting the silly little bugger over my knee, but come to think of it, it could make things awkward if he keeps thinking things like that. I mean, I'm having contact with Sergeant McNabb a dozen times a day on the job here, aren't I?' he said, frowning.

'Well, I say just forget the daft old cunt, Tony, I don't think you fancy his little darling anyway – or do you?' He burst into laughter.

Tony, ignoring the question, made for the door smiling. 'Come on funny boy, let's get on the job before Pike comes looking for us.'

65

'Do you think my arms are coming on with my new training schedule, Tony,' asked the young lad working out alongside him in the gym.

Tony finished his set, banged the barbell down on the thick mat and took a few deep breaths. He gave the lad a quick glance before replying, 'Sure, you look great kid, keep at it.' He went over to the coat hanger near the door where he'd hung his tracksuit top; glancing through the glass panel in the door, he saw a group of men dressed in jogging gear, filing into the gym from the main entrance. It was the wrestling team, led by big Sam Barns, puffing and blowing and oozing with confidence, as he yelled orders at the other lads. This was the first time Tony had seen him since they'd caught sight of each other in the Airmen's Mess. However, Tony knew Barns had seen him since then, because he was sure he'd been on the other end of the heavy punch he received that night in the darkened lane. Giving his face another quick wipe with the towel before throwing it down on a bench, he pulled on his track suit top and made for the door leading to the main hall.

Catching sight of Tony walking up the gym in his direction, Sam, laughing and shouting in the midst of his wresting team, suddenly froze – his eyes focused on Tony. Noticing this, the whole team went quiet, looking in the same direction. Reaching them, Tony pushed through the little crowd surrounding Sam and came to a halt in front of him. They stared at each other – Sam grinning, Tony expressionless.

'Well, if it isn't the clever Mr Ryan,' Sam chuckled. He pretended to look around the hall before he continued, 'You haven't got your skinny mate with you tonight, I see. I hope he hasn't slipped through a crack in the floor.'

As he leaned back laughing loudly, Tony said, 'Look, Sam, I haven't come to argue with you, I've come to try and end this animosity between us.'

Abruptly ceasing his raucous laughter, he replied menacingly, 'You – what? Have you forgotten, Ryan, you struck me a foul that night in the billet? I was out for over five minutes, the lads told me, now you expect me to shake your hand and say thank you, Tony.' Pulling a face he looked down at him, continuing, 'You realise, pal, I could have reported you for that and got you run in, old son.'

'No, I can't deny the incident, Sam,' Tony replied calmly, 'but as far as saying I fouled you – I don't know – I'd no other choice; don't forget you threw a punch at me first and you were on the point of putting another one on me, weren't you?' Sam stood silently glaring down at Tony as he continued, 'Anyway, seeing as we're both equal now, I think we should drop this vendetta and shake on it.' Tony then extended his hand towards him with a friendly smile.

'What do you mean equal, Ryan?' Sam enquired sarcastically.

Tony replied smiling, 'I'm sure your memory is better than that, Sam. By the way, I didn't report it either, even though Sergeant Prince asked me to at work in the Mess the next day,' he lied. The tittering little crowd surrounding them went silent, as everyone on the camp knew who Sergeant Prince was.

Sam, still looking down into Tony's face with a leering smile, said, 'Okay, Ryan, I'll shake on it.'

As Tony again extended his hand towards him, he grabbed it with his huge paw in a bone shaking grip. Tony realised what he was up to and responded, but Sam had the advantage of surprise and Tony felt his hand beginning to give way. Looking up into Sam's leering face, he heard his crowd of friends beginning to chuckle, expecting their tutor to make a fool out of him; Tony clenched his teeth, applied great mental concentration, and forced his aching hand to come back to life and retaliate.

Feeling the response, Sam's eyes narrowed and his grip tightened. Tony, now in deep concentration responded. Staring up into Sam's straining face, he saw for the first time now a look of fear gradually creeping into his eyes. Immediately the big man made another effort, but he could not loosen Tony's grip. Tony saw the veins beginning to stand out on Sam's forehead and knew then that he had him. Sam had now reached his limit in front of a crowd of his own friends, who respected him as their leader. Tony realised at that moment he had only one choice: if the vendetta was to be solved once and for all, he would have to lose the contest to win the peace between them.

Still looking up into Sam's contorted face he muttered, loud enough for all to hear, 'Okay, Sam, that's as much as I've got, I've had enough.' Saying this, he relaxed his grip and yanked his hand away, massaging it with a groan. 'Christ, man, you've got a grip like iron,' he gasped and a loud cheering followed from Sam's trainee wrestlers.

Wiping the sweat from his brow with the sleeve of his track suit, Sam stood looking at him with a puzzled smile on his face. 'Yes, I have, haven't I,' he said, 'and so have you without a doubt, mate. I'm surprised you packed up like that, Ryan, from my end I felt you had a bit more left in you.'

Still rubbing his hand Tony replied, 'No, I know when I'm beaten, Sam.'

Glancing at the group of lads surrounding them, then back at Tony, Sam replied, grinning, 'Yes and I know when you're not, mate. Do you think I'm a bloody fool, Tony Ryan? I'm a professional sportsman in civilian life, I've never had an opponent do a drop for me in my career, mate.'

Listening intently, the onlookers once again fell silent and Tony replied innocently, 'I'm sure you haven't, Sam, but what are you getting at anyway?'

'I'm saying that I'm no hypocrite,' he replied firmly, 'and that I can take a loss, as well as a win. What's more, I don't ever cheat in a contest whatever it is, even tiddlywinks,' he added, smiling. 'In my game you win some and you lose some, but always with grace, that's called professionalism, mister!'

Turning to his lads, he grinned and said, 'This bugger must think I'm a bloody fool, lads; he beat me there fair and square, I was knackered. Mind you,' he said, laughing and looking back at Tony, 'I'm going to insist on a rematch if the opposition agrees.' As the group of lads started laughing and clapping at his sportsmanship, Sam yelled out with mock anger, 'Right, go on you lot and get changed we've done enough tonight, I don't know about you but I'm buggered.' As they wondered away, he said to Tony, 'Do you want a lift down to the camp, Tony? I've got one of the Land Rovers outside and it's pissing down out there.'

Tony pleased at this friendly invitation accepted with thanks. When they reached the camp, Tony wanted to make sure the animosity between them was now at an end, so he invited Sam for a little refreshment in the NAAFI canteen.

66

The two men, sitting at a table and chatting, their plates piled high with fish and chips, looked like old friends. Suddenly Tony, glancing at the door over Sam's shoulder, spotted his mate, Jeff coming in. As their eyes met, Tony smiled and waved him over.

When Jeff arrived at their table and saw who Tony was sitting with, he was clearly rather taken aback.

Noticing his bewilderment, Sam said, smiling up at him, 'What's up Baxter, do you disapprove of me and your mate eating together?'

'No, no not at all, Sam,' he replied. 'Just a bit surprised; I didn't think you two had anything in common, really.'

'Nothing in common,' Sam repeated, feigning surprise, as he stuffed a big fork full of chips into his mouth. 'That's where you're wrong, matey; we've got a lot in common.' Glancing at Tony munching away, he said, 'Tony and me are both athletes; that's why we've crossed swords in the past, we're both basically competitive, neither of us will let anybody shit on us.' He glanced at Tony again and smiled, 'Right, mate?'

'Right, Sam,' Tony agreed, feeling sure now all the ill will had diminished. 'It's what's called a code of sportsmanship, Jeff; like any other group of people when it comes down to it, we always stick together. It's like a union you see, mate,' he said, smiling as he finished off the last bit of fish. He picked his pint pot and took a long and satisfying drink of tea before he added, 'As a matter of fact, Jeff, we're both lifelong members of the 'Health and Strength' organisation an'all.

'He doesn't seem such a bad old bugger when you get to know him, Tony, does he?' Jeff remarked, as the two were walking back to the billet later. 'I was bloody shocked, though, I must admit,' he went on, 'when I first saw you and him sitting there so chummy, eating fish and chips.'

Laughing, Tony said, 'Aye, we sorted everything out up at the gym earlier, Jeff.'

'What – you mean you had a scrap or something?' he asked.

'Not exactly, no,' said Tony, grinning, 'just a bit of a straightening out of the situation between us, Jeff, lad.' He told him about the whole incident, and also that they'd arranged to practise Acadia and Kung Fu together occasionally. 'I know quite a bit myself,' Tony told him, 'but Sam being a wrestler by profession is obviously far ahead of me.'

'Oh, looks like you've got another mate then now, Tony,' Jeff said, pretending to be jealous.

'Shut up, you daft bugger,' he laughed. 'I'm only pleased we're not at each other's throats any more mate, I don't like being hated, Jeff,' he said, shaking his head. He meant it too; Tony Ryan was basically a very sensitive lad.

67

'Ryan, I'd like word with you; will you come in my office for a moment,' called out Sergeant Pike, catching Tony hurrying past his open door.

'Yes Sergeant,' called back Tony, stopping in his tracks and turning abruptly into the office.

Sergeant Pike was sitting behind his desk at the back of the little room, pretending as always to be very busy – the usual pile of papers before him and the usual expression of work pressure and self-pity on his face.

'I've just had a phone call from the commanding officer, Ryan; he said the new carpets for the bar are to be delivered and fitted early next week. So, I calculate we should be able to get them down, and the bar all finished ready for Easter. However,' he went on, 'I do realise your team will have a tight schedule to get the bar floor prepared for the tradesmen, but I'm sure you can get things organised in that department, Ryan,' and he smiled.

'Oh, that's good then, Sergeant, it's about time, we've been waiting long enough for 'em,' replied Tony, 'but they haven't given us much notice to get everything sorted out, have they? It's a big area in there.'

'True, Ryan, but we can't let the side down, we'll have to just dig in and get cracking,' he said firmly. 'I want all the old carpets up, the floor cleaned and scrubbed by Tuesday 13.00 hours without fail, right?'

Swallowing hard, Tony replied, 'But Sergeant, it's Friday today, that doesn't give us much time; there's a lot of work involved getting a large area like that properly prepared by then.'

He looked down at the paper work on his desk for a moment, then without looking up he said casually, 'Well, from what I could gather, the suppliers have had the carpets delivered without much notice. Anyway, it's got to be done, Ryan,' he went on, giving him a quick glance. 'Carry on now, get the job organised, if necessary we'll have to work over the weekend.'

'Bloody lovely,' said Jeff, when the boys were told of their forthcoming task.

'I can't see it being done by then, Tony,' said Ted West. 'I mean when we scrub the floor boards it'll take a day to dry 'em out, they can't fit carpets on a damp floor, you know,' he pointed out earnestly.

'Right, Ted, that's why we've got to have the old carpets up and out in the yard by Saturday dinner-time, and the floor scrubbed and fully prepared by Sunday tea-time. That'll give the floor long enough to dry out ready for the carpet layers on Tuesday afternoon, right lads?' he stated positively.

The work was hard and dirty, but by midday on Saturday, the floor was clear of the old carpets and ready for a thorough cleaning. After a quick snack, the lads got stuck into their work once more and by mid-afternoon they were well on with the task. Tony was sure now that his timing for the job was going to work out just about right. Of course, as it was Saturday, they were disturbed by a few of the residents, the ones who didn't know the bar room had been closed for the afternoon. They'd come in grumbling, saying the bar should be open, and wanting a drink.

'To be expected,' said Jeff, 'with so many drunken buggers in the Mess.'

Tony was just about to call a halt for a tea break, when Eddy Jones, who was behind the bar counter with a claw hammer, checking the floor boards for protruding nails, yelled out excitedly, 'Ryan! Ryan! For Christ's sake come here, man, just look at this, we've struck gold.'

Tony and the others rushed over to him; he was sitting on the floor behind the bar, staring down at the place from where he'd lifted up a short piece of loose floorboard. 'Look, look at that lot,' he yelled excitedly, pointing into the hole.

'Bloody hell,' gasped Jeff Baxter, looking down over Eddy's shoulder. 'There must be over a hundred quid there; what can we do with it?'

'I say we split it five equal ways, before anybody else sees it,' muttered Ted West quietly, staring down into the hole.

'I agree with that,' said Eddy, making a move to grab a handful of the notes, mostly in small bundles with elastic bands round them.

'Hold it there, Jones!' Tony called out. 'Don't be a fool, man; do you want to follow Corporal Jackson to Colchester?' Looking down at the cash, he said to Jeff, 'Keep an eye on that lot, Jeff, while I go and get one of the NCOs to witness this; Pike went home at twelve and the new Steward isn't here because the bar is closed, so I'll have to find someone else with rank.' As he walked towards the door he called back, 'And don't any bugger touch anything near that money, if you value your freedom. Sergeant Prince and his boys will be checking for finger prints around that lot.'

Five minutes later Tony came rushing back in with his friend Sergeant Jerry Banks. Going straight behind the bar, Tony said, 'Has anybody touched anything, Jeff?'

He was assured that no one had. Pointing down at the pile of banknotes in the space from where the floor board had been lifted, he said, 'There you are, Sergeant Banks; what do you think of that lot, then?'

Staring down at the loot, the sergeant gave a low whistle. 'I reckon this is a bit more of little Barney Jackson's mischief, Yorky,' he replied quietly, 'and I reckon we'd better get Sergeant Prince up here soon as possible.'

Half an hour later, Sergeant Prince arrived with one of his corporals. They were accompanied by a tall morbid-looking civilian, who immediately went behind the bar counter and started powdering the floor area around the hole, taking special interest in the short piece of floor board that had been over it.

The sergeant forbade anyone else to go behind the bar, until the man had finished his investigation for finger prints; he positioned his corporal beside the gateway into the bar to make sure his order was upheld. Sergeant Prince then asked Tony and the others to tell him exactly what had happened, and asked if anything had been touched before he'd got there. He also informed them that he would require their prints to be taken in order to eliminate them. Tony said he understood, but assured him as far as he knew nobody had touched the money; and requested permission to resume work, as they had a deadline to meet.

They'd no sooner got stuck into the job again, when the door burst open and Sergeant Pike came storming in. Charging up to the bar, he was barred by the police corporal, so he made straight for Tony and Jeff, who working with the electric floor scrubber at the far end of the room.

'What the devil's going on, Ryan? Sergeant Banks just rang me at home to say you've found a load of money under the floor boards, behind the bar.'

Turning the machine off, Tony replied, 'Well, it wasn't me that found it, Sergeant, that was Jones, but I did make sure no one interfered with it. Also, as you were off duty, I asked Sergeant Banks to stand witness until the Police arrived.'

Glancing over his shoulder at the bar with a sigh, he replied nodding slowly, 'Good man, Ryan, what you did was just right and I appreciate your judgment in my absence.'

'Well, thank you, Sergeant, but I was only doing my duty after all, 'Tony replied smugly. Wanting to impress Sergeant Pike even more, he continued, 'Do you mind if we get on with our work now, Sergeant, we've a close deadline to meet, you know.'

'Pike, clearly still upset with the situation, was staring at the wall with a blank look on his face. Suddenly he was jerked back to reality, 'Yes, oh yes, carry on, Ryan,' he said abruptly. 'Get on with the job; you're right – we have a tight schedule to meet.' As he turned to go, he asked, 'Are you on duty in here overnight, Ryan?'

'Yes, and I'm afraid I'll have to stay all over the weekend, Sergeant too; I'm expecting three new residents: one male and two for the female wing.'

With a sigh, he replied, 'Bad timing, seeing as you've so much on, Ryan. Can't be helped though, it's all part of the job I suppose,' he added cheerfully, as he made for the door. No doubt pleased that he wouldn't be on call to receive them at some unknown hour himself, he called back as he disappeared out of the door, 'Good man, good man.'

Tony resumed his labours with a smile, knowing there was a good chance that he might have more favourable company in his bedding store over the weekend, if he could coax her.

68

'What bloody time do you call this, West?' Tony yelled, as Ted West sauntered into the bedding store on Tuesday morning. The others, who were sitting around having their tea break, all grunted approval.

'You'll be coming in at fucking dinner time next,' Jeff Baxter told him angrily, 'and you've done this before if I remember rightly – it's every time there's any heavy work about,' he sneered. Don't you realise, mate, the new carpets we've all been slaving our balls off for all weekend, are coming this morning.'

'Sorry I don't mean to let the side down lads,' he replied apologetically. 'I've been right bad, honest; I thought I'd got some sort of food poisoning. I've had the shits, mate,' he said forlornly. 'I've been sat on the bog since half past seven.'

Okay, Ted,' said Tony wanting to stop the growing argument. 'How are you now then, mate?'

'Bloody empty or I wouldn't have dared to leave the bog, Tony, I'll tell you.' He laughed forcefully.

'By the way, Ted, I've just been telling the others before you arrived,' said Tony. 'One of the sergeants told me earlier this morning that word is going around the Mess, that there was nearly a thousand quid in that bloody hole we found the other day.'

'Christ! A thousand?' gasped Ted.

'Yes, and he also told me,' he went on, 'that Corporal Jackson's prints were found on all the money, also around and inside the hole. Some of Eddy's were found on the surrounding floor of course, but that was to be expected seeing as he found the bloody stuff in the first place.'

Just then they heard the sound of footsteps coming up the corridor and Sergeant Pike called urgently, 'Come on, chaps, on your toes; the van's outside.' Reaching the store, he popped his head in. 'Come on, come on, never mind the tea break, we've work to do,' he yelled. By Friday morning the Mess was functioning as normal, the work in the bar had been fully completed; the whole building was, in fact, pristine, ready for the Easter weekend break.

The holiday weekend went well for the two friends and as at Christmas, they were on duty at the big social occasion on Saturday evening. As the evening progressed, they had, as usual, a little trouble now and then with a few drunken residents, but this was expected. One thing Tony was very grateful for, was that Sergeant McNabb was not present; neither was her pugilistic boyfriend, little Warrant Officer Bloomer. However, Sergeant Riley, the dust maniac, was also there, and to the mystification of both Tony and Jeff, he was in the company of a very attractive young woman with a most striking figure.

'Well, what do you think of that, then, Tony?' Jeff muttered to him out of the side of his mouth as the couple walked passed them stood in the doorway. Staring after the attractive young lady, as Riley escorted her onto the dance floor, he continued, 'I'm sure she gave us the eye as they passed – didn't you notice?'

Looking the young woman up and down from behind as they danced away, Tony replied quietly, 'I wouldn't have thought a twat like him, would have been capable of pulling a beautiful creature like that; no, not in a million years, Jeff.' He stared after them with a sigh. 'I'll tell you what, though, I'd willingly go in the boxing ring with him, for a session with her, mate.'

'Don't try kidding me, Tony Ryan,' Jeff said, giving him a nudge. 'You know you'd prefer your Sergeant McNabb.'

'Come on, clever boy,' Tony said, without further comment. 'Let's have a walk around the building to make sure everything's okay, then we can see if we can cadge a crafty pint off that new steward, in our beautiful new bar.'

The evening passed uneventfully; everyone appeared to have had a good time – apart from some gluttonous bugger who'd overindulged and brought it all up on the highly polished floor on the top landing. Eddie, of course, soon cleaned the mess up, first thing the next morning.

69

The holiday was over, everybody was back from Easter leave and the camp had returned to normal. Tony and Jeff were now making their arrangements for their own leave – as at Christmas, a week late.

'I think I can get a lift up to that camp near Doncaster, on one of them little Hanson transport planes on Friday, Jeff, Tony told him with a note of excitement. 'Warrant Officer Cox told me this morning, that he could fix it for me with one of his friends.'

'You lucky bugger, getting well in with the SWO man, eh, Ryan?' he said, laughing. 'Anyway, that'll save you time and money, won't it, mate.'

'Oh, I'll still have to get the train over to Leeds, but that's not much, only a few bob,' he said casually. 'Mind you, the bloody train will take as long again to get from Doncaster to Leeds, with it stopping at every little station on the way.'

Feeling on top of the world, Tony, dressed in his best blue uniform, weekend case in hand, walked out of the billet smiling, as he saw the others getting ready to return to their respective posts of employment for their afternoon' s work.

'Cheer up lads, you had your turn last week,' he called out, as he went jauntily through the door with a spring in his step. The time was one o'clock; Warrant Officer Cox had told him the little plane was due to take off at two o'clock, so he'd plenty of time to get down to the takeoff point at the bottom of the runway – or so he thought. Going through the big double gates as he headed for the guardroom to show his pass, he was already beginning to get that holiday feeling.

Reaching it he pressed the little bell button on the shelf in front of the long glass sliding window and almost immediately he was confronted by a surly young SP corporal eating a thick bread sandwich. Sliding back the window with a scowl, he asked, 'Yes, airman, what can I do for you?'

Tony casually handed him his pass sheet replying with a cheerful smile, 'Easter leave; relief staff, Corporal.'

The man, still munching at his food took it from him and glanced at it. He was just about to hand it back when, looking down at the shelf under the inside of the window, he paused and picked up a small sheet of paper. This he looked at for a moment, then turning back to Tony stood waiting patiently, he said sternly, 'Sorry, AC Ryan, this pass sheet has been overruled; you're to return to the Sergeants' Mess immediately and report to Sergeant Riley.'

Tony was dumbstruck, and took back the pass sheet cursing under his breath. Breaking into a run, he made his way back to the Mess seething with anger and thinking that if that bastard Riley hadn't got three stripes up, he'd knock his fucking head off. With time now being the essence, he charged through the main doors of the Sergeants' Mess into the dining room, where he saw Riley sitting at a table apparently just finishing his meal.

When he saw Tony, he got to his feet and made straight for him, with a peevish smirk on his face. 'So you're back then, Ryan, about time too,' he said threateningly, as he reached him.

'Yes, Sergeant, what's the problem? I'm not on duty, I've got a leave pass,' he told him.

Glaring into his face, Riley said in slightly raised voice, 'And I say you are on duty, man, when you leave shoddy work behind you; that bloody landing window outside my bunk is a bloody disgrace.'

Looking at him in disbelief, Tony replied, 'But the lads cleaned all the windows up there yesterday afternoon and Sergeant Pike inspected them this morning.'

Riley, his face going red with anger replied, 'Well, I say the one outside my bunk is filthy, get yourself up there man and get it cleaned now!' His glare intensified and he added, 'or you're going nowhere, man.'

Tony, fuming inside, turned to go and obey him saying, 'Yes, Sergeant,' but at that very moment there was suddenly a shout from the doorway.

'Ryan, what the hell are you doing here, lad; it's turned one thirty, the bloody plane takes off at two.' Warrant Officer Cox was standing there with a bewildered look on his face.

Going over to him, Tony explained the situation, but told him it wouldn't take long to clean the window again and that if he missed the plane he would have to go down to town and get the train.

Warrant Officer Cox would have none of it; realising the situation was nothing more than spite and rank pulling by Riley, he said, 'Oh, bugger that, lad, I've fixed you up with a lift up North and you're going to take it.' Glaring over at the bewildered Sergeant Riley, standing there motionless, looking over at them, he continued, 'You get yourself off, Ryan. I'll give the guardroom a ring, and I'll also sort this out with Sergeant Riley,' he added, staring at the now fidgeting man.

With only a few minutes left before take-off, Tony was sprinting up to the hanger at the bottom of Runway Two; he saw a little group of four young airmen, including a corporal technician, watching a small six-seater personal transport plane, taxiing down the track towards them. Reaching the group, Tony, not sure if they were waiting for the same plane, yelled out, 'Is this the lift up North, lads?'

Turning, one of them called back, 'Sure is, mate, and you nearly missed it.'

Entering the cabin, Tony was surprised to find the interior so compact; there were five small passenger seats, barely separated from the pilot by the back of his seat in the front of the little cockpit; sitting there was the grey-haired pilot, a flight sergeant.

As they shuffled in, he yelled out in a broad Glaswegian accent, 'Come on, come on, ladies, take your fingers out, we're late, as it is.' The door was no sooner slammed shut than the little old plane, with engines roaring, lurched forward and shot down the runway, like one of the jet fighters.

'Good God,' whispered one of the lads to Tony. 'What the hell have we let ourselves in for here? This bloody old crate will drop to bits, if he keeps pushing it like this.'

Within no time, they were clear of the runway by about a thousand feet and they continued soaring skywards like a rocket. However, when they reached the required altitude they settled down to level flight; the elderly pilot turned in his seat, and smiled. 'Good take off lads, eh?' Having said this, he reached into a leather bag at the side of his seat, pulled out a large bottle half-full of whisky, and took a long swig before starting to sing, 'I belong to Glasgow,' in his broad Scottish accent.

The passengers glanced at each other with looks of amazement. Tony, leaning over the shoulder of the man sat in front of him, whispered, 'Can any bugger else here, fly this old cart?'

Without turning, the man just muttered, 'I shouldn't think so, and if this pilot keeps knocking that stuff back, he won't be able to fly the fucker for long, either.

The next half hour or so passed uneventfully, and even though the pilot had taken a few more swigs from his bottle, his singing had not lost any of its volume – in fact it seemed to have increased somewhat.

Suddenly he shouted out, 'The lad that wants to be off for Birmingham, get ready; we're going down for your nearest landing point.' Within a couple of minutes the plane started to smoothly descend and as the runway come into view, everybody cringed, wondering if the pilot with all that whisky inside him was on the verge of killing them all. Tony made a lightning decision to get off and make for the nearest railway station, if they did survive the landing. However, they were all surprised when their plane made a most smooth, highly professional landing and taxied to a halt.

'Right, all out that want to, I'm in a bloody hurry,' the pilot yelled.

As the lad struggled out onto the runway with his case, he called back, laughing, 'Best of British, lads, you might need it.'

Considering the perfect landing, the boys began to think they might have underestimated their pilot; he couldn't have been as drunk as they'd thought. This, of course, could have been partly induced by wishful thinking, as they wanted to get home as quick and easy as possible; whatever the case, they seemed now to have developed a little more confidence in the man.

Tony, now having changed his mind about getting off, settled back in his seat and called out to the lad nearest the door, 'Come on, mate, pull that bloody door shut, let's be off.'

'We're doing a slight detour across country, boys,' called out the pilot, as they again began to climb. 'I've got a package to collect from a camp near Liverpool; might be a tricky landing though this one – it's just come through on my radio that there's a bit of fog over there.'

'Christ!' Tony whispered into the bloke in front's ear. 'Let's hope he leaves that bloody whisky alone now, or this could be our last hour, pal.' The lad slowly turned, giving him a very frightened look, accompanied by a forced weak smile.

Whatever the weather forecast ahead, where they were now was bright sunshine; looking down out of the little window; cattle in the fields below looked like flies and a train puffing away, looked like a piece of string winding its way along the track. The flight was smooth and the conversation had ceased; the only remaining sound was the pilot quietly humming some unknown tune. Tony was now beginning to enjoy the flight; in fact, he was feeling rather drowsy too. Settling back in his hard little seat, he glanced ahead at the pilot, hoping he wasn't feeling the same.

Suddenly he was brought back to full alert by the sound of a loud rasping noise followed by raucous laughter, 'Excuse me, gentlemen,' called out the pilot in pious tone, 'I'm afraid I broke wind.'

As the laughter subsided, Tony, now fully awake, resumed his gazing out of the side window; he could see they were flying over a large town or city with buildings stretching far ahead. They were too high to make out individual people, the streets looking like strings of cotton and the motor vehicles on them could just be made out like moving dots on the strings. Suddenly they hit a thick fluffy white cloud and all was wiped out instantaneously. A few seconds later they again emerged into bright sunshine; then they flew over another thick white cloud which looked so solid that it could have passed for a snow-covered mountain top. By the time they'd passed this beautiful sight they were back again flying over open countryside – green fields full of cattle the size of flies, and the occasional river or lake, until suddenly, it all began to fade and go misty.

'Fasten your seat belts, boys,' the pilot called out very authoritatively, 'We're going down and it's bloody foggy down there according to the control tower. In fact,' he added, 'they've advised me to abort the landing here.'

After a slight pause, the young corporal said hesitantly, 'With due respect, Flight Sergeant, may I ask why you've not accepted the advice?'

'Because the package I've been instructed to pick up from this station is of vital importance,' he replied casually.

'What's more, I also know the fog won't bother me, laddie; I could fly this little bus blindfolded,' he chuckled. Staring ahead and concentrating, he added, 'I served my apprenticeship flying these little kites through flak, not fog.' Breaking into laughter, he said, 'Most times, as I was weaving my way through the bloody Nazi anti-aircraft fire, I had a bottle of this good old Scotch by my side. As he spoke, he reached into his bag and pulling out the bottle, took a quick gulp, before he said seriously, 'Right, boys, make sure you're belted up; joking over, we're going down.'

Almost immediately they began to descend; Tony, looking through the porthole window, could see nothing but a thick wall of yellowy black fog ahead; as they hit it the tension in the little cabin was electric.

'Christ, you can't see a thing out there, and look – it's pissing it down as well,' yelled one of the young lads, a note of rising panic in his voice, 'looks like we've bloody had it, chaps.'

'Shut up, you silly young bugger,' said the pilot, without turning to see who was causing the commotion. 'We'll see the runway lights any second now.'

He was right; the runway lights almost at once came into view, but not in line with the forward motion of the aircraft. They were coming in sideways to the runway and furthermore, to their horror, directly in their path – barely a hundred yards away, was a row of high voltage electric pylons racing towards them. Gasps erupted from the passengers; Tony felt his stomach tighten, he'd never been so scared in his life, he was sure he was going to die. However, the old pilot never flinched and made no comment; he just stared ahead as though out for a Sunday afternoon jaunt in his little car. He'd obviously calculated that, as the high voltage wires between the pylons were about sixty feet from the ground and as they were approaching at a landing speed of just over a hundred mph, there was no chance he could lift that plane over them in time. No, they would definitely hit the wires, and the consequences would be being catastrophic – a fireball.

The same idea of this inevitable end was now apparent to all the passengers. Tony was thinking fast – would he have time to kick the door open and jump out before the plane blew up? It would certainly do that; they could hardly have used half their high octane aviation fuel up by now, he reasoned. While he was thinking, some of the others were gasping or shouting with fear; one young lad started openly weeping.

The pilot sitting coolly staring ahead at the approaching problem just growled out of the corner of his mouth, 'Aw shut up, you lot.' As he spoke, he dropped the plane down to within thirty feet of the ground roaring forward, engines screaming. Showing no sign of emotion as they passed under the wires he immediately climbed steeply, banking the craft sharply to port, swinging it round facing directly down the runway. Then, following the fog lights, he brought it down in a perfect landing. Tony and all the other young men were so impressed with the flying skills of their pilot that they gave a loud cheer – mainly gratified that they were still alive, no doubt.

Bringing the little craft to a halt near one of the hangers at the end of the track, the pilot muttered, 'Fucking shut up, you daft buggers. I don't know what you'd have done with the Luftwaffe, up your arse,' he chuckled. Turning off the engine, he got up, opened the door and kicked the stepladder down. 'I won't be a minute,' he said, 'and no lighting up when my back's turned,' he ordered.

However, before he'd gone down the four steps from the plane, a young corporal came running up with a box about two feet square and passed it up to him, shaking his head. 'I've been told to tell you, Flight Sergeant, the advice given you over the radio still stands, flying conditions remain hazardous; they say it'll be almost impossible to take off in this lot.'

'Bunkum,' he replied grabbing the box. 'We got down all right and we'll get back up. Then leaning into the plane he called out, 'Did you hear what the corporal said, you lot? They think we can't get back in the air through this muck.' He paused for any response and as there was none, he continued, 'Anyway, lads, if any of you agree with him, you can get off now and make your own way home, I'll understand,' he told them seriously. No comment was returned and nobody moved a limb so, climbing back into the plane, the old flight sergeant put the box behind his seat, sat down and fired up.

70

'Hello there, Landlord, mine's a pint of your best brew please, and make it quick, I'm thirsty,' called out Tony, with mock authority, in the near empty Dog and Gun that same evening.

Bernard bent down under the counter, and recognising the voice immediately, stood up smiling. 'Bloody hell, look what the wind's blown in,' he said. 'I hope you've brought some money with you tonight, AC Tony Ryan an'all, we've done away with that bloody old slate you usually use,' he laughed.

'Come on get that pint pulled, Bernard,' Tony laughed as he reached the bar. 'I'm dying for a pint of real beer after having to drink that dishwater down South.'

Leaning over the bar Bernard slapping him on the shoulder said affectionately, 'Glad to see you lad, how's things then?'

As he sat drinking his ale, Tony gave him a good rundown of his goings on back in the Sergeants' Mess, also his adventure flying home.

'You say this pilot flew one of them old wartime reconnaissance planes under a high voltage electric cable, between two pylons, and in fog,' gasped Bernard, standing with his elbows on the bar top looking flabbergasted.

'Aye, and it was pissing it down like hell, as well,' said Tony, 'What's more, he'd been taking swigs from a bottle of Scotch all the way up,' he told him, with a laugh.

'Christ, he could get bloody well drummed out of the service for that,' Bernard said, 'but he can't have been drunk, Tony, if he could fly the plane like that.' Pausing and shaking his head he went on, 'Mind you it was risky in them conditions apart from going under that wire, and what if another plane had been coming in to land as you'd crossed the runway?'

'Well, I must say that passed through my mind at the time Bernard,' Tony replied, 'but he'd no choice, if he hadn't gone under we'd have crashed. But he had been advised on his radio earlier not to approach for landing as visibility was not suitable for flying, so he knew, ten to one, the runway would be clear he said.

'Mind you, all us lads in the back nearly shit ourselves,' he added, grinning. Then he ordered another pint.

'Don't serve that bugger, landlord,' a shout came from the doorway.

Spinning around on his stool, when he recognised the voice, Tony leapt to his feet, and charged across the floor. 'Dave, Dave you rotten sod, why the hell didn't you let me know in your last letter that you'd be here,' he said wrapping his arms round him in a brotherly hug.

'I didn't know myself, mate, until last Wednesday,' Dave told him, as they walked back to the bar. 'Anyway, come on, let's get some ale inside us, Tony, old son, I'll put you in the picture then,' he said, looking over at the smiling Bernard.

Before they could sit down, there was a tittering from the back of the room and a man's voice called out, 'I think them two are in love, don't you, Fred?' This was followed by loud laughter.

Bernard said, 'Oh my God, don't say we're in for some scrapping, lads, and you've only just got home.' However, the two mates just turned, giving the two pasty-faced young men a brief glance, sitting down on bar stools without further comment.

'Two pints of best, Bernard, please,' said Dave, banging two half-crowns down on the bar. Nonchalantly, he reached into his inside jacket pocket for his silver cigarette case.

Watching him take out a cig and light it with his flashy gas lighter, Tony said with a sneer, 'I see you're still poisoning yourself with them bloody things, Mansfield.'

Dave taking a deep drag at his cig just replied, 'Yep.'

'Well, don't say I didn't warn you, old lad, when you end up coughing your lungs up and spitting blood,' Tony told him scornfully. 'Mind you,' he sneered, 'I should know better than to bother, I've been telling you since we were fourteen.'

'Oh, shut up,' Dave laughed. 'You sound like my mum. Anyway, it didn't hinder me on my training course, and believe me, mate, the Marine training course is one of the hardest in the world; I passed first time, an'all,' he told him proudly.

'I can back him up on that, Tony,' butted in Bernard, as he polished his beer glasses. 'I did the RAF Regiment course when I was younger and that's very similar; it's a bloody killer, Tony, I'll tell you.'

'We did a hell of a tough course for that display down in London,' Tony retaliated. 'Fourteen mile run every morning in working boots, then in the gym all bloody day. Some of the lads nearly passed out at first,' he told them, with a shake of his head.

'That's nowt,' said Dave, grinning. 'We had to do runs like that with a back pack full of house bricks, in battle dress, carrying a rifle and a survival kit. Then when we got back to camp, our Sergeant would turn us around and make us do it all again, with just a sup of water to keep us going.

'You're bloody kidding, Mansfield,' said Tony laughing. 'You couldn't do that on a roast beef dinner, never mind a bloody drink of water.'

'He's not, Tony,' said Bernard, again chipping in on their conversation. Looking at Dave, he said, 'Tell him about the three day survival course, sometime, Dave, lad; that'll make a pampered airman sit up and listen.'

Changing the subject completely, Tony asked, 'By the way, Dave, how long are you home for?'

Taking a long slug at his pint he answered casually, 'I'm on twenty-one days, mate, but it could be my last for two years, my lot are off to the Far East when we get back, and giving Tony a quick glance, he added, 'on active service.'

Tony and Bernard gave each other a startled look when they heard this. 'You're what?' Tony replied with a note of shock in his voice. 'You mean to say they're sending blokes straight from basic training onto active service?'

'That's right,' Dave said arrogantly, 'No problem to a marine, Tony. 'We're fully trained and ready for 'owt us, believe me, old lad.'

'Well, I think it's bloody disgusting,' said Tony. 'I hope you realise, dear silly boy, that the active service the bastards are sending you into will be jungle warfare, against hardened native jungle fighters, an'all,' he stressed firmly, glancing at Bernard leaning over the bar.

'Oh, you've no need to worry about me, Tony,' Dave replied, with a grin. 'We're not bothered about a load of rebellious natives, we're professional fighting men – the Royal Marines, the cream of the British military.'

'Aye, I know you are,' Tony said, with a frown. 'And you're also a silly bugger, not yet twenty year old, on your way to fight some of the most experienced jungle fighters on the planet, and in their own backyard as well.'

Dave looked at him for a few seconds without replying. He knew his mate was genuinely concerned, as he would have been if the tables had been turned. 'Look, Tony,' he said, staring into his face, 'to tell the truth, I'm not too pleased about the fucking posting myself, but it's my job now, mate, and like it or not, we've got to obey orders and make the best of it.'

'I realise that, Dave,' he replied, 'but I wish you'd have come into my lot for two years, done your National Service and then got out. After all, you should know the Services are only tools for the bloody politicians to exercise power,' he added bitterly.

'Right then, let's be more cheerful now, shall we?' Dave said, knocking the remainder of his pint back. What are we going to do now then, Tony, more ale or what?'

'Well, what's going off around here these days?' he asked. 'It's too early to start serious drinking. What about going out for a walk around, see if we can find some night life?' he suggested.

Dave, looking at him cautiously, said, 'I met that lass who runs that dance place that our Peggy has a share in this afternoon, Tony, you remember the plump lass, Sue; she asked me if I'd like to go up there tonight. What you think, mate, do you fancy it?' he asked tentatively.

Tony's eyes narrowed for a moment and then a wide smile crossed his face. 'Good thinking, Mansfield, good thinking; why not?' he said, with a grin.

Then, knocking back the remainder of his ale, he said cheerfully, 'Right, okay, let's be off – the ladies will be getting inpatient waiting for us.'

71

Going into the dance hall everything looked just the same as before, and many of the dancers were the same people. The first person Tony noticed was the tall skinny bank Manager that he'd crossed swords with in the excuse-me dance, when he had rescued Peggy from his clutches.

'Well, it's bloody full tonight,' Dave remarked, looking around the hall, 'and there's plenty of talent an'all, mate,' he said, nudging Tony in the ribs with his elbow.

Looking around without replying for a few moments, a solemn-faced Tony asked casually, 'Have you heard anything about your, Peg, lately, Dave?'

Before he could answer a woman's voice called out from behind, and Peggy's friend, Sue, came bustling up to them, smiling. 'So you decided to come after all, then, David,' she said. Smiling at Tony, she went on, 'You didn't say your friend, Tony here, was on leave as well, though, did you?'

'I didn't know myself, love, until half an hour ago; we met in the Dog, that's right, isn't it, Tony?'

'Sure is, strange but true,' he replied.

Smiling warmly, she continued, 'Anyway, I'm glad you've both come – but why didn't you wear your uniforms? You'd have had all the girls here in raptures, a couple of good -looking lads like you two.'

'Glad to get 'em off love,' Dave laughed.

'Aye, and we wanted to show off our new suits, as well,' added Tony, grinning as he dusted his jacket down with the flat of his hand.

'By the way, David, I was glad to see Peggy has just about got her affairs cleared up with that rat of an ex-husband,' Sue chipped in. She frowned. 'That must be a weight off her mind; I bet you and your mother are relieved for her now, after all the grief that man put her through.'

' Well, I know he's a nasty bugger, love, but I've heard nothing from her since she went back over there,' Dave replied, 'As far as I know, she's never written.

'She has David,' she replied with surprise. 'She told me she writes to your mum regularly, to keep her in touch with things – your mum being such a worrier.'

'When did she write and tell you about her affairs, then?' Dave asked. 'It's taken a bloody long time to get them sorted out, if you ask me.'

'She told me herself when we went over on holiday to see her; she's got a great job over there, good pay an'all.'

'Oh, I didn't realise you'd been to visit her,' Dave said, surprised. 'What sort of a job has she got, then, Sue?' he asked.

'She's an instructress in a big tennis club, belonging to the brother of a girlfriend of hers. He's rolling in money and gorgeous looking as well,' she replied.

Tony, who'd been standing in silence looking around the hall, pretending not to be listening, suddenly came to life as she told Dave this. 'Huh, that sounds very nice for her; rich and good-looking, eh? Lucky old Peg,' he said sarcastically.

Dave, realising that this had struck a sore point with his mate, said with a sneer, 'I'd have thought after all she'd been through with that other bloody yank, she'd have bloody well had enough of 'em. She must be going mad, getting herself emotionally entangled with another bugger, as soon as she'd just got rid of the last one.'

'Oh, you've got the wrong idea,' she replied, with a laugh. 'Peggy only works for him, there's nothing like that involved I assure you; anyway he wouldn't want to be involved that way with her,' she told him confidently.

'Come of it, Sue love, there's not many blokes would turn their back on a woman like Peggy, I can assure you of that,' Tony interrupted arrogantly.

Smiling at him, she said, 'Well, he would, my dear boy, he'd rather have you or Dave than her, even if she did want him, which she definitely doesn't,' she said firmly. 'He's got a regular boyfriend anyway.'

Hearing this Dave broke into a loud laugh and Tony smiling broadly, said sheepishly 'Well, I didn't say she did want him, did I?'

'Come on,' she said, grabbing his arm realising, how he was thinking. 'You dodged having a dance with me the last time you came in here; you're not getting away with it this time.' As she dragged him onto the dance floor, Dave stood watching with a very puzzled look on his face, shaking his head thoughtfully.

The rest of the evening went well; both lads felt a form of relief and contentment with regard to Peggy's situation, even though the reasons may have been for different ends. Tony of course insisted he was now resigned to the fact that she didn't want him anymore and that was that. Dave told him that he was pleased with this as he was sure it would never have worked out in the long run; however, he didn't really believe it, but kept his suspicions to himself. The rest of Tony's leave was a great success, irrespective of the worry at the back of his mind regarding Dave and his dangerous far Eastern posting.

Wednesday soon came; after the usual farewells at home, Tony was off to the railway station, accompanied by his mate, Dave, who insisted on seeing him onto the train.

After promising to write to each other regularly, Tony gave him a lecture on self-preservation, and how he must never volunteer for anything, plus lots more advice. Tony was on the train ready for his journey back to camp and was leaning out of the open window, waving farewell to Dave stood on the platform. He had a deep sickly feeling in his gut; could this be the last time he'd see his mate who he loved like a brother? However, although he didn't know it, there was an unexpected catastrophe in the Sergeants' Mess, waiting to greet him on his return to camp.

72

Walking up to the two steps in front of the guardroom, Tony rang the bell and waited to show his pass. He thought it seemed rather strange that everywhere was so quiet; usually the place was very active, but today it appeared to be deserted.

He rang again, and after a couple of minutes Sergeant Prince himself came walking up to the window. Looking very grave, he slid it open and accepted Tony's Pass. In a solemn voice, he asked, 'Hello, Ryan, have you had a good leave, then?'

'Yes, thank you, Sergeant,' Tony replied. 'It's quiet around here today, Sergeant,' he remarked cheerfully.

'Yes, most of my corporals are down on the airfield on supervisory duties. I've been down there half the night myself,' he said quietly. 'I've only come back up here to handle some outside communications.' Then noticing Tony's puzzled expression, he said, handing him his Pass sheet back, 'Of course, you won't have heard about the terrible accident last night, Ryan?'

'What accident, Sergeant?' Tony asked, startled.

'Horrible job, lad,' he replied, obviously upset himself. 'Several men were killed, two from our Mess; terrible, terrible,' he repeated. 'I knew 'em both, one for over five years. Grand blokes,' he added, shaking his head.

Shocked at this news, Tony said, 'Two Sergeants from our Mess killed, did you say, Sergeant – do you mind me asking who the two poor souls were?'

Looking back at him sadly through the open window, Sergeant Prince could see the anticipation on

Tony's face and realised he would have known the two NCOs. 'Well, there were four men killed, two young commissioned officers, Sergeant Miller and Flight Sergeant Long. Tony's heart missed a beat as he heard this.

'Oh, my God, no!' he gasped. 'Flight Sergeant Long, what a bloody shame, he was a lovely bloke, Sergeant,' he said, shaking his head. Sergeant Prince just nodded in silence. 'I was talking to him for fifteen minutes the morning I went on leave,' Tony went on. 'He'd called in at the bedding store to collect his laundry.' He stared into space momentarily. 'He was telling me, he'd just booked a holiday in Cornwall, and was taking his wife and little daughter. She's only four, he told me. They were going down there for a fortnight. Oh God, poor Flight Long – what a loss,' he whispered, staring down at his boots. 'I didn't know Sergeant Miller much,' he said. 'He hasn't been here long, only a young chap, though, wasn't he, Sergeant?'

'Yes, he was,' he replied, 'only twenty-five. Flight Sergeant Long was older, about my age.'

As Tony put the Pass sheet back in his jacket pocket and turned to go Sergeant Prince said, 'Mind you, how the one that survived got out is the biggest puzzle, four killed, the plane blown to smithereens and he got out without a scratch. The rescue team found him crawling on the track shocked, slightly concussed but otherwise unharmed.' Then reaching out to slide the window closed he said, 'Aye, a miracle how he got out of that lot, lucky man, Sergeant Riley, he must have a guardian angel.' Tony's jaw dropped when he heard this, he could hardly take it all in.

Walking up the road carrying his case, his mind was in a spin. There seemed to be a solemnity over the camp and justifiably so he thought – four men killed so suddenly like that. Then he thought of Sergeant Riley, and how he'd survived. 'He's a nasty bastard,' he muttered, 'but thank God he's safe, anyway.'

73

Walking into the Sergeants' Mess later, the atmosphere was of static depression; everybody he passed on his way to the bedding store looked in a state of shock.

As he passed Sergeant Pike's permanently ajar office door along the corridor, the sergeant called out, 'Ryan, Ryan can I have a word?' Stopping in his tracks and going in to the office, he was surprised when the sergeant said pleasantly, 'Hello, Ryan, I hope you've had a good leave.' Motioning to a chair in front of his desk he said quietly, 'Sit down, Ryan.' Tony did so and he continued, 'I don't know if you've heard, but there was a very bad accident here in the early hours of this morning.' He paused and stared down at the desktop for several seconds, before he went on, almost in a whisper. 'Tragically the Mess suffered two fatalities, two fine men,' he said, shaking his head slowly.

Looking back at him across the desk, Tony replied quietly, 'Yes, Sergeant, I know about it, Sergeant Priest informed me when I handed my Pass sheet in at the guard room earlier. He looked exhausted; he told me he'd been down on the runway himself, half the night.'

Leaning forward, his elbows on the desk top, Pike replied, nodding sadly, 'Yes, apparently, he was one of the first down there; must have a mind of steel that man,' he said, shaking his head. 'I was told the explosion was so violent that no-one on board could possibly be recognised. Body parts and debris were found all over the track; even entrails from the victims were discovered hanging on the surrounding bushes – the explosion was so horrific.'

'Oh, my God,' said Tony. 'It's a rough job the police have; I don't think I'd have the stomach to face sights like that, especially if it were chaps I'd known.'

'No, no, Ryan, me neither.' The sergeant frowned, 'Sergeant Riley was lucky though,' he said, 'Did he tell you about him managing to get out of the plane before it blew up?'

'Yes, but how do you think he managed to do that, Sergeant, with it all happening so quick?' Tony asked, screwing up his eyes.

'Only God knows that, Ryan, but he did, that's all that matters,' he replied. Then getting to his feet he said, 'Anyway, Ryan, I've got two commissioned officers coming over this afternoon, to take stock of the contents in the bunks of the deceased men, so I'll be busy all afternoon.'

Nodding and getting up to leave, Tony said, 'Don't you worry, Sergeant, I'll try and hold the fort, while you're sorting everything out.'

'Good man,' he replied in his usual brisk tone. As Tony made for the door, he called out, 'Oh, and Ryan, make sure you keep all the cleaners away from the two bunks in question; I don't want the inspecting officers disturbed in their duties.'

Eventually reaching his bedding store, Tony found the door open and the sound of the radio playing softly; going quietly in, he found Jeff sitting with his back to the door, a cup of tea on the table beside him and reading a newspaper.

'Out of my chair, Baxter!' Tony yelled, making the poor lad nearly jump out of his skin. 'Go and get that mop and bucket,' he chuckled.

'Hi there, Tony, old son,' Jeff smiled. 'Have you had a good time, mate?'

'Not bad at all, Jeff,' he replied, 'and you?'

'Oh, not bad, mate. How's that pal of yours getting on in the Marines? Did you see him, then?'

'Aye, he was home on leave, he'd got three weeks. Huh,' he grunted, 'deserves them, the silly bugger – got himself posted to the Far East – on active service an'all,' he added,   despondently.

'Yuh what?' he replied. 'Better him than me. By the way, Tony, have you heard about the crash?'

'I've heard nowt else since I got back, mate; bloody awful Jeff, I can hardly believe it. Poor Flight Sergeant Long and the other Sergeant killed, terrible' he said sadly. 'But Riley was lucky, though,' he stressed, 'fancy him being able to get out of a situation like that without a scratch.'

'Yes, old Pike told me all about it earlier, 'said Jeff, ' but them kids were there, an'all; if it had happened on the first landing they'd most likely all have been killed; doesn't bear thinking about, Tony, does it?' he sighed.

'What kids?' Tony asked, with a blank expression on his face. 'Nobody said anything about any kids being involved to me, Jeff?

'Didn't Pike mention the young boys from the local ATC group?' Jeff said. 'They were being given the experience of night flying as a treat. Different groups of them often come up here for that experience he told me. Anyway, they'd been up for well over an hour, out over the North Sea, an'all, Pike said. Then when they came back, the plane landed on Runway One for them to get out; their coach was parked there, apparently. Then it took off again, circled, to come down to land at the top end on Runway Four, so it could be put in the big hanger up there,' he nodded, 'that's when it happened.'

Tony stood listening intently, asked, 'Yes, but Jeff, what caused the bloody accident, anyway?'

'Well, of course, nobody knows for certain until after the inquiry, mate,' he shrugged, 'but from what I've heard, it looks as though part of the front landing gear collapsed when it hit the track; bloody terrible the crew getting killed like that though,' he sighed.

'Christ, it was lucky all them young boys weren't still on it,' Tony said. 'That would have been terrible.'

74

For the next few days a morose atmosphere hung over the Mess; however, by the weekend, things seemed to be getting back to normal. By the end of the following week the initial investigation into cause of the accident had been done but, as was usually the case, the final results were expected to take several weeks. However, it was generally presumed unofficially that the accident had been caused by metal fatigue on the front suspension.

An inquest was conducted on the four deceased casualties, and arrangements made with their next of kin for the release of the bodies. It was decided they were to be buried in the local Churchyard down in the village, with full military honours. The bearers of the coffins were volunteers, recruited from the residents of both the Officers' and Sergeants' Mess, each to carry their own. A small party of airmen were selected to be the guard of honour at the church ceremony and Tony and Jeff had willingly volunteered for this duty. Tony was not surprised to see that his fellow Yorkshireman, Sergeant Jerry Banks, was one of the six bearers of the remains of Flight Sergeant Long. He knew they had been very good friends and members of the camp tennis team together.

Later on, back into the billet, the two lads were lying on their beds discussing the afternoon's activities, when Tony suddenly groaned, 'I'll tell you something, mate; I'm fucking starving.'

'So am I, but it's a bit early to go over for tea, it's only just gone four fifteen,' said Jeff. 'Are we having the sale tonight, then, Tony? Don't forget it's Friday and we didn't have it last night.'

'Of course we are, you pillock,' Tony said in startled tone. 'The show must go on, you know, business is business. Anyway, it doesn't matter whether we have it on Thursday or Friday, as long as the punters haven't spent all their money yet, does it?' he said, with a laugh. Jumping off his bed, he yelled, 'Come on, lazy bugger, let's get over to the Airmen's Mess, it'll be half four by the time we get there.' Making for the door, he added, 'When we get back, you can get the stall laid out on your bed, ready for when the lads get in.'

'Why – my bed?' Jeff grumbled, as he ambled behind him. 'We used my bed last time we had a sale, why not yours, this time?'

'Because,' Tony said, firmly, 'You're handling the job tonight.' With a smile he went on, 'You're fully in charge of the business tonight, Jeff, have you forgotten? I've to go back to work after tea; I'm on duty all weekend. I can't be in two places at once, you know,' he told him, nodding arrogantly.

'Aye, you were on duty the last time we had a sale, if I remember,' Jeff grumbled.

'Come on, let's get our bloody tea and don't be so ungrateful, Baxter, there's not many people I'd trust to handle the business on their own, you know. Don't forget you're a shareholder an'all, so you've a right to hold the fort when I'm on duty. By the way,' he said, 'make sure you get cash for everything you sell tonight, no tick for anyone.'

75

Tony was feeling very pleased with himself as he walked up to the main front door of the Sergeants' Mess, a couple of hours later. Jeff was organised, and the items of clothing, repaired shoes and other bits and pieces had all been laid out on his bed. Tony was still dressed in his best blue dress uniform, not having bothered to change. As he was going into the Mess, he was just thinking he really ought to have put his working gear on, when he was hailed by Sergeant Pike, who looked as though he'd got the problems of the world on his shoulders.

'Ryan! Ryan! Thank God, you're here, Ryan,' he yelled, going towards him with a look of panic on his face. 'Emergency, Ryan! We've got a flood in the main kitchen – it just happened about ten minutes ago; thank God we've got tea over. Sergeant McNabb is going mad,' he raved on. 'I've tried wrapping towels around it, but it can't be stopped, Ryan,' he gasped. Staring up at Tony, he continued passionately, 'I've even tried ringing the Maintenance Department, but there's no reply.' He stood wringing his hands and frowning for a few seconds. 'You'll have to run down there, Ryan and see if you can get anybody who knows anything about plumbing to come and stop it, before we're flooded out.'

'I suggest we go and have a look at what the trouble is first, Sergeant,' said Tony calmly. 'I've seen things like this before, how did it happen?'

'They were rearranging some of the benches,' he told him. 'One of the silly buggers accidentally hit a copper pipe running along the back wall, and it broke into two.' As they began to hurry in the direction of the kitchen, he wailed in panic, 'Do you think you'll know how to stop it, Ryan? There's water spurting out all over the place.'

'Well, I was in the building trade before I came into the Service, Sergeant,' Tony told him reassuringly.

Going into the kitchen the scene resembled a war zone; the staff were all running around in great excitement. Some were mopping, some moving things back from the squirting water pipe, and Sergeant McNabb, who was trying to stem the flow of water with a large towel, was wet through.

'Please calm down everyone,' called out Tony, as he walked around the kitchen looking under all the wall benches and shelves. Suddenly he spotted what he was looking for on the far wall, under one of the vegetable racks; yes, there it was – the mains stop tap; crawling under the big rack which smelled strongly of cabbage, he managed, with great difficulty, to turn it off.

Suddenly the kitchen fell silent. 'Thank God for that, Ryan,' yelled out Pike, coming over to Tony, as he struggled out from under the smelly vegetable area. 'However did you do that, man? Good work, good work,' he said, smiling with relief. Looking around, he smiled at the sight of Sergeant McNabb, drying herself with the wet towel. Then, regaining his authority, he said to Tony, 'You'd better get down to Maintenance now, and find someone to come and mend that pipe, Ryan.'

Dusting himself down, Tony said, 'It might not be necessary, Sergeant. As I said, I've seen things like this before; I'll just have a quick look at that damaged pipe fitting first, I think I might be able to put it right myself.'

Going over to the now stable pipe, Tony made his inspection with great authority while Sergeant McNabb and her staff stood around watching. 'Where's the tool cabinet, Sergeant?' he asked confidently.

'It's over there.' Pike pointed behind the door. 'What is it you require, Ryan?' he asked, subserviently.

'The spanner box, Sergeant,' he replied. 'Would you mind going and getting it for me please, I'll soon have this sorted out,' he told him, looking the damaged pipe over with a professional eye. 'Hopefully this won't take long,' he said, 'then I can get on with my own duties, I've a lot on tonight, you know – I've got three new residents due in.'

'Oh yes, I realise that, Ryan,' replied Pike, dodging over to the tool cabinet for the spanner box, sounding greatly relieved that the situation had been sorted out.

76

'By God, you're looking a bit wet, Yorky,' shouted Sergeant Banks, seeing Tony pass his open door on way to his own abode.

'Aye, they've just had bloody calamity down there in the kitchen, Jerry,' he called back. 'You'll never believe it,' he chuckled stepping into the doorway of the Sergeant's bunk, 'some silly bugger knocked a nut off a copper pipe coming from the mains, while scrubbing out. Christ, I could hardly believe the naivety of 'em,' he laughed. 'Not one of 'em, not even Sergeant Pike, knew how to turn the bloody stop tap off.'

Laughing like hell, Jerry Banks got off his bed, where he'd been lying, reading a novel, and followed Tony across the passage into the bedding store. 'You must be kidding, Yorky, he spluttered, laughing. 'You mean to say that Cyril, with all his knowledge, didn't know how to turn the bloody stop tap off? Were they flooded out then, or what?' he asked, gleefully.

Taking his wet jacket off and hanging it on the pipes, Tony replied, laughing, 'They'd have all drowned, if I hadn't turned that bloody tap off for 'em, Jerry. By the way, I saw you down at the funeral this afternoon,' he said, seriously. 'Sad job that; you can't be feeling too good yet yourself yet, Jerry, having just buried your mate, Flight Sergeant Long,' Tony said sadly.

Staring back at him for a few seconds in silence, he replied almost in a whisper. 'Yes, Gordon was a great guy, Yorky. I'm going to miss the big bugger, he's left a lovely wife and a beautiful little daughter you know;

they've taken it so bad an'all,' he told him, with grief in his voice.

'The ceremony went off well, anyway, didn't it?' Tony said, more cheerfully, when he saw the sad look on his friend's usually jovial face. 'I was in the funeral parade you know.'

'Yes, yes, I saw you; very smart you looked an'all.' He smiled weakly.

'Do you know Jerry, I know it's daft but whenever I go to a funeral, I'm always on tenterhooks when the bearers are carrying the coffin, thinking because it's heavy, one of them might trip up and they drop it.'

Looking back at him with the same sad expression on his face, Jerry said quietly, 'Not much weight in them we were carrying today, Yorky – light as a feather, there was hardly 'owt in 'em,' he muttered, looking down at the floor frowning.'

'What do you mean?' replied Tony, with a look of disbelief. 'Your mate, Flight Sergeant Long was a big lad, he must have weighed at least thirteen and a half stone, Jerry,' he said.

'Oh yes, you're right there,' he replied. 'He was a big lad, but there were only bits of them lads in them boxes. Gordon had to be identified by his dental records; I suppose it was the same with the others,' he said, staring into space.

Tony listening intently, replied softly, 'You know, it's hard to believe something like that could happen to someone you knew so well; I mean, I was talking to him in here for fifteen minutes the morning before I went home on leave.' Looking at Jerry sadly, he added, with a nod, 'He was standing just where you are now, Jerry.'

Moving slightly to one side, Jerry replied, 'Well, that's what happened to them, Yorky, with 'em being involved in an explosion like that, I suppose it was to be expected though. I mean, there was very little left of the bloody plane itself,' he added, staring down at his feet, shaking his head slowly.

'Good God, it must have been terrible for them when it happened,' muttered Tony. 'Sounds as though they were lucky to find anything left at all of the poor blokes, if it was violent enough to blow the plane itself to bits like that, Jerry.'

'Well as I said only parts of the bodies were retrieved,' he replied. 'Sergeant Priest was one of the first on the scene; he told me it was a horrific sight when he got down there. He said there were body parts, such as liver and other internal organs, hung on the bushes at the side of the track; one of the men's legs was found over a hundred yards down the runway,' he grimaced, shaking his head. Tony cringed on hearing all this as Jerry continued, 'Of course, Sergeant Priest and his boys got it all cordoned off before my transport chaps got there with the heavy lifting gear. Not much for us to do anyway when we did get there, as it was nearly all in small bits scattered about the runway,' he muttered. 'Anyway it's all in the past now, Yorky,' he went on with a false smile. 'Life must go on, this sort of disaster was an everyday occurrence during the war, they had to just grin and get on with it then, didn't they?'

Smiling, Tony replied, 'Well, I didn't know much about the war, Sergeant Banks, I was nowt but a bairn, as my granny would say, but no doubt you're right.

'Well, I was only a young bloke when war broke out,' Jerry said. 'I joined up straight away and served right through. Gordon Long was a few years older than me,' he smiled thinly. 'Got his wings within six month of joining the service; flying with Bomber Command throughout the war, he was.'

'Pausing in thought for a moment, he went on, 'Do you know, Yorky, he never got a scratch either,' he said, nodding.'

'Fate seems to work in strange ways, doesn't it, Jerry?' Tony replied sadly.

'Yes, unbelievable, he flew through all that bloody Nazi anti-aircraft fire untouched, then he gets his lot in a freak accident like this. He was a squadron leader by the end of the war, an'all, you know,' he told him, with a shake of the head.

Giving him an enquiring look, Tony said, 'Squadron leader, well, how was it he was only flight sergeant here then, Jerry?'

Chuckling with another the shake of his head, he replied, 'Well, I don't know really, but I've heard it said that they used to give rank out like bird seed to aircrew in the war.'

'Aye, my granddad told me, that in the first war they'd give stripes and commissions out like hell to get the job done, then, when it was all over they decommissioned a lot of the officers who were not from the posh end of society,' Tony said with a sneer.

'Well, as I said I don't know much about it really, but it could be something to do with money, pensions or summat of that sort,' Jerry pointed out. 'They say it was cheaper in several ways for a commissioned officer to volunteer to be demoted to a non-commissioned senior rank, if he wanted to stay on in the service after the war. It could be Mess fees, or that sort of thing,' he shrugged. 'We don't have to pay them in the Sergeants'

Mess you see; but commissioned ranks do in their Mess.'

'Sounds like a bloody con trick to me,' Tony said haughtily. 'By the way have you heard how my friend Sergeant Riley is getting on in hospital, Jerry, I know the old sod didn't like me much but I'm glad he managed to get out of it okay; lucky bugger, though.'

'Aye, that's an understatement,' he replied, ' unbelievably lucky; no bugger knows how he did it either, he's got no physical damage as we know, but he's very badly shocked they tell me; they say he was stone deaf for three days after the accident.'

'He'll get over that,' Tony grinned. 'I was deafened at Padgate on the shooting range. I was firing a bloody big Sten gun and silly bugger me turned my head as I pulled the trigger. The blast hit me straight in the bloody lug hole; I was deaf in my right ear for three days after.' He laughed. 'But do you know what I did on impulse,' he continued, still laughing, 'I threw this bloody big gun down at the feet of the instructor, an RAF regiment flight sergeant no less, and yelled out at him that I'd never fire one of them fucking things again.'

'Oh Christ, what happened then, Yorky,' Jerry asked, grinning. 'Did he put you on a fizzer for your cheek?'

'No, he just laughed like hell and walked away telling me to grow up. I was very surprised myself,' he laughed, 'but I bet he'd seen that happen countless times with the raw recruits.'

Hearing the sound of quick footsteps coming up the corridor, Tony said, 'That sounds like a woman's walk; I'm expecting a woman sergeant and two male sergeant technicians this weekend.'

'I'll be off then, Yorky.' Jerry turned to go, but before he could get out of the door the footsteps arrived and he was confronted by a short, plump sour-faced woman sergeant of about forty, whom neither of them had seen before.

Jerry had been in the process of getting ready for a Friday night social evening before coming over to the bedding store, and was dressed only in trousers and sleeveless vest; apparently, seeing him in this attire didn't seem to impress the lady.

Staring up at him for a few seconds with a look of extreme disapproval on her face, she yelled, 'What the devil are you doing on duty dressed like that, airman, do you realise this is a mixed sex Mess?'

Tony slightly startled came up to the door smiling friendlily, but before he could say anything she shouted at him, 'And you don't look too smart either, on duty without your jacket.' Then, glancing back at Jerry, she said scornfully, 'but you're half-naked, man!'

Jerry, turning to Tony with a broad grin on his face, said, 'Looks as though we're in trouble, AC Ryan.'

Seeing this as insubordination, the lady, now red-faced, yelled angrily, 'You deserve a lesson, man, acting like this with a superior officer.' Reaching into her jacket pocket she pulled out a small note book, saying quietly to the still grinning Jerry, 'Right then, name and number, you're on a 252, man.' With a frown, she added, 'That'll wipe that grin of your face, I'm sure.'

Standing there in his sleeveless vest still grinning, Jerry, pretending to come to attention, stamped his slippered feet on the floor and called out with mock respect –'1234567, Sergeant Banks, J.' Walking past her without further comment on his way back to his bunk, he said casually to Tony, 'Hope your jacket dries out, okay, AC Ryan, after getting it so wet saving the Mess from being flooded.'

77

'Are you in there, Tony?' Jeff called out urgently, tapping on the bedding store door next morning, 'Come on, open up, mate, it's nine o'clock.' There was a groan heard from within, then a shuffle of feet was heard and the door slowly opened to reveal Tony standing there bleary-eyed, in his underpants and vest.

'What the hell are you making all that bloody noise about? I've had a right night of it here,' he grunted. 'I bet I haven't had more than a couple of hours sleep all night.'

'Why, what's up, mate?' Jeff asked, grinning.

Beckoning him in, he grunted, 'Well, like any Friday night in here, they've been rolling out of the bar in the early hours, making a hell of a din. Then, just when it had all quietened down, there was a braying on my door; one of them bloody sergeants I've been expecting, arrived. He was also pissed as a newt, and fucking three o'clock in the morning an'all,' he moaned.

'Shut that bloody door, Jeff, while I get dressed,' he went on grumpily filling the kettle; then pointing to a big black leather case behind the door he said, 'That's the drunken bugger's luggage, you can take it up to his bunk when we've had a cup of tea.'

'What's he left it here for, Tony?' he asked, staring down at it.

Buttoning his shirt up, Tony grunted, 'I left the bloody thing there in the middle of the night when I was trying to get the drunken old fart up to his bunk; I couldn't manage him and his bloody big case as well,' he grumbled.

'Huh, that far gone was he?' Jeff laughed. 'How come he arrived so late then?'

'He told me he's based near London. He'd been to a stag party before driving up here he said, he's a metallurgist or some bloody thing,' he told me. 'He's only here for a few days; he's part of an inspection team investigating the cause of that crash.'

'Christ, you say he drove a car right from London, pissed? Jeff said with a whistle.

'Aye, that's what he said,' Tony replied, as he mashed the tea. 'Mind you, that's nowt compared to that drunken pilot I told you about, who flew us home when we went on leave,' he laughed. 'By the way, how did you go on with the business yesterday evening, Jeff? More importantly,' he stressed, 'Where's the takings?'

'Sales not too good, Tony,' he replied, reaching into his pocket and passing him an envelope. There's four pound ten and six in there, mate, and I kept the stall laid out until ten o'clock,' he told him.

Counting the money Tony sneered, 'Poor do, that, Jeff. I thought you'd have had better takings than that with all that good gear you had last night. Anyway, could be worse I suppose,' he sighed, putting it in his pocket.

They finished their tea and Tony, pointing at the big black case behind the door, said, 'You'd better get that up to the sergeant's bunk, Jeff, he'll most likely have all his togs in there.'

Picking up the case, Jeff said, laughing, 'I'd better not go braying on his door like he did here, Tony, ten to one the old bugger will be hung over.'

A little later, Tony, walking into the busy kitchen, called out, 'Good morning, Sergeant McNabb. I've just come to see if that damaged pipe is still okay.'

'Standing there in a spotless white smock and hat she gave him a warm smile. 'Yes, it's fine,' she replied, looking him up and down. 'You don't look fine, though,' she told him, with a note of concern in her voice.

'As a matter of fact, Sergeant, I don't feel all that lively. I must admit,' he told her in a self-pitying voice, 'I've only had about a couple of hours sleep all night, I really feel exhausted I'll tell you,' he moaned.

'Oh, poor you, what's been the trouble, then?' she enquired with concern.

After he'd told her all about his rough night – grossly exaggerated of course – and how he'd overslept because of it, thereby missing his breakfast, she was visibly distressed for him.

'Oh, you poor boy,' she sympathised, looking at him affectionately. 'I can soon sort the breakfast problem anyway,' she said, smiling. Turning, she glanced around the kitchen; seeing Ruby coming in from the dining room with a tray full of empty plates, she called out, 'Pritchard! Put that lot in the sink then come here, woman and get AC Ryan a full breakfast; set it out on that table over there,' she yelled pointing across the kitchen. Tony had no sooner got stuck into the huge plateful of sausage, bacon, three eggs, fried bread and tomatoes, when Pike came striding into the kitchen.

'Oh, you're there, Ryan,' he called out, seeing Tony sitting at the table eating, 'I've been looking all over for you. We've got another problem on the top landing, Ryan; two of the lavatories are blocked up with newspaper.' Pausing in his speech, he said, 'What the devil are you doing, Ryan, sitting there eating, when you're supposed to be on duty?'

Before Tony could reply, Sergeant McNabb came over from the oven where she was checking the temperatures. Looking down at the cocky little Pike, she yelled, 'Because the poor young man has been up all night on duty, Cyril.' Staring aggressively into his face, she continued in a slightly raised voice. 'He missed his breakfast in the Airmen's Mess by attending to late arrivals, so I insisted he dined here under the circumstances; surely you've no objections to that?' She still stared intently into his shocked face.

'Oh, no of course not, under those circumstances, Mavis,' he replied, looking up into her frowning face. Turning to go, he said in a friendly tone, 'Anyway, I'll be in my office, Ryan, when you've finished your breakfast, we'll sort that ablution problem out then.'

The job in question ended up being given into the capable hands of Ted West and Eddy Jones, who were the most experienced men in that type of work.

Walking into the billet later the same afternoon, Tony yelled out, 'I've bloody well had enough today, Jeff, that third flight sergeant turned up half an hour ago, just as I was coming out of the front door; I had to go back and open up again just for him, the twat,' he said. Then getting a coat hanger from his locker, he discarded his tight-fitting best blue uniform. 'Glad to have that monkey suit off, an'all,' he grunted, flopping back on to the bed in underpants and vest.

'What about us going down into the village tonight, Jeff,' he suggested, yawning, 'It's Saturday night, let's go mad for once and get bloody drunk, mate, eh?'

'Good idea,' Jeff replied eagerly. 'We could go to that dance in the village hall; there were some lovely birds there last time we went, if you remember.'

'Aye, you're right, Baxter, there were,' Tony chuckled. 'We might get a bit of "that there" if we're lucky an'all,' he laughed, waving two fingers up and down.

78

The band was thumping away at 'Twelfth Street Rag' as the two lads walked into the packed dance hall; the smell of sweat and thick cigarette smoke was everywhere, while the floor vibrated under the feet of the enthusiastic dancers.

'Christ, Jeff, it's packed,' shouted Tony, leaning towards him, so that he could be heard above the band and the inarticulate conversation within the crowded building.

'What did you say, Tony?' Jeff yelled, gazing around the hall. Tony repeated it again, only louder, leaning nearer to his ear.

'Sure is mate,' Jeff yelled back. 'I were right an'all eh, there's some real talent in here tonight, I'm glad we came aren't you?'

Looking over the heads of the dancers to the top end of the hall Tony noticed a small bar had been set up since their last visit; it appeared to be doing a roaring trade. 'Come on, Jeff,' he yelled. 'Let's get over to the bar before the dance ends or we'll never get served, it looks bloody enough busy now,' he added, pushing his way through towards it.

Looking around as they struggled through the crowd, Tony remarked, 'There's certainly some nice floosies about, Jeff, I reckon we'll score here tonight, mate, if we play our cards right.' Suddenly his conversation froze and he stood staring tight-lipped, blankly into the crowd.

Glancing at him slightly baffled, Jeff said, 'What's up, Tony? You look as though you've seen a ghost.'

'Worse than that, mate,' he replied, still staring into the thronging mass. 'It's Father Fletcher, and he's dancing with a real beauty. Christ, they're snogging as they dance, Jeff,' he gasped.

'Well, what the hell's wrong with that, Tony,' Jeff said, with a laugh. 'You do it yourself, don't you?'

'Yes I do, but that's Father Fletcher,' he repeated, still gaping in disbelief.

'Anyway, who the fucking hell is this Father Fletcher, Tony and whose bloody father is he?' He laughed. 'What's more, why are you so bothered anyway, it's nothing to do with us; don't tell me you're jealous as well as bloody hypocritical.'

Spinning round to face him, Tony said sternly, 'I'm not bloody jealous, you fool, and yes, I've said I do snog birds on the dance floor, I admit it, you twit, but I'm not a Catholic Priest,' he almost yelled as he turned glaring, and headed for the bar.

'How do you know who that bloke is then, Tony?' Jeff asked, after they'd been served and had found a seat at the wall side.

'I met him when I had to go on Church parade last month, he was serving Mass.' As he sipped his beer, he muttered, 'It's unbelievable; fancy, a Catholic Priest snogging a bird on the dance floor, my mum wouldn't believe it in a thousand years, Jeff.'

'I didn't know you were religious, Tony,' Jeff replied, casually lifting his glass to drink.

'I'm not bloody religious,' he said sharply, 'but my mum and my granny are; I was brought up a staunch Catholic, in a Catholic school, so I know what the rules are, even though I think they're all rubbish myself,' he shrugged.

'Huh, you still sound a bit religious to me, mate,' said Jeff, with a laugh.

'Ho, I didn't believe all the shit they used to try to pump into us at school, Jeff. I saw through all that by the time I was about seven. No, I only stuck it out because I was forced to,' he said with a little laugh. 'They couldn't brainwash Tony Ryan, mate, I'll tell you.'

'They're coming up to the bar, Tony,' hissed Jeff, nodding in the direction of the dance floor.

'I must say I like his choice of women,' remarked Tony, watching the young Priest in his smart modern suit and flashy tie, escorting his girlfriend in the direction of the bar area.

'He can't be much older than us though,' he said quietly, still looking at the couple. 'He looked much older dressed in his cassock at the altar, serving Mass,' he added, watching him direct the young girl to a seat, his arm around her protectively.

'Right, come on, Baxter,' he said, banging his empty glass down on the table, to emphasize his lack of continued interest. 'It's about time we went on the prowl for some female company. I'm beginning to get fed up of looking at your ugly mug,' he laughed.

Within the next fifteen minutes they'd achieved their goal; Tony was dancing around the hall with a sweet little blonde girl called Sally, who told him she worked in one of the local chemist's shops. Getting a couple of gin and tonics down her, while he drank only a half of beer shandy, so as to keep reasonably sober, he suggested a walk in the fresh air might be a good idea. She, being only a young naive girl and him, a very persuasive young man they were soon around the back of the dance hall, huddled in a door way, snogging passionately.

They hadn't been there more than a few minutes, when Tony, his back to the wall looking over Sally's shoulder, saw Father Fletcher and his girl friend coming towards them along the path. As they got nearer, Tony, watching them closely, held Sally to him and leant back into the shadows of the doorway, while the couple passed. However, to his surprise they went into a similar doorway straight across the path from themselves and immediately fell into a passionate embrace.

Tony, although not in the least religious, for some reason just couldn't stand to see a Catholic priest behaving in this manner. 'Come on, darling, let's go back in now, its getting cold out here,' he said, giving her a little peck on the forehead and escorted her quietly up the path back into dance hall. He looked around for Jeff as they entered and spotted him talking to the girl he'd picked up – a nice-looking ginger-haired girl with a pony tail – and waved him over.

'I thought you'd gone out for a walk, mate,' Jeff whispered in his ear, when the girls weren't looking.

'We had,' Tony whispered back, 'but you wouldn't believe it,' he said, shaking his head 'Father Fletcher came out with his bird and they went into a doorway straight across the path from where we were. I couldn't stand the sight of it, mate,' he said grimacing. 'They were going at it like hell; I had to come in Jeff, it was disgusting,' he said, frowning.

'Oh bugger him, now, Tony,' replied Jeff. 'I'm fed up of hearing about him.' Grabbing his girlfriend's arm, he said jovially, 'Oh listen, darling, they're playing a quickstep, come on let's all get on that floor and show 'em how it's done.'

After half an hour of dancing, the four young dancers were beginning to feel thirsty.

'I suggest we pop over to the bar for a little liquid refreshment,' advised Tony with a grin. All heartily agreed, and they proceeded to move off the dance floor; ironically, and without Tony noticing, so did Father Fletcher with his girl friend. Engrossed in conversation, there was a slight collision as they proceeded.

'Sorry, mate,' he said turning and smiling apologetically; however, the smile faded as he realised who he'd bumped into. The two men looked into each other's faces wide-eyed; it was obvious by his reaction that the Priest recognised Tony as an airman from the camp, even though he didn't know him by name.

'Oh sorry, Father,' Tony spluttered repeating his apology. 'I didn't realise it was you.'

Slightly flushing, the young man leaned closer to Tony whispering, 'Don't call me that in here, pal, my name's Tim. Giving his girl friend a smile, he took her arm and whispered to Tony as they moved on, 'I'll explain later.'

'What was that about, Tony?' Jeff asked, as the couple moved on.

Tony just stared after them without reply for a moment. 'Oh, bugger him, you were right, Jeff, it's nowt to do with us. Come on, let's get them drinks – I'm parched.'

The last dance reached its end and as the girls had already told them they were being picked up by Sally's dad in his car, the lads decided to get a bottle of ale each from the bar, for a refreshment break on the three-mile walk back to camp.

Setting off along the lonely country road with great vigour, the two pals felt on top of the world. A little drunk, they were singing 'Rock around the clock tonight' at the top of their voices and giving every car that flashed past them the cheeky two-fingered V sign. They'd covered about half a mile, and were well out of the village, still singing at full volume and now walking in near pitch darkness, when Jeff suddenly began to dance around in the middle of the road; apparently he was feeling the effects of the alcohol more than his mate.

'Stop acting the fucking goat, Jeff,' called out Tony angrily, 'You'll get run down.'

'Oh, stop worrying, you sound like an old woman.' He laughed, continuing his dancing.

Glancing back up the road Tony saw headlights in the far distance and warned his friend again. Jeff still took no notice as he laughed and danced in the middle of the road.

The lights rapidly approached and Tony realised there were two cars, both going like hell, with headlights blazing; what's more they appeared to be racing each other, one about fifty yards behind the other, and closing fast. Tony darted out into the middle of the road as they neared, and grabbing hold of Jeff's arm, he flung him sideways off the road, to where he ended up cursing in the ditch.

The first car flashed past – missing Tony by a hair's breadth, as he sprang to safety –followed closely by the second car, in hot pursuit. Suddenly there was a loud screeching of brakes and the second one came to a halt, some hundred yards up the road – then it began reversing slowly back towards them. As he helped Jeff out of the ditch and reprimanded him, Tony noticed the reversing car.

'Look, one of the bastards is coming back, Jeff, feeling guilty I suppose,' he said angrily. 'We could have got fucking killed there,' he added, now feeling very sober.

They stood dusting themselves down, both fuming, preparing to give the driver of the little Morris Minor car a right bollocking, when it reached them. However, as it pulled along side, the window rolled down and a friendly voice called out, 'Come on, you guys; jump in before some silly bugger runs you down.' Going over to the rolled-down window with a string of four-letter words, Tony suddenly froze when he saw the driver. Father Fletcher was sitting with his elbow through the open window, grinning like a Cheshire cat.

79

'Not a bad sort of a bloke though is he, Tony,' Jeff
remarked as the little car, having dropped them off,
sped away up the road just inside the camp gates.

'No, I suppose not,' he replied. 'He seems to be
just a normal bloke like us, wanting the same things
that we do.' Shaking his head as they walked along he
continued, 'but him saying he likes to have a good time
now and again, and he doesn't care what anybody
thinks, seems wrong really, Jeff somehow; you know,
him being a Priest. I always thought they were a bit
different that way to anybody else,' he muttered, as
they reached their billet. Going through the brightly-lit
entrance lobby, they marched into the dimly-lit billet, to
be met by a foul stink of vomit.

'Christ Almighty!' Tony yelled out, grimacing and
pointing at the repugnant mess in the middle of the
floor. 'Look, some buggers spewed their guts up right
in front of our beds, Jeff. 'Ok! Who's the dirty, drunken
bastard that's responsible for this, then?' he yelled out.
Getting no reply other than a chorus of snores and
drunken grunts, he repeated the enquiry even louder,
with only the same results, including a loud rasping fart
this time. 'They're all pissed, Jeff, they must be, to be
able to sleep in here with this rotten stink,' he said
angrily.

'Well it is Saturday night, mate, and we've had a
few, don't forget,' Jeff replied, with slightly slurred
speech.

'But who's going to clean this fucking mess up,
Jeff?' he asked, staring down at the vomit. 'We can't
sleep here with this stink right at the foot of our beds.'

'Oh, it'll be all right, mate,' he replied, with a laugh. 'We'll find the culprit responsible in the morning and make him clean the fucking stuff up.'

'Bugger that,' Tony grumbled, 'if you can sleep with this lot at the foot of your bed I can't, I'm going over to my bed in the Mess; I'm supposed to be on duty over there all weekend, anyway.'

'But you're in civvies, Tony, 'Jeff pointed out. 'If you're going over there, you'd better put your uniform on mate, hadn't you?'

'Don't matter,' he replied, as he made for the door. 'I've got my second working-blue uniform on a hanger over there, it's just come back from the laundry,' he called back as he went out.

80

Going stealthily through the small entrance hall that divided the male and female wings at the back of the Mess, Tony crept silently down the corridor to his bedding store. He went in, quietly closed the door on the Yale lock, and put the radio on very low, playing Jazz music from some pirate station.

He'd just taken his jacket off and hung it away, when he heard a soft tapping on the door. 'Oh Christ, who the hell can this be?' he said out loud. Taking his tie off and throwing it onto the shelf behind the bed, he went to the door, frowning. However, his frown turned to a look of shock when he saw the person standing outside the door, smiling down at him. He could hardly believe his eyes – in fact he had to look twice to make sure it really was her – she actually looked rather glamorous. She was dressed in a short, black, tight-fitting skirt, with a low-cut, silky red blouse and although about six foot two without them, she had fancy high-heeled shoes on and fishnet stockings. Tony just stared, open mouthed in disbelief; she looked a different person; in fact, so tasty he felt himself getting hard.

'Good evening, Sergeant McNabb,' What can I do for you at this late hour?' he asked, trying not slur his speech.

Obviously noticing he'd been drinking, she only gave him a lingering smile, then producing a bottle from her large handbag, she said sweetly, 'I'm just on my way from a little get together in the bar, Tony. I noticed you were in, so I thought I'd call to thank you for saving my kitchen from a major flood last night; can I come in for a moment?' she asked politely.

Tony couldn't believe it; was this the same woman who yelled her head off at everybody that crossed her path, the tyrant of the kitchen, as she was known, standing there before him purring like a lost kitten? For a moment he didn't know what to reply. Then he thought, well, she had been kind that morning, providing him with his breakfast, she'd also sent Pike off with a flea in his ear, when he had started moaning about him eating on duty. What's more, he wouldn't mind another little drink, as he felt he was beginning to sober up.

'Yes, please come in, Sergeant,' he replied, with a smile stepping back in the doorway.

Tripping in on her high-heeled shoes she said coyly, 'By the way, Tony, I'm not on duty now, so you'd better drop the formalities; please call me Mavis, it's more friendly,' she said, giving him a seductive glance and closing the door behind her with a click of the Yale lock.

Tony, although he was still not thinking too straight after the booze he'd already consumed, began to wonder if he'd done right to invite her in, considering his experience with her the last time she came to see him late at night. However, he reasoned, she was drunk then and she was far from that tonight.

'Have you got two glasses in here, Tony dear?' Mavis said sweetly, opening the large bottle of Johnnie Walker whisky.

'Yes, here we are,' he replied, producing a couple of half pint beer glasses off the sink shelf, wondering as he did so whether he dare risk trying to get her on the bed; she certainly looked sexy tonight he decided.

'Oh dear, you are a glutton,' she laughed. 'These are big glasses.' Taking one from him, she half-filled it with whisky, before passing it back to him with a smile. Taking the large measure of spirit from her, Tony took a good swig, as he was used to beer drinking and failed to notice that she only put a very small measure into her own glass.

'By God, Mavis, this is bloody strong stuff,' he said, slurring his speech slightly. 'I'm not used to this sort of thing you know,' He shook his head. 'I'm strictly a beer drinker as a rule you know.'

'Go on you silly boy,' she giggled, sitting down in the big, old armchair beside the wall. 'A big, strong boy like you can take a few whiskies, surely,' she told him, with a coy glance at his slightly bulging crotch area.'

'Of course I can,' he boasted. 'I've supped over five pints of ale tonight already, down in the village,' he bragged, standing there swaying; then draining his glass.

'Come here give me your glass, Tony.' She smiled and took the glass from him; still smiling, she proceeded to pour him another large measure of the very potent spirit.

'Steady there, Mavis, darling,' he said, laughing drunkenly. 'You'll get me pissed if you're not careful, love.'

'Go on, silly lad,' she cooed, sitting back down in the chair. She lay back so that her short skirt hitched up, showing her big, firm, stocking-covered thighs and black suspenders. Tony took another swig at his whisky and, although now feeling very inebriated and unsteady on his feet, couldn't help noticing her manoeuvres with arousing interest.

Seeing him staring at her stocking tops, Mavis giggled. 'What are you staring at, you cheeky boy? I think you've got evil thoughts on your mind tonight.'

As she said this, she leaned back further in the big chair, making her tight dress hitch even higher to show the legs of her brief, frilly, red underwear.

Standing waveringly looking down at her, Tony really didn't know what to think; however, taking another drink of whisky, he continued to hungrily stare at her provocative pose.' Slurring his speech, he eventually managed to say, 'I think you're playing with me Mavis; it's called cock-teasing, darling, where I come from.' He followed this with a drunken laugh.

Looking up at him smiling and crossing her ample thighs seductively, she said softly, 'Don't you like what you see before you then, Tony?'

Standing there swaying, he replied, with a glassy grin, 'I didn't say that, Mavis darling. I've got to admit I never thought you could look so sexy, once you got that bloody big kitchen smock off.'

Swaying more now, he stepped sideways, putting his empty glass on the table. Sitting down with a bump on the bed he muttered, 'Oh, bloody hell, love, I feel as pissed as a newt.'

Mavis could see he wasn't kidding; getting up out of the chair she went over to him and stroked his forehead affectionately.

'Poor darling, looks as though you've had a bit too much tonight, Tony,' she said warmly. Saying this she unbuttoned his shirt collar, and smiling continued in a coaxing tone, 'Come on, we'd better get you into your bed, my lad.' Tony sat on the edge of the bed with his head spinning, he felt as though he was going to pass out at any moment. He did not even notice what she was doing, or hear a word she was saying; he just sat there stupefied, doing exactly as he was bid. As she managed to get all the buttons on his shirt undone, it pulled out of his pants, and she began to peel it off him, while he sat there with a blank look on his face.

Suddenly realising his pants were about to come down he said, 'Hey, what you doing, Mavis?'

Cupping his face in her hands, and putting hers close to it, she whispered with a smile, 'I'm putting you to bed, where all naughty boys who have drunk too much should be.' Then, pulling his shirt off, she threw it onto the old chair and proceeded to loosen the belt of his pants. Only half aware of what she was doing, Tony tried to object and struggled to get to his feet, but the room began to spin faster and he fell back on the bed, his head banging down on the pillow. Feeling his shoes being taken off, and then his pants being pulled down, he tried to focus his eyes to see what was happening.

Through the haze he caught a brief glimpse of Mavis removing his clothing; she was gaping wide-eyed at his naked body. 'Oh, you beautiful boy,' she said in a hushed voice, dropping down on her knees alongside the bed.' Lying there with his head spinning, Tony, realising he was very drunk, tried to concentrate all his mental strength to stop himself from passing out; but he felt at any moment that this would happen. He made a supreme effort to sit up but failed, and he fell back onto the pillow once more, in a cloud of semi-consciousness.

Flat on the bed naked and submitting to his condition, he felt relaxed; the warm hands stroking his naked loins and caressing his genitals created a state of deep relaxation and contentment. Then, as the caressing continued, he felt himself being fully aroused, even though he was too intoxicated to appreciate it. Suddenly in the far distance, he heard a sigh from Mavis; then, feeling the warmth of her mouth as she took him, he faded out into an oblivious drunken stupor.

81

Coming groggily to his senses several hours later, with the sun blazing in his face through the little window, Tony grimaced. Sitting up in the bed, his head thumping, his mouth tasting like the bottom of a bird cage, he tried to remember what had happened the previous night. He'd been well tucked up in his bed but was surprised to find that he was quite naked; he always slept in his tracksuit bottoms when on duty, in case of emergency arrivals. Thinking nothing more of the matter but still feeling half-drunk, he rolled over cuddling the pillow and decided to go back to sleep. Suddenly, he sat bolt upright and wide-eyed; he'd begun to remember everything and as he did so, he began to feel angry and humiliated.

He'd had many experiences with women of different age groups, even though he was so young, but for some reason he didn't understand himself at this moment. He was no prude –never had been – but the feeling of disgust and anger within him now at what had happened, so disturbed him that he felt as if he'd been raped.

Going to the sink he stuck his throbbing head under the cold tap and filled a pint glass with the cooling liquid. He drank it back in one go, hoping to clear his system and the hammering in within his head. Then getting into the old track suit he kept for sleeping in when on duty and putting on his working boots, he slipped quietly out of the building with the intention of a going on a long, long jog, to clear both mind and body.

How far he'd run, he'd no idea, but it was lunch-time when he came jogging back through the main gates of the camp, feeling hot and sweaty, but much better physically than when he'd set off, over four hours earlier. After a good shower and a good Sunday lunch in the Airmen's dining hall, he put on his working blue uniform and made his way back to the Sergeants' Mess. He'd got duties to attend to, and also he intended to have a straight talk with Sergeant McNabb. Irrespective of her superior rank he wanted an explanation: his manly pride had been hurt by being taken advantage of like that, by a woman.

82

'Hi there, Yorky,' Sergeant Banks called out from his open bunk door, as Tony stood rummaging in his jacket pocket for his keys. 'What were you up to last night, then,' he asked, coming out of his bunk and standing behind him, grinning?

'Hi there, Sergeant,' Tony called back, fumbling to unlock the bedding store door. 'Jeff and me went down to the village dance and had a few pints down there,' he answered.

Still grinning, Jerry went on, 'I mean after that you scoundrel, about two in the morning as I was coming back from a little get together we'd been having in the bar, I saw big Mavis McNabb creeping out of your place there, looking very bloody sheepish indeed.' He laughed.

'Sheepish, why should she look sheepish?' Tony called back casually over his shoulder, as he went into the store.

'Well as I just said, it was after two in the morning, you bugger.'

'As a matter of fact, if you must know, Jerry,' Tony said piously, 'she'd just popped in to offer me a whisky, as a token of her thanks for mending that broken pipe in the kitchen the other day.'

Following Tony into the bedding store, Jerry said with a laugh, 'So that's what she came back and bought the whisky for then, is it?'

'What do you mean?' Tony asked with a frown.

'I don't know if she told you, but several of us had a bit of a party to cheer ourselves up last night, she was there with her boy friend, little WO Tommy Bloomer.'

'I don't know 'owt about that, Jerry,' he told him. 'Hope you all had a good time, though,' he smiled.

'Yes, yes, we did, Yorky, but Mavis left when her boyfriend passed out drunk. Two of the lads had to get him up to one of the empty bunks, he was too drunk to get back to his own place,' he chuckled. 'That was about an hour before the party broke up. But the funny thing was,' he continued, 'Mavis came back about five minutes after she'd left, and bought a bottle of whisky over the bar counter; then she left without talking to anyone, except the steward. We all thought she was going to have a session on her own when she got back to her room, as she'd only had about two drinks all night, what with trying to keep little Bloomer sober.'

Looking over at him with a nod, Tony said sternly, 'Aye, she didn't drink much in here either, but I bloody well did, she made sure of that; I got pissed as a bloody fart, Jerry.'

Laughing, he replied, 'Oh, bloody hell, she got you pissed did she, Yorky? Well, she was the only one in our crowd who remained sober – but I'll give her one thing, Yorky,' he went on seriously, 'she was very attractively done up, I didn't recognise her when she first came into the bar, with little Tommy.'

Instead of replying, Tony went over to the old radio and after fiddling about, found the required station. As the music started, he turned back to Jerry and nodded. 'Well, I must agree with you there, Jerry, the big bugger did look bloody fit in that outfit she was wearing. A lot better than she does in that big baggy smock she wears in the kitchen.'

'Anyway, so she brought you some whisky then, Yorky, eh?' Jerry said in a suspicious tone, together with a sly smile.

'She certainly did bring some whisky, Jerry,' he grunted, 'but I wish she bloody hadn't.'

'Oh dear, why's that?' he enquired with added interest.

'Aw nowt really,' he replied hesitantly. 'I like a drink as much as next man, Jerry, but I don't like to get paralytic,' he said giving him a sulky glance.

Jerry being an older man, nearly old enough to be his father in fact, realised that the young chap had something on his mind; and being a fellow Yorkshireman, felt concerned and wanted to help if possible. 'Come on, Yorky,' he said thoughtfully. 'You can tell me to mind my own business if you like, but by the look on your face there's something bothering you, lad.'

Tony gave him a fleeting glance before looking down to the floor. 'It's nowt really, Jerry – best forgotten I suppose,' he replied quietly.

'Well, that's up to you, lad, I'm not trying to be nosey, you know,' he smiled warmly.

'Oh, the thought never crossed my mind, Jerry,' Tony replied. With an effort, he continued, 'Well, there is something really bothering me, but it's more a matter of principle than anything else.' He looked down at the floor with a quick, forced laugh.

Walking over to the old armchair that had previously been used by the lady in discussion, Jerry plonked himself down into it heavily. Staring up at Tony for a few seconds in silence, he said, 'Well, come on then, Yorky, let's be having it; what's on your mind?'

Sitting down on the edge of the bed, Tony, avoiding direct eye contact, spoke quietly. 'Well, as I said, it's mainly a matter of principle, really, Jerry, but I admit I feel bloody annoyed about it. I don't want anybody else to know, though,' he said firmly. 'I'm not even going to tell my mate, Jeff, about it. 'Oh no,' he said hastily, 'I'd never live it down, Jerry.' After being assured by Jerry that anything discussed would only be between the two of them, Tony told his fellow Yorkshireman everything that had happened between himself and Sergeant McNabb, on her late night call with the whisky.

Having listened to Tony's explanation of his experience for over ten minutes, without interrupting, Jerry sat back in the chair with a whistle. 'Christ, the scheming cow,' he sighed. 'She certainly took advantage of you all right; she's around my age an'all, she should have more sense,' he said. 'Do you realise, Yorky, it would be termed as a form of rape; if I'd done that to a young woman your age under the same circumstances, I'd have got sent to Colchester for about ten years and dismissed with dishonour from the Service,' he told him, shaking his head in disgust.

Getting to his feet, Tony said firmly, 'Well, as I told you, Jerry, I don't want any bother, and I definitely don't want anybody else to hear about it. Phew, if ever the lads heard how she stripped me naked and put me to bed, they'd be taking the piss till kingdom come. Mind you,' he went on with a grin, 'It's not what happened that bothered me, Jerry, I'm no prude and I'm definitely no virgin either, but it was the way I was used I didn't like – getting me into a state where I'd no option.' Grinning slyly, he continued, 'Actually, I was thinking about trying my hand with her until I got too pissed – as I said, she did look tasty, last night.'

'Sure, I see what you mean, Yorky,' Jerry replied, nodding. 'I must say I agree with you on both points there.'

'I mean, there was no need to encourage me to drink all that lot,' Tony went, on scowling. 'She knew I was a bit drunk when she came in, then she coaxed me to bloody well sup about half a pint of whisky. I told her, Jeff and I had supped five pints of ale each in the dance an'all; that was a fair skinful in itself,' he stressed, with a sharp nod. Then, looking down at Jerry sitting there listening intently, he continued with a smile, 'I mean, if she was so hard up for a bit of the old man, there'd have been no need to go to all that trouble. The way she looked, sitting there in that chair you're in now, Jerry, flashing her fishnet stockings and fancy suspenders, believe me, I'd have soon had her on the bloody bed and leg over, big as she is,' he grinned boastfully. Then, becoming serious again he said, 'but I'm going to have it out with her, you know, Jerry, sergeant or not; no, I've got my limits and my principles; as I said, sergeant or not, nobody treats me like a bloody toy,' he stated, shaking his head.

Getting out of the old armchair and smiling, Jerry said, 'Spoken like a true Yorkshireman. But don't get yourself in any trouble, Yorky,' he added looking serious. 'Be careful what you say, don't forget she could cause you a lot of bother; she is a sergeant after all.'

83

'Any problems last weekend, Ryan?' Sergeant Pike called out, as he passed Tony, who was walking into the main entrance door of the Mess, first thing on the Monday morning.

'No, Sergeant, everything went like clockwork, apart from a very late arrival in the middle of the night,' he told him.

'Good man,' he replied cheerfully, without breaking his stride. Suddenly he paused as if just remembering something and called out over his shoulder, 'Oh, Ryan, I nearly forgot, we've two female NCOs arriving today, short term, a sergeant and a flight sergeant. Make sure there are two rooms prepared as soon as possible; I haven't been given any definite time for their arrival,' he yelled, as he marched off again.

'Where the hell have you been all the weekend, Mr Ryan?' Jeff asked. He was standing waiting for him in the corridor, when Tony finally reached the bedding store, carrying a bundle of dirty tablecloths under his arm.

Tony unlocked the door to his abode without reply, went in and threw the dirty linen into the laundry basket, and grunted, 'Nowhere much; I had a rotten hangover yesterday and went for a long jogging session to get rid of it.' Struggling with some blankets on the back shelf, he went on, 'You'd better get them three lazy buggers cracking on the passages on the women's wing; Pike's just told me we've got two new residents expected today. I'll attend to their rooms myself – I should be able to get Ruby to prepare them, if she can be spared from the dining room.'

'You'd better be careful down there, mate,' warned Jeff, turning to go, 'I've just passed through the kitchen, and that big bugger McNabb nearly bit my head off. Little Betty said she's in a hell of a mood, she's been like it most of the weekend, according to Betty.'

'Oh bugger her,' Tony replied. 'Go on, get them idle buggers stuck into them floors up there, we don't want any complaints.

A little later on, Tony was going through the dining room with a pack of clean tablecloths under his arm, when he caught sight of Ruby. ''Hi there, Ruby, love,' he called out. 'Have you got a second? I'd like a word with you, darling,' he said, making for her across the floor.

Turning towards him with a smile, she asked, 'Where have you been hiding yourself, Tony Ryan? I haven't seen you for a while.'

Thinking she looked beautiful, as he returned the smile, he said, 'Ruby darling, I've got two female residents coming today; do you think the "dragon" will let you get their rooms ready, when you've done with the tidying up in here?'

'I suppose so,' she said, glancing around to see if the dreaded sergeant was anywhere within earshot. 'But you'd better ask her yourself, Tony, she's been in a terrible mood for the last two days,' she said with a scowl. 'Been at everybody's throat she has; it's been a hellhole here in the kitchen.'

'Huh, she has, eh?' he grunted. 'Well, I'm not bothered about her, Ruby; I've got to have a member of the female staff for preparing rooms on the female wing, that's Mess standing orders,' he said adamantly.

As they were talking, the door to the kitchen opened and little Betty came scuttling out with an empty tray followed by an angry-looking Sergeant McNabb. Seeing Ruby standing there with a tray full of dirty plates, talking to Tony, she yelled out, 'Prichard! Haven't you got anything better to do than stand there gossiping to other members of staff.' Poor Ruby, red-faced, shot off towards the kitchen with her dirty crockery, without a word. The sergeant, now back to her usual dictatorial self, yelled, 'and what are you doing hanging about in here, Ryan, haven't you any thing better to do, either?'

Tony just stared at her, without replying for a moment, and then he walked slowly across the room towards her. 'I've come to request the help of ACW Pritchard to prepare two rooms on the female wing, Sergeant,' he said politely, 'and also to request an appointment with you to discus a personal matter. I've been trying to catch you since the weekend about that,' he added.

Going bright red in the face when she heard his second request, she replied, 'Yes, you can have Pritchard when she's done her cleaning up in here.' Fidgeting with her apron strings, she asked aloofly, 'but whatever do you mean, Ryan, to discuss a personal matter with me?'

84

'Okay, you three better get up on the top wing,' Tony told Ted and his two mates, as they were finishing their afternoon tea-break in the bedding store, 'Pike said he wants all the ablutions cleaned and polished by four thirty.' As they made to go, he added, 'Oh and by the way, lads, he told me that one of the bogs up there is blocked up; he said some bugger's been wiping his arse on newspaper again.'

'Hang about, Jeff,' he said to him quietly, as the other three left. Pausing until they were out of earshot, he went on, 'Go up there and keep an eye on them three, Jeff, and make sure they don't come back here to the store for anything before three thirty. Oh and by the way,' he added seriously, 'you stay with 'em an'all.'

'Yes, fair enough, Tony, but why? Don't tell me you've got Ruby coming to stroke your tired brow,' he said, laughing.

'No such fucking luck, mate,' he replied, pretending to be disappointed. 'As a matter of fact, I've got Sergeant McNabb coming to see me, because she goes off duty at three o'clock and we've got a bit of business to sort out.'

Looking back at him with puzzled concern on his face, Jeff asked quietly, 'You're not in any bother are you, mate?'

'No you silly bugger,' he replied, grinning. 'It's just to discuss arrangements for the preparing of rooms on the female wing, you know – so there'll be no hassle in the future,' he lied.

Within several minutes of Jeff's departure, he heard footsteps coming up the corridor. Recognising them as being a woman's, he sat down at the old table he used as a desk, and reaching out for his big infantry book from the shelf above, pretended to be deep in concentration studying its contents. As he sat there and the footsteps drew nearer, he cringed as he anticipated the boisterous entry of his guest – however, it was not to be, instead he was surprised when he heard a gentle tapping on the door, and a soft voice called out, 'Hello? Is there anyone there?'

'Come in!' he called out authoritatively. As she came quietly in, Tony, sitting at the table with his head buried in the big infantry book, and pretended to look very busy in the manner of Sergeant Pike, didn't look up for a long moment. Eventually, pushing the book away from him, he sat back on his chair with a sigh, shaking his head. 'Phew, work,' he muttered, looking up at the silent Sergeant. 'Work, it never ends, Sergeant.' Before she could reply, he pointed to the old armchair that she'd previously used to exhibit her charms, and said, 'Would you care to sit down, Sergeant McNabb?'

Meekly, she accepted the offer, but this time with great modesty holding her uniform skirt close to her as she sat down. 'Well, what is it you want to discuss, AC Ryan?' she asked him with a weak smile.

Without answering her question, he said, 'I realise that what I'm going to say to you, Sergeant, you could consider as insubordination. I further realise that you're in the position to reprimand me; but I've got to say it on principle.'

To his surprise, she just looked at him expressionlessly, and replied in a friendly tone, 'If, as you told me, a personal matter, I'm quite willing to consider the conversation completely unofficial and just between the two of us.' A slight smile creased her mouth. 'Right then, Tony, your turn now.'

Tony proceeded to tell her what he thought of her conduct with regard to the incident between them previously, and how he thought it very unprofessional of her, as a senior NCO, to take advantage of him sexually, whilst he was in an inebriated state.

She sat quietly listening to everything he had to say without comment, and then staring down at the floor with a guilty, forlorn look on her face, she whispered, 'Sorry, Tony, I just got carried away. I felt so lonely and unwanted – even that little fart, Bloomer, got himself pissed and had to be carried back to that spare bunk.' Then raising her eyes to meet his, she said sadly, 'Nobody wants me really, Tony, I'm just that bloody great big McNabb, six foot two and thirty eight years old; I'm a social failure, ' she whispered, bowing her head.

Tony, basically being very soft hearted, felt sorry for her. 'Oh, I wouldn't go that far Mavis,' he told her sympathetically, 'but it can't be denied you were out of order, doing what you did.'

After a slight pause, looking over at him forlornly she replied, 'All right, I admit I stripped you whilst drunk and had sexual contact – but I'm so sorry it's upset you so much, Tony, really,' she stressed, misty-eyed.

For the first time in the conversation, Tony laughed. 'I'm not bloody well upset at you stripping me and doing what you did sexually, Mavis; you're a woman and I'm a man and that's the game we play. The trouble was, on that occasion, I'd no choice. I was pissed when you arrived and you primed me more with whisky; I wasn't in a condition to say yes or no –that's what annoyed me,' he said, nodding at her.

Looking slightly baffled, she replied, 'but I've admitted performing a sexual act on you Tony, without your consent, you could report me for that.'

'Mavis,' he said seriously, staring down into her face. ' I've had women do what you did to me loads of times – they all like doing things like that to a bloke; what's more, if you hadn't got me so bloody drunk I'd have enjoyed it. No, it was the fact that you connived to get me incapable of deciding for myself, Mavis,' he told her firmly. I'm a man of principle you see, I don't like my intelligence being underestimated, even by attractive women.'

'But surely, Tony, you don't think me attractive, do you?' she asked, with surprise and disbelief on her face.

'Huh,' he grunted. 'I must say you wouldn't make heads turn when you're in your big baggy smock and cap, but when you came here the other night, you looked very tasty.' Smiling slightly, he continued, 'If I hadn't been so pissed, I'd most likely have done similar to you, as what you did to me and a lot more things.' He laughed, and changing the subject abruptly, he continued in business-like tones, 'Sergeant McNabb, I've said all I wanted to say now, so if you'll kindly excuse me, I'd better get on with my work or I'll be in trouble with Sergeant Pike.'

'I see your point, Tony,' she replied subserviently, getting up out of the chair, 'but can't you please forgive me? I didn't realise you thought so deeply – after what you've just told me, I feel so angry with myself. '

'I don't know whether I can, Mavis,' he replied. 'As I told you, I'm a man of principle,' he insisted aloofly.

Turning away without further comment, she made for the door with a sob, her eyes brimming with tears, just in time to meet Sergeant Pike striding briskly up the corridor.

'Hello there, Sergeant McNabb,' he called out. 'Everything in order?' he enquired, in his usual brisk tone of voice. Then, noticing her distressed state, he said with great concern, 'Dear, dear, is there something wrong, Sergeant?'

Ignoring the question she shoved passed him roughly, saying with a sob, 'Mind your own bloody business, nosy little bugger, Cyril Pike.' Puzzled, at this unexpected reception, he just stood staring at her in silence as she trundled away down the corridor, wiping her eyes.

Going into the bedding store, the bewildered Sergeant Pike looked at Tony suspiciously and asked, 'What's the matter with Sergeant McNabb? I hope you haven't done anything to upset her, Ryan.'

'No, Sergeant,' he replied casually. Thinking quickly, he continued, 'we were just talking about the tragic accident; she liked poor Sergeant Long, she'd met his wife and little girl too I think,' he added sadly.

'Oh, I see why she was so disturbed then, Ryan,' Pike said, nodding. 'I never thought I'd ever see her in tears though, everybody thinks she's as hard as nails you know,' he told him.

Smiling and nodding in approval, Tony replied, 'Well, she's only a woman underneath really, Sergeant, however big and hard she appears on the surface.'

'Yes, I must agree, you're right, Ryan,' he sighed condescendingly. 'I suppose we've got to make allowances for them – they're only women after all, as you say,' he said, shaking his head. Changing the subject abruptly, he continued, 'The boys have got that toilet unblocked, Ryan, but we've got to find who the hell it is that's too miserly to buy toilet paper.' Frowning, he snapped, 'We can't have this bloody carry-on every time this man wants a shit.' Saying this he turned and marched out onto the corridor, clearing his throat several times angrily.

'What's up with you, Tony? You're looking glum, mate,' Jeff enquired, meeting him in the corridor later that afternoon.'

'Nothing really,' Tony replied, without stopping or even breaking his stride. Turning to accompany him, Jeff said, 'Well, by the look on you're face, you're not too happy about something. It's not that bloody McNabb been bollocking you again, is it mate?'

'No, no, it's nothing like that, Jeff,' he replied miserably. 'I've just picked my mail up – I've got a letter from Becky.'

'Oh, good for you, Tony,' he smiled. 'Has she got her home posting yet, then?'

'Has she, hell!' he replied sharply. 'Refused, bloody flatly refused, after all this time she's spent applying; it's that fucking wing commander that's blocking it I bet, bloody Conrad, the bastard,' he said passionately.

85

'Expecting any new arrivals this weekend, Tony,' Jeff asked, sitting eating dinner in the Airmen's Mess, later in the week.'

'Could be,' he replied, his mouth full. 'Most likely, Saturday or Sunday; I won't know for sure until I see Pike in the morning, though. By the way, Jeff,' he went on, 'you haven't forgotten what day it is today, I hope.'

'Of course I know it's bloody Friday,' Jeff grunted. 'Do you think I'm stupid? Why? What are you on about anyway?'

'Business, Jeff, my lad,' Tony said, smiling, you're on the stall after tea, don't forget; we've got some good stuff this week an'all,' he pointed out proudly. 'You should have good takings with a bit of luck tonight.'

'What me again,' Jeff grumbled. 'What about you having a go for once? You're not on duty tonight,' he said, sulkily.

'No, I'm not, Jeff, and I'd love to do it. As you know, I enjoy selling, especially when everything's a bargain like tonight's stuff,' he added, smiling. 'However, it's my training night, so, unfortunately I can't make it – much as I'd like to.' He shrugged, before continuing to stuff his mouth again.

The weight training room up at the gym was empty as Tony walked in, whistling merrily. He felt on top of the world physically, and having left Jeff with his bed piled up with gear, he had visions of money rolling in, while he was here working out. Loading the barbell, he could hear the commotion made by the men in the wrestling class, throwing each other about in the gym hall, accompanied by the loud voice of big Sam Barns, shouting orders at them.

'Hell, I couldn't work out in there, with that bloody noise going on,' Tony said out loud.

He'd been working hard for about half an hour and was feeling well pumped up with his efforts, when his concentration was broken; the door opened and big Sam came in, looking rather serious.

'Sorry to disturb you, Tony,' he said, closing the door behind him. 'But there's a little 'WO Bloomer' out there, looking for you, mate; he told me he'd been to your billet, and they'd told him you were up here.'

'Oh Christ, sound like bloody hassle, Sam,' he moaned, reaching for his towel and mopping his sweaty brow, with a scowl.

'Well, you'd better come out and see him, Tony; I told him I'd find you for him. What's his problem, anyway?' he asked.

Shaking his head in frustration, Tony said, 'The silly little bugger thinks I'm after his woman – it's not true, of course,' he added firmly. 'What's more, he threatened to get me in the boxing ring and disregarding rank, give me a bloody good thumping.'

'Fucking hell-fire,' said the big man, laughing, 'sounds as though you're in the shit here, mate; if you do a runner he'll track you down and if you go in the ring with him you might end up in the glass house for murder. Anyway, you'd better come out and see him; you might be able to talk your way out of it before he gets stuck into you.'

'Oh, you're there, Ryan, are you?' the little WO yelled, as Tony came out into the main gym hall followed by big Sam, both stern-faced. 'I warned you what would happen if you didn't stop making a nuisance of yourself with Sergeant McNabb, didn't I, lad?' he said angrily, staring up into Tony's baffled face as he approached. 'But apparently, you weren't prepared to listen,' he went on. 'Now you've been at it again, according to what I gather from Sergeant Pike. Well, you're going to get it – as I promised,' he stated firmly, staring at Tony, wide-eyed.

'Sergeant Pike, Sir?' Tony repeated, still looking baffled.

'Yes, he told me he saw her coming out of your bedding store in tears the other day, and you told him she was upset about the accident – but we know better, don't we, Ryan,' he said, glaring at him with hate.

'You'd been trying to gain her affections again, hadn't you, lad?' he rattled on. 'Forcing yourself on her, weren't you? You just won't take no for a bloody answer, will you?' he barked up into his face, 'but you bloody well will now, when I've done with you,' he yelled, prodding him on the chest with his forefinger.' Having said this, he proceeded to take off his tunic, and pointing at one of the young lads in the group who were watching the fiasco in shocked silence, he yelled, 'You man, go and find me a pair of boxing shorts and a pair of size six training shoes from the kit room.'

'Excuse me, sir,' chipped in Tony nervously, 'but I told you before, you're under a misapprehension regarding Sergeant McNabb, sir. What's more I really can't box, sir,' he added with sincerity.

'Anyway, sir,' he went on submissively, 'if you ask Sergeant McNabb herself, I'm sure she'll assure you that your suspicions are groundless; we're just working companions, sir, she's far superior to me, of course,' he added and stood silently, awaiting a reply.

Glaring at him for a moment, the little man said haughtily, 'I wouldn't dream of asking her; obviously as she's so soft-hearted she'd shield you, even though you're annoying her.'

Still glaring at him, he went on, 'However, regarding all the excuses for your behaviour, I just don't believe them; as for the boxing I'll soon give you a bloody good lesson on that when I get you in that ring there,' and he glared menacingly in that direction.

The ring was set out ready within ten minutes, and the two fighters climbed in and sat down in their respective corners, each with his second standing behind him. Tony had big Sam; his little opponent commandeered one of the young lads from the wrestling team.

Waiting for the bell, Sam immediately started whispering advice in Tony's ear like a professional trainer, while Tony was wondering how the hell he'd got himself into such a predicament. 'Just go easy on him, Tony, keep pushing him away every time he gets near you,' advised Sam in a whisper. 'He'll soon get worn out, the silly little bugger.'

At the sound of the bell, Tony got to his feet clenching his gloved fists in preparation, but before he knew it, the little WO had crossed the ring like greased lightning and delivered a flurry of punches. The first punch hit Tony in the solar plexus with great force, sending him staggering back onto the ropes, gasping for breath and shaking his head to clear it. There was also a gasp from the little crowd, and big Sam's jaw dropped; he stood staring at poor Tony in amazement. As Tony was an athlete in fine condition he soon recovered, but he realised that he'd made a mistake to underestimate Warrant Officer Bloomer.

Tensing his abdominals, and with his gloved fists held before him, he stepped forward to face the opposition once more, but this time with great respect and caution. Again Bloomer came in with lightning speed, but Tony, being a fast learner, kept his fists and forearms held in front of his face and upper body, for protection. Then, using his eight inch height advantage and longer reach, he got in the occasional jab, and managed to keep the more skilled boxer at bay for the remainder of the round.

Sitting in his corner after the first of the three rounds, Tony muttered, 'Christ, Sam, I'd never have believed it, that little bugger's good; he'll drop me if I don't watch out.'

'You're right,' Sam agreed. 'He surprised me, Tony, I'll bet he's been a pro in his time to be able to fight like that. You'll have to keep a lookout for him, mate, or he'll cop you one without a doubt,' he warned him seriously, glancing respectfully towards the opposite corner.

Coming out at the bell the WO waded in fast as usual, but being more prepared, Tony turned sideways slightly and swung a heavy blow at the side of his head; however, he only connected with air and received another flurry of sharp blows to his face and head in return.

This sort of situation continued through the rest of the round; by the time the bell went Tony was beginning to think the man was impossible to hit and that he himself was a punch bag.

'I'm bloody glad this is the last round Sam,' he said, sitting in his corner feeling sore and bruised, while being rubbed with a towel by his stern-faced second. 'I just can't hit the little bugger, he's never there long enough,' he said, as Sam wiped the trickle of blood from his nose, dabbing it with a wet cloth.

'Look Tony, obviously you don't know much about boxing,' Sam said thoughtfully, 'and he's definitely a very experienced boxer, so I say, keep your back to the ropes and let him come to you. Then, keep him at arm's length with your much longer reach and if you see a chance to get one in then get the bugger in hard! You might just be lucky and drop him.'

At the final bell, Tony was quick on his feet, meeting the smaller man mid-ring. Keeping his arms up and shielding his face, he took several fast heavy blows to the body; these were not of much consequence however, as he was so muscular. Absorbing them easily, he took Sam's advice, and backing onto the ropes, shielding his head and jabbed hard at his fast, very determined opponent. After taking several flurries of hard punches to the body and a few nasty clouts to the head and face, Tony saw an opening. The little WO got too confident and

Tony, leaning on the ropes weaving, shielded himself as the WO charged forward with both arms flailing, fully intent now on finishing him off.

Realising his intention, Tony rolled sideways along the ropes, and at the same time he lashed out a straight right-hand drive to the jaw. The little man, with his unbelievable reflexes, managed to avoid the intended full contact however, although he did catch a heavy glancing blow which sent him reeling across the ring, to a loud cheer from the crowd of wrestlers. In true professional style he was on his feet in a split second and flew at Tony with renewed venom. Fortunately for Tony, after receiving only a few more punishing body blows, to his great relief the final bell sounded – his lesson was over. This was greeted with loud cheers from the audience and to Tony's great surprise, a sporty hug and a warm handshake from his opponent.

'Good show, lad for a novice,' he said smiling, wiping his own face with a towel handed to him by his second. 'Let's hope it's taught you a lesson in more ways than one,' he beamed up at him.

As he walked into the billet later, Jeff, seeing his bruised face, called out, 'Bloody hell, who's hit you this time, Tony?'

'Oh, just a bit of a boxing lesson this time mate,' he replied grinning, and then told him all about it.

'I can hardly believe it, Tony; that little fart Bloomer bashed you about like that, he must be nearly fifty – if he's a day,' he added, shaking his head.

'That's just how I felt, mate, before I got into that bloody ring with the little bugger; by the way he's fifty-two,' he said casually.

'He's what, how do you know?' Jeff asked, surprised that he was still boxing at that great age.

'Jerry Banks told me, but seriously Jeff,' he went on, 'he can really handle himself; Sam recons he's been a pro. I'll tell you what,' he said, laughing, 'I'm bloody glad he wasn't my size, he'd have fucking killed me.'

Next morning, Ruby, meeting him bringing in the kitchen laundry, called out, 'Tony, whatever's happened to your face?'

'Nothing to worry about Ruby, my love,' he told her, with a cheerful smile. 'I've just been having a few boxing lessons; anyway, I'm pleased that you're so concerned for my welfare, darling,' he said, with a cheeky wink.

'You two gossiping again, are you?' called out Sergeant McNabb across the kitchen. 'Get on with your work, Pritchard,' she yelled. Noticing Tony's bruised face, she came over to him and said sympathetically, 'Oh dear, AC Ryan, whatever have you been up to? Have you been fighting with some ruffian in the pub or something?'

Laughing, he replied, 'Well, not in a pub, Sergeant.'

86

'He's gone Tony; he's gone,' yelled Jeff boisterously, charging into the bedding store. I've just helped him load his stuff into the car.'

'I don't know what you're looking so pleased about, you silly bugger; you've still got to do the same job, whether he's here or not,' Tony replied, without looking up from his newspaper.

Two weeks had passed since Tony's painful boxing lesson, and now another challenge lay ahead. Sergeant Pike had gone on a ten day refresher course and before he went, AC Ryan had been officially appointed by him as head man – fully in charge of the cleaning staff in his absence.

Getting to his feet and throwing the newspaper down on the chair, Tony sighed, 'Oh well, we'd better get up there and see if them two lazy buggers are getting stuck into them floors. I sent Jones outside around the back to clean out the grates; they're full of leaves again,' he grumbled.

'We're not going to sit on our arses and neglect the work, you know Jeff, just because Pike's not here,' he said, throwing the paper down and getting to his feet. 'Come on, let's get upstairs and make a start.'

'No, I realise that,' he replied, 'but we won't be getting a bollocking every time we miss a bit of dust, or a greasy sink, will we?'

'Who said you won't?'Tony laughed as they started up wide stairway to the top landing.

'Christ, you're letting your new power go to your head now, Tony.' Jeff said, with a laugh. 'You sound just like Pike.'

Grinning, Tony replied, 'Shut up or I'll put you on a 252, Baxter.'

'Ryan, can I have a word, please,' called out a firm voice from above; they were half way up the stairway and both their faces dropped when they saw who it was.

'Oh hell, here we go,' whispered Tony, from the side of his mouth. It was Sergeant Riley looking fit and well, every inch his old self.

'Certainly, Sergeant,' Tony called back, quickening his pace up the stairway. As he reached him, looking meticulous in his best blue uniform, Tony said, 'Very pleased to see you back fit and well, Sergeant Riley.'

Tony waited motionless in front of him, with Jeff a couple of paces behind, anticipating the usual complaint to be yelled out, but it never came; Riley just stood looking at him in silence. Tony was now beginning to wonder what could possibly be going on in his mind; had he gone mad or something caused by the accident he wondered? Was he going to explode crazily about some dusty problem he'd made up? Or was it a dirty bath or sink? However, suddenly, his fear of an angry complaint turned to unbelievable shock; the sergeant's face slowly softened into a warm smile.

'As you obviously know, AC Ryan,' he began. 'I was involved in that terrible accident a few weeks back, and I've only today been released from hospital.' Still smiling, he continued warmly, 'This is the first time I've had the opportunity to thank you.' Saying this he held out his hand to Tony, who just stared back at him looking baffled.

Wondering what he was on about, Tony slowly extended his arm accepting the handshake and replying blankly, 'Thank you, Sergeant, but I don't know why I deserve thanks; I only do my job in here like any of the other chaps.'

'I'm not talking about your duties in here, young man,' Riley said, still holding Tony's hand. 'I'm talking about the night of the crash.'

More baffled than ever, Tony said, 'but I'm sorry, Sergeant, I don't understand; I didn't do anything to be thanked for on the night of the crash, in fact,' he added, 'I wasn't even on camp at that time; I was on home leave, Sergeant.'

Releasing his hand, Riley said smiling, 'Anyway, AC Ryan, whatever you say, you've got my heartfelt thanks.'

Glancing over his shoulder at Jeff, standing silent and motionless behind him, Tony, looked back at the Sergeant and enquired, 'Would you mind telling me what I've done to deserve your thanks, Sergeant Riley?'

'For saving my life, of course, AC Ryan,' he smiled. 'If it hadn't been for you, my friend, I'd have either been fried, or blown to pieces like my never to be forgotten colleagues.' Tony looked at him in shocked disbelief, as he went on, 'When we hit the ground and the plane eventually dragged to a halt,' he paused, staring into space momentarily, 'the front of the fuselage burst into flames, engulfing the lads in the cockpit. Their screams were horrific,' he muttered, grimacing. 'I was lucky there,' he nodded. 'My instruments being at the back end meant I was shielded for several seconds from the initial inferno.' Tony could see now that he was sweating profusely as he continued. 'I tried to open the side door to jump out onto the runway, but it was stuck. I kicked it and shoved it, but the bloody thing wouldn't move,' he said excitedly. 'Then, I fell back exhausted with the heat, fully expecting to die like everybody else in there.' By now, Tony was wondering if the poor man should still be in hospital, but he just looked back at him, as continued.

'That's when I saw you, AC Ryan,' he said, staring wide-eyed at Tony, 'you just stood smiling down at me there on the floor, didn't you?' He paused momentarily as he looked warmly into Tony's baffled face. 'Then you just calmly turned and took a mighty kick at the side door, and it flew open off its hinges with a bang. Good God, lad, you must be strong,' he said, shaking his head. 'Then you grabbed me off the floor as though I was a doll, and bundled me out onto the runway, yelling at me to "bugger off" fast. I half ran and half crawled away and when I'd gone about forty yards I fell down exhausted; looking back I saw you, standing in the doorway of the plane, smiling.' Tony just stood open-mouthed, listening.

'Why didn't you follow me, Ryan? You could have been killed when the lot blew up. I thought you had been until Jerry Banks told me you were okay, when he called in to see me at the hospital a week later,' he added. Then clasping his hands together passionately, he said staring again into Tony's face. 'What I can't understand though, Ryan, is how the hell you managed to get out yourself. I was sure you were dead man; I saw the plane go up like a bomb, in a ball of flames with you still there in the doorway, waving at me and smiling.' Tony could not believe what he had heard. God, this poor guy really had been through a trauma, he thought.

After saying all this, Sergeant Riley stared at Tony affectionately for several moments in silence, without further conversation. Eventually relaxing slightly, he smiled and giving a nervous little cough, he said, 'Anyway, AC Ryan irrespective of all that, I think I owe you an apology for my uncalled for behaviour towards you over the past months here in the Mess. I don't really know why I did it, I can't understand myself, there was no reason and I apologise profusely; furthermore, I assure you it will never occur again,' he stated firmly.' Then without further comment, he turned, walked back along the corridor and went into his room, closing the door behind him.

Tony, open-mouthed, slowly turned to face Jeff, still standing looking mesmerized behind him. 'Christ, Jeff, what do you make of that lot, then?' he asked almost in a whisper.

'Sounds to me as though he's gone bloody mad, Tony,' he replied shaking his head, 'but I must say he sounded very convincing, didn't he? What do you think really happened, though, to make him think you saved him like that?' He was deadly serious. 'I mean you weren't really there, were you?' he said.

Laughing for the first time since the meeting with Sergeant Riley, Tony replied, 'Don't be such a silly bugger, Baxter and stop taking the piss; when all that happened I'd be on the train somewhere between Leeds and Birmingham – and fast asleep,' he said.

'I bloody well know you weren't there, Tony,' said Jeff, laughing. 'But seriously, do you think he's gone bloody crackers and dreamed it up or something like that? I mean he's fully convinced you were in there with him, that's for sure.'

'He's not crackers, Jeff,' Tony replied sternly. 'That poor sod has been through hell, he's been concussed; he's still in a state of mental trauma. Do you realise, it could take months, or even years for him to get over it? Some people never get over things like that; it remains at the back of their minds until the day they die. My granddad was one of 'em from the First World War,' he told him with a nod.

Just then, they heard the sound of loud laughter and shouting coming from the ablutions at the end of the corridor. 'Come on, mate,' Tony said angrily, setting off at a brisk pace. 'Just listen to that. It's them lazy bastards at it again; they think they're on holiday now Pike's gone on that course. I'll soon get that out of their fucking minds,' he muttered, as the pair charged towards the sound of merriment.

87

Saturday morning was like a madhouse for the cleaning lads in the Sergeants' Mess after the usual Friday night social. With Pike on leave, Tony had even more responsibility on his plate.

'Are you going to the dance in the NAAFI tonight, Tony?' asked Ted, coming into the bedding store for a new mop head. 'The lads say it'll be a good one tonight. They're bringing a bus load of army birds over from that camp near Oxford,' he said, with a dirty grin. Not looking up from the infantry book he was studying on the table before him, Tony replied casually, 'You'll get nowt out of them, mate, they'll be watched like hawks by the SP's.

No,' he repeated, looking up at him, grinning, 'you'll never get one of them outside, believe me, Ted, I've tried before myself,' he said, returning to his perusal of the book, with deep concentration.

'Where do you keep the new mopheads, Tony?' Ted asked, getting a cigarette out of a crumpled packet, he'd produced from his jacket pocket.

Looking up from his work, Tony yelled sharply, 'Hey West! Don't you light that bugger in here, mate. How many more times have I got to tell you? I don't like being bloody gassed. The mopheads are over there in the top cupboard,' he snapped, pointing.

'Huh, a bit of smoke won't hurt you,' Ted said, stuffing the cigs back into his pocket, as he went to get his mop. 'You're not smoking the bugger anyway,' he moaned.

'No, I'm not breathing any second-hand smoke into my lungs, either, mate,' Tony told him emphatically. 'I've always thought that more damaging, than the smoking of the cig itself.' He gave him a black look. 'Especially when it's already been through a pair of smoke-sodden, contaminated lungs like yours, West. By the way,' he went on, changing the subject, 'I've got two male sergeants coming this weekend, so you and Jones better get them two rooms that were vacated last week, cleaned out as soon as possible.'

No sooner had Ted gone, than Jeff came bustling in, arms loaded with a bundle of dirty bed sheets. 'McNabb said she couldn't spare Ruby to get that room ready on the female wing, Tony,' he grunted, straining with his load, 'but you can have Betty,' he said, banging his bundle down on the floor.

'Fair enough,' he replied. 'She's not as experienced as Ruby at that job, but I suppose she's got to learn,' he sighed. 'By the way, Mr Baxter,' he went on with a sly smile. 'How are you getting on with that young lady these days – have you managed to get her bloomers down yet?'

Freezing in his labour of stacking the dirty linen in the big laundry basket, Jeff replied angrily, 'You're at it again, Ryan, aren't you? I've told you before, Betty's a decent girl, not like some of them sluts you go chasing after in the NAAFI.' He returned to filling the huge basket, with renewed vigour.

Faking shock, Tony replied, 'Oh, Mr Baxter, you are so protective; I was only being concerned for your welfare. Anyway, I'm sure Betty wouldn't mind, you getting her bloomers down now and again,' he told him, with a little smile and a wink. 'By the way,' he said, 'regarding the NAAFI, I assume you're referring to Jean, her with the big tits, aren't you, Mr Baxter?'

'Huh, well, she's one of em, yes,' he grunted, without turning.

'I thought so.' Tony laughed. 'You're a bloody hypocrite, then.'

'What do you mean – a hypocrite?' Jeff replied, stopping his work and turning to face his tormentor with a scowl.

'Well, don't tell me you wouldn't like to have your hand up the leg of her knickers, Jeff. I've seen you walking away from the counter in there with a sandwich in your hand and a bulge in your pants, more than once, mate.' Tony laughed uproariously.

Without returning to that subject, Jeff turned back to his laundry basket and asked with casual piety, 'Are you going to the NAAFI dance tonight, Tony?'

Still tittering with laughter, he replied, 'Of course I am, mate, and I'm going to have a go at getting that big beefy Jean round the back an'all, if I can. I'm sure she won't mind having her pants dropped,' he sniggered. Jeff, made no reply and went briskly on with his work.

'Hi there, Yorky,' called out Sergeant Banks a little later, walking past the open door.
Tony, still at his paper work replied, 'Hi there, Sergeant.' Then, pushing the pile of papers away he jumped to his feet, and called after him, 'Excuse me, Sergeant, can you spare a minute?'

Freezing in his stride he turned back going into the bedding store, 'Sure I can, Yorky; what's the problem this time, then?' he asked with a smile.

'It's about Sergeant Riley, Jerry,' Tony said. 'I met him on the landing the other day, he said he'd just been discharged from hospital.' Tony told him the whole conversation that occurred between them.

'Yes, I know about most of that, Yorky,' Jerry said, nodding.

'Aye, as he told you, I did go see him; I was down there in the Medical Centre on other business though, but aye, he told me a similar story. He looked all right physically, when I walked into his ward,' he continued. 'He was dressed and reading a newspaper; however as soon as we started talking, it was obvious that he was somewhere else within in his own mind. What he said about how you saved him sounded so genuine, I could have believed it myself, if I'd not known you were on leave,' he said, grinning.

'I know, he really does think it all happened like that,' Tony said. 'In a way it's bloody scary, Jerry; do you think it could be caused by some sort of guilt complex, you know, because he's been groundlessly hounding me over the past months?'

'Could be, he did apologise, didn't he?' Jerry replied. 'But after I'd been in to see him I felt so concerned I went to have a word his doctor. He told me it's just the shock; it takes time to get over it.' With a laugh, he said, 'Anyway, you've no need to worry, Yorky – they know it's all in his mind, and you'd nowt to do with it.'

'Thank God for that,' said Tony, grinning. 'Anyway, he's gone on sick leave this morning, so we won't be bothered with him for a couple of weeks or so.'

'By the way are you on duty this weekend, Yorky?' Jerry enquired, as he was about to leave.

'Yes, but I'm going to the camp dance until about midnight,' Tony replied, with a sly grin. 'Why? Or shouldn't I ask?' he chuckled.

'Well, there's a chance I might have an overnight visitor, if I'm lucky,' he told him with a wink. 'Mind you, we'll keep things quiet, if you know what I mean.'

'Oh, I know what you mean, you lucky bugger,' Tony said, shaking his head and grinning.

88

'Huh, not a bad turn out,' remarked Jeff, as the pair walked into the NAAFI dance that evening; they were both smartly dressed in best blue uniform, smelling strongly of Yardley's Old Spice aftershave.

'Aye, not bad,' agreed Tony, scanning the room. 'Mind you, I think some of them Army girls are a bit overfed, Jeff,' he pointed out, watching them gliding around the floor. 'I'm not too fond of fat lasses, you know, mate,' he added frowning. He pointed onto the dance floor. 'Them two jiving together aren't bad, Jeff, come on mate let's split 'em; I'll have the ginger one with the big arse,' he said, with a note of urgency.

Several dances later, with several different ladies, all of which had proved fruitless, the two boys decided it was time for a little liquid refreshment.

They were just ordering their second pint at the bar when Jeff called out excitedly, 'Oh look, Tony, Betty's just walked in – she said she was coming.'

'So that's why you've been staring at the door every two minutes, you crafty bugger, why didn't you tell me; is Ruby coming with her?' he asked, craning his neck to see if she was following in Betty's wake.

'No sorry you've had it there, Tony,' he laughed. 'McNabb put her on duty in the bar, there's a little party in there tonight; it's somebody's birthday she told me.'

'Huh, bloody big Mavis, trust her to spoil things for me there,' Tony moaned. 'She hates poor Ruby, you know, Jeff.'

'Mavis' – oh, is that Sergeant McNabb's name? I never knew that,' he said. 'How did you know, Tony?'

'I don't remember really,' Tony lied. 'I think I heard Sergeant Pike call her that one day in the dining room or somewhere.'

'Hello boys,' cooed Betty, coming up to them at the bar. She was smiling and looked fresh and sweet in her nice little pink dress and stiletto-heeled shoes.

Jeff, flushing with pleasure, enquired, 'What would you like to drink, Betty, dear?' He went to the bar to get it.

When the three were sitting at one of the tables with their drinks, Tony said, 'Your mate's on duty in the bar tonight then, Betty, eh?'

'Oh, Ruby, you mean,' she replied, sipping her cherry wine, 'Yes, Sergeant McNabb singled her out for the job this afternoon; she hates poor Ruby for some reason,' she sighed.

'Aye, poor Ruby,' Tony said, before finishing off his pint with a long swig. Glancing over to the food counter, he got to his feet. 'Anyway, I'm not staying here playing gooseberry with you two lovebirds, I'm going over to have a word with Jean on the food counter. I think she finishes her stint at ten o'clock, she might like to have a dance.' He grinned as he walked away.

Later, Jeff smooching round the floor with Betty held close, suddenly noticed Tony with Jean, the buxom NAAFI girl, dancing alongside him. They exchanged smiles, and then nearing the door, Tony suddenly guided Jean off the floor. She then made her way behind the counter, leaving Tony alone.

Excusing himself from Betty for a moment, Jeff went up to him, and asked him with a laugh if he'd been dumped.

'Definitely not,' he was told. 'It was a plan to beat the SPs.'

Tony said he was giving her time to get out of the back door, before he went out the normal way to meet her outside, thus avoiding any hassle from the SPs. Wishing him the best, Jeff then went back to his own dream girl.

'Where's Tony gone, Jeff? He hasn't gone back to the billet, has he?' Betty enquired, as they made their way back onto the dance floor. 'It's not even eleven o'clock yet, and the dance doesn't finish till midnight.'

'He's got a bit of a thick head, love, he's gone out for a breath of fresh air,' he lied.

Less than ten minutes later, they were dancing around to a jaunty quickstep, when he saw Tony come walking back in on his own, with a black look on his face.

'Tony's soon back; I hope he's all right, Betty,' he said drawing her attention to his observation. 'You go up to the bar, my love,' he told her. 'I'll go over and ask him if he'd like to join us; he doesn't look too happy for some reason,' he chuckled.

'Now then, mate you're soon back,' Jeff said, approaching his scowling friend. 'I didn't expect to see you in here again for at the least half an hour – don't tell me you've lost your touch.'

Glaring back at him, Tony mumbled, 'Stop the piss-taking, Baxter. It don't suit you, mate.'

'What's wrong, Tony?' he asked, now slightly concerned as he could see that Tony was genuinely upset. 'You haven't had any bother with the SPs out there, have you?'

After a slight pause, he replied mournfully, 'No, bloody worse than that, mate; it's ruined my night an'all – I was so building up to it.'

'What? What the hell's happened, Tony? Come on, mate, spit it out; where's your girl, Jean, anyway?' he asked.

'She's gone in the back door.' Looking at him sadly, he said, 'Just my bloody luck – we had a great snogging session for a few minutes, then as soon as I dropped my hand she shoved me away and said it was the wrong week.'

Trying to keep a straight face, Jeff said sadly, 'Oh hell, so what happened then?'

'Huh, nowt,' he grunted. 'I said it was getting cold and we'd better go back inside.'

'Anyway Tony, come on, have a drink with Betty and me; she's waiting for us up at the bar,' he said, nodding in that direction.

'No thanks, Jeff, I've had enough, I'm off back to the Mess; that female flight sergeant hasn't arrived yet. I hope she doesn't come knocking on my bloody door in the middle of the night,' he added, turning to go.

The building appeared deserted as Tony walked through the highly polished front doorway of the Sergeants Mess, and so was the long corridor leading to his bedding store. However, passing the plate glass entrance door to the bar, he could see a throng of activity within.

Back in the bedding store, standing at the little sink dressed only in his underpants, giving his teeth a final scrub before getting into bed, he suddenly heard a soft tapping on the door. 'Oh Christ,' he muttered. 'Here we go, fancy turning up at this time of night.' Grabbing his tracksuit bottom and a tee shirt he quickly slipped them on and called out, 'Coming, just a minute.' Opening the door with a big smile on his face, expecting to be confronted by the new resident, Tony was surprised to see standing there in front of him the tall elegantly dressed figure of Sergeant McNabb.

'Sorry to disturb you AC Ryan,' she said, sober as a judge and smiling at him, 'but a Flight Sergeant Brown came earlier looking for reception; however as you weren't available I booked her in and sent Pritchard to escort her to her room, using the Mess master key. I told her I'd get her personal key when you returned and deliver it to her myself,' she added with a weak smile.

Hardly being able to believe she could be so considerate, Tony replied, 'That was very nice of you, Sergeant, I'll go get it for you right away.' He turned and went over to the notice board on the back wall where all the room keys hung, but as he did so, he couldn't help thinking how nice she could be when she wanted to be. Also, how sexy she looked in her tight black cocktail dress; he now realised Mavis was a very attractive woman out of her working gear. She was quietly waiting and he went back with the key, passed it to her and enquired sweetly, 'Had a good time tonight then, Sergeant?'

'Not too bad,' she said, frowning. 'They're all bloody drunk in there, as usual,' she added, curling her lip.

She paused for a moment looking into Tony's face, smiled warmly and said, 'Well, good night, AC Ryan.' Turning to go she continued, 'Sorry if I got you out of your bed.'

Looking at her lustfully, his randy feelings once more aroused, he eyed her sexily – a trick that rarely failed – and said quietly, 'Well, it's not all that late,

Mavis; can I invite you in for a cup of tea, seeing as you've been so kind as to help me tonight?'

Turning back to face him she smiled sadly. 'I'd love to, Tony, but I don't think I'd be very good company tonight. I'm not feeling too good,' she moaned softly, shaking her head. 'That's why I had to leave the bar party.' With an exaggerated frown she added, 'and now I'm beginning to develop stomach pains, I think I need a good night's sleep.' Surprising him once more, she leaned forward and stroked his face. 'Normally I'd love to take up your offer – some other time, perhaps.' She smiled affectionately and turned to go, looking down at him mournfully. 'I hope you understand, Tony dear.'

Watching her walking away up the corridor he certainly did understand; turning and slamming the door behind him, he said out loud, 'Unbelievable, bloody well unbelievable, same thing; twice on the same fucking night, I must be jinxed.' Then stripping off down to his underpants, he jumped into his – for tonight at least – most virtuous bed.

89

'I'm back, chaps,' called out Sergeant Pike, walking
briskly up the corridor to his office, arms loaded with a
thick leather brief case, plus several Quattro size folios.
West and his mates were busy polishing the floor; Jeff
and Tony were up ladders, fixing a broken pelmet on
one of the big side windows.

Seeing Pike, they all put more effort into the tasks
to show their keenness and Tony called out, 'Hope you
did well on the course, Sergeant!'

'Yes, thank you, Ryan; passed with flying colours,'
he called back, straining to reach into his jacket pocket
for his keys. 'Can one of you boys go and fetch my big
suitcase out of the car boot? It's open,' he added,
struggling on.

Getting down from the step ladder, Tony, sending
Jones for the case, followed the sergeant into his office,
'I suppose you'll want a full work report on
happenings, while you've been away, Sergeant?' he
said, as the little man dumped his load down on the
desktop with a grunt.

Puffing, Pike replied, 'Well, yes, of course, Ryan,
but not just at the moment if you don't mind, that will
do later,' he said, with a smile. You're too darn keen,
you are, Ryan; I'm sure everything's gone like
clockwork with you at the helm,' he said cheerfully.

'Oh yes, of course it has, Sergeant,' Tony said
confidently, 'but I just want to make sure you're kept
right up to date of all goings on in your absence. I think
it only right, considering the responsibilities you have
to bear in this Mess,' he said seriously.

'So true, Ryan,' he sighed. 'I can't afford to miss a
trick in this establishment, but I really do appreciate

your loyalty. Do you know, Ryan,' he went on, 'I was just thinking, haven't you ever considered signing on as a regular in the Service, I'd recommend you for promotion immediately if you did; of course as National Service man, I couldn't,' he told him, with a shake of his head.

'Well, I must admit I have thought about it, Sergeant,' Tony replied. 'Thank you for your consideration and confidence in me. I really take that as a compliment from a man of your military experience, Sergeant, an'all,' he added nodding. Tony knew how to boost the little sergeant's ego.

Just then Jones struggled in with the huge case; glancing at him, Pike called out, 'Put it over there, Jones, near the window, then get back to your duties.'

'Well, I'd better go back to mine as well, Sergeant,' said Tony, as Jones went out of the door,

'Yes, yes, of course, Ryan, I suppose you want to keep an eye on them lads of yours out there. He sighed again. 'That's another bit of responsibility you take off my shoulders, Ryan, thank the Lord.'

Confident he'd scored again, using his flattery with the conceited little Pike, Tony said, as if by way of an afterthought, 'By the way, Sergeant, I was wondering if you could manage to get me a forty-eight hour pass this weekend, something's cropped up at home I'd like to attend to.' Of course he got it.

90

Seeing Sergeant Prince leaving the dining room after his midday meal, Tony approached him with a smile, 'Excuse me, Sergeant,' he said respectfully, 'I wondered if you'd had any contact with SWO Cox recently, I've been looking out for him in here without any success over the last few days.'

He looked at Tony enquiringly for a moment, his little black beady eyes scanning his face; then his mouth slowly stretched into a tight begrudging little smile. 'Hello, Ryan. Yes, he came into the guardroom first thing this morning. He's been on home leave for the last fourteen days. Nothing wrong professionally, that I could deal with, is there, Ryan?' he replied, looking deep into Tony's eyes, causing him to feel an unwarranted guilt.

'No, no, nothing like that, Sergeant,' Tony replied, smiling uneasily. 'No, if it was anything of that nature, I'd have come straight to you, of course,' he said. 'No, the fact is I've got a forty-eight hour pass this weekend and I wanted to ask SWO Cox if he could get me a lift up North on one of the transport flights. He told me, last time when he got me one, that anytime I wanted a lift he'd help if he could – just to ask him – he told me.'

'I see,' the Sergeant replied, his face softening somewhat. 'Well, he hasn't been in here for his dinner yet as far as I know,' he said. 'So, if you keep a look out, you'll no doubt spot him. He'll have been catching up on his backlog, that's why he's running late I suppose. I don't know about him being overloaded with work, though, Ryan.' He frowned. 'I got two raw young corporals posted to me yesterday. Consequently after the weekend, on top of my own work, I've got them to bring up to scratch,' he grumbled, turning to leave. Going out of the door he called back with one of his rare grins, 'Anyway, Ryan, behave yourself up there in Leeds; don't get into any trouble with that gang of ruffians you told me about before.'

Laughing Tony called back, 'I'll try not to, Sergeant.'

91

'Good evening, Bernard.' Tony grinned as he walked into the Dog and Gun, dressed smartly in his best light grey suit with all matching accessories.

'Hello there, Tony, my old love,' Bernard replied, reaching automatically for a pint glass off the shelf. 'It's a nice surprise to see you, lad. Home for long, then? I suppose it's pint of best, as usual,' he said, smiling broadly, as he filled it.

Sitting down on a bar stool watching Bernard pull his pint, Tony replied with a sigh, 'Aye, got home late this afternoon, Bernard; I'm only on a forty-eight hour pass, though. How are things for you then, Bernard?' He glanced around the nearly empty room. 'Not much activity in here for a Friday night, is there?'

Passing him his drink, he replied, 'Yes, it is a bit quiet tonight, Tony, but it's only eight o'clock, plenty of time to fill up yet.' He leaned over the bar towards Tony. 'Bad do about your mate's mother, Tony, weren't it?' he said quietly.

Just picking his glass up for the first drink, Tony put it back down on the bar with a bump. 'What do you mean Bernard,' he asked, shocked. 'What's up with Mrs Mansfield?'

Looking back at him, shaking his head thoughtfully, he replied, 'She's being victimised Tony, haven't you heard? Aye, she keeps getting bricks through her windows and dog shit pushed through her letterbox – that sort of thing, you know.'

'When did this lot start then, Bernard?' he asked angrily, and who the bloody hell is doing it?'

'Well, the first brick went through her kitchen window the weekend after Dave got posted abroad,' he told him. 'Then, off and on, she's had nowt but trouble with the bloody louts, since. Usually Friday or Saturday night after pub's chucked out; but police can't cop em,' he said.

'Sound like it's some bugger that doesn't like Dave, and they're taking it out on her, instead,' Tony said, taking a sip from his pint.

'Well, Dave and you always did things together around here, Tony,' Bernard pointed out. 'Has there been any trouble at your house, then?'

'No, not as far as I know, Bernard,' he replied, 'but my dad's there, ain't he, whereas poor Mrs Mansfield's there on her own.' He frowned. 'Anyway, I've an idea who it could be,' he said angrily. 'I think I'll go to see Mrs Mansfield at closing time, Bernard, and if they try 'owt tonight, whoever the buggers are, they'll be in for a bloody big shock,' he told him, taking another swig from his glass.

After serving a group of young people further down the bar, Bernard came back, and asked quietly, 'Who do you think could be nasty enough to do that to Dave's mother, Tony?'

Hesitantly, he replied, 'Well, I'm not positively sure, Bernard, although I've a good idea; but whoever the bugger is that's doing this to my mate's mum is going to answer to me, if he comes tonight, you can be assured of that,' he said firmly.

Mrs. Mansfield's little semi was situated at the bottom of a cul-de-sac. The back of the house was approached by an unmade, dark road and Tony, knowing that the kitchen – the scene of the first assault – was at the back of the house, had decided to take that approach. His idea was first to go and inform Mrs Mansfield of his intentions, then come back out, conceal himself and wait. However, his plan was swiftly changed, when suddenly, just before he'd reached her house, he heard voices approaching, way down the dark back road.

Slipping behind a nearby garage he stood concealed, waiting with baited breath. As the voices got nearer he realised that his suspicions had been correct, he recognised them distinctly. Yes, it was the stocky little fart, Harry Proudfoot with another of their gang, a big bonehead of a lad who worked with Harry down the local pit, and whose nickname was 'The Brute.'

They were tittering as they passed Tony, hidden in the shadow of the old garage. He heard Proudfoot say, 'We'll put that bloody kitchen window through again tonight, Brute; that'll shift the old cow, she'll shit herself.' He laughed. Then bending down, he picked up a half-brick off a pile of rubble on the grass verge, and was just preparing to throw it over the fence into the kitchen window, when Tony made his move. Slipping out of the shadows in silence like a cat, he was on them before they knew it.

The first blow caught Harry Proudfoot smack in the face and sent him spinning into the gutter, groaning, with blood oozing from his nose. Brute was a big bloke, but not very bright, and therefore a bit slow to appreciate what was going on – it all happened so fast. Before he could be of any trouble, Tony delivered several heavy blows to his face and head, sending him down, groaning and cursing, to join his friend Harry.

Looking down at the two pathetic figures sitting on the grass verge, mopping the blood from their faces, Tony said, menacingly, 'Right, are you going to get to your feet or have you had enough?'

Both lads remained silent, just sitting on the grass with sorrowful expressions on their faces, and Brute, although big and rough-looking, began to cry. 'I didn't do 'owt to Mrs Mansfield's house, Tony Ryan, it were Harry that threw that tin tray through her kitchen window the other day; he put that shit in her letterbox, an'all,' he said, giving Harry a dig with his elbow, 'didn't ya?'

'Shut your cakehole, Brute, you're in it as much as me,' he replied angrily. 'You know why we did it, you agreed from the start, when Terry Ward told us.'

Brute, looking up at Tony like a naughty little boy, said, 'I didn't want 'owt to do with it, Tony, he talked me into it; I've nowt against Dave or his mum,' he told him, wide-eyed and tearful. 'He said Dave scratched his dad's car and let tyres down, the week before he went away and we're getting our own back. I don't believe Dave would do a thing like that, though, Tony,' he said innocently.

Knowing Brut was a simple lad, and his mate a cunning little bugger, Tony said, shaking his head in disgust at the pair, 'Anyway, you were both in it, whatever. Also, the police have been informed, as you'll no doubt know; what's more,' he stressed, 'if they get you, you'll both do time for a serious thing like this. Do you realise, you could have killed Mrs Mansfield, if one of them missiles had have hit her,' he told them angrily.

Just then he noticed a light way down at the bottom of the road, coming towards them slowly; as it passed under the only street lamp in the road, Tony could see it was a policeman on a bike. 'Watch it, you two,' Tony said. 'It's bobby Smirthwaite coming up on his bike, come on get to your feet before he gets here.'

'Oh Tony, you're not going to report us, are you?' moaned Proudfoot, all the fight now out of him. 'My dad'll kill me, if we get a summons.'

Looking back at the pathetic sight, struggling to its feet he said, scornfully, 'No Proudfoot, I'm not going to grass on you, but you're going to pay for all the damage you've done to Mrs Mansfield's property. What's more,' he added, 'you're going to pay her a fiver for the hassle you've put her through, personally.'

'Now then, what have we got here, then?' the old policeman called out, as he slowly dismounted. Seeing who the three figures were, he said to Tony, 'Oh, you're home, are you, Tony Ryan?' Then, glancing at the others suspiciously, he asked sternly, 'What's been going on then?'

Harry and Brute just stood in silence looking at Tony, waiting to see his response. 'Oh, it's nowt, Mr Smirthwaite,' Tony said, casually. 'It's these two silly buggers scrapping again, they're always at each other when they've had a few, you know,' he said laughing.

'And what about you then, Tony Ryan,' he replied, looking him up and down. 'Have you been having a go as well, then?'

'No, oh no, Mr Smirthwaite,' Tony replied, with a little nervous laugh. 'I'm past all that sort of stuff, since I joined the RAF; if I got into any trouble with you, whilst on leave, I'd be in front of the CO when I got back,' he told him with a sharp nod. 'No, I was just on my way to see my mate's mother, Mrs Mansfield, when I saw these daft buggers at it and separated em, that's all; then you came,' and he shrugged.

Continuing to look them up and down suspiciously, the wily old copper said, nodding at Harry and Brute, 'Right you two, bugger off home before I change my mind and lock you both up.' As the pair shot off, breaking into a sprint, he turned to Tony, saying seriously, 'I suppose you know your mate's mother has been having a bit of bother with vandals, don't you, Tony?'

'Aye, I do, Mr Smirthwaite,' he replied. 'Bernard told me in the Dog and Gun tonight, that's why I'm going to see her now,' he said, glancing over at her house.

'Have you any idea who it could be then, Tony?' the officer enquired, staring into his face suspiciously.

'If I did Mr Smirthwaite, they'd be very bloody sorry, I'll tell you,' he replied sternly.

Pausing for a moment, obviously churning the situation over in his mind, the officer said, 'Aye, I see, well you'd better get off to see the good lady before she goes to bed, lad; it's getting a bit late for visiting.'

As Tony walked off towards Mrs Mansfield's back gate, he called after him, 'You sure you'd no part in that scrapping then, Tony, lad?' As he slowly peddled away on his old bike, he continued, 'I just thought the results bore some of your trademarks, that's all,' and he chuckled, as he rode away.

Walking up to the bar the following evening, Bernard asked, 'Did you get things sorted out last night, then, Tony?'

Smiling, he replied, 'Well, I think so, Bernard, I can't see there'll be any more trouble from that department,' adding smugly, 'A pint of best please, Bernard.'

Passing him his drink, Bernard quietly leant across the bar. 'It was two of my regulars wasn't it, lad? They were in here at lunchtime.' He smiled knowingly. 'You certainly gave them a going over, black and blue they were,' he laughed. 'They went straight into the tap room and stayed there all the time they were here, they daren't show themselves in the main bar, apart from when they wanted a re-fill,' he chuckled.

Grinning Tony said, 'You don't miss much Bernard, do you? Aye, it was Proudfoot and his thick mate. Proudfoot was the ring leader, of course,' he said, taking his first sip of ale. 'I caught 'em right in the act, Bernard,' he told him, gleefully. 'They won't want any more of what they got last night for a long time, I'll tell you,' he said, laughing, and he went on to tell all that happened.

'Anyway, Bernard, if they come in tonight just let me know, will you? I told Mrs Mansfield they were going to pay for the damage and I'd like to sort it all out before I go back to camp. On my mate's behalf, you know,' he said, with a nod.

Sitting on his own in the half-empty room, with his elbows on the bar, staring into his half-full pint glass, Tony was miles away. Suddenly, a voice called out right behind him in true military fashion, 'Airman, attention!'

Spinning round on his stool shocked out of his daydream Tony's face broke into a wide grin when he saw who the culprit was. 'Hi there, Steve,' he said warmly, 'how's my favourite corporal? What are you having, mate, a pint or what?' he asked.

The two friends had been sitting with their drinks, talking for about half an hour; Tony had been telling Steve about the trouble he'd had to sort out the previous night, when suddenly Bernard, behind the bar, came up to them. Leaning over, he whispered, 'They've just gone into the tap room, Tony.'

Thanking him, he got to his feet, pulled a sheet of paper with writing on it from his pocket, stared at this seriously for a few seconds and chuckled to himself. 'This is their bill for the damage they caused,' he said, waving it at Bernard, grinning. Then, telling Steve he wouldn't be long and to watch his half-drunk pint, he put on a stern face and made for the tap room. As he went into the little tap room, Tony was first confronted with the strong smell of pipe smoke, given off by two old men in cloth caps sitting at the far side of the room, talking intimately. Not far from them a young courting couple were sipping what looked like cider, and gazing into each others' eyes with adoration. The only other occupants were the two members of the Canal street gang that Tony was looking for.

'Ah, this is where you're hiding out then, is it?' he said sternly, going up to where they were sitting side by side at a table, facing the wall.

They automatically turned to face him, and he gasped at the sight, 'Christ, you two look as though you've been in the wars,' he chuckled.

Proudfoot had a black eye and a split nose and poor Brute had two black eyes and a very swollen lip – which he kept licking. 'Stop gloating, Tony Ryan,' said Harry, giving the impression that it was painful even to speak. 'What do you want anyway, don't you think you've done us enough damage already?' he said, grumpily.

Tony replied seriously, 'You got off very bloody lucky, you two, believe me; if bobby Smirthwaite had known why you got that lot, he'd have run the pair of you in, and you know it, Proudfoot. Anyway,' he went on, 'I've talked to Mrs Mansfield and she's worked out the cost of the damage you both did to her house.'

Pulling the sheet of paper out of his pocket again, he looked it over once more and then went on seriously, 'Right, here we are; the damage to the glass and window frame, plus the curtains, etc. came to four pounds, nine shillings and sixpence.

Hearing this, both lads gave a groan.

'Hold it, hold it,' said Tony, 'I haven't finished yet, on top of this is her personal discomfort; the cleaning up of the dog shit you shoved through her letter box, having to scrub the carpet and providing the necessary cleaning materials, this comes to a further five pounds, ten shillings and sixpence.' Staring down at them, he said, 'That's exactly ten pounds you owe her.'

'Ten quid,' moaned Brute, 'I ain't got ten quid, Tony.'

'Neither have I,' said Harry, in the same moaning tone.

'I didn't say ten quid each, you silly buggers,' Tony replied. 'That's the full cost of the damage; you owe half each,' he told them.

'Even so, I don't expect you to pay it all in one go,' he said, benevolently. 'How much have you both got on you, now?' he asked, firmly fixing them with a hard stare. Reaching into their pockets, they both pulled out a handful of change and proceeded to count it.

'I've got twenty-seven and six,' said Harry, begrudgingly.

'And I've got twenty-six and six, Tony,' Brute told him.

'You both must have been on a spending spree then,' he grunted. 'It's only Saturday and you get paid at the pit on Friday, so where's it all gone then?' he enquired. Then going up to their table he sat down opposite them, saying quietly, 'Come on, the pair of you, out with them wallets.' Slowly, they both reached into their inside jacket pockets, scowling, and pulled out the wallets.

Harry, producing a further one pound note, said forlornly, 'This is all I've got to last me 'till next pay day, Tony, honest.'

'And you Brute?' Tony asked, glaring at him.

'Same here, Tony, just a quid, my mum only gives me three pound pocket money you know,' he told him mournfully, 'and I've to buy my clothes out of that, an'all.'

'OK, give me two quid each, now,' Tony said, 'and you'll be left with a balance to pay of six quid between you, then.' Moans came from the pair as Tony continued, 'so, if you both give Bernard another two quid next pay day, and a quid each the following week, you'll be straight then, okay? Bernard will make sure Mrs Mansfield gets it.' As they handed it over, he said, 'Don't forget, boys, will you? I'll be home again at the end of the month, and if Mrs Mansfield hasn't received her money in full – I'm not going to soil my hands on you again. No, I'll have a little talk with Mr Smirthwaite,' he threatened firmly. Then Tony put the money into his pocket, got to his feet and made off back to the bar, leaving them staring after him, cussing and grumbling to each other.

92

The rain was belting down as Tony stepped out of the railway carriage into the hustle and bustle of the busy railway platform; he'd got only fifteen minutes to get to the bus depot, if he were to catch the first hourly bus up to camp. The train had been running late; the time was seven fifteen in the morning. With his weekend case under his arm, he broke into a fast jog across town, and just managed to jump on the bus, as it started off out of the depot. Uniform sodden, water running down his face, he settled into his seat, knowing he'd be even wetter when he'd walked the half-mile from the bus stop, over the airfield to his billet.

Half an hour later found him trudging up the side of the runway in the long wet grass; by now looking like a half-drowned rat, and feeling utterly miserable. Getting nearer the camp, he met several lads he knew, going to their different departments of employment and he took a few friendly jibes from them about the state he was in. Nearing the guardroom at the main gates, he noticed two SP corporals standing like ramrods, sheltering under the veranda that protruded from the front of the building. One, the shorter, was a heavily-built man, the other a tall gangly fellow; both were immaculately dressed in their white-topped peak caps, white belts and gaiters, with canes held firmly underarm.

Noticing the bedraggled figure of the soaked Tony coming closer, the taller one yelled out at the top of his voice, 'Airman!'

Then beckoning with his arm he yelled, 'Come here, man, at the double!'

'Oh Christ, this is all I need,' Tony mumbled, turning to obey the loud command from the corporal, who made sure, of course, that he didn't come out from his sheltered position under the veranda, into the teeming rain.

'I said at the double!' he yelled again, as poor Tony, squelching in his shoes, trudged towards them. The corporals stood staring down at him from their sheltered position. Struggling up the steps onto the veranda he dropped his case with a clutter; it burst open, depositing a few pairs of clean socks and his vacuum flask on to the veranda floor.

'You stupid fool!' yelled the corporal, as Tony stooped to pick up his belongings and shove them hastily back into the case. Slowly, cane under arm, the corporal walked towards him, smirking. Tony stood up to face him and he continued menacingly, 'You horrible, scruffy –' he got no further. Both he and Tony just stared at each other open-mouthed, while the thick-set corporal in the background looked on with a puzzled expression on his face, surprised at his colleague's sudden silence. Neither man spoke for a long pause, which seemed like an hour, they just stared at each other, transfixed.

The baffled corporal behind was beginning to fidget, no doubt wondering what the hell was going on. Suddenly he called out, 'Everything all right, Corporal?'

Without turning, he replied, 'Yes, go and put the kettle on, Percy, I'll see to this.'

As the man disappeared into the office, the Corporal, still staring into Tony's shocked face, hissed with a smirk, 'Bloody Tony Ryan; well, well, this is a surprise!'

'I'll second that,' replied Tony, staring back at him. 'I knew you were in the Service, but I never thought they'd have had a bugger like you in the RAF police. Chris Simpson? No, never in a thousand years,' he said, shaking his head.

Scowling, he replied, 'Well, you were wrong, weren't you? AC Ryan.' Then, leaning forward and glaring at him, he continued in a threatening tone. 'And don't you forget, airman, you'd better have respect for your superiors from now on and address me as Corporal; do you understand, Ryan?' he yelled in Tony's face.

Fully realising the situation, Tony replied, 'Yes, Corporal.'

'Good,' he snarled, curling his lip and looking Tony up and down. 'Stand to attention when you speak to a superior officer, Ryan,' he yelled, 'or I'll be tempted to put you on a 252, for insubordination.' Tony obeyed promptly, standing there looking like a half-drowned rat in his saturated uniform, as Simpson raged on. 'You're a disgusting sight, Ryan,' he sneered, 'and apart from your uniform, your hair's half-way down your back; get it cut!' he yelled, staring at Tony, wildly.

'Yes, Corporal,' Tony replied calmly, while thinking what he'd do to him next time they met in the Dog and Gun.

Glaring and obviously annoyed by the calm response he'd got from Tony, the angry corporal was just about to find more fault with him, when the main door to the guardroom opened and a strict voice called out, 'What's the trouble there, Corporal Simpson?'

'Now you're for it, Ryan,' he whispered. 'It's my boss, Sergeant Prince.' Jumping to attention as he turned to face the advancing, immaculately-dressed figure, he called out, 'I've had to pull this man over, Sergeant, for improper dress.'

Coming up to them, his small black eyes flicking as he eyed the pair, he said to Tony 'What have you got to say, airman?'

Still to attention, Tony glanced at his old enemy standing smirking, waiting to see him get further chastising, when, without turning, the Sergeant said curtly, 'You can go now, Corporal Simpson, I'll attend to this man myself.'

He reluctantly departed and Sergeant Prince enquired, 'Now then, Ryan, what have you got to say for yourself; what was it my corporal stopped you for?'

Speaking formally, Tony replied, 'Improperly dressed, Sergeant, and then he pointed out the length of my hair.' The Sergeant looked him up and down as Tony continued, 'and justifiably so, I suppose, Sergeant, the condition I'm in after walking about for the last couple of hours in this torrential rain.'

'Well, you are a disgusting sight, Ryan, I must admit,' he replied quietly, still eyeing him.

'All I can say, Sergeant,' Tony went on formally, 'is that I offer my apologies and assure you, I'll do all in my power never to get into a situation like this again.'

With the slightest hint of a smile behind his stern face, the Sergeant spoke in a friendlier tone of voice, 'Well, I don't suppose you could have foreseen this downpour, no more than anyone else. But of course the corporal is technically correct; you do look a disgrace to the uniform.' He shook his head and paused in thought for a moment. 'However, these are mitigating circumstances and I'm prepared to overlook it this time with a caution. By the way,' he said, 'my other corporal told me that you and Corporal Simpson appeared to recognise each other when you met, is that so Ryan?' he asked, staring into Tony's face as if he were reading his mind.

'That is true, Sergeant,' replied Tony. 'Chris Simpson and I have known each other all our lives, we were in the same class at school,' he told him.

'I see,' he said, 'so you've been friends for a long time, then?' Smiling slightly, Tony replied, 'Well, I wouldn't say we've been friends, Sergeant, but we always respected each other. We've exchanged black eyes on many a Friday night after closing time at the back of our local pub, 'The Dog and Gun'. He was the leader of a local gang you see, Sergeant,' he said seriously, 'The Canal street boys' they called themselves,' he added, 'they never liked my mate, Dave and me.'

'Canal street boys; well, well,' Sergeant Prince muttered, nodding thoughtfully.

'Mind you, Sergeant,' Tony went on – feeling reluctant to harm his old enemy professionally – 'that's a long time ago, we were only young lads then; I'm sure Chris is a fine police officer now, Sergeant. He's a great guy to have with you in a rough situation,' he added. 'Knows how to handle himself, I'll give him that,' he said, positively.

'Is that so,' Sergeant Prince replied, with a slight nod. 'Anyway, you'd better get off, Ryan, you're beginning to steam, lad.'

Tony turned smartly to go, and as he went down the steps, Sergeant Prince called out, 'By the way, Ryan, you'd better get your hair trimmed as the corporal suggested; we don't want any more trouble, do we?'

Wetter than ever, Tony walked into the billet block; his mate, Jeff, was still there, although the time was past nine o'clock. 'What the hell are you doing here at this time, Jeff? Pike will be going bloody mad, do you know what time it is?' he said. As he turned to face him, Tony was shocked to see a large swelling on the side of his jaw. 'Fucking hell, Jeff, what's up with your face, mate? Don't tell me you've been scrapping with some bugger over that little Betty of yours, while I've been away?' He started to laugh.

'I've been to work, Tony,' he said mournfully, 'and Pike gave me a note to report to sick bay; hope you've had a nice weekend, mate,' he said, stroking his jaw.

'Well, what is up with you, then, Jeff? You look a right sight, have you been scrapping or what?' he asked, getting more concerned.

Pathetically, Jeff replied, 'I've got a bloody big gumboil, Tony, and it's driving me mad; I couldn't sleep a wink last night. Sergeant Pike said it looks as though they'll have to pull the tooth out.'

Tony, realising that infections like that could be more serious than most people thought, said condescendingly, 'Looks a bad job that, mate; I'd better come down with you and make sure you get prompt treatment, Jeff. I'll have to get a hair trim on the way, though,' he said. 'They've just had me down at the bloody guardroom for the last half-hour.'

'What for?' he asked, maintaining his moaning tone of voice.

'Never mind for the moment,' Tony replied, commencing to strip off his wet best blue uniform. 'Just let me have a quick change into my working togs and then we can get off and sort things out; I'll tell you all about it on the way.'

'How's your face then, Jeff?' Tony asked, at afternoon tea break in the bedding store.

'A lot better now they've pulled the bloody tooth out, thanks, Tony,' he said, trying to smile. 'Unbelievable about that SP you told me about, though; I'll bet you were surprised when you saw him, weren't you?'

'Sure was, mate,' he grinned, as he poured the tea, 'but it's not the first time I've met a bloke from home out of the blue like that. I met a lad at Padgate who'd been a mate at home, he just walked into the Mess one day as I was having my dinner; that was a surprise an'all,' he said, with a laugh.

'I bet he wasn't a nasty bugger like this Simpson, though, was he?' Jeff replied, trying to laugh.

'Oh no, little Nigel Lacy is a nice lad, he was in the ATC for years before he joined this mob,' he told him. 'No, Chris Simpson's a different bloke altogether,' he went on, 'he was always a cocky bugger, he even ruled his own gang with a rod of iron; they were all scared to bloody death of him.'

'Did he scare you as well, Tony?' Jeff teased.

'What! He fucking didn't,' snapped Tony. 'I've blackened his eyes many a time,' and he laughed as he passed him his tea.

'Mind you,' he continued, 'I must admit he's blackened mine a few times as well,' he chuckled. 'Anyway, bugger him. I bet you didn't do as I asked you, last Friday evening,' he said abruptly, changing the subject.'

'Well, that's just where you're wrong, Mr "bloody clever" Ryan,' Jeff replied, reaching into his inside pocket and pulling out his wallet. 'I was wondering how long it would be before you remembered about money.'

'Oh, so you did have a sale, then,' he smiled. 'Huh, wonders never cease; how did it go then, Jeff, my old mate?' he asked, suddenly in a good mood.

Opening the wallet slowly, Jeff pulled out a handful of pound notes and passed them to him. 'Not a bad night, Tony, eh; I think if you count that lot, you'll find it's exactly fifteen quid, and here's the rest,' he said, passing him a half-crown coin.

'Good God: fifteen pound two and six,' gasped Tony. 'Bloody hell, that's the best night we've ever had, Jeff.' Counting the money carefully, he stuffed the notes into his own wallet, slapped Jeff on the shoulder, and pressed the half-crown into the palm of his hand benevolently. 'Here, Jeff, a little bonus to be going on with for your business talent and loyalty to the firm,' he said, with a smile.

Their conversation was broken by a tapping on the door. 'Come in. It's open,' called out Tony. 'Hello there, my little darling,' he said, as Ruby entered with a strained look on her face. 'What can I do for you, kitten?' he asked, with a dirty little laugh.

'Stop trying to be funny, Tony Ryan,' she snapped. 'It's Sergeant McNabb – she's in a roaring mood, playing hell with everybody down there. She's sent me to tell you to report to her as soon as possible, without fail,' she stressed, looking at him wide-eyed.

'Oh, bugger her,' Tony grunted, sitting back in his chair sipping his tea. 'I've too much on this afternoon, getting rooms ready for them new residents we're expecting. I've no time to waste listening to her gabble.'

'You'd better go, Tony, she's really on the war path. I'm not kidding – she's bad enough to put you on a charge if you ignore her order,' she told him, with concern in her voice.

'What the hell have you been up to, Ryan?' said Jeff, sitting in his chair and laughing. 'I hope you've been behaving yourself.'

'I've done nowt that could upset that silly bugger,' he replied casually. 'How could I? I've been away all weekend. She's probably blaming me for something that you, or them other daft twats have done,' he grunted. 'I think a better idea than going down to listen to her ranting and raving, is for you to piss off Baxter, and leave Ruby and me to have a nice cosy hour together here behind closed doors. What do you think darling?' he said, giving her a sweet smile.

'I think you're a daft sod, Tony Ryan,' she said blushing and turning to leave. 'Anyway, if you don't go to see what she wants, don't say I didn't warn you,' she told him firmly. She stamped out of the door and a chorus of laughter followed her.

'I think I'd better go down and see what McNabb has been ranting about, Jeff,' Tony said, finishing his tea and getting to his feet with a sigh. You'd better get up there and make a start on them two rooms on the top landing,' he added. 'I'll join you when I've sorted her out.'

'Oh, you're there, Ryan,' yelled out the big lady, as he walked into the dining room. 'I was just about to come looking for you; Pritchard told me you were too busy to obey my request,' she roared, glaring at him.

Ruby and another young girl, who happened to be passing by, with their trays full of crockery, glanced at him with a look of pity, as they hurried into the kitchen.

'I was only joking with her, Sergeant,' Tony said. 'I intended to come – as soon as I'd finished the job I was undertaking at the time.'

'What drinking tea?' she huffed. Anyway, you'd better go through to the kitchen and wait in my office,' she told him. 'I'll be with you in a few minutes, when I've got this lot sorted out in here.'

'What's she say, Tony?' Ruby asked in an urgent whisper, as he passed her, on his way the through kitchen.

'Nowt,' he muttered. 'She just told me to go and wait in her office until she comes, and by look on her face there's trouble forthcoming.'

'Oh dear,' Ruby replied sympathetically, glancing at the kitchen door nervously, to see if the sergeant was coming. 'It sounds serious, Tony, if she told you to wait in her office.'

'Office, it's more like a bloody broom cupboard,' grumbled Tony to himself, as he sat waiting for her in the cramped little room. 'Stinks rotten of fish in here, an'all,' he muttered, sniffing. Then he saw her through the glass panelled door, striding towards the office with a hard expression on her face. Oh shit, he thought, it must be them silly buggers; what the hell have they done while I've been away?

However, as she walked in, to Tony's great surprise her expression softened, and closing the door behind her, a pleasant smile emerged. 'Sorry to have had to put that act of aggression on, Tony,' she said softly, sitting down at her little desk, 'but them waitresses out there miss nothing, you know; that Pritchard especially,' she added, frowning.

Now realising that he'd been summoned for something less than a good bollocking, Tony said, 'Oh, she's not that bad, Sergeant, she's only a young girl, you know.'

'Huh, she's a scheming lazy little bitch,' she grunted. 'Anyway, Tony, I haven't got you here to talk about her – I've got a proposition to put to you,' she said, with a very pleasant smile.

'What's that, then?' he asked gingerly.

Reaching into her desk drawer, she pulled out a large pink envelope, from which she produced two fancy-looking silver tickets. 'These,' she said, waving them in front of his face. 'I've got two theatre tickets going to waste here, Tony, box seats too,' she pointed out. 'Do you like theatre?' she asked, smiling sweetly, into his baffled face.

'Oh aye, I like a bit of entertainment, Sergeant,' he replied. 'I've heard from the lads that they put some good shows on at the 'Theatre Royal' in town.' Grinning, he said, 'Everybody calls it the bug hut, though.'

Rather shocked, she replied indignantly, 'The bug hut, Tony! I'm not referring to a hovel like that; the theatre these tickets are for is a highly respected establishment down in London. These tickets cost two pound ten shillings each,' she said, looking down at them.

'One of them posh places, Sergeant, eh,' he said, 'but how the hell are we going to get right down there? It's about thirty miles or more from here to London; when are the tickets for anyway?' he enquired.

'This Saturday evening,' she said, smiling.

'Well, I appreciate your offer, Sergeant, I really do, but I can't see how we're going to make it to London and back in one evening; the train service around here is not so good you know.'

Smiling again, she replied, 'Tony, my dear boy, stop worrying about getting there; it's less than an hour's drive from here to London, by car.'

'I realise that, Sergeant,' he replied. 'But neither of us has got a bloody car; if we had, there'd be no problem.'

'What are you talking about, you silly thing – haven't got a car, are you trying to be funny with me?' she giggled.'

'No, I'm stating a fact, Sergeant,' he replied. 'Neither me or my mate, Jeff own a car, so we'd have to make our way there on the train; no other way I can see,' he said, with a shrug.'

Staring back at him frowning, she said indignantly, 'Jeff, your mate? I suppose you mean that clown Baxter, don't you?'

'Well, yes I do, Sergeant,' he replied.

'I'm not suggesting you go to the theatre with that fool; no, Tony, I mean you and I go together in my car.' She smiled again.

Rather shocked, he said, 'Oh I see, Sergeant; you mean you and me go to the theatre together in your car?'

'Of course, you silly boy. What else?'

'Well, I've nothing else to do on Saturday, so yes, that's okay with me, Sergeant.' He smiled and then his mind ticking over, he went on, 'Oh, I didn't realise that you owned a car – what sort is it anyway?'

'It's a black Austin 10,' she told him proudly. 'You must have seen it, Tony. I always park it under that lamp on the side of the Mess wall.'

'Is that yours?' he said, surprised. 'It's a little beauty is that, it's just like my dad's, lovely to drive, aren't they? I've driven miles in his,' he said. Actually, he was thinking that if he played his cards right here, he might be able to coax her into letting him borrow it on occasions, like his dad did at home.

Smiling, she said, 'but I didn't realise you were a driver, Tony. Have you got a full licence, then?'

'Of course I have,' he replied cockily. 'I've had one for over a year, I passed in my dad's old car, the one he had before he bought the one like yours. But I've just been thinking, Sergeant,' he went on, frowning slightly. 'You and me going to the theatre together – it would be all right wouldn't it, you know, you being my superior in here, like? Then there's WO Bloomer,' he pointed out, shaking his head. 'What about him? I don't want him on my back either; if he gets jealous 'owt could happen,' he said, remembering the boxing match.

Leaning over the desktop smiling, she replied in a soothing tone, 'Don't you bother yourself about that sort of thing, Tony dear; anyway,' she said, still smiling, 'We won't be in uniform, so rank won't come into it.' She went on sternly, 'as far as Tommy Bloomer is concerned, I can soon sort him out if he gets out of hand, believe me, but we can forget him, Tony,' she tittered. 'He's not on camp, he's gone off up to Scotland on a month's compassionate leave, his mother's very ill. Mind you she's ninety-six, so she's had a good run,' she added, nodding. 'By the way,' she continued, with a mock stern frown, 'my name is Mavis to you, behind closed doors, I'm fed up of you calling me bloody sergeant all the time, after all we're friends, aren't we?' She smiled coyly.

Tony smiled back weakly, while he mulled over the advantages of borrowing her car. 'Anything you say, Mavis darling,' he replied.

Walking back across the kitchen floor, frowning, he met Ruby, who enquired with great concern, 'Oh, you look upset, Tony, what happened?'

Frowning more, he replied, 'A right bloody bollocking I'll tell you, dust in the dining room she reckoned – it was them lazy buggers, while I was away. Wait while I get at 'em, Ruby,' he threatened. 'I'll bloody kill 'em for this,' he told her, stamping away determinedly.

Just then there was a loud yell from the office, 'Ryan!'

They both turned abruptly, to see Sergeant McNabb standing framed in the office doorway and glaring. 'Don't forget the new curtains for the dining room are due tomorrow, so make sure the windows are ready for them, or you'll have me to answer to.'

Noticing Ruby standing there cow-eyed, she yelled, 'How many more times have I to tell you about gossiping, Pritchard? Get on with your work, girl!'

Walking up the corridor back to the haven of his bedding store, Tony felt very pleased with himself, as he thought about his ideas for Sergeant McNabb's car. 'It would be great if I could manage to talk her into it,' he muttered to himself, 'it would be handy to have a car at my beck and call. I'll have to give her a bit more of the old Ryan charm,' he chuckled, as he walked along.

93

The boys were very pleased with their commission this week, mate,' Jeff remarked, coming into the bedding store later.

'I should think so,' Tony replied as he sat reading a newspaper. 'If we keep having sales like last week, Jeff, I'll be considering lowering their commission rates – they're being spoiled,' he muttered, staring down at his reading. Then glancing up, he chuckled. 'Put the kettle on then, Jeff; I've just pinched a bag full of chocolate biscuits out of the kitchen. By the way, mate,' he called out cheerfully, as Jeff filled the kettle, 'how did you go on in here, over the weekend?'

'Oh fine,' he replied. 'The two new residents both came before seven o'clock on Saturday evening, so there was no need for me to stay overnight.

'I don't mean them, you daft bugger,' said Tony scornfully. 'I mean your love life, man. Why do you think I gave you the run of this place for the weekend?'

Looking a little embarrassed, Jeff said, 'How do you mean, Tony?'

'Christ, man,' he sighed. 'I thought you could have had a night of passion with that little Betty of yours,' he said, with a note of disgust creeping into his voice. 'Don't tell me you threw a chance like that away, Jeff?'

'Well, I know how you feel, Tony,' he moaned, 'but I'm different to you, as I keep telling you; Betty's a decent girl, you know.'

'Aye, and you're a bloody fool, Baxter. The sooner you get her bloomers down, mate, the happier she'll be, Jeff lad, believe me,' he told him firmly.

'You're absolutely, bloody well disgusting, Ryan, suggesting that Betty has desires like that,' he replied, angrily banging his cup down on the table and stamping out of the store.

'Well, if you don't believe me,' Tony called after him, 'pop down to the kitchen and send her up here for half an hour, I'll soon have 'em down.' He laughed coarsely.

Later that day, Tony was at the top of a step ladder, struggling to hang one of the long velvet curtains, when a voice Tony recognised, called out, 'Don't hang those curtains upside down, Yorky,'

Glancing over his shoulder with a grin, he shouted back, 'Hi there, Sergeant Banks, are you having a day off, then?' Clicking the curtain rod into position, Tony climbed down off the ladder. 'It's okay for you bosses, you can have a day off anytime you like, not like us poor serfs, worked to death.'

'Huh, bosses,' the Sergeant grunted, 'I'm not having a day off, I've just had a bloody telling off, though, by a bloody snotty SP corporal, who looks wet behind the ears; he don't look any older that you, Yorky,' he said, shaking his head in disgust.

'What's he look like – this corporal then? Tony asked, smiling slightly.

'He's a tall, lanky, young sod,' he grumbled. 'Must be new, I've never seen the bugger before, and as I said he's only about your age.'

'Not quite, Sergeant Banks, he's a few month older than me,' Tony replied, adding with a grin, 'and a lot bloody dafter, I'll tell you.'

Surprised, he replied, 'How do you know, Yorky, who told you?'

'Nobody told me, Sergeant, I was in the same class at school as him; he hates my guts does Chris Simpson. He pulled me over as I was passing the guardroom the other morning, on my way back from leave. Pulling rank he was, told me I was scruffy and to get my hair cut. Aye, a nasty bugger, Simpson,' he said with a nod, 'had many a scrap, behind our local pub – him and me. There'll be another an'all, when I meet him back home in civvies,' he said nodding. 'Anyway, what did he get at you for, then? Couldn't you tell him to piss off or summat, you being a Sergeant, like?' he enquired.

'Not on police duty, Yorky,' he replied. 'He's got powers to check any rank that he thinks is breaking military law,' then with a sigh, he added, 'and strictly speaking I was doing just that.'

'Oh, how do you mean?' Tony asked, looking surprised.

He sighed again. 'He stopped my car as I went through the main gate into the industrial site, to check my identity; of course, I told him who I was, and that everybody knew me, but he insisted on seeing my 1250. Well, me like a pillock had forgotten my wallet with that in it. I've done it before, it's easy done,' he said, 'but I was in the wrong, your 1250 should be carried at all times, as you know, Yorky.'

'Oh aye, but there's limits,' Tony said with a head jerk. 'I mean he'd know you were only going to work, you were also in uniform; I think he's trying to impress Sergeant Prince,' he sniggered.

'Anyway,' he shrugged, 'that's why I'm here at this time in the morning, he wouldn't let me through, I've had to come back for the bugger; but I'll keep a look out for him in future,' he said, as he walked away.

'Might have thought you were a spy in disguise, Sergeant,' Tony called after him, laughing. 'After all your car is a Volkswagen.'

'Less of that, AC Ryan,' he called back, pretending to be stern, 'or I'll get you locked up for being bloody cheeky.' He walked off, grinning.

'What's this then, being cheeky to the sergeant, Mr Ryan?' Jeff Baxter said, coming up to him, as he went back to his curtain hanging.

'Just a joke, mate,' he said, laughing. 'He's just been telling me, though, he's been pulled up at the gate on his way to work, and guess who by?' he said, smirking, 'No other than that bloody swine, SP Corporal Chris Simpson.' He recounted the whole incident to Jeff. ' Do you know, Jeff, the first time I meet that slimy bastard, after I'm demobbed out of this lot, I'm going to give him the biggest bloody thumping he's ever had in his horrible life, mate.'

94

Friday morning found the Sergeants' Mess staff, hard at work cleaning, polishing, and preparing for the weekend. Jeff and Tony as usual were working together – this time cleaning the sinks and polishing the brass taps in the bottom floor ablutions.

Suddenly, Tony glancing behind him, grimaced and said, 'By God, Jeff, there's a foul stink coming from one of them bogs.' Immediately investigating, he yelled from within one of the cubicles, 'It's this one, Jeff, you'd better go get Eddy – he's on the top floor cleaning the windows. Tell him it's urgent and to bring his bucket and mop, he might need a little shovel an'all,' he added, followed by a volley of four letter words.

Emerging from the cubicle nipping his nose, he gasped, 'Phew, God! Some bugger's been at it again, mate; tell Eddy to bring his rods as well as the other things – it's fully blocked up, brimming over the top with shit.'

'Oh hell,' Jeff groaned, screwing his face up. 'It don't half stink, mate; what's happened?'

'The usual,' Tony replied indignantly. 'Some miserly bugger's been wiping his arse on newspaper again. The bloody thing's blocked solid, it's all over the floor an'all,' he moaned.

Just then Sergeant Pike came bustling in. 'Now then, chaps, everything all right?' He got no further, before he grimaced and coughed, 'Good lord, what's the cause of that terrible stench, Ryan?'

With a note of exasperation in his voice, Tony replied, 'The usual, Sergeant, one of our residents has been using newspaper in place of toilet paper, again!

I've just told Baxter to get Jones down here at the double, with his bucket and pipe rods,' he added.

'The dirty, thoughtless devil,' raved Sergeant Pike, angrily stamping his foot. 'I don't know what to do about this carry-on, you know, Ryan; it's got to stop, there's no doubt about it, it's got to stop,' he repeated, stamping his foot again.

'Yes, you're right, Sergeant,' Tony agreed, 'but we've been trying to catch the chap for weeks – this is the fifth time it's happened. It's not always in the same ablutions either,' he moaned. 'He's doing it all over the place; we don't know where to expect it next.'

He pointed at the excrement now sliding under the toilet door, and continued angrily, 'It's all right for the thoughtless bugger that's causing the trouble; he ain't got to clean the stinking stuff up. Do you know, Sergeant,' he went on in a serious tone, 'It would be cheaper to supply toilet paper free, rather than make the men provide their own. At least,' he said, glancing at the offending cubicle, 'there'd be no excuse for using newspaper then.'

'Yes, yes, I think you've got a point there, Ryan; that could stop it. Doesn't look as though we've much chance of catching the devil in the act, does it?' he said, biting his lip. 'I'll have a word with the secretary at the next general meeting about this lot, without fail.' He blew his nose hard into a big white handkerchief, and hurried out into the corridor, leaving the lads to it.

95

'Who is the lucky bird tonight, then, Tony?' yelled out John, sitting on his bed across the room, watching him getting dressed up, on the Saturday evening.'

'Nobody you'd know, mate,' Tony called back, without turning.

'He's a secretive bugger, is my mate, John.' Jeff laughed, lying back on his bed, reading the evening paper. 'Aren't you, Tony, love,' he taunted.

'I'll love you in a minute, Baxter with a kick up the arse, if you don't stop trying to be funny,' Tony said with a laugh, as he finished buttoning up his new white shirt, before zipping up the pants of his smart, dark grey suit.

'Is it that the young bird you went out with the other week then, Tony?' Jeff asked quietly after a pause, the one you said was "hot-arsed".'

'That's the one, mate,' he replied, without giving the question much attention, as he fixed his dark red, clip-on, bow tie.

'By the way, I'm staying in the Mess all weekend, Jeff,' he said, 'there's a chance of a new arrival. Pike said he could arrive anytime; a medical technician, he told me,' he added, with a sharp glance.

Fifteen minutes later, Tony, dressed like a tailor's dummy and smelling of Old Spice aftershave, walked round the side of the Sergeants' Mess to see Sergeant McNabb, who was sitting at the wheel of her shining black Austin 10. As he got nearer, he could see her looking him up and down through the windscreen, with a pleasant smile on her face.

'Good evening, Mavis,' he called out, getting into the passenger seat beside her. 'The car looks nice and shiny, are you pleased with it, love?' he enquired, settling back in his seat.

Starting up the engine she smiled, 'Yes, I definitely am, you've done a fine job on it Tony; it must have been hard work too – it was covered in mud from all that bad weather we've been having.'

'Well, actually dear, I didn't do the cleaning myself,' he told her aloofly, 'I put West on the job this morning, I was too busy myself in the Mess.'

'Oh, I see,' she replied, staring ahead with a knowing smile, as the little car moved forward. 'Anyway it looks beautiful.' Giving him a quick glance, she said, warmly, 'and so do you, Tony. You look like a young, country gentleman,' she said, smiling. 'I can hardly believe you're the same man. I'll feel so proud to walk into the theatre on your arm – I mean that sincerely, Tony,' she said, patting his knee.

'She's a lovely little runner, as smooth as silk an'all,' Tony commented, as they sped along the main highway to London.

'Who are you referring to, Tony?' Mavis asked innocently.

Laughing, he said, 'Your car of course, who the hell did you think I was on about?'

'Oh, silly me, 'she tittered, staring ahead into the ever increasing build up of traffic, as they neared the Capital.

When eventually they arrived at the theatre, she pulled the car onto the large parking lot at the side, giving Tony a cautious glance. Stopping the engine and turning to him with a thin smile, she said, 'Tony dear, before we go in I've something I'd like to ask – I hope you won't be offended.'

Looking back at her for a moment, puzzled, he replied, 'I don't think there's much chance of that Mavis, I'm pretty thick-skinned you know; anyway, love, I can always say no, can't I? We're not on duty now,' he chuckled.

'Of course, yes,' she said, smiling. Reaching for her handbag, she produced a currency note, which she passed over to him tentatively.

Taking it, Tony gasped, 'What's this for, Mavis? A twenty quid note – what's this for then?' he said, looking down at it in awe.

'I hope you're not offended, Tony,' she said. 'It's towards the expenses; things are very expensive in these posh places in London, you know,' she pointed out, with a nervous smile. 'Anyway, she continued, it's not my money really; when Tommy got his emergency call regarding his mother, he told me to use the theatre tickets and take a friend; he left the money to cover the cost of the night's expenses.' Looking into his face, she asked softly, 'you don't mind, do you, Tony?'

Shoving it into his wallet, he replied, giving her a bright smile, 'Of course not, dear; anyway, Mavis, you and I are friends, aren't we – and that's what he told you to do with it. 'Mind you love,' he hastily added, 'For God's sake, though, don't tell him you chose me to accompany you for the night out, will you?

A little later, as they descended the wide, thickly carpeted staircase, amidst a crowd of others, Mavis remarked, 'Very good show, Tony, don't you agree?' She smiled and suggested, 'Shall we call in at the cocktail bar for a nightcap, before we set off back?'

'Good idea, Mavis, just what I was thinking myself,' he replied, 'Mind you, I don't know about cocktails – I'd prefer a pint of ale.'

'You don't have to have a cocktail, you silly boy,' she said coyly. 'They do sell beer as well; mind you,' she said, 'it's a little more expensive than in the pub, you know.'

'Don't worry about the cost tonight, Mavis, my love,' he told her with a grin. 'I'm sure WO Bloomer won't mind; he'll want us to enjoy our evening at the theatre, won't he?'

Sitting at a little table in the corner of the room, sipping their drinks, Mavis suddenly leaned towards him, beckoning with her eyes across the room. 'Look Tony, over there, sitting at that table under the window, on his own,' she whispered, 'it's that big stout man who looks like a retired Major, he keeps staring at us.'

'Who – the bloke that was sitting near us in the theatre?' he replied, glancing quickly across at him. 'Aye, it's him,' he said. 'Who the hell is he? You don't know him, do you, Mavis? It's obviously you he's looking at, he won't be interested in me, will he, now?' he said, giving the man another quick glance.

'Oh, you never know, Tony, there's some funny folk about these days,' she teased, 'it could be you – one never knows.'

'Huh, better bloody not be, darling,' he said, 'or there'll be some bother. Oh look,' he said, suddenly, 'the old bugger's coming over.'

'Mavis, you're sure you don't know him from somewhere, aren't you? He's got a very determined look on his face, without a doubt,' he whispered.

Before she could answer, the man came up to the table, smiling at Mavis. 'I hope you don't mind me asking, my dear, but have we met before somewhere? I've been trying to place you all evening.'

Rather taken aback, she replied, 'No, I'm sorry you must be mistaken, we don't come from around these parts.'

'I was so sure we'd met before,' he said. 'My name is Sergeant Major William Stanley, Dragoon Guards, retired. By the way, dear,' he continued, looking straight at Mavis, 'may I get you and your son a drink? I wasn't thinking.' He laughed cheerfully.

Mavis, looking up at him standing there in his loud tweed suit, twitching his short bristly moustache as he laughed, replied curtly, 'No thank you, sir, as I told you, I've never seen you in my life before tonight.'

'Oh, but I know we've met before dear,' he went on, starting to pull a chair out from under the table, obviously intending sit down to join them.

Noticing the situation was getting a little out of hand, Tony slowly got up out of his chair, looked the man straight in the eye and said politely, 'The lady told you she's never met you before, sir, so if you don't mind, we're trying to enjoy a quiet evening together; good night, sir!'

'Oh, I see,' the man replied, pushing the chair back under the table; 'Sorry to have intruded, young man.' As he turned to march back to his own table, he said, looking at Mavis, 'Spunky young devil, this lad of yours, my dear, could do with some Military Service, without a doubt.

Watching him strutting back across the floor, Tony grinned. 'Cheeky old bugger, fancy thinking you were my mother, Mavis, you don't look old enough for that, that's for sure,' he told her, hoping to cheer her up.

'But I am, Tony,' she said sulkily. 'I'm thirty-eight and you're just twenty, aren't you? Anyway,' she went on, staring down at the table top, 'I have got a son your age – well, Robin is nineteen, that's near enough,' she said, avoiding his eyes.

Feeling a bit sorry for her, Tony said cheerfully, 'Well, I suppose you are old enough to be my mum, but that means nowt, love; who's bothered anyway? My mum is your age, well thirty-nine to be precise. So you've got a lad, have you, Mavis?' he went on with a smile, 'Nineteen, eh, is he doing his National Service, then?'

'He's deferred,' she replied, still looking a little disturbed. 'He's at university, studying economics.'

'Oh, a brain box, eh,' said Tony, 'economics, an'all. I might to be able to offer him a good job, when I get out of this lot, Mavis; I'm starting up in business on my own, you know,' he told her, nodding confidently.

Seeing she still looked a bit upset, he leaned towards her, putting his face up close to hers, and smiled. 'Come on darling, cheer up; forget that silly old bugger, drink up and let's get off.

'I'll tell you what,' he suggested. 'It's only just gone ten o'clock. Let's go to one of them posh restaurants and have a nice supper, before we hit the road, shall we? There's plenty of Mr Tommy Bloomer's money left; I'm sure he wouldn't like us to waste it,' he told her with a little laugh.

The small plush bar was beginning to fill up, as they made their way to the door. Suddenly, the sophisticated atmosphere was abruptly shattered and they both froze in their tracks.

Over the chatter of the drinkers, a loud voice called out, 'That's it; I've got it! Tommy Bloomer!' This was followed by hard, raucous, uninhibited laughter.

Both Tony and Mavis looked at each other in utter surprise, then turning towards the commotion, observed the retired sergeant major, staring at them red-faced, grinning broadly.

Going over to him, followed by Tony, Mavis said, 'You know Mr Bloomer, then, sir; do you?'

'Of course I do, my dear lady, that's how I know you.' He laughed. 'You were with Tommy, at the annual regimental ball last Easter. We weren't actually introduced,' he said. 'You were talking to a group of several other ladies, I was at the bar with Tommy; he pointed you out to me,' he told her, grinning.

'You must be that friend he told me was trying to sell him some Irish sweepstake tickets,' she replied.

'That's right, my dear,' he chuckled, then with further raucous laughter added, 'didn't have to try too hard with Tommy – he bought half a dozen, loves a gamble he does.'

Tony's streetwise mind was ticking over rapidly, as he stood listening to the conversation; his first thought was how to get away from this man. He realised that this situation could easily be the cause of big trouble in the future when he thought about the response he'd get from a very jealous WO Bloomer – if his Sergeant Major friend mentioned their coincidental meeting.

Stepping forward smiling, he said to the man, 'So you know, Mr Bloomer, then, sir. Mum has been friends with him for quite a while; nice man,' he added, with a nod.

'Yes, yes, first class NCO is Bloomer,' the man agreed firmly, 'he was a champion featherweight boxer when he was about your age, you know, young man,' he said. 'You want to get him to give you a few lessons in the art,' he told him, with a sharp nod.

'Oh, I don't know about that,' replied Tony smiling, thinking he'd had enough boxing lessons from him to last a lifetime. 'Anyway, sir, it's a small world and we're pleased to have met you. However, we're in a bit of a hurry, I'm afraid: we're meeting my uncle and aunt for a family meal, so we'll have to be off now. By the way, sir,' he said, as an afterthought, 'I apologise for being a little abrupt earlier, but we didn't realise who you were at the time.' Taking Mavis by the arm, he said, 'Come on now, Mum, we're going to be late – they'll be wondering where we are.'

'Oh yes, don't let me hold you up,' the man said in a patronising tone. 'You've got a very protective boy there, dear,' he told Mavis, with a smile, 'make a good military man,' he added. He looked at Tony, 'Yes, don't you ever forget, young man – always look after your mother, your mother's your best friend, you know.'

As they made their way out of the building, Mavis just stared ahead in silence. Tony, realising she'd been upset by the meeting with the old sergeant major chap, gave her the occasional glance and made some jovial comments. Reaching the car, Tony opened the passenger side door saying cheerily, 'Come on love, in you get; you did say I could drive back, didn't you?'

Giving him a sulky look and passing him the car keys, she said, 'Yes, here you are.'

Tony sat back in the seat behind the wheel, with a smile on his face. He loosened his jacket buttons and started up the engine. Driving out of the car park, the conversation was all one-sided, until eventually Tony said, 'Come on now, Mavis cheer up, darling; forget about that bloke, we're going for a nice meal, don't forget.'

'I don't feel like it now, Tony, 'she replied. 'I can't forget him – what if he tells Tommy? He'll go mad, spending his money on another man; he's a jealous bugger, you know,' she said. 'He'll play up like hell.'

'Forget it, Mavis, how many more times have I to tell you, 'he replied, with a laugh.

'Why do you think I kept up the idea he'd created in his mind, that you were my mother?'

'Insulting old sod,' she replied. 'Why did you, anyway?'

'Come on, love – surely you realised what I was doing, playing along with him like I did. You went to the theatre with your son, Robin, didn't you? Mr Bloomer won't mind that, will he?' he said, patting her leg.

After a pause she said, smiling, 'Oh I see; you crafty devil, Tony Ryan, but Tommy's met our Robin a couple of times you know,' she told him cautiously.

'Aye, but that old guy back there hasn't, it's a million to one chance he ever will either; even if he, did he'll have forgotten what I looked like by then. Just one thing though, love.' he asked, 'would your Robin play along with our little scheme?'

'Oh, no problem there,' she replied, 'he's a cheeky young bugger like you; he'll think it a big laugh.'

'Right, where's this posh restaurant, then?' Tony yelled out, 'I'm bloody starving, darling.'

A little later on, as they drove away from the Boar Hotel, where they'd just consumed a beautiful meal, Tony asked, 'Now then Mavis, do you feel more cheerful after that?'

'Definitely, Tony,' she replied, settling back in her seat. 'Beautifully prepared and the service was first class – I couldn't have done better myself.'

'Well, it's better than the usual place, my mate Dave and I go to, at home,' he said, putting his foot down and heading for the main highway.

'Is that a hotel in Leeds, then, Tony? she asked him casually.

He laughed. 'Hotel – no love, it's a little café at the back of Mr Blackburn's fish and chip shop on Market Street; my mate Dave and me go there for a fish and chip supper most Friday nights, after we've had a skinful in the Dog and Gun,' he told her.

'Oh, sounds very nice,' she lied. 'I suppose it's much cheaper than the 'Boar Hotel,' though, isn't it, Tony?' she chuckled.

'Yes, it sure is,' he huffed. 'We have fish, chips, mushy peas, tea and bread for two bob,' he boasted, 'and just think that meal we've just had, cost twelve and six apiece; glad I hadn't to pay for it,' he added, with a laugh.

After a long pause in the conversation, driving along the near empty highway, Mavis broke the silence. 'I suppose you've got a steady girlfriend at home, haven't you, Tony?'

'No, I haven't got anyone special at home, Mavis, ' he told her, 'but I have got one, well, I think I have,' he sighed, ' but I haven't seen her for around a year now, though.'

'Dear, dear, it sounds an unusual relationship that, Tony,' she said. 'Where does she live – can't you go visit her? A year's a long time not to see each other,' she sympathised.

'I know it is, Mavis,' he replied, staring ahead, frowning

'She's in our mob, on an overseas posting, though,' he told her, after another long pause, 'and if you don't mind, Mavis love, I'd rather not talk about it, it'll spoil my night,' he said, reaching out and patting her nylon-clad knee.

'Fair enough, Tiger,' she replied, lifting his hand off her knee, with a giggle. 'You just concentrate on your driving for the time being,' she added, 'we don't want to end up in the ditch, my lad.'

'What's that ahead?' Tony said, seeing lights flashing in the road, as they neared the camp.

'Looks like a disturbance of some sort,' Mavis replied, leaning forward to get a better look. 'Could be a car crash,' she said. 'There's certainly a lot of activity there.'

96

As they approached the main gate, they could see plainly by the full moon that a large furniture van had run into the boundary wall, knocking down the metal gatepost and dislodging the big gate. This had been dragged to the side of the road, supposedly by the police officers, but was still partially blocking the entrance. They could also make out four Service policemen buzzing around it with flashlights, two of them directing traffic.

Reaching the scene, Tony pulled the car up behind a police van, its roof light winking, and was immediately approached by one of the officers. Rolling the window down, he recognised the man as the one he'd met, when Chris Simpson had pulled him over, on his way back from leave. Asking him what the trouble was, Tony was told the van had suffered brake failure, and they were waiting for a breakdown crew to drag it away. They were talking for only a few seconds, when another flashlight came swiftly towards the car; Tony groaned when he saw the bearer.

Shining the torch into the car, the second officer said icily, 'Well, well, what have we got here –if it isn't the great, Tony bloody Ryan.' He focused the dazzling light on Mavis, who was sitting in silence, and said sarcastically, 'And – as usual, he's got a little floozy with him.' Shaking his head, he again shone his torch into Tony's face. 'You do realise, Ryan, that it's a chargeable offence for you to bring your women onto a military camp, don't you, especially at this hour,' he said, glaring at him and stabbing the torch beam at Mavis.

While he was yelling out the law at Tony, there was a click as the door on the passenger side swung open, and Mavis stepped out onto the road, with a stern expression on her face. This was no longer the flirty Mavis; this was the kitchen dragon, the fearsome Sergeant McNabb. Slamming the door shut behind her, she marched round the front of the car, with an air of military determination that extended her six foot two, plus stiletto heels height, and shocked Corporal Simpson into utter silence.

Nearing him, she reached into her handbag, producing her 1250 (identity card) and held it up six inches from his gaping face. 'Little floozy, eh?' she yelled, and Tony recognised the same tone she normally used, when addressing poor Ruby.

Staring at the card, he replied, faltering, 'Oh, I didn't realise, Sergeant, please accept my apologies.'

Disregarding this, she said icily, 'Now I'd be obliged, if I could see yours, Corporal.'

Looking shocked and surprised, he reached into his jacket pocket, and passed it to her, enquiring tentatively, 'May I ask why you need my identification, Sergeant, seeing as I'm a police corporal on duty?'

Looking at his card, in the light of the car headlamp for a moment in silence, she replied as she passed it back, 'For my report sheet, Corporal Simpson. Your comments regarding myself, just now, were on the verge of insubordination; I intend to make an official complaint through Station Warrant Officer Cox, first thing on Monday morning.' Then, turning abruptly, she proceeded to walk back around the car.

'But, Sergeant,' he called after her, 'I was only doing my official duty; the men are not in order, bringing women onto a military camp without permission.'

Turning in her stride, she replied curtly, 'Unless they're resident military personnel, Corporal, and you never requested my identification at that point, did you?' she yelled in draconian tones.

Tony, watching him squirming, was delighted; just what the bugger deserves, he thought – he's met his match with her and no mistake.

'Well, er, no, Sergeant, but no disrespect was intended I assure you,' the now panicky Corporal replied, 'and I have apologised,' he pointed out.'

Mavis stood looking at him for a moment, with curled lip, and eventually replied, 'Well, you are new to the job by the look of you, but no doubt you've had your training course, and passed out, so you should know better.' Then she said, nodding towards Tony, sitting at the driving wheel with the window rolled down, 'and with regard to my driver there, I consider he deserves an apology too; after all he's broken no laws. What's more,' she told him sternly, 'he happens to be one of my subordinates in the Sergeants' Mess, who had the kindness to escort me on a compassionate endeavour tonight, completely on a voluntary basis,' she pointed out firmly.

Swallowing hard, he glanced down at Tony, 'Yes, AC Ryan, I'm sure the Sergeant's right, I was a little quick off the mark, I'm sorry.'

Without further comment, Mavis got back into her seat, and Tony started the engine. As they moved slowly forward, he gave his old enemy a nod through the open window, calling out with a smile, 'Thank you, Corporal, good night.' But he could see the hatred behind the expressionless stare he got back.'

'You were great there, Mavis, you certainly put that clever bugger in his place.' Tony laughed, as they drove into the camp.

'No need for thanks, Tony, that man was completely out of order,' she said haughtily. 'The first thing he should have done when he saw me, not knowing who I was and dressed in civilian clothing, was to ask for identification, which he didn't do. He just assumed that you were breaking camp rules by bringing me in with you, for your own gratification; that was completely out of order,' she said adamantly. 'It was also against his training the way he approached you, even though he's of superior rank,' she added, 'in fact it was discourteous to talk to anyone like that. Glancing quickly at Tony, she said, 'The man was acting as though he had a personal vendetta against you, Tony; have you ever met him before?'

'Your right on every count, dear,' Tony said soothingly, 'but come on now, let's forget that pillock, I know him of old. I'll tell you all about him later, Mavis,' he said, laughing and patting her knee.'

'All right,' she tittered, 'but fools like him get me so annoyed, you know, Tony.'

Yes, I've noticed on other occasions,' he agreed, still laughing. 'I don't suppose you're referring to anyone we both know, of course, like poor Ruby Pritchard.'

'Don't mention that young fool to me, I know you've a soft spot for her, Tony Ryan,' she told him, putting her hand, on his hand that was still on her knee.

'Well, my love here we are, back home safe and sound,' he said, with a sigh, as he pulled the car to a halt at the side of the Sergeants' Mess. 'Have you enjoyed your night out, then?' he asked, smiling close up into her face.

'Very much so, Tony,' she said, smiling back. 'Very eventful too – you're a very protective escort,' she told him, stroking his cheek.

'Well, I was only doing my duty, darling, keeping you safe for Mr Bloomer. He laughed. 'After all he paid for event, didn't he?'

Pretending to slap him, she giggled, 'Oh, you are a devil, Tony; after what you said he accused you of, he'd kill us both if he knew who I'd gone to the Theatre with, would Tommy.'

'Aye, I know, you're right there, love,' Tony said, nodding. 'He's a jealous old bugger; for Christ's sake, love; don't let him ever find out, will you?'

Then, cupping her face in his hands, he kissed her lightly on the mouth, saying as he gave her the car keys, 'Well, Mavis darling, I'd better get to my bedding store, and my virtuous little bed.'

'Oh, virtuous is it, you poor boy,' she giggled, as he got out. 'Poor boy,' she repeated.'

Bending down and leaning back into the car with a cheeky grin, he said, 'Well, it's not forced to be, Mavis, my darling, I'm a very sociable sort of chap, I hate being lonely you know,' he winked.

97

'Morning, you bugger, had a good weekend, then?' Jeff called out cheerfully, walking into the bedding store on Monday morning.

Tony was sitting at the table, messing about with the old radio set. 'Aye, I have mate, apart from this thing, I think it's fucked: it'll only get one bloody station,' he replied grumpily.

'I'm not referring to that,' Jeff said, with a grin. 'I wondered how your date went on Saturday night.'

'What, what did you say?' he replied, looking up from the old radio. Then he remembered that Jeff was under the impression that he'd been out with a 'girl he knew'. 'Great time, mate,' he replied, 'She's a right little darling is that one.' Changing the subject abruptly, he said, 'Pike's just been in to tell me we've got a VIP inspection in the Mess on Wednesday afternoon, some bigwigs are coming to inspect the camp, Pike said; they should get to us about mid-afternoon.'

'What's it all about then, Tony, did he say? I hope we don't have to bullshit the billet up, an'all,' he moaned.

'No, it's not that sort of inspection, Jeff; apparently it's a new idea that they've come up with to create competition within the service: best camp facilities or some bloody thing or other.' He started to mess about with the radio again. 'Anyway we've got to get our fingers out for the next two days, you'd better go and get the others and make a start on the windows; that'll be a full day's job for the lot of us. Start at the bottom landing and work up,' he told him. 'I'll join you, when I get this bloody thing back together.'

Soon afterwards, Tony, perched at the top of the extended step ladder, cleaning the upper panes of one of the big hall windows, heard, 'Ryan, can you come down for a moment – I'd like a word with you.' Sergeant Pike was standing looking up at him. Cursing to himself, he called back, 'Sure, Sergeant,' and proceeded to climb down.

'I've just been informed we've got three new residents coming at short notice, maybe today, Ryan, two female and one male,' Pike said, in his usual brisk tone. 'I realise you boys are under pressure, what with the inspection coming up, but it can't be helped.' With a little smile he added, 'No doubt you can handle it, Ryan.'

He was turning to march off when Tony enquired, 'Excuse me, Sergeant, but are they all coming today, or what?'

'I'm not sure about that,' he replied. 'The male is a warrant officer and he's due this afternoon, but the two female sergeants could arrive anytime, might be late tonight or even tomorrow.'

'Oh, I see, so that means I'll have to stay on duty here this evening and overnight then, Sergeant?' he said with a worried look.

'Afraid so, Ryan,' he said, nodding.

'Well, I was just thinking, Sergeant, seeing as we've got all this work on over the next few days, and now we have these new residents arriving out of the blue, it puts me in a bit of a fix.'

'Bit of a fix, how do you mean, Ryan?' he asked, with a puzzled frown.

'Well, I'm not going to be able to keep an appointment I've arranged up at the gym, either this evening, or at all until after the inspection on Wednesday,' Tony replied, looking back at him, wide-eyed.

'Well, it's just one of them things, Ryan, can't be helped,' Pike replied. 'Anyway, a gym appointment is not that important, you'll have to make it later in the week.' He smiled and turned to go.

'Yes, I suppose you're right, Sergeant,' Tony replied, sounding melancholy. 'But I'm not sure SWO Cox will understand,' he said.

'What's he got to do with it?' Pike enquired, abruptly alerted.

'He asked me if I'd give two of the sergeants in the tennis team, a bit of instruction on arm development to strengthen their drive. I'd booked the first for this evening, but I think he might understand, when I explain the circumstances,' he said frowning.

'Well, I hope he does,' Pike said nervously, 'he can be a very funny man, the SWO, if anyone gets on the wrong side of him.'

'Very true, I agree,' Tony said, nodding. Then, a smile crossed his face. 'I was just thinking though, Sergeant, if I could tell him I'd got the afternoon off on Thursday, for a long session with the tennis boys, I'm sure that would please him.'

The little sergeant's face broke into a relieved smile. 'Good thinking, Ryan, good thinking; we don't want to get on the wrong side of the Station Warrant Officer, Ryan, now do we?'

'What have you been saying to Pike then, Tony to make him look so happy,' asked Jeff, watching the smiling sergeant walking away up the corridor, with a spring in his step.

'Oh, not much, mate,' Tony replied, grinning. 'I just put the wind up him a bit to get him to give me the afternoon off on Thursday, so as I can spend it up at the gym. I don't want to lose my form you know, mate,' he winked. 'Mind you, I also promised Mr Cox I'd show two of the tennis team a few exercises when I'd got time, to strengthen their arms you know,' he added.

'Did you ask Sergeant McNabb if you could do them two rooms out on the women's wing, Ruby darling?' Tony called out seeing her coming towards them smiling.

'Yes, I was just coming to look for you, Tony,' she said looking up at him, back on the stepladder. 'The dragon said I could have as long as it takes after dinner, she was so nice about it too,' the young girl told him, with a note of surprise in her voice.

'Well, well that's a change for her,' he laughed. 'I thought you were going to say she went bloody mad, as usual.'

'No, I couldn't believe my ears when I asked her,' Ruby said, smiling.

'I must say in all honesty, Tony, she's been so friendly for the past couple of days – it's unbelievable. Not only to me,' she stressed, open-eyed, 'but to all the staff – she even dished out cream buns at our tea break this morning,' she told him, with a baffled expression on her face.

'Aye well, probably somebody's told her it's not becoming to be so dictatorial with people,' he replied, with a knowing smile.

98

Thursday afternoon was hot and dull; in the weight training room at the gym Tony was well into his allotted schedule. He'd arranged with SWO Cox to meet his tennis players at two-thirty, and he had arrived an hour earlier to give himself time for a serious workout before their arrival. He had just completed his final sets and was preparing to go for a quick shower before his pupils arrived, when he was startled by an unusual spluttering sound of a low flying aircraft.

Going to the window, he saw it – one of the large four-engine transport planes coming in from his right, appearing to be preparing for a normal landing, at the head of Runway One. However, at the last moment it lifted its nose and gained height, making a very unusual engine noise, as it flew away into the distance out of view. Just then, the two sergeant tennis players came into the room; Tony was surprised to see one of them was his Yorkshire friend Sergeant Banks.

'Hi there, Yorky,' he called out to Tony, as he came in with his pal. 'So you're going to give me a more powerful right arm drive, are you?' He grinned, 'Mind you I don't expect to have biceps like yours in one lesson.'

Only half listening to him, Tony said, 'Did you see that plane that's just gone over, Sergeant? I thought it was going to land, then at the last moment it lifted off again and flew away; I'm sure there's summat up with it, it's making a funny engine noise,' he said, with a frown. The two tennis players had just changed into tracksuits ready for their training session, when the sound of the clearly stricken aircraft was again heard approaching the airfield. 'It's here again,' yelled Tony, charging back to the window, quickly followed by the other two. 'That plane isn't right,' he said. 'Just listen to it Jerry, it sounds like an old tractor,' he said, straining to catch sight of the craft.

'And look at the undercarriage,' Jerry Banks said, pointing at the descending plane as it came into view and once again aborted its landing. 'I'm sure there was a wheel missing on the left front axle, Bob,' he said anxiously, turning to his mate.

As they were discussing the stricken plane, they heard the scream of sirens coming from the airfield enclosure across the road. Looking out, they saw a fire engine and an ambulance speeding up the runway, followed by a police Landover.

'Christ, it's an emergency, Bob,' Jerry Banks called out to the other sergeant. 'They've sent your biggest fire engine an'all, they must think there's risk of a catastrophe,' he said.

'Yes, I agree, Jerry,' his friend replied, himself transfixed. 'And I should be there in control of that engine; trust me to take an afternoon off when something like this happens.' Pulling his tracksuit top off, he sighed, 'I'd better get dressed and get over there. It's one of them big transport jobs, you know; if that crashed God knows what would happen.'

'It's coming back, Sergeant,' yelled Tony, still looking out of the window, straining his eyes.

'Oh aye, he's sure to bring it down this time,' Jerry said, hurrying back alongside Tony and straining to see. 'He'll have been waiting for the emergency services to get in place, before he dare attempt a landing; must be summat serious,' he said, shaking his head.

'You can forget trying to join your fire crew, Bob,' he called out over his shoulder. 'You'll never get there in time.'

'I bloody well will,' he replied, still dressing. 'It's only a couple of hundred yards across the airfield to the runway.'

'What about the eight foot security fence with the barbed wire topping?' called back Jerry. 'There's no way over that, mate – the only way is through the main gate and that's four hundred yards down the road. We walked up here an'all don't forget,' he added.'

Talking ceased abruptly as Tony called out, 'He's coming down this time. Oh Christ, Jerry, look – it's wobbling like hell, and one of the engines is smoking.'

The three of them stood at the window, all eyes fixed on the stricken plane. All three gasped, as it bounced down on the tarmac. Immediately there was a blinding flash, followed by a stream of sparks at one side of the front landing gear, as it continued to career down the track. The cockpit and front part of the craft, engulfed by the ever increasing smoke from the damaged engine, were now only partly visible. Slowly it came to a halt, leaning sideways with its nose down on the track. The activity around it increased as the rescuers rushed into full gear.

'God, I was right,' said Jerry, staring open-mouthed out of the window. 'They've lost a wheel in some way. Good pilot flying that plane,' he said shaking his head. 'No mean task to get a craft that size down, with a wheel missing. I wonder what's caused the engine trouble?' he asked anxiously. 'Funny combination of damage; it's the sort of thing you'd expect in wartime, after being shot at.'

Although the three spectators were a good two hundred yards distant from the action scene, they could easily see the emergency crews preparing for immediate action, now that the big plane had come to a halt on the runway. The fire crew drove as near to it as was safe; the firefighters jumped off the vehicle, dragging the thick hose pipes straight towards the craft, and sprayed the smoking engine with a foaming substance.

'Well, your lads seem to have got to that hot engine in time, Bob,' Jerry said.

'Fingers crossed,' replied the other, watching every move out there. 'I've seen those buggers blow, even when they've been covered in foam,' he said, without turning his head. 'I wish I could make out who's giving the orders over there, though,' he said, straining to see; 'it's just too far away to make individuals out.'

'That engine is still burning, you know,' Tony said, engrossed in his observation. 'The bloody thing just gave another flash and it's still giving off smoke, even though it's covered in foam.' Noticing a scramble of men charging towards the craft, he yelled out, 'Look they're going to board the bloody thing to get the crew out, by the look of it,' he added excitedly.

'The crew must have been stunned on that rough landing,' remarked Jerry, 'or they'd have been making an effort to get out themselves by now.'

Suddenly, there was a loud bang and the faulty engine burst into flames, even though it was still being sprayed by the big fire hose. The charging rescuers stopped abruptly, with the exception of two men, who continued to rush towards the side door.

'Good God, they're going in, Jerry,' said Bob, the fire officer. 'That plane could go up any minute,' he yelled, gripping his chin with tension.

'Well, somebody's got to try and save the poor sods in there,' Tony called out firmly, forgetting his inferiority in rank. 'Whoever the two guys are, they're brave men and no mistake about that,'

'Sure are,' agreed Jerry Banks. 'Can you make out who they are, Bob?' he asked, trying to focus on them himself, through the window.

'No, too far away,' he replied still straining to see. 'Looked like it could have been our guys, or there again, it could have been police or ambulance, I couldn't make it out, but as you say they're bloody brave lads,' he agreed.

All three men stood at the window gaping open-mouthed, as they watched the ongoing attempt to rescue the trapped crew.

The two making the rescue attempt, went straight for the side door of the doomed craft, ignoring the din of the flaming engine and the shouting of the firemen working like the devil to overcome the flames. Pulling the door open, they were met by a gush of smoke; undeterred, they both climbed up and scrambled in. Several of the firemen then went forward, standing around the open door shouting warnings about the risks, to the men inside. Within a minute a man was being passed out of the door into the arms of the men outside, then in quick succession four more were pulled out in the same way.

The last one had hardly got clear when there was another loud bang and a sheet of flame shot through the full length of the fuselage, engulfing the two rescuers still standing in the open doorway. One was blown out with such force that he went rolling several yards across the runway, before any of the ambulance staff could grasp him and roll him in a blanket to extinguish his burning clothing.

The other, who had been standing slightly nearer the opening, managed to make a last minute dive as the flames hit him – ending up on the runway, his clothing in flames. Both men were bundled into the waiting ambulance, which then drove away at high speed down the track, siren blaring. The three in the gym remained at the window staring blankly at the scene of desecration, as the police and ambulance staff departed, leaving the fire crew working hard to control the burning craft.

'Right, gentlemen – what now,' Tony said, trying to sound cheerful. 'Shall we carry on as planned, or what?'

Bob, the fire officer, insisted on going to join his men, but Jerry said, 'Well, I've nowt else to do this afternoon, Yorky, so we might as well get on with the job, eh? Old SWO Cox will be expecting big things from me at our next match,' he said.

99

The talk in the billet that evening was all about the earlier catastrophe and Tony was the star of the conversation, having being a first hand, on the spot, observer.

'So you've no idea who the two heroes were then, Tony?' Jeff asked, after they'd broken away from the discussion; the two were on their way over to the NAAFI for a little refreshment before retiring.

'No, they were too far away, but I suppose it'll be all over the Mess tomorrow; anyway, let's forget it for tonight, Jeff – I've had enough of it for one day. 'I've just decided though, I don't know about you, Jeff, but I think I'll have a couple of pints of ale tonight, even though it's not the weekend; just a couple,' he added.

The following day, Tony was on his way down to the dining room with a bundle of laundered tablecloths in his arms; as he dashed passed Pike's office door, the Sergeant called out, 'Morning, Ryan, have you got a minute?'

Tony, in a hurry, cussed under his breath. 'Certainly, Sergeant,' he replied putting his bundle down on the nearest window sill. Going into the office he was confronted by the little Sergeant sitting behind his desk, with a wide smile on his face.

'Sergeant Banks told me that you, he, and his friend Bob, had grandstand view of the sad event yesterday afternoon, Ryan,' he said, with a note of excitement in his voice.

'Well, not quite that, Sergeant,' Tony replied. 'We only saw it from the gymnasium window and as that was at least two hundred yards away, the view was only vague,' he pointed out.

'Yes, so Sergeant Banks told me,' he replied. 'Pity you couldn't make out who the two heroes were, Ryan. Sergeant Banks reckons the Group Captain will recommend them both for recognition of some sort.'

'Well, I wouldn't be surprised in the least for what they did,' replied Tony. 'An act of valour if ever there was one,' he said nodding.

'Yes, yes, brave men, the pair of 'em – saved five lives without a doubt,' Pike agreed, also nodding. He paused thoughtfully for a moment, tapping his desktop with the end of his pen. Suddenly looking up, he said, 'By the way, Ryan, you've got two more new residents coming this weekend, both are flight sergeants, one male, one female.

'Oh dear, and I'd planned to go out off camp on Saturday evening, Sergeant,' Tony told him. 'You haven't got a rough idea when to expect them, have you?'

'Sorry, Ryan, no,' he replied, without raising his eyes from some paperwork he'd just decided to attend to. 'But I'm sure you'll be able to sort them out in one way or another; as you usually do,' he added, looking up and smiling momentarily at Tony. Then he resumed his literary work with deep concentration and Tony turned and walked out.

Crossing the dining room, bustling with activity, as the girls prepared the tables for the midday meal, Tony went straight towards the kitchen. As he plonked the clean tablecloths down on the nearest bench inside the doorway, he noticed Ruby approaching him.

As usual when she saw him, she had a shy smile on her face. 'Hello, Tony, your mate, Baxter, told me you were an on the spot witness at the scene of that crash yesterday,' she said excitedly.

'Oh aye, well he told you bloody wrong, then,' he answered sullenly. 'I only saw it from the side window of the gym and that was from a distance of nearly three hundred yards.' Then he smiled. 'But look what I've brought for you, darling,' he said, indicating the tablecloths. 'I thought I'd deliver the clean laundry myself this morning to save you the trouble.' He grinned. 'We can't have you tiring out them lovely long legs of yours fetching them, now can we?' he said with a cheeky wink.

'What's all this about lovely long legs, then, Ryan?' A stern voice rang out right behind him.

Recognising it, he froze, and saw Ruby's face flush bright-red, staring wide-eyed over his shoulder. Turning slowly with a broad smile, he said, 'Oh, good morning, Sergeant McNabb, I've just brought the clean tablecloths down for you – I was just saying to WAC Pritchard that it would save her the trouble of collecting them.'

'Well, well, that's very considerate of you, Ryan, being so concerned about the welfare WAC Pritchard's "lovely long legs" as you so kindly put it,' she said, sarcastically.

Laughing nervously, he replied, 'That was only a figure of speech, Sergeant; just being friendly, you know.'

'Oh, was it now?' she replied, giving him a doubting look. 'It sounded like a flirty remark to me, Ryan.' She looked at Ruby. 'What do you think, Pritchard?'

Fidgeting, the still highly flushed Ruby stammered awkwardly, 'Oh, AC Ryan is always joking Sergeant, I take no notice.'

Giving her a slight smile, McNabb said with a sigh, 'Well if you don't mind him looking you up and down and assessing your legs like that, I suppose that's your prerogative.' Shaking her head she added, 'Go on, then, get on with your work, girl; I'll sort Casanova here out. You're a bugger you are, Ryan, I always knew you had a soft spot for her,' she said, watching Ruby hastily scuttle back to the tables.

Trying to laugh it off, he replied, 'I don't look at the poor lass like that, Sergeant; as I told you before, I pity her and I just like to help her, that's all,' he said shaking his head sympathetically.

Scanning his face as he spoke and smiling knowingly, she replied, 'I don't know about helping her, but I think I know what you would like to do for her, Ryan, you bugger. Anyway, seeing as you're so kind and considerate, you can take the dirty laundry back with you and save her lovely legs the trouble of walking up to your bedding store with it,' she chuckled.

Realising she could see through him, he said smiling, 'It's a pleasure, Sergeant. I was just going to ask if you'd got it ready.'

She gestured behind her. 'Over there on that table – it's packed up and ready for you.'

On his way to pick up the large bundle of dirty linen, Tony suddenly paused. 'Oh, I've just remembered, Sergeant, he said, 'I've just been informed that we have a new female resident coming this weekend and –' he got no further.

'Yes, yes, you can have her after dinner, Ryan,' she said in a bored tone.

'Oh, thank you, I'll tell Pritchard on my way out, Sergeant.' He smiled and gathered up the linen.

She looked at him for a moment, shaking her head. 'Right, if you're sure there's nothing else you require from me, Ryan, I'll get on with my work.'

'Well, as a matter of fact there is, Sergeant,' Tony called out. Turning slowly, she looked at him suspiciously. 'What's that, then?'

Going up to her, his arms full of soiled laundry, he said hesitantly, 'Well, you see, I've been invited to an old friend's birthday celebration tomorrow evening. However,' he paused, looking up at her forlornly, 'with new residents arriving, I'm on call over the weekend.'

'Well, that's nothing to do with me,' she said, frowning.

'Well, you see, Sergeant,' he sighed, 'the problem is I can't be away from the Mess too long you see, I'd have to be back by eleven at the latest,' he told her with a distressed look on his face.

Looking at him dubiously, she replied, 'Fair enough, but what's this leading up to –where do I come into it, Ryan?'

With pleading eyes he continued, 'Well, you did say you'd lend me your car occasionally, Sergeant, didn't you?' Now that would solve all my problems; you see, the celebration is to be held down in the village, and with my own transport I could easily get back here on time to attend to my duties,' he smiled thinly.

She looked at him in silence for a few seconds, nodding slowly. 'I suppose this old friend is that bloody idiot, Baxter, the place of celebration is that mucky little dump, the Pig and Whistle down at the bottom end of the village and the main course is draft bitter – am I right, Ryan?' she asked, smiling.

'You must be a mind reader, Sergeant,' he replied, returning the smile and shaking his head with pretence of surprise. 'I really don't want to go,' he stressed, 'but I feel obligated –the poor lad's got no other friends, you see.'

Moving closer to him she said quietly, 'Look, Tony, I don't mind you borrowing the car, but I don't want it all over the Mess that I'm loaning it to one of the AC'S on the staff. OK?'

'Oh, no problem there, you know me, Mavis, I'm the height of discretion,' he whispered.

'I've no doubts about you, you're a crafty sod,' she said, 'but what about your stupid mate? He's the type that can't hold water. If Tommy found out I was lending my car to you, he'd go mad; he's a jealous little bugger, I've told you before,' she said firmly.

'I know you're right there, Sergeant,' Tony grunted. 'You've no need to tell me that; but as far as Baxter's concerned, don't worry, he's not very bright, as you know. I can easily handle him.' Chuckling, he added, 'I'll tell him I did you some sort of a favour – he believes anything I tell him.'

'Yes, most folk do, Ryan,' she agreed, scowling. 'But I don't, and if you let me down, your life won't be worth living,' she growled. Tony, smiling weakly, knew that she meant every word. 'I'll drop the keys into your bedding store tomorrow, when I go off duty at four o'clock,' she told him, as she walked off.

100

'Ready for another, then, mate?' Jeff asked, draining his glass.'

'No thanks,' Tony replied, his own still half-full. 'I don't like to have too much when I'm driving, especially when it's not my car.'

'Right, fair enough, but I think I'll have one, Jeff said. 'It's my birthday don't forget.'

'Yes, of course, you have what you want.' He shrugged, 'but I must look after the Sergeant's car, after all she was good enough to trust me with it.'

Coming back with his full glass, Jeff said, as he sat down, 'You know, Tony, it's still hard to believe that McNabb would loan you her posh little car, just for you getting the Mess table linen done quick.' He took a sip of his fresh pint and chuckled. 'Are you sure she hasn't gone round the bend or something? I'd have thought she'd have been the last person in the world to do a favour like that for any bugger, especially you.'

Realising his mate was not quite as easy to convince as he thought, Tony said, 'Well actually, Jeff, I did a little more for her than that, but it's very confidential.'

Looking back at him wide-eyed, Jeff muttered, 'Oh aye, mate, you can definitely trust me, Tony; you know that.' With a laugh he added, 'Don't say you've been taking her pants down an'all, mate, eh?'

Ignoring the question, he said piously, 'I'm sure I can trust you, Jeff – if I can't trust my best mate, I can't trust any bugger. 'Well, it's like this, Jeff,' he continued, in a low confidential tone. 'Sergeant McNabb has just gone through a very rough time connected to a compassionate situation in her personal life. Now I know on the surface she appears to be a very hard, tough woman,' he explained, 'but recently she's been a very worried one.' Jeff sat intrigued in front of his full, hardly touched pint, just staring back, nodding agreement and waiting for the plot to unfold. 'But believe me, Jeff,' Tony went on, 'you can't always judge a book by its cover, and in her case, very much so. That poor lady has got a very soft core,' he told him, looking down at the floor, nodding sympathetically.

'Oh, has she, Tony?' Jeff replied quietly, with a puzzled look. 'It's hard to believe though, isn't it, mate; I mean, she frightens the shit out of everybody in the kitchen with her dictatorial behaviour.' He shook his head.

'Yes, I've got to agree with you there, Jeff,' Tony replied, with a thin smile, 'but you must realise, a man of your intelligence, that's it's all part of her job; she's a Sergeant in charge of staff, she's got to maintain discipline. She doesn't like being so strict with the staff, she told me that,' he added, shaking his head, 'but after all, somebody's got to be in charge to get the job done – if it wasn't her, somebody else would have to do it.'

'Yes, oh yes, I see the point there, mate,' Jeff chipped in, looking back at him blankly. 'I can also see why them lesser intelligent buggers in the kitchen, think she enjoys being so heavy on them all the time. I mean they don't understand like us, do they, Tony?' he added, with a grin. 'But what's this compassionate situation she's been involved in, Tony?'

Tony looked at the table top for a few seconds before replying. Then he stared solemnly into Jeff's face. 'Well, Jeff, I don't suppose you know, mate, but she's got a son about our age; it partly involves him.' Seeing his mate's jaw drop, Tony knew he'd got him;

he knew he was going to suck everything in that he fed him now.

'Bloody hell, mate,' gasped Jeff. 'I can't imagine McNabb being anybody's mother.'

'Well she is, and a very loving, protective mother, too,' Tony stressed. 'Anyway,' he continued, leaning towards him confidentially, 'I can't say much about it, Jeff; what's more, I wouldn't have gone this far with anyone else but you, mate,' he impressed upon him, staring into his face. 'However, the situation I helped her with involves very serious illness and her only son.' Looking his mate straight in the eye again, he said sadly, 'You do understand don't you, Jeff? I'm under a promise of secrecy to the poor sergeant.'

'Oh yes, I fully understand, Tony,' he replied, nodding with a sad expression on his face. 'The poor woman, fancy having all that on her mind and at the same time, having to keep that ferocious front up in the kitchen. Anyway, Tony,' he said cheerfully after a pause, 'you haven't done bad out of the situation have you; I mean, it looks as though you've got a nice new car whenever you want one now, don't it, mate.'

Without further discussion, Tony said, 'Come on, Jeff, sup up, I'm getting hungry; let's get to that bloody fish and chip shop before the pub chucks out, or there'll be a queue a fucking mile long.

101

Thursday morning of the following week was bright and sunny, and Tony Ryan walked into the Mess with a spring in his step, feeling on top of the world. 'Morning, Sergeant Pike,' he called out to the little man, who was scurrying down the corridor from his office with a very worried look on his face.

'Oh, you're here at last, Ryan; I've been waiting for you, terrible news, Ryan, terrible. I don't know what we're going to do about it, I really don't,' he said, frowning and wringing his hands in frustration.

Rather shocked at seeing the distressed state Pike was in, Tony enquired, 'What's the trouble, Sergeant, has the boiler burst or something?'

Still wringing his hands, Pike replied, 'No, worse than that, Ryan, it's terrible – blood all over the place; no, Ryan,' he continued, with a note of panic in his voice, 'it's that new resident you booked in last weekend, next room to Sergeant Banks – he's cut his own throat. Sergeant Prince is up there now with the orderly officer,' he continued passionately, 'he said he wants to see you as soon as you arrive; Baxter and the other lads are all there cleaning up. I sent over to the billet to get them in, earlier; they said you were out jogging.

'Oh my, God,' Tony gasped. 'What a catastrophe; he's only a young guy an'all,' he said. 'I put him in that room we've just had decorated out, that one straight opposite my bedding store; he seemed a very nice straight-thinking guy. Is he dead, Sergeant?' he asked hesitantly.

'No, no, he's not dead, Ryan; well, he wasn't when they took him away in the ambulance,' he said, shaking his head. 'Apparently, the Doctor said he missed his jugular vein, or he would have been dead within seconds. No foul play involved though,' he went on. 'He'd left a note for his ex-girlfriend; looks as though she'd just abandoned him for a commissioned officer, a wing commander no less,' he stressed.

'Huh,' Tony grunted, 'using his rank, no doubt. Old bloke this wingco, is he, then, Sergeant?' he asked haughtily.

'No, quite young actually, only about thirty-nine, I've met the officer myself as a matter of fact,' he said, 'seemed a very nice man.'

'Aye, but you'd think an old bugger of that age would have more sense than to go chasing after young women, wouldn't you? I mean you'd think he was just about past thinking of sex and things like that, wouldn't you?' he added, frowning in disbelief.

'I definitely wouldn't – he's only a young man,' yelled Pike, suddenly springing to life. 'I'm the same age as that, Ryan, and believe me, I'm not in the least past it,' he told him angrily. 'I can handle my women better than I could at your immature age,' he stressed, glaring at him. 'Experience, Ryan, experience, that's what captivates the ladies,' he nodded defiantly.

Rather shocked at the little outburst, Tony said apologetically, 'Oh, I'm sorry, Sergeant, no offence meant. I always looked upon you as a man just a little older than myself, certainly nowhere near thirty – let alone thirty-nine,' he said, with mock surprise.

Smiling, Pike replied, 'Don't worry, Ryan, that sort of mistake has been made before. I've always been taken for a much younger man – I suppose it's with being an athlete in the past; I was a good cricketer when I was your age, you know, Ryan,' he told him smugly. Then abruptly, as though suddenly remembering the attempted suicide, he said sharply, 'Anyway, Ryan, you'd better get up there at the double; Sergeant Prince seemed very keen to have a word with you about that poor young fellow.'

Passing a young flying officer coming the other way along the corridor, Tony assumed he was the orderly officer, and having concluded his inspection was now departing. He also noticed the grim look on the man's face and his very pale complexion. It must be an awful sight in that room, he thought, as he continued on his way. Reaching the room, he found Sergeant Prince standing in the doorway, watching Jeff and one of the other lads on their knees, scrubbing away at the carpets.

'Morning, Sergeant,' Tony said formally. 'Sergeant Pike has just told me everything, and informed me that I'd to report to you.'

The Sergeant replied quietly, his little black eyes watching every move Tony made. 'Yes, I've got a few points I think you might be able to help me with, AC Ryan.'

The soul-searching stare, plus the way he said this, sent the usual quiver of guilt through Tony, even though he'd done nothing wrong. It was just the professionalism of the man, he thought. Smiling at the blank-faced Sergeant, Tony said, pointing across corridor, 'Would you like to come into my bedding store and sit down, Sergeant? I'll obviously give you any help I can,' he told him subserviently.

With a stiff nod, he muttered, 'Right,' and followed him across the passage out of the blood-spattered room.

After answering all the questions Sergeant Prince fired at him, about his knowledge of the unfortunate victim, Tony pointed out that he didn't seem the type of person who would take to such drastic measures. Then he enquired politely, 'Sergeant, do you mind me asking who found him?'

Looking at him in silence for a moment, his face softened into a slight smile. 'Sergeant Banks next door,' he replied, with a sigh. 'He heard a bang, like someone falling and went to investigate; getting no reply from his knocking on the door, he got a chair and looked through the fan-light window above. He saw the chap on the floor covered in blood and was obviously shocked; then he went for Sergeant Pike. They got into the room with a duplicate key. He's a lucky lad, though,' he went on, 'not knowing how to do the job right, he missed his jugular, but only by a fraction, or he'd have been dead within about five minutes.

Tony asked Sergeant Prince if he could make him a cup of tea, but he refused – he did not have time. 'You're very busy lately, Sergeant, what with the recent plane accident and now this,' Tony said.

'That's an understatement, Ryan,' he replied, getting up to depart, and I've got two of my corporals off an'all, one on leave and the other in sick quarters, injured in the plane job.'

'Was he one of the two that went in to rescue the crew?' Tony asked. 'Very brave men them two, Sergeant, it looked as if it was ready for blowing, even as they went in, didn't it?'

Looking at him with a frown, he replied, 'Yes they did a good job, saved five men's lives without a doubt; but how do you know so much about what went on, Ryan, you weren't there, were you?'

'No,' Tony smiled. 'I was in the gym working out and I saw it all from the roadside window. As a matter of fact, Sergeant Banks and his friend, a sergeant from the fire department, were there with me. I was giving them a little help with their tennis training,' he said, with a smile. 'We saw it all, right from the beginning, but of course we were too far away to see much detail,' he added.

'Yes, we all tried to do our best,' Sergeant Prince said quietly. About to leave, he paused at the door and turned slowly to face Tony. 'I don't know whether it would interest you to know which one of my men went into that inferno the other day, would it, Ryan?'

'Yes, of course it would, Sergeant,' Tony replied, his heart missing a beat; he only knew one corporal at the guard room and the Sergeant knew it.

Seeing the shocked look that crossed Tony's face, Sergeant Prince looked him in the eye and nodded slowly. 'I think you've guessed, Ryan,' he said quietly. 'Yes, it was that old enemy of yours, Corporal Simpson.'

Gulping, Tony said, 'What! Sergeant, you mean it was Chris that went in there with that other chap? Oh my God, is he hurt bad, Sergeant?' he asked hesitantly. The expression on his face showed genuine concern.

'Well, he got caught in the blast jumping from the plane, suffered burns to the back of his legs,' he said. 'Mind you the other poor young man was the Medical Officer in charge of the ambulance team, unfortunately he lost his right foot; he had it amputated at a specialist unit in London. He sighed, 'but, as I said, they saved five lives.'

'But what about Chris Simpson, Sergeant,' Tony asked, eagerly. 'Where is he now, is he in London, as well?'

'No; he got badly burnt as I just told you, but no, he's down in our sick bay. We tried to inform his parents about the situation,' he went on, 'but apparently they're touring in Scotland on holiday and can't be contacted.'

Tony stood silent for a moment with a look of despair on his face. 'Do you think they'll let me in to see him, Sergeant?' he asked. 'Poor Chris,' he sighed. 'Mrs Simpson will go mad when she hears he's been hurt like this.'

Rather surprised at Tony's reaction, Sergeant Prince replied, 'Oh yes, Ryan, no problem there – I'll give you a chit myself that'll allow you to visit him. But I was under the impression that you and Corporal Simpson didn't get on with each other,' he said, with a puzzled frown. 'I'd have let you know about him sooner, if I'd have realised your concern, Ryan,' he added, almost apologetically.

'You're right in a way, Sergeant,' replied Tony, with a weak smile. 'We never have got on together Chris and me; we've been scrapping with each other since infant school. Then of course, after leaving school, he was the leader of the 'Canal Street Gang', as I told you before. But a thing like this is different,' he said seriously. 'We do have our differences, but we're like a big family really, where I come from, we always stick together in a crisis, you know.'

'I see,' said the Sergeant condescendingly, realising the youthful side of the young man was showing.

'Mind you,' Tony went on, laughing lightly, 'I suppose we'll be still knocking hell out of each other back home, down at the Dog and Gun, for years to come.'

'That so,' he said with a nod. 'Anyway, Ryan, as long as you both keep sorting your differences out at the Dog and Gun and not on this camp, I've no objections,' he told him, taking out his pocket book and writing out the chit for Tony.

102

'Corporal Simpson is in Number Two Ward,' the young ACW at the reception desk told Tony, as she read Sergeant Prince's chit. 'The second door on the right,' she smiled, pointing along the passage.

Looking through the glass-panelled door as he went in, Tony could make out only one bed occupied in the little four bed ward. In it, he could see a figure laid out on its back with a Para shield protection unit covering the lower part of the body. Going through the door, he at once recognised the man as Chris Simpson; he appeared to be asleep, his face looked pale, drawn and most of his hair was missing; obviously it had been singed off in the fire blast, as he jumped from the doomed aircraft.

Closing the door behind him, the patient slowly opened his eyes. Seeing Tony, he called out, 'Oh, bloody hell, Tony Ryan, you've come at last; I knew you would, mate, as soon as you heard I was in here.'

Grinning at him, Tony replied, 'Now then, Chris, you old bugger; what the hell have you been up to? Your boss has only just told me or I'd have come to sort you out sooner.'

'Oh, I'm glad to see you though, Tony,' he said. 'It's all right being among all these bloody foreigners when you're fit, but when you're not, you want to have your own around –someone you can trust,' he replied, with a hint of self-pity in his voice. 'They say they can't contact my mum and dad, Tony,' he went on, 'but of course they'll be off in that bloody caravan for a month; as you know they do every year.'

'Oh, I'm sure they'll be contacted before long, Chris,' Tony assured him with a smile. 'Anyway, you're in one piece that's all that matters,' he said, grinning.

'Aye, but my legs are burned like hell, Tony,' he moaned. 'I could hardly bare the pain for the first two days; they had to give me injections to numb it, it's not bad now though,' he told him, forcing a slight laugh.

'Have you been told how long you'll be before you're out of here, Chris?' Tony asked.

'No, but I bet it won't be inside the next two weeks, mate, and I'm bloody fed up by now,' he grumbled.

'Oh, you're a fit bloke, Chris,' Tony said reassuringly. 'You'll soon heal; as far as your mum and dad are concerned, I'll see if I can find anything out as to where they might be.'

'How can you do that? Sergeant Prince said the local police are having difficulties,' he said.

'I'll give Bernard at the 'Dog and Gun' a ring, I'll bet he'll have a good idea; him and your old man talk to each other a lot when he's in there boozing, as you know,' Tony said confidently.

'Oh aye, that's a good idea, Tony; I never thought to tell 'em to ask Bernard,' Chris said more cheerfully. 'Aye and while you're at it,' he went on with a grin, 'you can tell Bernard to send me a few pints of his best over, an'all, mate.'

'You won't be able to get hold of any ale in here though, will you, Chris?' Tony said seriously.

'Huh are you trying to be funny, Tony, lad,' he replied scornfully. 'All we get in here is tea, tea, and bloody tea – like witch pee.'

'Oh, we can't have that, Chris, my old son,' Tony said, with a laugh. 'I'll pop back this evening on my way to the gym, with a few pint bottles of strong ale for you.' With mock concern, he added, 'But we want no scrapping; think on when you get the bloody stuff inside you; I know you of old when you get some bloody ale down you.'

103

The next couple of weeks passed uneventfully for Tony, apart from one occasion when, as a Catholic, he was ordered to attend a special Sunday service in the camp church. This, he reasoned, was thought up by some religious nut trying to brainwash the lads. The hypocrisy of it was confirmed when the pious service was very formally conducted by the same priest that had been flirting with the young woman at the village dance – the nice lad, the one that had given him and his mate, Jeff, a lift back to camp, when they were drunk.

He also met SWO Cox, a devoted Catholic, who thanked him for the arm strengthening instruction he'd given the two sergeant members of the station tennis team. He told him proudly that they'd won the cup and he himself, being honorary secretary had been presented with it, on behalf of the station. He asked Tony once more, if he'd made his mind up yet about a career in the Service, and assured him again of his help, if he decided to go ahead.

Tony, as before, thanked him for his concern, and told him that he was still thinking very seriously about it; but he was also still rather keen to start his own business in civilian life.

After the church service, walking back to his billet, Tony found himself beginning to think it might not be such a bad idea after all to stay in the Service for a few years. Dave had signed on in the Marines, and he seemed happy enough. Then his mind turned to Becky; it would certainly please her, as she'd suggested it to him several times. However, thinking of her a wave of depression crossed his mind, 'Huh, if ever I see her again,' he said out loud, quickening his step.

104

'When is your friend, Baxter, due back from leave, Ryan?' Sergeant Pike called out, as he hurried past him coming into the Mess on the Monday morning.

'Wednesday, Sergeant,' he called back without breaking his stride, 'and about time too,' he added.

Jeff Baxter had timed his dates just right; he happened to be taking his leave during the annual special cleaning week for the domestic section of the Mess; consequently he was avoiding the extra work. Furthermore, all the other lads had a suspicion that he'd planned it.

'Anyway, it's no use grumbling,' Tony told them, 'he was due for leave like anybody else, and that's all there is to it.' However, on his return on the Wednesday morning, he told him what a lazy scheming bugger he was; furthermore, the first job he allocated to him was with the use of a lavatory brush.

Sitting at the little table in the bedding store, a pint mug of tea before him, his head buried in the laundry book, Tony was suddenly alerted by a tap on the door, 'I see your friend is back, Yorky, looks fit an'all,' Jerry Banks said, popping his head round the door, grinning.

'Oh morning, Sergeant Banks,' Tony replied, looking up from his task with a smile. 'I've just given him a nice job cleaning out the lavatory pans in the top floor ablutions to get him back into his stride,' he told him, with a laugh.

Looking back at him blankly for a moment he said, 'You've what, Yorky? Who are you talking about?' he asked, frowning.

'My mate, Jeff Baxter, he's just come back off leave this morning; well, you just said you'd seen him, didn't you, Jerry?'

'Oh, I don't mean him,' he replied, starting to laugh. 'I'm talking about your friend, Sergeant Riley. He's just back from sick leave; looks as though he's made a full recovery, looks fit and sounds cheerful, just like his old self – well better,' he added.

'Well, good luck to him,' Tony replied, 'but I hope he sticks to his word and remembers the apology he gave me before he went; I don't want a bollocking every time he sees me, like I've had to put up with in the past,' he said, frowning.

'I'm pretty sure you've no need to worry on that subject, Yorky,' Jerry said. 'He's moving out this morning, anyway; he's got a posting to a base up in Scotland. Actually,' he continued, 'that's the main reason I've popped in to see you – he asked me if I'd mind giving you a message. He said he would appreciate it if you'd go up to his room at eleven o'clock and give him a hand out to the car with his luggage.'

'Oh, bloody hell, Jerry, just as I thought,' Tony moaned, 'he wants a final bash at me before he buggers off; I'll send West or Baxter, I'll keep out of his way,' he said, shaking his head.

'Well, as a matter of fact, I did say should I ask one of the other lads, if I didn't see you,' Jerry replied, 'but he said he would particularly like you yourself to go up. I don't think he intends to be offensive,' he added, 'I got the feeling he just wanted to say goodbye, or summat like that.'

'Aye, I know, what sort of a goodbye he's most likely to dish out, Jerry,' Tony grunted, 'now he's feeling better – but I suppose I've no choice really – I'll have to go and take a final salvo before, he buggers off to Scotland.'

Just before eleven, Tony was outside Sergeant Riley's bunk door.

'Hello there, AC Ryan,' smiled Sergeant Riley, answering his knock, 'please come in. It's nice of you to agree to help me out with my gear; I do appreciate it's not part of your official duties,' he said, in a very friendly tone.

'No problem at all, Sergeant,' Tony replied, smiling – although he was finding it hard to believe his reception. 'I'm very pleased to see you looking so fit and well after the turmoil you went through,' he smiled.

It took several trips out to the car with the sergeant's cases, and as they worked together, they talked continuously in the most warm and friendly manner. By the time everything was loaded, and Sergeant Riley himself got behind the wheel, no one would ever have believed the antagonism over the past months. Tony stood beside the rolled-down window, the sergeant sat ready for off, his elbow protruding out laughing and chatting – they looked like old friends bidding farewell.

Tony was beginning to think what a nice guy Sergeant Riley had turned out to be. He must have been under some sort of stress he thought; the treatment he'd had after the accident must have relaxed him. Whatever it was, he reasoned, Riley was a different man now; his mind was as clear as a bell and he looked as fit as an Olympic athlete.

'Well, AC Ryan I thank you for your kind assistance,' the now friendly sergeant said, starting the engine up, with a smile. Then he reached into the inside pocket of his tunic and pulled out a small oblong package, wrapped in brown paper and looking up at Tony through the open window he passed it to him. 'This is a small offering for everything you've done for me, Tony,' he said, 'I hope you'll accept it with my eternal gratitude.'

Tony stared back at him, genuinely shocked; considering the way this man had treated him in the past, he was lost for words. Slowly reaching out his hand, he took the little package from him in silence – he just nodded with a blank expression on his face. Sergeant Riley's car had disappeared up the road before Tony's mind defrosted; then slowly turning, he made his way back into the Mess with the little package in hand, wondering what the bloody hell was in it.

On his way back to the bedding store, he noticed Sergeant Banks' door was slightly ajar. Tony tapped on it. 'Are you there, Jerry, can I have a word?' he called softly.

'Aye, come in, Yorky,' he called out cheerfully. Tony wondered in, looking bewildered, holding the small present wrapped in brown paper fearfully, as though it was a bomb.

Looked up from a newspaper he was reading, Jerry said with a smile, 'Bloody hell, you look glum, what's up – has Riley given you a rough time, Yorky?'

'No, oh no, just the opposite, Jerry, no look – he gave me a present.' Holding out the little package, he said, 'with his gratitude for my help an'all.' Still staring at the little package he went on, 'but I only helped to carry his cases to the car; I couldn't believe it, he was so very nice and friendly,' he added. Still looking down at the package, he shook his head.

'Most likely he's still feeling guilty for being so nasty to you before; anyway what is this present he's given you?' Jerry asked, nodding at the little package in Tony's hand.

'I don't know,' he replied quietly, staring at it again. 'I daren't open it.' He chuckled. 'It might be a bloody bomb or summat, Jerry; the sod might be still trying to get me, after all.'

Laughing with him, Jerry said, 'Come on then, get the bugger opened up; let's be seeing what it is.'

Thrusting the package at him, Tony said, 'Huh, it could be 'owt – here you open it if you're so curious,' he smiled.

'Christ, he's stuck this up firmly,' said Jerry, tearing off the sticky tape binding the package. When he finally got the thick brown paper off it, he said, 'Hell it's wrapped in tissue paper an'all.' Finally, getting all the wrapping off he held it up – a small, oblong, black velvet covered box about six inches long. 'By God, this looks like summat expensive,' he said, quietly looking down at it. Slowly taking off the lid, he gasped, 'Good God, it's a dress watch with a gold expanding bracelet, Yorky.' Passing it over to him he added with a whistle, 'It's a beauty; it must have cost the best part of fifty quid, a thing like that.' Suddenly noticing a slip of paper among the wrapping, he grabbed it up. 'Oh look, there's a note here,' he said passing it to Tony. 'Go on read it, it's for you; let's see what the bugger's got to say, then.

Taking the slip of paper from him gingerly, Tony read it out in a low voice,

'Dear AC Ryan, (Tony),

This is a small token of my gratitude for saving my life and also, for your tolerance and forgiveness regarding the unjustified treatment you received from me over the past months.

I don't suppose we will ever meet again, but I wish you all the very best on life's journey and

I sincerely thank you again. Without you I would, no doubt, not be here now,

Sergeant Tim Riley

(PS) But I'm still baffled as to how you got out yourself.'

As he finished reading it out the two just stood staring at each other in silence for a moment, then Jerry said, 'Well, I'll go to hell! And I thought he was back to normal. It looks as though there's a lot more to be done on his mind yet; he still believes you were on that crashed plane with him,' he said shaking his head, adding with a chuckle, 'You weren't though, were you, Yorky?'

105

'You mean to say, Sergeant Riley gave you that bloody expensive watch for nothing, Tony?' gasped Jeff, as they sat chatting in the bedding store, later.

'Well, not exactly for nothing, Mr Baxter,' Tony replied indignantly. 'He insisted it was for saving his life and also for me having to tolerate his unjustifiable persecution over the last few months prior to that. Grinning he added, 'Mind you, mate, I don't know about the former, but I definitely agree with him regarding the latter.'

Giving him a blank look, Jeff said, 'What do you mean, Tony, you don't know – but you do?'

Getting up and going over to put the kettle on the gas ring, Tony sighed, 'Oh, never mind you thick bugger, I haven't time to explain; do you want a pot of tea before we make a start upstairs?'

After tea, Tony, seeing two of the other lads working away polishing the linoleum on the landing, called out proudly, 'Hello, you lot; what do you think to this then?' He held his raised arm out in front of them, showing off his new watch.

Gathering round looking at it with admiration, Eddy Jones, beside him, said quietly in his ear, 'Tony can I have a private word, please?'

Walking away from the others, Tony said, 'Okay, Eddy, how much this time?'

Grinning sheepishly, he replied, 'Ten bob, same as last week, Tony, if it's okay with you.'

Reaching into his pocket for his wallet, Tony said, 'Ee, you're a bugger, you are, Jones. I don't know what you do with all your money. I want it back a week today, same terms an'all,' he stressed, 'so that means a quid back next Monday, okay?'

Taking the ten shilling note eagerly from him, Eddy said with a wide smile, 'Oh, no problem there, Tony – I've got another little job this weekend, with that rich friend of mine down in London; I'll be able to pay you back on Sunday night, if you want.'

'Aye,' replied Tony, eyeing him up and down. 'I don't know what you get up to with him, but I hope it's legal, not pinching or 'owt like that,' he said, watching him put the money in his trouser pocket.

'No, I wouldn't do anything like that, Tony and you know it,' Eddy replied, with indignation, 'No, he's a friend; I just help him with his personal matters – he's a lonely man,' he told him, shaking his head sympathetically.

Back in the bedding store later, Tony said, 'You know, Jeff, I don't know what to make of that bugger, Jones.' 'I'm sure he's up no good on these trips to London. I mean, I've been loaning him money for cigs and booze regularly now, every week for ages; he spends that, also all his wages from here, then buggers off down London at the weekend, just about broke. After the weekend he comes back, loaded; it's beyond belief, Jeff,' he said, screwing his face up, looking baffled. Jeff just nodded and avoided Tony's eye. 'He spends a lot more money than he gets here in his wage packet, you know,' Tony continued, 'and that's every week,' he pointed out, 'He's up to summat, I'm sure,' he said, frowning. 'I only hope it's legal.' When Jeff just sat there nodding, again without comment, Tony looked down at him suspiciously for a moment, and then said quietly, 'You're not saying much about him, Baxter, you don't know 'owt I don't know, about his little escapades, do you? Because if you do you'd better spit it out and let me know, before the silly bugger gets himself into any bother.

Sitting in silence for a while, staring at the floor, Jeff said, 'Well, he did tell Ted and me about this bloke, Basil, in London.'

'Who, him he gets his money from?' Tony almost yelled.

'Well, yes,' Jeff said, 'but he made us promise faithfully not to tell anyone else what he'd told us; especially you, Tony,' he said, glancing at him sheepishly.

Frowning and pursing his lips, Tony said angrily, 'Just as I bloody well thought, he's a sly little bastard – but why does this Basil give him all this cash, Jeff? Is he a fucking gangster or summat like that?'

Pausing, Jeff eventually said, 'You know, Tony, I feel awful breaking my word to Jones, after I made a solemn promise not to tell anybody about how he gets his money.'

More inquisitive than ever now, Tony was determined to get to the bottom of the matter. Walking over to where Jeff was sitting, he stood straight in front of him staring down into his upturned face, 'Jeff, I always thought you and I were real friends,' he said softly, 'and real friends have no secrets between them, am I right?' he enquired with a raised eyebrow. 'Well, yes I suppose so,' he replied meekly, 'but I did promise, and what he told us was very unusual and I don't know if I believe it really, Tony.'

Beginning to feel a little exasperated Tony said, 'Look, mate you leave that to me – just bloody well spit it out; for Christ's sake, let's know what the silly bugger is up to.'

As though struggling to break a mental barrier, Jeff suddenly burst out, 'I think it could be some sort of sex thing, Tony.'

Stepping back smiling, he replied, 'Just as I thought, shady goings on, eh? He's mixing with old puffs, is he?'

'Well, I don't know about that,' said Jeff, beginning to forget his promise and opening up, 'but he did say that this Basil chap gets dressed up in a bloody schoolgirl's uniform, with black stockings and suspenders.'

'Oh Christ,' said Tony, 'and what about Jones, does he wear an outfit like that, an'all?'

Smiling slightly, Jeff said, 'No he told us the bloke insists that Jones wears his Service uniform, because he likes men in uniforms and it's part of the act.'

'What act?' yelled Tony, 'What the hell goes on, Jeff? Jones doesn't shag his arse, or 'owt perverted like that, does he?' he asked, screwing his face up in disgust.'

Laughing now, Jeff replied, 'No, he doesn't go that far, no; this Basil just walks around the room dressed like a sexy schoolgirl and Jones stands there in his uniform shouting out orders and throwing balls of horse shit at him.'

'Bloody hell,' gasped Tony, 'and this old guy, Basil, pays him good money to throw horse muck at him?'

'Yes, that's what he told me and West,' Jeff replied. 'What's more,' he said with a grin, 'he gets three quid a session for doing it, an'all; easy money that, eh, Tony?'

Tony, hands on hips, laughed loudly. 'I only hope he wears gloves when he's handling that shit, though, Jeff – what do you say?'

106

Jeff and Tony were busy cleaning the sinks in the downstairs ablutions, when Eddy Jones came in grinning, holding out a pound note to Tony. 'There you are, Mr Ryan – repaid Monday with interest as promised,' he said cockily. Eddy always repays his debts,' he added, with a shake of his head.

'Aye, that's because he knows it's best for his health where I'm concerned,' replied Tony, with mock aggression. Then in a very serious, concerned tone, he enquired, 'And how was Basil this week, Eddy? I hope he's keeping well.'

Without noticing the question, he replied cheerfully, 'Oh, he was fine, just his normal self.' He stopped, realising what he'd been asked and by whom and turned towards Jeff with an angry, menacing look on his face. 'You big-mouthed prick, Baxter,' he yelled. 'I'll tell you nothing else in confidence.' Heading for the door amidst a chorus of laughter, he added with venom, 'You're like a big tart; you can't hold fucking water, Baxter.'

'Now then, you lot, what's going on, what's all the noise about?' Sergeant Pike called out, walking in looking stern.

'Oh, we're just having a joke, Sergeant,' Tony told him, trying to subdue his laughter.

'Oh, are you Ryan,' he said gruffly, 'Well, you'd better forget your joking and get down to the main phone in the entrance hall; there's a call for you and the caller is hanging on – so you'd better hurry yourself up.'

Tony at first thought with excitement – it must be Becky; 'God! I'll bet it's Becky,' he whispered to Jeff, rushing past him to the door.

Ten minutes later, he came walking slowly back into the ablution, ashen-faced. Jeff, left on his own, scrubbing away at one of the sinks, called out without turning, 'How's she going on then, mate? Has she got her home posting sorted out, then?'

'It wasn't her,' was Tony's barely audible answer.

Hearing the tone of his reply, Jeff spun around to see him, standing there with tears in his eyes, wringing his hands together.

Going over to him, Jeff put his arm around his shoulder. 'Tony, old mate, what's up? What's happened, Tony?'

Wiping his eyes with the back of his hand, Tony muttered, 'It was Mrs Mansfield, Dave's mum, she rang to tell me Dave's been in an ambush in the jungle; he's been shot, Jeff.'

Oh God,' Jeff said, with a gasp. Is it bad, Tony?'

'That's all they've told her at present, she said; several of the boys have been hit and they're going to give her more detailed information, as soon as possible.' Almost in a whisper he said, 'Oh my God, Jeff, Dave is more than a mate, as I've told you before; we've been brought up together, we're like brothers – and he might be dead,' he said, leaning on the wall with his face in his hands, sobbing.

Patting him on the shoulder affectionately, Jeff said, 'Come on, mate, let's go down to the store and have a pot of tea and talk this out – things are not always as black as they seem at first you know. A little later, sitting in the bedding store with their mugs of tea, chatting about the matter, Jeff was trying to point out the brighter possibilities to make Tony a little more hopeful.

They were just about to get back to their duties in the ablution, when Sergeant Pike, seeing the door ajar and hearing the conversation within, popped his head through the doorway. 'Now then,' he said, frowning. 'What's all this, then?' He was just about to continue his scolding, when he noticed the look on Tony's face and asked tentatively, 'Is there something wrong, Ryan?' After being told what the phone call was about and realising Tony was very upset, he said, 'but is that all they could tell his mother about the condition of the lad, Ryan? I'd have thought they could have told her whether he was dead or just injured.'

'The report was delivered by the local police,' Tony told him, despondently. 'They told her that as soon as they got any further details, they would inform her.'

'Uh-huh,' the little sergeant grunted, getting up. 'Well, I think this is disgusting, completely out of order; surely they know more about the casualties than that. Huh, leaving next of kin with worry like that on their minds; out of order, out of order, that's as I see it,' he snapped.

Tony nodded. 'Yes, that's what I said to his mum on the phone, Sergeant – she's so upset,' he said.

'No wonder,' Pike replied curtly. 'The poor woman – it could be days before they get round to contacting her again. Not like in the war, you know, Ryan,' he rambled away. 'On the ball in them days, you know; no messing about then.'

'I'll tell you what,' he suddenly said, as if the thought had just struck him. 'Have you got your friend's name, service number and camp address,

Ryan? I'll see if I can get some more light shed on the matter,' he told him, with a determined nod.

Reaching into his jacket pocket, Tony pulled out a recent letter he'd received from Dave; he tore off the top part of the first page which bore Dave's address and personal credentials and passed it to him. 'Do you think you can find out anything more definite, Sergeant?' he enquired meekly.

'Well, I think I might be able to improve on the situation at least, Ryan,' he replied, taking the paper. 'Well, with the aid of my friend, Flight Sergeant Broadbent,' he added, 'he's in charge of telecommunications.' Just as he was leaving, he suddenly turned. 'Oh, I nearly forgot what I came to tell you, Ryan,' he said, with a smile. 'I've just had a phone call from Personnel regarding a temporary resident, a flight sergeant expected later tonight.'

'Oh, we haven't got any rooms prepared, Sergeant,' Tony replied apologetically. 'Is the person male or female?' he asked.

'That, I'm afraid, I don't know, Ryan. They failed to mention it when they rang me up, but I presume it's a male the way the young corporal down there was talking. It's only a very short temporary stay, anyway,' he told him. Smiling again, as he made to leave, he called over his shoulder, 'No doubt you'll sort it out – as you usually do, Ryan.'

As his footsteps faded away along the corridor, Jeff, who'd been silent throughout, said angrily, 'That's bloody beautiful that is, he must think we're fucking psychic.'

'Well, you should know what he is by now, Jeff,' Tony grunted. 'Never mind, we'll manage,' he assured him.

'Yes, because we'll bloody well have to,' Jeff moaned, 'but if he doesn't know himself if the new resident is male or female, how the fuck, are we to know where to get the bloody room prepared, for him or her?'

'Easy but inconvenient,' Tony replied with a sigh. 'We get two rooms prepared, one here on this side and one on the female wing. Anyway, come on, Jeff lad,' he continued, 'you get yourself up to that room on the top landing that was vacated yesterday, number 26, wasn't it?'

'Aye, 26,' he replied.

'Anyway, get on up there and get working on it,' Tony told him. 'I'll pop down to the kitchen to see if we can borrow Ruby for an hour before lunch, to get that one ready on the female wing, then I'll join you.'

107

'Well, that's that sorted out,' Tony said with an exaggerated sigh on rejoining his pal. 'The kind Sergeant McNabb said I can have the lovely Ruby's services for an hour, when they've cleared the tables after lunch.'

'Oh, that's very nice for you Tony, eh – her services for an hour, eh? Mind you,' Jeff said with a grin, 'I suppose that's no new experience to you, mate.'

'Aye, watch it Baxter, mind what you're implying,' he said, raising his fist in mock anger. 'Ruby's a decent girl,' he added jocosely.

Laughing, Jeff replied, 'I know that, Tony, it's you I'm bothered about, you bugger.'

'Shut up and get on with the bloody work,' he said, chuckling. Becoming more serious, he said, 'I wonder if Pike can find out anymore about Dave's shooting, Jeff?'

Realising Tony was still worrying about his pal, he replied confidently, 'Well, he seemed sure of it, mate, I've a feeling that things will turn out okay,' he told him, resuming his work.

As they both got stuck into the job, Tony asked casually, 'Have you found anything worth having in here for the business, Jeff?'

'I found two pairs of boots under the bed, but they'll want mending,' he replied.

'Is that all?' Tony moaned. 'I thought we'd have done a bit better than that; he was a dandy type guy that was in here – I expected a few nice shirts at the very least,' he grumbled.

'Well, there was nothing else but a pile of them mucky books full of bare women; I've put them in that carrier bag over there to chuck away,' he said, pointing at a large paper carrier bag on the floor, in far the corner of the room.

Suddenly coming to life, Tony said sharply, 'What the fuck are you talking about, Jeff, chuck away; you don't chuck anything away before I see it, mate. Don't you realise, Jeff, them mucky books, as you call 'em are in great demand; how many are there anyway?' he asked.

'Oh, about fifty at least,' Jeff told him, huffily.

'There you go then,' he went on sternly. 'You'd be chucking between a quid and thirty bob down the drain throwing them out, perhaps more,' he added, nodding seriously.

'Do you realise we'll get at about a tanner apiece for them, mate, at our billet sale on Friday evening? Well, you will,' he added aloofly, 'I'm in the gym that night – it's one of my training nights again,' he said, smiling.

'Aye, it's your bloody training night every week these days when we have the sale, 'Jeff said, grumpily. 'I'm beginning to wonder what the hell you do in the business, Tony Ryan. I know you make most money out of the fucking venture,' he told him sulkily.

Tony was stunned. 'What did you say, Jeff? I can't believe what I've just heard,' he continued, without waiting for a reply. 'Are you implying that I get a disproportionate share of the business takings?' He stared at him indignantly, hands on hips.

'Well, no, I'm not saying that really, Tony,' he said, avoiding his stare, 'I just thought you didn't do much of the work yourself, that's all.'

Shaking his head from side to side in disbelief, Tony gave a long sigh. 'You obviously don't understand the workings of a modern business, Jeff, old son. You've got to understand that the head of any organisation spends most of the time thinking and planning the next move. Without a good business plan, Jeff,' he lectured, 'there'd soon be no bloody business at all; surely you can see that – a man of your intelligence,' he nodded, staring at him with a hurt frown on his face.

Looking back at Tony's sad expression, Jeff replied in a quiet, guilty tone, 'Well, I suppose you're right, mate; I didn't mean to say you didn't do anything – anyway let's forget it, shall we?'

Shaking his head again, and smiling condescendingly, Tony replied, 'I realise how you were thinking, Jeff, I also know you've never had any business experience.' With a slight laugh, he went on, 'You just listen to me, mate, you'll soon learn.' Pointing at the bag full of dirty magazines on the floor in the corner he added, 'and remember, throw nothing away until I've seen it, okay?'

During afternoon tea break, when Ruby came tripping into the bedding store, Tony asked, 'Have them lazy buggers finished polishing that corridor floor on the women's wing, Ruby?'

'No, they're still buffing away with the polishers,' she replied handing him the key to the room she'd just prepared, 'but I'll tell you what,' she said with disgust, 'they're smoking their heads off up there, Tony, it stinks like an opium den, it does.'

'What! I've told them about that bloody mucky game, filling the place with fumes – especially on the women's wing,' he said angrily. Then turning to Jeff, he said, 'You'd better get up there, mate; tell 'em to put them bloody fags out, and open all the windows, an'all,' he added.

'Anyway, Ruby, darling, thank you for your kind help as usual,' he said, when Jeff had departed. 'And don't forget my love, I'm always here – willing and available, any time, to do anything for you,' he said, adding the usual wink.

'Oh, you are a one, Tony Ryan,' she replied, blushing. 'You've a one track mind, you have.'

'By the way, darling,' he called out, as she made to go, 'Will you ask Sergeant McNabb if she could let you bring me a meal up here at tea time? Explain to her that I can't leave the Mess, I'm expecting a new resident at any time; tell her it's an emergency booking.'

Looking a little doubtful, the poor girl replied, 'I don't think she'll do that, Tony, I don't know whether I dare ask her either,' she said nervously.

'Just tell her you're passing a message on from me, Ruby, and tell her why I want it, okay? I'm sure she'll oblige when she knows the circumstances,' he said, with a smile.

Ruby had only been gone a couple of minutes when she was back with a worried look on her face; 'Tony, Sergeant Pike just asked me to tell you, he's got some information for you about your friend, David Mansfield; he'd like you to go down to his office as soon as possible.'

Noticing his face darken on hearing this, she said tentatively, 'I hope it's not some sort of bad news, Tony.'

Hurrying to the door, he said, 'I hope not an'all Ruby, I'll tell you about it later, love,' he muttered as he ushered her out of the door, locking it behind him.

'Come in,' called out Sergeant Pike, hearing the tap on his office door. 'Hello, Ryan, you haven't wasted much time getting here,' he smiled across his desk. Beckoning to one of the little wicker chairs in front of it he continued solemnly, 'Well, Ryan, Flight Sergeant Broadbent sent off a message regarding your friend this morning.' Tony's heartbeat increased as he waited for his next words. 'His department sent it on one of those marvellous teleprinter machines, you know.' He continued with a little smile. 'And, he's just rung me on my phone here within the last few minutes to say they've received a reply.'

'Did they find out anything about Dave, then?' Tony chipped in, anxiously.

'Yes, yes they did, Ryan, but it's not all good news,' he said with a cautious frown. 'He's alive and his injuries are not life-threatening.' Hearing this, Tony leaned forward in his chair, his elbows on his knees, and gave a long sigh of relief. 'Oh, thank God for that, Sergeant, thank God,' he repeated, holding his head in his hands.

'However,' went on Sergeant Pike, 'as I said, it's not all good news, Ryan, he's been quite badly injured with rifle fire to his right leg; they've transported him and several more chaps, to a large military hospital on the south coast of Australia.' Watching Tony's face carefully to gauge his reaction, he went on, 'The initial diagnosis is, that there's a good chance of complete recovery; however, looking on the black side there's a chance that there may be reasons to amputate part of the leg.' He again looked at Tony, obviously worried about his reaction to this news.

'What are the chances of that, then, Sergeant,' Tony said frowning. 'Did they say?'

'Apparently the people on his station won't know, until they get further reports on all the injured men in Private Mansfield's group,' he told him. 'This of course has been promised as soon as possible by the military hospital in Australia. However, we hope to get more news for you by midday tomorrow,' he said, with a little smile.

Tony thanked him for all his help, saying that it had taken a large weight off his mind. He also enquired if it would be in order to try contacting Dave's mum with the news, which he said would put her mind at rest; the sergeant condoned the idea. Tony told him that contact could be made through Bernard, the local pub landlord; he also hastened to point out that Bernard was an ex Station Warrant Officer, still on reserve.

'Oh, ex S.W.O, Ryan, eh,' he said, when he heard that. 'It couldn't be in better hands there, then.' By the way, Ryan,' he called out, as Tony was halfway out of the door. 'I've also made a phone call to Personnel regarding the new resident you're expecting; a young woman down there assured me it was a male.'

Then with one of his very squeaky little laughs, he added, 'I told you it would be a male of course, so I hope you've got a room prepared on the male wing.'

'Yes, I certainly did, Sergeant,' Tony told him, 'and don't you worry, everything is under control. I'm also staying here on duty tonight, so it doesn't matter what time he arrives either,' he said, on his way out.

108

'It's a bloke we're to expect, Jeff,' Tony called out, meeting him on his way back to the bedding store. Pike's just confirmed it. Oh and by the way, he'd got some news about Dave, an'all; he's been shot, but he's not too bad, thank God.'

'That's great then, Tony, I thought you looked a bit more cheerful,' he smiled, turning and following him along the corridor. Going into the store, Jeff picked up a large paper bag at the side of the door; taking it in with him he said, grinning broadly, 'Wait while you see what's in here, Tony.'

'Oh aye, what have you got now,' he mumbled with little interest. 'Ruby left it outside the door of that room she's just been cleaning out on the women's wing,' he chuckled. 'One of the lads brought it down for you to go through.'

'What the hell is it?' Tony enquired, putting the kettle on.

'Clothes, two sweaters, underwear, plus other bits and pieces for the business, mate,' Jeff   told him. 'You said not to throw anything away until you'd seen it, didn't you?'

'We won't be able to sell women's frocks and bloomers to the blokes in the billet, you pillock,' Tony told him, laughing. 'Well, I don't think so,' he added, laughing more. 'I hate to think what narrow-minded Pike would say though if he found the bloody stuff in here, he'd think the place was a den of iniquity. I mean, what with a great pile of dirty books and now a bag full of women's clothes, he'd think we're a load of perverts.'

'Well, you never know, mate, we might get him as a customer,' Jeff said, with a laugh.

'Christ, Jeff, just look what we've got here,' Tony stood in front of the wall bench with the bag of women's clothing, grinning and holding a pair of silky French knickers in front of him.

'Very nice, very nice – better not let West see them, though,' Jeff said, laughing – as he's partial to that sort of thing.'

'Oh aye, we better be careful with him, after what happened when he found them others in the waste bin upstairs,' Tony said, laughing boisterously.

'The lads in the billet will bite our hands off for 'em, I'll bet,' Jeff tittered.

'I don't know about that,' Tony said, waving the lacy garment in the air, 'they might for what's been in 'em,' he said, still laughing. Just then they heard fast, heavy footsteps coming up the corridor. Pushing the pile of clothing up to the far end of the bench, behind a stack of laundry, Tony said with urgency, 'Come on, Jeff, on your feet, this sounds like Pike in a hurry, could be bother.'

'Catastrophe, Ryan, catastrophe,' yelled out Sergeant Pike, charging into the bedding store in a state of panic. 'Those stupid fools down at Personnel have got us into a right mess, the bloody incompetent idiots,' he raved.

Looking back at him blankly, Tony asked, 'Why, what's the problem, Sergeant?'

Breathing heavily and shaking his head, he replied through clenched teeth, 'Wrong sex Ryan, bloody wrong sex; it's a woman.'

I presume you mean the new resident flight sergeant?' replied Tony calmly.

'Who else, Ryan, who else?' he yelled. 'She's arrived too, she's on her way up here now with her luggage,' he moaned, clenching his fist. Then, wringing his hands together, he continued, 'Where the devil are we going to put her up, Ryan? We haven't got a room prepared for her now, because of their incompetence.'

Smiling, Tony replied, 'Don't worry, Sergeant, there is a room on the female wing all prepared and ready for occupancy; you see I wanted to make sure myself, so I got one prepared on each wing.'

Sighing with relief, Pike gasped, 'Thank God! Good thinking, Ryan, good man, good man.' Hearing the sound of footsteps he said in hushed tones, 'Sounds like her now, Ryan, she said she'd only be a few minutes getting her things out of the car.'

But Tony wasn't listening, he was staring through the doorway, open-mouthed over Pike's shoulder, where the smartly dressed young flight sergeant had now come to a halt in the corridor, and was looking in, smiling. Seeing the look on Tony's face, Pike glanced behind him at the young woman and then back at Tony with a puzzled expression. He was just going to say something but before he could, Tony as if mesmerised, pushed past him and ran towards the young woman standing beside her suitcase, outside the door.

Reaching her, he took her in his arms and pulled her tightly to him, kissing the top of her head and muttering, 'Darling, oh, my darling.'

Poor Sergeant Pike thought Tony had gone mad. 'Ryan! Ryan!' he yelled out. 'Have you lost leave of your senses, man, you'll be in the guardhouse for this.' Then stepping towards the embracing pair, he yelled, 'Come on Baxter, give me a hand – the man's gone mad; I can't believe this is happening with Ryan,' he yelled, making a grab at Tony, with the intention of pulling him off her.

However he released his hold when the young flight sergeant, who now had both her arms around Tony's neck, and was looking lovingly up into his face, turned to him, smiling. 'Don't worry, Sergeant Pike, everything is in order. Tony is my boyfriend – we haven't seen each other for around a year; I've been on an overseas posting, you see.' Then, she gently pulled Tony's face down towards her, and kissed him firmly on his lips, in full view of the two onlookers.

Standing in silence for a few moments, his mouth agape as he observed the romantic scene, Sergeant Pike, red-faced with embarrassment and coughing nervously, suddenly said sharply, 'Well, well I think I'd better get back to my office, the job must go on.'

Glancing back into the bedding store, he called out to Jeff, who had been quietly watching the whole episode, 'And I should think you've got something better to do than standing there like a zombie, Baxter. Come on, man, let's have you back on the job,' he yelled, as he strode away, 'I'm sure, Ryan can manage to handle the flight sergeant without any assistance from you.'

'Oh yes, I'm sure he can, Sergeant Pike,' replied Jeff, following in his wake with a smile.

109

'By, your Sergeant Pike sounds a strict little taskmaster,' Becky tittered, as the pair disappeared down the corridor.

'Oh, he's not a bad sort, love,' Tony said, ushering her into the bedding store with his arm around her shoulder, 'he's helped me a lot these last few days, with a domestic problem that cropped up.'

Slightly startled, she enquired, 'Domestic problem, darling, nothing serious I hope.'

'Well, very serious, really,' he replied. 'Anyway, you sit yourself down,' he said pointing to the old armchair, 'while I make you a cup of tea, then I'll tell you all about it.' Going for the kettle, he added, 'you can tell me about your adventures in Cyprus an'all; I was beginning to think I'd never see you again.'

'Heaven forbid, darling,' she said, with a start. 'That would be the end for me, you know how much I love you, don't you, Tony?'

'Of course I do, darling, and I love you; I was on the verge of coming over there to get you,' he chuckled, passing her the teacup. 'Anyway,' he went on, 'so you didn't know you'd got this posting until the weekend, then? That's quick action,' he added, 'it's only Monday and you're here.'

'That's right,' she replied, 'but as you know, I've been constantly applying all the time. I've been over there, Tony. Anyway, come here,' she said, putting her cup down and going up to him, smiling. 'You haven't given me a proper greeting yet,' she cooed, slipping into his opening arms.

Ten minutes later, the passionate greeting satisfied, she continued, 'This offer came through out of the blue;

it was due to some sort of emergency with the guy I'm replacing. I don't know exactly what the reason was; anyway I grabbed it, obviously,'

'Great, the camp you're on is less than fifteen miles from here, an'all, eh? Couldn't be much better than that, darling,' he said, grinning.

'Sure, that's right, actually it's about twelve miles; similar distance as the previous one, but in the other direction,' she told him. 'By the way, I've been told the gym I'm in charge of, is one of the most up-to-date in the country,' she said, with pride.

'Terrific, I'll be able to come over now and again for a workout then, love, it'll be like old times, won't it, Becky,' he said, giving her another little hug.

'Sure will, darling, but it's still twelve miles, you know; I'd have to chauffeur you both ways, unless you walked,' she said, laughing.

'Who said anything about walking Becky, dear,' he replied, with mock disgust. 'I'll have you know, young lady, Tony Ryan is in a position to provide his own wheels on occasions.'

'You mean somebody is daft enough to loan you their car, love,' she replied with a cheeky chuckle.

'Well, as a matter of fact there is,' he replied. 'It's a little beauty an'all,' he told her, snootily. Changing the subject, he went on, 'How would you like to come up to our gym this evening, Becky, I was going to have a workout tonight, you could loosen up a bit yourself, after all your travelling.'

'Oh, I'd love to,' she told him, enthusiastically.

'Right then, pet, that's fixed then.' He smiled and leaning forward, pulled her playfully out of the big armchair and kissed her responsive lips, 'Come on, let's get you up to your room, and you can get yourself settled in.'

As he went over to the sink with her empty cup, Becky suddenly called out, 'Good Lord, what have we got here?'

Turning, he was shocked to see her looking through the bag containing the dirty books and waving the fancy French knickers in the air. Thinking fast, he went over to her, pretending to be surprised, 'Oh, that bloody Baxter!' he said, pursing his lips. 'I told him to get rid of that load of rubbish; I don't know why he brought it in here in the first place,' he said angrily. 'Jeff Baxter,' he stressed, 'the lad you've just met in here; that stuff was found while cleaning a room out on the female wing.' He shook his head, grimacing with disgust and said, 'You'd be surprised what we find in here, you know, Becky.'

Standing looking into his face, full of false piety, she said, bursting out laughing. 'Who do you think you're kidding, Tony Ryan, blaming your poor friend, Jeff? I know what you lads get up to when you get together; I wouldn't be surprised if you hadn't been planning to hang them knickers on the regimental flag pole in the square,' she laughed.

'No, it's the truth, pet,' he said, now feeling genuinely embarrassed. 'As I said, the clothing was found in a room that Ruby was cleaning out, in fact it was the room that you've got,' he said, nodding.

'Oh, I see and who is this Ruby, anyway?' she asked.

'Ruby – oh, she's just one of the rough-looking little ACWs from the kitchen staff,' he said nonchalantly, brushing the question to one side.

'And what about the sexy books?' she asked, smiling. 'Were they found in there too?'

'No, oh no, they were found on the men's wing of course,' he replied, with a snigger. 'They were left in some dirty old Sergeant's room that Jeff Baxter cleaned out. I don't know, pet,' he went on, 'I told the silly bugger he should have put them straight in the kitchen stove – disgusting things,' he said shaking his head.'

'Oh, did you, and how long have you been disgusted at the sight of a shapely female body, Tony Ryan; you always gave me the impression that you were an ardent admirer,' she giggled, tormenting him.

Before he could reply, there was a tap on the door and a soft female voice called out, 'Tony, I've brought your tea tray, dear.'

Giving Becky a cautious glance, he called out in a business-like tone of voice, 'Oh, bring it in, Ruby,' saying to Becky, casually, 'I'm officially on duty tonight, Becky, so they provide me with a teatime meal.'

As the good-looking, leggy Ruby came in with the tray covered with a stiff white cloth, she paused, slightly shocked when she saw Becky standing there at Tony's side. 'Oh, I hope I'm not intruding on anything, Flight Sergeant,' she spluttered, 'but I was told to bring AC Ryan his meal at this time.'

'Don't worry, Ruby,' Tony said. 'The flight sergeant is here for personal reasons.' Giving Becky a little smile he continued proudly, 'This is my girlfriend, who I told you about, Ruby, she's been on overseas posting, she's having that room you got ready earlier.'

'Putting the tray down on the table, Ruby said, with a nervous smile, 'Your girlfriend, Becky?' Then freezing, she turned to Becky with a shocked expression, 'I'm sorry Flight Sergeant, no disrespect intended; I've just got used to Tony referring to you by your first name when he's talking about you.'

Smiling, Becky replied, 'Don't worry, Ruby, that's my name anyway; I don't mind in private,' she added.

'Tony never said you were a flight sergeant, though,' Ruby said, smiling shyly, 'and with him saying you were the same age as we are, I just thought you'd be one of us,' she said nervously.

'Did you have any difficulties with Sergeant McNabb, when you requested my meal be brought up here, Ruby?' Tony asked, changing the subject.

'No, I was very surprised, too,' she told him wide-eyed, 'she was very nice about it, she told me to give you ample proportions of salad and double pieces fish.'

Laughing, he said, 'Well, she knows I'm in special training, and need extra nourishment, Ruby. By the way, while you're here, would you mind helping Becky up to that room with her luggage, while I have my meal,' he asked, smiling.

'Of course I will,' she replied, giving him a quick glance and grabbing the big suitcase at Becky's side.

The smile on Tony's face faded somewhat as Becky, following Ruby out, gave him a very suspicious look. At the door, she paused and leaned towards him, whispering sarcastically, 'One of the rough-looking little ACWs – eh, Ryan?'

110

'By God, Tony, you've been in there a long time,' Jeff called out, breaking off from his floor polishing when he saw him coming out of the phone box. 'You were on it when I came into work fifteen minutes back,' he added. It was early morning in the Sergeant's Mess, several weeks later; Becky was now well-established on her new camp and Tony, as expected, was spending as much time with her as possible – they were both very happy.

'Aye, I've been talking to Becky, she'd left a message for me to ring her at the gym as soon as I got in, so I had to obey orders,' he said, with a laugh.

'Nothing wrong, I hope?' Jeff enquired. 'Or are you both too much in love?' He laughed.

'No, to be frank, mate, I'm a little puzzled myself,' he replied, frowning. 'She seems worried about something; she wants me to go over to her place again for some reason, before I go home for my leave on Saturday.'

'You were over there all last weekend; I'd have thought she'd have been glad to see the back of you for a while.' Jeff laughed and resumed his labours. 'It was a bit of good luck, though, her getting that house to rent on the married quarters, wasn't it, though?' he said.

'Yes, it was, but there's quite a few empty on her camp, they must not like married folk over there.' He grinned. 'Mind you, Jeff, if it wasn't for wanting to see Dave now he's home after his brush with death, I'd spend my leave over there with Becky.'

'So you're only going home on leave see your mate, Dave, then, Tony, eh?' he replied. 'Mind you, I can see your point about staying with her,' he said with a smile, 'she's a lovely woman, is Becky. By the way, mate,' he said, with sincerity, 'I'm glad Dave's going to be okay after his troubles.'

'Oh thanks,' he replied distantly; then nodding thoughtfully, he said, 'I'll have to go over there again though, Jeff, and sort this little problem she's got before I go home. I'll see if I can borrow Mavis's car again,' he went on. 'She'll let me have it for a few of hours, I'm sure, if I tell her Becky's bothered about something. They got on well together while Becky stayed here, you know, Jeff,' he said. 'You wouldn't have thought it really, would you?' He chuckled. 'Mind you, Mavis was an athlete when she was younger apparently, so Becky said, so they did have something in common.'

'Aye, they went to the swimming baths together one morning, didn't they?' Jeff remarked.

'Oh aye, Becky said Mavis is a terrific swimmer – used to swim for the Service apparently, anyway I'm sure Mavis won't let me down,' he said with confidence. 'I'll nip over on Friday evening; I've got to keep my little darling happy, you know, Jeff,' he said, grinning.

'I understand that Tony, but it'll be a rush to get prepared for your early start on Saturday morning, won't it?'

Tony shrugged. 'Aye, but I'll manage, mate; I wouldn't enjoy my leave if I thought she was worrying about something.'

111

'Hello darling!' called out Becky, seeing Tony standing on the door step outside her little semi in slacks and a sweater. She slipped into his open arms as he stepped inside and they embraced affectionately. 'Sorry if I've inconvenienced you, love, but I just had to see you again before you went on leave,' she murmured.

Looking down into her serious gaze, Tony replied warmly, 'You haven't inconvenienced me, darling, I'd be here with you all the time if I could, you know that.'

Looking back at him for a moment in silence, she suddenly held onto him more firmly, her arms tight around his neck. 'Oh, would you, Tony, truly darling?' she said with a sob.

Rather shocked at this behaviour, Tony held her firmly for a moment, then looking down into her flooded eyes, he said paternally, 'Now then, you silly girl, what's all this about?'

Sniffing and trying to give a little smile she stepped back and reached into her pocket for a little handkerchief to wipe her eyes. 'I'm sorry, Tony,' she said softly, 'but I love you so much. Come on' she went on, 'let's go into the sitting room and I'll make us some tea.

'Good idea, my love,' he replied cheerfully, although he was rather worried as to what was going through her mind.

Coming out of the kitchenette and putting the tea tray down on the little side table, she dropped down beside him on the settee, put her head on his shoulder and sighed. 'Phew! I've had a full day today, Tony, how about you?'

Realising she wasn't going to come straight to the point, he replied cheerfully, 'I have a full day every day, darling, with the silly buggers I have to put up with in that Sergeants' Mess.'

Laughing a little, she said, 'by the way, your mate, Dave, seems to be making a quick recovery; are they going to send him back on active service after his convalescent leave?'

'I don't know, pet,' he replied, with a note of disapproval. 'I've told him to try to get out of that bloody mob, but he won't listen to sense.' Tony couldn't stand the suspense of not knowing what was troubling her any longer. 'Right, Becky, come on now, let's be knowing what's troubling that pretty little head of yours?'

Snuggling up to him, she said quietly, without looking at him, 'I know I'm being stupid, Tony, but I can't help it; I'm so worried, darling.' Looking up into his face, she repeated, 'I'm so worried, darling.'

Pretending to be surprised, he said, with a little laugh, 'Worried, worried about what, love?'

'Losing you,' she replied, almost in a whisper. 'I know it sounds silly, but I've got this uncanny feeling that I could lose you; I can't help it,' she stressed. 'I couldn't sleep for worrying it last night, Tony,' she said, with a look of desperation. 'I realise you're only going away for a week,' she continued. 'It's probably with us being separated for so long, me being in Cyprus; I don't know.'

Pulling her closer and kissing the side of her head, Tony said softly in her ear, 'You're a silly girl, Becky Stanhope and I love you; you've no need to be worried about losing me, darling, you'd have a job getting rid of me,' he said, pretending to bite her ear lobe.

Sitting back on the sofa with her head on his shoulder, she said softly, 'I know love, but I just got this overwhelming feeling, as I said; I couldn't sleep for worrying about it last night,' she repeated, with a sigh.

Sitting up straight on the sofa, Tony gently put his hand on her cheek and turned her head to face him. 'Becky, baby, just listen to me,' he said lovingly. 'I really don't know what you are fretting about, I love you – and if it wasn't for seeing Dave after his troubles, I'd be spending my leave here with you.'

He gave her a little peck on her forehead and said, 'Look, pet, if my going home is causing you all this worry, I'll forget the idea; I'll stay here with you instead. Dave will understand,' he assured her, looking into her face with a smile. 'I'll ring Bernard at the pub – he'll pass my message on to him,' he said, pulling her closer.

'Oh no, Tony, I wouldn't want you to do that,' she said firmly. 'You must go and see the lad, after what he's been through; anyway, I feel better now I've seen you again, love.'

'Now are you sure, Becky, I don't mind, you know,' he told her seriously. 'Personally, I'd rather stay with you anyway.'

'Yes, I believe you, Tony, but I think it better you go as planned, darling,' she said, smiling. 'I've got to face the fact that you've got other people close to you apart from me, Tony.' It's just that sometimes I can't help worrying about things out of my control,' she added glumly.

'You've got nothing at all to worry about, Becky, regarding us,' he assured her with a smile. 'Believe me, pet, there's only one person on this planet that could keep me away from you – her face paled and she looked at him in awe as he said this – and that's you yourself,' he told her, kissing the end of her nose.

Staring back at him expressionlessly for a few seconds, she said, in a whisper, 'and what about Peggy?'

Immediately realising what was troubling her, he replied, 'Becky darling, I've just told you, nobody other than you could come between us – I love you, pet, honest,' he stated emphatically.

Still staring into his face, she repeated, 'but what about Peggy, Tony; what about Peggy?'
Seeing the tension in her eyes, he repeated, 'Nobody darling.'

However, as he attempted to pull her closer, she pulled away, and stood in front of him looking coolly down into his face. 'Please, Tony, please – say it; for God's sake, say it if you really mean it – what about Peggy?'

'Getting up from the settee, he stood in silence looking into her taunt face for a moment. 'Becky', he said quietly, 'I swear nobody could keep me from you, but you yourself, darling.' Pausing momentarily, he put his hands on her shoulders and swallowing hard, said, almost in a whisper, 'Not even Peggy.'

Falling into his arms, she sobbed, 'I had to hear you say it, Tony, I just had to hear you say it because I know you still love her, you told me that,' she said, gripping him tighter.

'Yes, darling, I did tell you that, because I love you so much Becky; I couldn't bear to lie to you, darling, but I can't control my feelings either, my love.' He continued on a lighter note, 'but you can forget her, darling, she dumped me as I told you, and she's living in the lap of luxury in America now, according to Dave.

He told me that on the phone only last night. He also told me,' he continued, 'that she only sent him one letter when he was in that hospital in Australia; just think,' he added disapprovingly, 'he could have been killed out there, an'all. I'd have thought she'd have had more feelings for her brother than that,' he said, shaking his head.

'Yes, I agree that doesn't sound like the same person you described to me previously, Tony,' she said, giving him a doubtful look. 'Mind you he was only there for a very short time for correspondence over that distance,' she pointed out. 'Anyway, Tony,' she went on, 'all I want is for you to be happy, darling, so I've got something to request,' she said seriously.'

'Anything pet, anything you say.' He smiled, gratified at having put her mind at rest.

'Well, I want you go off as to planned, spend a week with your pal and have a good time; but always remember, my darling, I love you whatever, and I always will.' With a little smile she continued, 'however, if for any reason you decide while you're there, that there's somebody else you'd prefer rather than me, I want you to promise, never to try to see me again and don't contact me in any way. I'd rather you just forget me completely; do you understand darling?' she said, calmly.

'What! What are you on about Becky?' he yelled, his heart rate increasing rapidly. 'Please don't talk like that darling, please, please!' he repeated passionately, grabbing her and pulling her to him possessively.

112

'Hello there, young Tony,' called out Bernard, as Tony – in his best blue uniform – walked into the 'Dog and Gun' at seven o'clock on the Saturday evening. 'What you supping, lad –this is on the house,' he added cheerfully.

'Hi there, Bernard thanks. I'll have the usual please,' he replied. 'Have you seen Dave?' he asked looking around the room anxiously. 'We arranged to be in here around seven.'

'Aye,' said Bernard, as he pulled at the big wooden pump handle. 'He told me, when he came off the phone the other night, Tony.' Glancing up at the wall clock as the beer glass filled, he said, 'but it's only just seven now, give him a chance, lad,' he chuckled, banging the full pint glass down on the bar top.

Reaching out for it, Tony took a long swig, followed by an exaggerated sigh, 'By God, Bernard, they don't brew ale like that where I'm stationed,' he said, wiping the froth off his mouth with the back of his hand.

Bernard gave a little laugh, 'Ee, lad, you say that every time you come home; ale can't be that bad down there.' Suddenly he said, 'Ee up, lad, thy mate's coming, he's just passed the window outside.' Within a couple of seconds, Dave came slowly walking in, and seeing Tony standing at the bar, his face broke into a wide grin.

Tony charged across the room to greet him and called out, 'Get him a pint in, Bernard, he looks thirsty.'

The lads threw their arms around each other and hugged in genuine warm affection.

'Now then, you bugger, what the bloody hell have you been up to behind my back, getting yourself shot up like that,' Tony said, stepping back and grinning at his mate.

Laughing, Dave replied, 'I think them buggers over there must have taken a dislike to me, Tony; I didn't try to shoot them, as a matter of fact I never saw the buggers – first thing I knew I was on the floor covered in blood.'

Turning to the bar, Tony said, 'Come on then, you go and sit at that table over by the window,' he pointed with a nod. 'I'll bring the ale over; you can let me know all the news then.'

They sipped their drinks and Tony remarked casually, 'I only arrived home in the last hour, Dave, I missed the early train this morning, had to come on the midday one.'

'How come,' he asked, 'don't they mind the lads sleeping in on your camp, then?' he teased.

'I wasn't on our camp,' Tony replied. 'I stayed overnight with, Becky, my girlfriend; I told you about her posting,' he added. Pulling out his wallet, he showed Dave a postcard- size photo he'd taken of Becky only the previous week, dressed in running gear.

Taking a prolonged look at it, Dave said with a jerk of his head, 'Phew, very nice if I may say so, Tony, I don't know how you do it,' he muttered, still gazing at the photo, 'I can't see what the hell all the good-looking ones see in you,' he chuckled, handing it back.

'Shut up and get some ale down you, you pillock,' Tony said, laughing. He signalled to Bernard for two more pints.' 'Bloody hell,' Dave suddenly said, frowning and pointing to the doorway, 'Hope we're not going to have any bother tonight.'

'Oh Christ,' muttered Tony, 'the remnants of the 'bloody Canal street gang; anyway they haven't got their glorious leader to support them tonight,' he said, laughing.

'You know, Tony,' Dave said, still watching the newcomers, 'I made my mind up to give that big-mouthed Proudfoot a bashing when I got home, when you told me in that letter about him shoving dog shit in our letter box.'

'Don't worry, Dave, old love, I gave the pair of 'em enough of that, when I caught him and his big, ugly friend 'Brute' in the act,' Tony said, glancing quickly at the gang. 'I had 'em squealing on the deck, you should have seen 'em, Dave,' he said, laughing. After taking a long drink from his pint, he continued, 'and just then Mr Smirthwaite came up the road on his bike and I threatened to report 'em to him, if they didn't behave themselves.'

'Well, as I said, I was going to look for Proudfoot as soon as I got home, but Mum talked me out of it,' Dave said. 'She told me that he came around to see her saying he was very sorry. And then, unbelievably, he offered to look after her garden for her, and for nowt an'all,' he stressed, shaking his head. 'What's more, the little buggers have done it ever since,' he added, with a laugh.

'Look, he keeps glancing over here,' Tony said, pointing across the room. 'I'd say he's still wondering if he's in for another thumping, mate,' he said, taking another long sup of his ale.

'Oh, Tony, look, Steve Grimes has just come in; he's in uniform an'all,' Dave said smiling and waving to the corporal.

Waving back at the pair, Steve went straight to the bar. Returning with a tray holding three foaming pints, he chuckled, 'and how's AC Ryan going on then, still keeping your foot drill up to scratch?'

'Definitely, Steve,' said Tony, smiling, 'and how are things at my favourite camp?'

'Just as you left it, mate,' he replied, sitting down with a sigh. 'I've had a right time today, though, I've only just arrived here; I haven't been home yet,' he said, sipping his ale.

Staring across the room, Dave said suddenly, 'Tony, I'm sure them buggers down there are talking about us.'

Glancing at them, Tony replied disinterestedly, 'Oh, bugger 'em, Dave, they're only a bag of wind without their mainstay, Chris Simpson.'

'Who are you on about, that 'Canal Street' lot?' Steve enquired, glancing in the same direction.

'You don't know the latest about Simpson, do you, Steve,' Tony said excitedly. He told him all about the meeting he'd had with Chris, and his posting to his own camp.

'Bloody hell, that must have been a shock for you, Tony, meeting your old enemy like that, and him being a corporal in the police an'all,' Steve said with a laugh.

'Sure was, mind you he was as bloody shocked as I was at first. He soon got over it, though, realising he'd got one up on me; he gave me a terrible bollocking then.' He laughed. 'But what got me most was, that I had to be so subservient and let him get away with his bloody cheek; he was in his element, Steve, I'll tell you.'

Laughing Steve said, 'Well, I wouldn't hold any malice against him for that – he was only getting back at you, because he was the boss for once.'

'No, there's no malice, Steve, other things have happened since then,' he said seriously. He went on to tell him about the crash, and Chris Simpson's involvement in that.

'Aye, I was surprised when you told me about the rescue, and how brave he was,' chipped in Dave, who had been listening in silence.

'Well, I must say they were two very brave lads, him and that young officer, doing what they did without regard for their own safety,' Tony said, nodding sincerely.

'Oh yes, there's no doubt they were brave chaps going into an inferno like that,' Steve agreed.

'Well, if it's true,' continued Tony, 'I heard a rumour in the Mess, only yesterday, that they've both been recommended for acknowledgment by the camp Commander, Group Captain Sanderson. They're saying that the young medical officer who lost his foot is expected to get the George Cross, and Chris is to get the George medal.'

Their conversation was suddenly disturbed when Dave – who hadn't taken his eyes of the gang drinking down at the bottom end of the bar – remarked quietly, 'I think them buggers are coming over here, Tony.'

Looking across the room again, Tony said, 'Aye, looks like it; Christ, I'm in uniform. I don't want to get into any scrapping; I'll get the Service a bad name, won't I, Steve?' he added, glancing at him.

'You could be before your CO if the local police got involved,' he told him seriously.

'Hold it,' Dave chipped in, still watching them closely, 'the gang aren't coming, Tony, just Proudfoot on his own,' he said, sounding surprised.

'Thank God for that,' Tony sighed. 'He wouldn't dare come on his own if he was after bother.'

'Good evening, gentlemen,' called out the stocky little Proudfoot, coming up to their table with a wide smile.

Rather taken aback at this courteous approach, Tony replied in a bored tone, 'And what do you want, Harry?'

Still smiling, he replied, 'I've just come over to thank you for being so kind and helpful to Chris, when he sustained his horrific injuries,' he replied, holding out his hand to Tony.

'What the hell are you talking about, you silly little bugger.' Tony laughed, ignoring the handshake. 'I only took him a few bottles of Bass when he was caged up in that bloody hospital. How the hell do you know so much anyway?' he asked.

'He wrote to tell me about it, as a matter of fact,' Harry replied with a smirk. 'He also said you'd told him about the little misunderstanding we'd had with Dave's mum.' He glanced sheepishly at Dave.

'Aye and you're lucky you didn't get a bloody knuckle sandwich for that from me, Proudfoot,' butted in Dave. 'You would have got one if my mum hadn't stopped me, I'll tell you that,' he told him menacingly.

Forcing a little smile, Harry continued, 'Well, there'll be no more bother from any of our lot again, I can assure you of that.'

'Huh, I'll believe that when I see it,' Tony chuckled, taking another sip from his glass.

'No, there won't, Tony,' he said, adamantly. 'Chris said in his letter, I'd to tell all the lads that if there is any trouble caused by any one of 'em, he'll sort the culprit out himself when he comes home.'

'Right, Harry, thanks,' Tony said dismissively. 'It sounds as though Chris has grown up, at last.'

'Actually, there was something else I came over tell you RAF guys,' Proudfoot went on, with a proud smile. 'I'm leaving the pit; I passed my medical for National Service last week.'

'Oh, bully for you, Harry; what are they putting you in then, the Pioneer brigade? Or as they're better known – the shit-house diggers,' Tony laughed.

Still smiling proudly, Harry replied, 'No, as a matter of fact, Tony Ryan, I've got special orders to report to RAF Padgate on Monday week. I'm joining your mob,' he said, smirking down at the uniformed Steve and Tony, who were looking startled.

'Oh Christ,' exclaimed Tony, turning to look at Steve. 'What's the bloody Service coming to, Steve?' he said, shaking his head.

'Well, he's going to a good camp, anyway,' he replied, keeping a straight face. 'I've been okay there for the last couple of years or more; I've no complaints,' he said, with assurance.

Hearing this, Harry chipped in with great enthusiasm, 'Oh, so you're stationed at Padgate, then Steve, eh? That's great, we'll be able to get together and straighten the buggers out when I get there then,' he said, laughing coarsely.

'Oh, it's a great place to straighten people out, is Padgate, Harry, I can assure you of that,' Steve told him, with a nod. 'When did you say you're reporting for duty, then?'

'Monday week, Steve,' Harry replied, grinning, 'and it can't come too soon for me, mate, I can't wait to get into that uniform.' He looked down at theirs, with glowing admiration.

'Don't worry, Harry,' Steve called out to him, as he turned to go back to his mates, 'I'll keep a look out for you, I'm sure you'll learn a lot at Padgate,' he promised him, still keeping a straight face.

'I'm sure he will, you bugger,' Tony laughed as the little stocky figure strutted away across the room.

'Well, we managed to knock a bit of sense into his boss, Simpson,' Steve said, 'So I think we should be able to do something with him. There's one thing for sure,' he continued, with a chuckle, 'he'll be in for a bit of a shock when he does get there.'

'I'll second that,' said Tony, with a laugh. 'You certainly gave me a shock or two, Corporal Grimes.'

'By the way, you two,' Steve said changing the subject. 'Do you fancy a ride out to some nice, little country pub tomorrow lunchtime, for a change?'

'Great idea,' they both replied. 'In your car or do you want me to try borrowing my dad's?' Tony asked.

'Ours, of course,' Steve replied. 'It's the wife's father's birthday tomorrow, so if I drop her off there for lunch with him, I'll have the car for the afternoon; I can pick you two up in here at about twelve thirty then, if that's okay?'

'Perfect old son,' said Tony, with a laugh. 'Now then, what are we having – it's my round, come on, let's get drunk.'

Not for me Tony,' Steve said, finishing the remains of his drink. 'I'd better get off home – the wife will be wondering where I've got to, I haven't been home yet, as I told you.'

As they watched Steve going out of the door, they heard the loud boisterous voice of Harry Proudfoot call out, ' Good night, Corporal Steve, mate, see you at Padgate,' followed by loud cheering from the gang, as they all started slapping him on the back and pretending to salute him in military fashion.

'Bloody ale's taking effect on them buggers, Tony,' Dave remarked, sounding cautious.

'I can see that,' Tony replied, frowning. 'I hope it don't mean bother, after all Proudfoot's talk.'

'No, I don't think so, mate,' Dave replied, shaking his head. 'If Chris threatened 'em, as Proudfoot said, they wouldn't dare; they know he'd drop 'em when he gets back home.
Come on now, sup up, let's have another,' he said, with a grin.

113

The lounge at the 'Dog and Gun' was throbbing with Sunday lunchtime drinkers, as Tony entered, dressed in black single-breasted blazer and grey flannels. Seeing his mates, Dave and Steve, sitting at a table at the top end of the bar, his face lit up. Waving, he proceeded to make his way across the crowded floor to reach them.

'What you having, Tony?' called out Steve, getting to his feet as he approached.

Seeing their pints were untouched, Tony realised that they must have just arrived themselves. 'Never mind, I'll go get my own,' he replied, and headed for the bar.

Dave, who was sitting there in silence with a rather worried look on his face, called out 'Hang on a tick, mate; I'd like a word with you first.'

'Won't be long, Dave, won't it wait?' Tony called back, still making for the bar.

'Tony please,' Dave insisted. 'I've got summat to tell you, mate, it's very important.'

Turning and seeing the look on his face, Tony paused and went over to him. 'What's up, Dave, are you all right, mate? What's bothering you?' he asked, beginning to feel anxious.

Looking back at him for a moment in silence, Dave said quietly, 'She's back, Tony; she was sitting talking to my mum last night, when I got back from the pub.'

Tony froze, his face drained; he stood there like a zombie for what seemed an age, then he whispered, staring down into Dave's eyes, 'How is she, David?'

'She looked fine, just like she always does.' Dave looked back at him expressionlessly.

Staring into space for another long moment, Tony suddenly asked, 'Where is she now?'

'Last night she went back to her flat to go to bed, that's the last I saw of her,' Dave told him. 'She said she'd been travelling for about twelve hours; she'll still be there I suppose, mate.' Without another word, and to the surprise of the other two, Tony slowly turned, making for the door. 'Where are you going mate?' Dave called out.

'I'm going home,' he muttered, continuing towards the door.

'Why?' Dave yelled, jumping to his feet intending to follow him, but Steve, who'd been sitting in silence throughout the conversation, put his hand gently on his arm to restrain him.

'To put my uniform on,' Tony called back to him.

'I don't think you'd be able help him, if you did go after him, Dave,' Steve told him as Tony disappeared out of the door, 'I presume the pair of you were talking about your sister, Peggy, weren't you?'

'Yes, yes, we were,' replied poor Dave, clearly very upset about the matter. 'I know he told me he loved her, Steve, but now he's got this other girl – I thought he'd got over our Peg, but he looked pole-axed when I said she'd come back, didn't he?'

'Sure did, but this is the type of problem he'll have to sort out on his own, Dave, lad,' the older man told him. 'This other girl, have you met her yet, Dave?' he asked.

'No, but he told me that they're in love with each other, and he showed me a recent photo he'd just taken of her; she's gorgeous an'all, you know, Steve,' he said, nodding his head with approval.

'Well, that's it, then, Dave,' Steve said, smiling. 'As a matter of fact, I've seen her photo myself if you remember, and I agree she's beautiful, so he's probably just going to see Peggy to clear the air; after all he's got to meet her again sometime, she is your sister.'

'I suppose so,' Dave mumbled dubiously, 'but I don't know, Steve; he was so upset, he really was, he never calls me David, unless he's really uptight about summat, you know.

At home, Tony found the house empty; his mum and dad had gone out in the car for a day to Bridlington, and his sister was most likely out with her latest boyfriend. Going straight up to his bedroom, he did a quick change into his best blue uniform, gave his cap badge a little rub on the sleeve of his jacket, put the cap on and went over to the big wardrobe mirror. Standing there looking at his reflection, his mind went back over the past long months since he'd last seen her, suddenly he thought, what the hell am I doing? Sitting down on the bed, he took off his cap and put it down beside him; elbows on knees and chin in his cupped hands, he gave a long sigh of frustration. 'Tony Ryan you're a right pillock,' he said out loud. 'You've been dumped by this girl once and you're going back for more.' Reassuring himself, he thought, well, facts have to be faced – after all, I've always believed in taking the bull by the horns and I've never run away from a problem in my life. What's more, I'd have to meet her again sometime, being so close to her family, he reasoned. Finally, sitting up straight, he slapped his hands down on his knees saying again out loud, 'Right, pull yourself together, Ryan; think in your usual logical manner.' Yes, he thought, getting to his feet and putting his cap back on, I'm getting all worked up about nowt.

Scanning his reflection again in the big mirror, he said firmly, 'I'll go and greet Peggy in a nice cheerful, friendly, platonic manner, and then return to the pub, showing nothing of the past feelings I had for her.' After all, he reasoned, there'd been other women he'd thought a lot about, before her. Yes – she was just another experience and she obviously didn't want him, he assured himself as he marched out of the house.

Pressing the bell on the white-painted Georgian door, Tony stood smartly to attention as though on guard duty, as he waited for a response. When none came after a few seconds, he was just about to turn away, thinking she must have gone out, when he heard a slight movement and the door slowly opened. His heartbeat quickened when he saw Peggy framed in the doorway, looking stunningly beautiful. She was dressed in casual clothing and looking exactly as he'd seen her at their first meeting on that Friday night, at the dance class.

They looked at each other in silence for a long moment – then Tony, nonchalantly tilting the peak of his cap back slightly with his thumb, said with a nervous smile, 'Hello, Peg, I've come to show you my uniform.'

Peggy continued to remain silent, looking back at him expressionlessly; then slowly a faint smile crossed her face and rather nervously she said, in her low husky voice, 'Oh, hello Tony, you'd better to come in, then.' Closing the door behind them, she led him into the big, comfortably furnished lounge, the one he remembered so well.

Looking around, he saw the curtain pelmets he'd so carefully made for her on that first day they'd spent together, and the ornamental wall shelves he'd put up in the corner of the room. Everything looked just the same, as though he'd never left – even the big, gold velvet sofa against the wall and the two matching armchairs were in the same positions. In fact, he thought, he could have gone through a time warp, and this Sunday was still the Sunday of their first togetherness.

'Well, it's been a long time, Tony,' she said chirpily, turning to face him, as they reached the middle of the room. 'I hope you've enjoyed your time in the RAF.'

'Aye, it's been a great experience up to now,' he replied, in equally confident tones, although the atmosphere was clearly tense. 'How about you, love?' he asked. 'Have you had a good time over there in America? Dave told me you'd got a good position in a tennis club,' he added. She went on to tell him about the club, but he wasn't listening; he was looking at her clear blue eyes, the flash of her white teeth as she spoke, and the body movements of her athletic figure. She hadn't changed a fraction since he'd loved her so passionately, all those months back. As he glanced across the room into the open door of the bedroom they'd shared, he caught sight of the big double bed with the same deep purple-coloured eiderdown on it. Out of the blue, he interrupted her flow of forced small talk. He almost snapped at her, 'And how's life now, Peggy, are you happy?'

Slightly startled at the abruptness of his question, she froze in mid-sentence and looked blankly back at him; he also stood in silence staring into her face. Suddenly, Tony noticed her lovely blue eyes were beginning to cloud over as she gazed back at him, and her lip was beginning to quiver.

Feeling a lump rising in his throat – he could stand no more. Taking a step towards her with open arms, he engulfed her in his powerful embrace. She melted instantly, throwing her arms around his neck sobbing, as their hungry mouths met in a deep, passionate kiss. Their pent-up emotion was released as they clung to each other, their faces wet with mutual tears.   As she sobbed, he murmured between their hot wet kisses, 'Oh, you devil woman, Peggy, you bloody devil woman, I love you so much – but you've put me through hell.'

He gripped her even tighter as the passion of their embrace heightened; his cap falling off the back of his head onto the thick Wilton carpet and rolling away across the floor, as they fell back onto the big sofa.

The End
Or is it?

Lightning Source UK Ltd.
Milton Keynes UK
UKOW050613201211

184093UK00001B/2/P